RELENTLESS

JONATHAN MABERRY

RELENTLESS

A JOE LEDGER AND ROGUE TEAM INTERNATIONAL NOVEL

 ST. MARTIN'S GRIFFIN
NEW YORK

First published in the United States by St. Martin's Griffin, an imprint of St. Martin's Publishing Group

RELENTLESS. Copyright © 2021 by Jonathan Maberry. All rights reserved. Printed in the United States of America. For information, address St. Martin's Publishing Group, 120 Broadway, New York, NY 10271.

www.stmartins.com

Library of Congress Cataloging-in-Publication Data

Names: Maberry, Jonathan, author.
Title: Relentless : a Joe Ledger and Rogue Team International novel / Jonathan Maberry.
Description: First edition. | New York : St. Martin's Griffin, 2021. | Series: Rogue Team International series ; 2 |
Identifiers: LCCN 2021004761 | ISBN 9781250619303 (trade paperback) | ISBN 9781250619310 (ebook)
Subjects: GSAFD: Adventure fiction.
Classification: LCC PS3613.A19 R45 2021 | DDC 813/.6—dc23
LC record available at https://lccn.loc.gov/2021004761

Our books may be purchased in bulk for promotional, educational, or business use. Please contact your local bookseller or the Macmillan Corporate and Premium Sales Department at 1-800-221-7945, extension 5442, or by email at MacmillanSpecialMarkets@macmillan.com.

First Edition: 2021

10 9 8 7 6 5 4 3 2 1

This is for Thomas C. Raymond, Anne Pryor-Raymond,
Ben Raymond, Babette Raymond, and Kelly Powers
Superfans, friends, family

And, as always, for Sara Jo

RELENTLESS

WHEN DARKNESS CALLS

PART 1

Cross charred bridges all you want,
If you're lucky, you won't find me on the other
    side,
Waiting to exact the toll.
"Exactly what?" you may ask . . .

Well—don't ask.

Just remember (*don't you dare forget*)
When you see me
Placidly waiting by your roadside's soft
    shoulder,
We were never friends.

Under my smile lurks a thousand convictions,
And two thousand preemptive persecutions,
And my eyes see sharp enough to pierce
Your very strongest veneer.

I will assume everything until you validate
    otherwise.
I will suspect and distrust your every intention
    until
You prove them pure . . . not an easy task.
And when you can't, you will be vilified.

I will rip you to shreds—don't FUCK with me.

I only look like a paper tiger.

—*A SNAKE IS NEVER A KITTEN*
BY JEZZY WOLFE

CHAPTER 1

They say that no plan ever survives contact with the enemy.

My enemies thought that if they hurt me badly enough, if they took away the people I love, that it would break me. That it would cripple me so thoroughly I would give up the fight, that my hands would be too numb to pick up my weapons ever again. That I'd be too ruined to come after them.

That was their plan.

They were wrong.

CHAPTER 2

TRSTENIK ISLAND
SOUTH DALMATIAN COAST OF THE ADRIATIC SEA
CROATIA

We came out of the darkest corner of the sky.

Silent and hungry. Gliding on the thermals, propelled by muffled motors that let us approach the island low enough to spook our way under the radar. Our avenue of approach was narrow, but we didn't need much space. Havoc Team rode the night wind on TradeWinds MotorKites. Something my boss, Mr. Church, had commissioned long ago from a company that made ultralight aircraft. The frame was made from an aluminum-magnesium alloy that was lighter than a lawn chair but far stronger. Big silk bat wings filled the frame and extended beyond it, ribbed with flexible polymers. The motors were tiny two-strokes built for stealth rather than speed. Virtually silent. And they had a surprisingly hefty weight capacity, which is good because I'm a bit over two hundred pounds, and my combat dog, Ghost, is only fifty pounds lighter.

We wore Google Scout glasses—another gizmo concocted by one of Church's many "friends in the industry." He seems to have reliable friends in a lot of useful industries. These glasses were synced with our tactical computers, which were extensions of the MindReader Q1 computer system. The glasses could cycle from standard vision to ultraviolet, infrared, and adaptive night vision. Most NVGs cast the world in a thousand shades of luminescent green and black, and they're fantastic as long as someone doesn't turn on a light. The adaptive tech in ours used ultrafast reactive lenses to modify the light intrusion, keeping us from being blinded and also bringing in some natural colors that would otherwise be washed out.

My boss loves his toys. Got to say, I'm a bit of a fan, too. We all were.

I led our little flight of bats through the black night, following a line of swells that humped up as they climbed from deep water to shallows and then curled over into gentle waves. Those waves weren't big, but they were continuous, with the soft hiss and sigh of tons of water hitting the sand and sliding back into the inky vastness of the Adriatic. Behind me, flying in a loose vee, was the rest of Havoc Team.

There were four of them, apart from Ghost and me. Our mission intel told us that we'd be more than enough for this gig. Trstenik Island was a tiny patch of wooded nothing off the coast of the much larger island of Korčula off the coast of mainland Croatia. Trstenik was only 3.66 acres, densely wooded, with some low hills and sandy soil. One of the islands nations try to lease or sell so that someone comes in and develops it into something that pays taxes. In this case, the buyer was Mislav Mitrović, a tech billionaire who'd made his fortune with some kind of doohickey that made a gizmo work for a business that I couldn't give a cold shit about. Not that I'm a Luddite. Hardly. It's just that the owner of the island was actually a front man for a group of other rich assholes who had their fingers deep into the global black market. And we're not talking guys who sell knockoffs of Galaxy phones. No, these cats were in vending technologies that were giving small groups of very angry extremists the kinds of toys that allowed them to do considerable damage to their industrial, political, and religious competitors.

Through six or seven removes, Mitrović and his little crew of mad scientists were selling high-end guidance systems that turned the already dangerous RPGs into guided missiles capable of taking down passenger liners, military jets, and even ships at sea. Stuff like that. He also sold special depleted uranium loads for those RPGs that could punch right through the skin of any of the smaller navy vessels, including hospital ships.

Here's the thing. Normally, if my crew—Rogue Team International, currently based on Omfori Island in Greece—caught wind of something like this, either Mr. Church or our COO, Scott Wilson, would pick up the phone and make a discreet call. Someone in the Sigurnosno-obavještajna agencija—the Security and Intelligence Agency, or SOA—and the SOA would send in a few helicopters crammed with shooters.

But this was a special case for us. The RTI computer team, led by world-class super nerd Bug, peeled back all the layers of the cover stories and shell corporations Mitrović was using to hide who he was really in bed with. The name *Kuga* floated to the top of that particular cesspool.

Kuga.

Yeah, we wanted him really badly. There aren't words to describe exactly how badly.

Kuga was an international criminal empire specializing in black market sales of everything from polonium for assassinations to the sale and distribution of the most lethal bioweapons you can imagine. Kuga was also very likely the code name for the chief executive of that group, and there was a good chance the person behind it all was a former CIA superstar and self-made billionaire, Harcourt Bolton. For perspective's sake, imagine if James Bond and Tony Stark had a love child, and that kid grew up to be Doctor Doom. That's Harcourt Bolton. Smart, rich, ruthless as fuck, and he holds the number-two spot on my bucket list of people whose lives I want to destroy in very ugly and painful ways.

The number-one spot is held by Kuga's right-hand man, Rafael Santoro. The most feared and effective manipulator, blackmailer, and extortionist the world has ever known. He has the subtlety and tradecraft to deconstruct the lives of key people and then turn them into weapons for the Kuga empire. Not willing converts—he's not into changing hearts and minds through motivational speaking. No, his method is to make it very clear what will happen to the target's loved ones. He shows photos and videos of what *has* happened to the families of people who defied him. He's broken Navy SEALs, and that is something that's supposed to be impossible, and breaks my heart that it, in fact, *had* happened.

Nothing is impossible, though. Santoro follows the Archimedes philosophy of:

"Give me a lever long enough and a fulcrum on which to place it, and I shall move the world."

But here's the thing . . . and this is why Santoro, not Kuga, was in my number-one must fucking eviscerate list: Santoro is also the man who murdered my entire family on Christmas Eve last year.

Yeah.

So there's that.

Mitrović was in bed with Santoro and Kuga, which meant that he was not going to be very happy at all to wake up and have me bending over him.

CHAPTER 3
TRSTENIK ISLAND
CROATIA

"Coming up on it, Outlaw," said a voice in my ear. It was the voice of my second-in-command, Bradley "Top" Sims. Combat call sign was Pappy because he was the oldest active shooter in the RTI. Oldest, not weakest or slowest. No, sir.

"Going in," I said, and I tilted the MotorKite to spill wind. Ghost, dangling from a harness, wriggled against my thighs. He likes this part of it. Idiot dog likes parachutes, hang gliders, and these kites. I, as a rule, do not.

I angled down and followed just behind a wave, my boots less than a yard above the creamy white foam. The wave broke, and I touched down as it began to slide back, landing with short running steps. I made it to the high-tide line and knelt, popping the harness release to let Ghost jump down. He moved off a dozen yards and then stopped, raising his head, ears high, nose sniffing the breeze. I kept my hands on the MotorKite's controls until I heard a soft *whuff.*

All clear.

I killed the motor.

"Havoc Actual to Havoc Team," I said quietly, "down and safe. Split two and two on my three and nine."

They came in like pelicans, gliding softly, landing on either side of me, switching off their machines. We all detached from the cradles of straps and immediately collapsed the MotorKites. They folded up like beach umbrellas, and we pulled canvas bags, thrust them inside, and buried them quickly in the soft sand farther up the beach.

"On me," I said, and they clustered around, taking up stations like compass points, looking both ways along the beach, out to sea, and inland. Each one of them murmured an all clear.

"Weapons check," ordered Top, and there were a few quick movements as guns were unslung, magazines secured. Hands patted the various pockets to make sure nothing had been lost in flight. We'd come armed with a lot of nasty little toys.

I tapped my coms unit to cycle onto the main channel with the TOC—the Tactical Operations Center—where Church, Wilson, Bug, Doc Holliday, and a room crammed with mission specialists were waiting.

"Havoc is on the deck," I said.

"Copy that, Outlaw," said Wilson. "Good hunting."

Unless they had a reason to speak, the TOC would remain quiet so as not to distract us with chatter.

"Jackpot," I said, using the call sign for Andrea Bianchi, our utility infielder, "get some birds in the air."

"*Subito,*" he said. *Immediately.* He had a big equipment bag slung across his back and slipped it off. From it, he removed a handful of what looked like dead cormorants. But these were sophisticated surveillance drones fashioned to look like Adriatic coastal birds. From any distance greater than six feet, they were totally convincing. He activated them, holding them one at a time next to a sensor on the small tactical computer strapped to his forearm. Then he handed them to Harvey Rabbit, a hulking giant of a man affectionately known as Bunny, who threw them high into the air. The birds' wings deployed, and they flapped off into the night. As soon as the birds were in flight, they began sending telemetry to a screen on Andrea's tac-com. *"Bellissima,"* he murmured approvingly.

Bunny—combat call sign Donnie Darko—shifted closer to me, his rifle up, stock tucked into his brawny shoulder.

"Call the play, boss," he said.

"You and Jackpot go inland one klick until you find the service road by the gate," I said. "Locate the watchtower and wait. And prep a couple of Lightning Bugs. As soon as I give the order to pull triggers, I want you to kill all communications from those towers."

Lightning Bugs are one of Doc Holliday's wonderful new toys. These are small drones carrying e-bombs that consist of a metal cylinder—the armature—which is surrounded by a coil of wire called the stator winding. The armature cylinder is filled with the desired amount of explosive based on the desired area of effect. Once airborne, it flies to the designated height and location and then—*bang.* The explosion travels as a wave through the middle of the armature cylinder, and when it comes in contact with the stator winding, it creates a short circuit that compresses the magnetic field, generating an intense electromagnetic burst. All electronics in the blast radius are fried. That means no radios, no sat-phones, no cells. They also kill night vision, body cams, and—well, anything that runs on a chip.

We have to be very careful to make sure we're outside of the effective range. Havoc Team carries a lot of very expensive gear, from MindReader uplinks to special targeting systems for certain kinds of guns, to the RFID telemetry chips we all have implanted so that we—or our bodies—can be located.

"Hooah," he said. Bunny and Andrea melted away into the night.

I turned to Top and the fifth member of my team, a slender woman named Belle—no last name—who carried a Sako TRG 42, a superb Finnish bolt-action long-range sniper rifle chambered for .338 Lapua Magnum cartridges. I've worked with a lot of snipers over the years, including the legendary John Smith and the cold and precise Sam Imura, but Belle was her own breed of shooter. She had neither the years of practice nor the military experience of either of those men, but she brought a natural coldness and precision that set her apart. Belle was not a hunter or competitive shooter. She had no trophies, no stuffed heads on her walls—but if she wanted you dead and could

　　　　　　　　　　　　　　　　JONATHAN MABERRY

line you up in the sights, you had better be right with Jesus. Belle's call sign was Mother Mercy. She was personally trained by Violin, a woman who is arguably the deadliest sniper alive.

Yes, I run with the cool kids.

"Mother Mercy," I said, "you and Pappy go along the beach and up through the ravine we saw. Establish an elevated firing position where you can see both towers."

She said nothing and gave only a small nod. Lethal but not chatty.

Top said, "Hooah," and they moved off together.

That left me there with Ghost. He came and sat down next to me, pushing at me with his muzzle. Ghost is a big white shepherd who has been through a lot of kinds of hell with me. Like me, he was badly injured when Santoro blew up my uncle's house. Like me, Ghost healed in body but less so in spirit.

Like me, he wants some payback. He couldn't say it in words, but he didn't have to. There's a kind of telepathy between pets and humans, and it's a bit stronger between combat dogs and their soldiers.

I said, "Let's go get them."

Ghost gave me a wag of his bushy tail and flashed his teeth in the starlight.

Then we went hunting.

INTERLUDE 1
THE PLAYROOM
UNDISCLOSED LOCATION
NEAR VANCOUVER, BRITISH COLUMBIA, CANADA
SEVEN MONTHS AGO

It was called the Playroom, but there wasn't a lot of fun or games happening there.

With only a few exceptions, Rafael Santoro disliked jokey or ironic nicknames. He felt it cheapened what they did and made sport of what they had planned. It was, after all, a mansion, a lab, a training center, and a staging area for what was to come. It didn't need to be named at all, but Kuga liked the name and he paid the bills.

Once upon a time, Santoro had been the conscience to Hugo Vox, the King of Fear, a founding member of the Seven Kings. That had been a real name for an organization that ran miles deep in terms of subtlety, maturity, and elegance. Now he worked for the ex-CIA master spy who called himself Kuga—taking the pseudonym from the Bosnian word for *plague*. That much was fine; there was a certain panache to that. And although his new boss was quite capable of subtlety, he was hardly as refined as Vox had been. Capable of it, perhaps, but not inclined to it. If anything, Kuga saw himself like some kind of absurd blend of Hugh Hefner and a James Bond villain.

On his more tolerant days, Santoro wondered if maybe that was an artifice designed to keep *him* off guard. And to provoke Santoro. Kuga was certainly manipulative and petty enough to do that, even to his allies. It was, however, a bad habit shared by powerful narcissists. It tended toward excess, and Santoro was not much of a fan of excess when it came to running a global criminal empire. He preferred true subtlety—to vanish into the woodwork, to be unseen and unfelt until the blade slipped between the ribs. To stay many layers removed from anything actionable; to let other people take the blame.

But, no. Kuga had styled himself after Professor Moriarty from the Sherlock Holmes stories. He wanted to be *known* as the master manipulator, the Napoleon of crime, who crouched like a spider at the center of thousands of webs of criminal enterprise. And, after the events in Korea and Norway last year, he had accomplished that. There was probably no one except bushmen in Africa and unnamed tribesmen in the Amazonian rain forest who did not know the name *Kuga*. No one was more fiercely sought by the world's many—*many*—law enforcement agencies and intelligence networks. And as a result, Santoro's own name shared those Most Wanted lists.

These thoughts, in infinite variation and levels of gloomy speculation, ran through Santoro's head as he sat next to Kuga on an Adirondack chair in the shade of a canopy, watching three very lovely young women swim slow laps in a massive pool. Kuga was on his third bourbon of the morning; Santoro was sipping *café con miel*—coffee with honey, a shot of espresso, and steamed milk. He'd made it himself, layering the ingredients and adding touches of ginger, cinnamon, and cardamom.

The two of them had been sitting there for nearly an hour, with

JONATHAN MABERRY

Kuga slowly getting smashed while watching the women in the pool. One—a petite brunette—splashed and floundered, her head up above the water the way the inept do because they don't know what they're doing. She was a pretty woman, but the poor form made her ugly to Santoro. He disliked weakness in any of its manifestations.

The other two women were taller, fitter, and better at it. They'd gone into the water with the sleek efficiency of experts, barely making a splash and arrowing along for many yards before settling into mechanical crawls. Lifting their heads every other stroke to take quick breaths. One was a woman from Cameroon who had intensely dark skin and a shaved head, and the other was a strawberry blonde wearing a tight swim cap. All three wore Olympic-style swimsuits with racer backs. Santoro had not bothered to learn their names. He did not care to dive into the endless river of beautiful women who came and went through Kuga's Playroom. Like so many things, Santoro's sexual life was kept private, and he found fleshy excess quite distasteful.

As if reading his thoughts, Kuga said, "Can you at least *pretend* to enjoy the fucking view?"

Kuga was shirtless and wore a tight and skimpy red Speedo that was clearly chosen because it displayed his phallus to great effect. His body had long since lost the pallor of prison and was now an even golden brown. Kuga wore a white ship captain's cap with the brim tugged down to shade his face and a pair of Dita Epiluxury Black Palladium sunglasses. A short red-and-white swizzle stick bobbed between his teeth when he spoke.

"Yes," drawled Santoro without enthusiasm, "quite charming."

Kuga snorted. "Pretty sure none of these broads ever went to charm school."

Santoro declined to comment. Another thing he disliked were degrading epithets. Kuga apparently knew this and had recently begun using them more often.

The sky above the pool was a faultless blue, with no trace of haze or clouds. A few birds rode the thermals high above. Santoro squinted up, shielding his eyes with his hand. Were they vultures? He thought so. How odd. How lovely.

"Not exactly sure why you have a stick up your ass today, buddy," said Kuga, "but I can take a guess."

"Oh, please enlighten me," said Santoro.

"You think I'm wasting valuable time watching three fuck-bunnies play splish-splash when I should be working on the American Operation."

Santoro said nothing.

"You don't have a lot of faith in me, Rafael."

"I have a great deal of faith in the operation we mapped out."

"Heh, nice evasion." Kuga sipped the bourbon. It was not a particularly expensive brand, but when Kuga saw it in a store, he immediately bought two cases. Larceny Barrel Proof. Kuga thought it was the best thing he'd seen in months and smiled like a naughty kid whenever he opened a new bottle. "Of course you like the American Operation," he continued. "Hugo Vox cooked it up, and you mapped it out. And in case you think I'm ungrateful, I appreciate you sharing the details on all those Seven Kings ops that were in the pipeline. This one is a fucking doozy, and talk about *timely*. Vox was a visionary, that's for damn sure. He had his finger on the pulse of my *ex*–mother country. It's so right on that nobody will think we had any hand in it because—hey, even the fake news has been calling this for years. It'll make that freak Church shit a twenty-four-karat gold brick."

Santoro stared into the depths of his coffee. "And yet here we sit, like a couple of foolish middle-aged tourists on a Princess cruise."

"You see," said Kuga, pointing a finger at Santoro with the hand holding the whiskey glass, "that's the part about being executives that you don't get."

"Pray enlighten me about that, too."

"You think we need to get our hands dirty. How do you still have that thought? You think we should be down in Texas micromanaging the whole G-55 thing? Hugo Vox never got blood on his hands—or dirt under his fingernails, for that matter. Neither did his mother—your goddess."

"*Cuidado*," murmured Santoro, the warning clear in his tone. But Kuga ignored it.

"We have people working for us," continued Kuga. "Very smart people. The best money can buy. Loyal, too, because they know that you're around to give lessons in efficiency and to spank them if they step out of line. They are doing the heavy lifting while we are enjoying a gorgeous morning, drinking good bourbon—well, in your case, some fruity-ass coffee drink—and watching three insanely gorgeous women. The sun is shining, and all's right with the motherfucking world."

"You're drunk."

"Mmmm-hm. That was my actual intention. Happy to report that I've met my life goal for the day."

Santoro lapsed into a bitter silence. When Kuga was like this, there was no shot at a real conversation. It was a petty response to being scolded, and Kuga had no peer when it came to childish obstinacy or obfuscation.

The women swam and talked and laughed. Their voices were musical, but the day had soured, and so they seemed to be nothing more than noise.

After a long time, Kuga said, "Besides, Rafael ol' buddy, I called in some help."

"Help? What's that supposed to mean?"

"Someone with a little more oomph than that Barbie doll you're mentoring."

"Do not mistake Eve's lack of education for a lack of intelligence. She has great potential to—"

"Yeah, yeah, she has great potential to become a criminal mastermind, blah blah blah. At best, she's a useful knife at the end of your arm. But since Ledger killed her boyfriend, she's been . . . Well, let's face it, Eve's crazier than a honey badger on crack."

"Those extremes are useful to me for certain operations," said Santoro coldly.

"Sure. Fine. Whatever. But my guy is on a whole different level. He'll be able to take over the sales—and I guarantee you he'll send that up like a rocket—freeing us up to work on the American thing."

Santoro studied Kuga's profile, and it became slowly apparent that Kuga might not be quite as drunk as he pretended. He had that little inward smile. The one he wore when he was playing a game on everyone in the room.

"Who is this person?"

"Oh, you've met him. Did some work for the Kings once upon a time."

"*Who?*"

Kuga sipped his whiskey and watched the splashing. "He's currently calling himself Mr. Sunday. Not his real name, and I know you're superstitious and don't like to hear his real name spoken out loud."

The warmth seemed to leach itself out of the day, leaving the Spaniard shivering despite the sunshine. He was unable to speak for a moment.

Kuga grinned. "Let's just say he's the right man to piss in Mr. Church's punch bowl. And he's definitely the right guy to get our sales process back on its wheels."

Santoro frowned, and then his eyes went wide.

"No . . . ," he breathed.

"Yup," said Kuga. He laughed and threw back the last of the bourbon. "Abso-fucking-lutely."

CHAPTER 4
TRSTENIK ISLAND
CROATIA

We moved inland, following a narrow game trail. Above and around us, the trees swelled with wind as the breeze freshened from the southeast. Far away in the direction of the big island nearby, I heard a boat cutting across the darkened waves, the motor sound like an idling chain saw. An early fisherman heading out to the blue water between Croatia and Italy.

I heard soft rustling and turned, looking up to see that the trees around me were thick with birds. It was hard to pick out details, but from what I could see, they looked like crows or ravens. Scruffy, though, and ragged, as if they'd all been standing in a cold blast of winter wind, but this was early summer. They reminded me of something I'd once read in a book, or perhaps a poem. What was the line?

Night birds . . . the prophets of apocalypses large and small.

For some reason I will never understand, I waved to them. A few rustled their wings. One opened its beak to give a call, but if any sound came out, I didn't hear it. And so I turned away, feeling uneasy. Maybe I should start reading limericks instead.

Ghost ranged ahead, and every time he encountered an obstacle, he stopped and waited for me to catch up. The first time was—of all things—a kid's red tricycle that looked like it had been rusting there for thirty years. That made no sense, because until Mitrović bought the island, there had been no habitation here. No resorts or even a small family home. Ghost looked from the bike to me and endeavored to cock an eyebrow.

"Beats me, furball," I said, and we moved on.

And almost immediately jolted to a stop. I quickly dropped to one knee. Up ahead, to the left of where Ghost was sniffing, I saw a figure. A man. Tall, slender, fit-looking. Standing in the woods with his back to me. He was silhouetted against the faint glow of lights from the mansion, which was over a series of low hills.

I murmured into my mic, "Hostile spotted." I gave the approximate location and details but ordered my team to stop and hold positions.

Ghost, for some reason, did not seem to see the figure, although they weren't more than a dozen yards apart. Ghost is trained for exactly this, but he kept moving.

I tapped the Scout glasses to bring up the zoom function, but the figure was too dark and at a bad angle. So I rose, silent as the shadows around me, and moved in the direction of the man. He was unmoving, apparently looking down at something I couldn't see. Ghost has his own coms unit, and I shifted to that channel and ordered him to do a lateral search. I could see him lift his head, suddenly tensing as he stretched out with his canine senses. Then he moved to his left so that he and I were heading in roughly converging lines.

And then Ghost walked right past the man.

Not a pause, not a flicker. It almost looked like he walked through him, but that was clearly a distortion of bad light and dense foliage. I raised my rifle and followed the barrel to the spot.

A bat suddenly broke from a hole in a tree and fluttered straight at me in its panic. I shifted to avoid it, and when I looked again—the man was gone.

The spot where he was standing was empty.

I hurried up, signaling Ghost to close on me. He did, looking expectant but not troubled. I moved through the whole area, using the Scout glasses on the thermal imaging setting.

But there was nothing.

I knelt once more at the exact spot where I'd seen the man. The soil was dry but not hard, and it was loose enough to take a print. Except there were no prints anywhere.

It made no sense. I'd seen the man for sure. This wasn't a case of me seeing a shrub or stunted tree and being confused. He had been tall, maybe middle aged, with gray hair, trousers, and a sweater with some kind of pattern on it. He had been right goddamned here.

There was a double click of squelch as Top sent a wordless inquiry.

"Wait one," I told them.

Ghost stood by me, his body rippling with tension that he was no doubt picking up from me.

I searched all around the spot.

Nothing.

Then as I straightened, I saw something. Not a man, but a faintness of a line that ran like a strand of silver through the leaves maybe two feet from where I stood.

Had I not seen that man, I would have walked right through it.

The wire ran across the various natural walking paths and vanished into the leaves. I followed it to a small metal box attached to the base of a pine tree. It was a kind I'd never seen before, but that didn't matter. It was without a doubt an antipersonnel mine.

I tapped into the team channel. "Havoc Actual to Havoc Team, stop and listen." I described what I found.

A few moments later, Andrea said, "Copy that, Outlaw. Same over here."

And then Top verified that he and Belle found the same thing.

"What about the hostile?" asked Top.

"Sighting uncertain," I said. "Stay alert."

I scanned for laser trip wires but found nothing. There were more advanced versions of trip wires, but despite dealing in technology, Mitrović liked it old-school. Physical trip wires were still one of the most effective methods of ambushing foot patrols like ours. I could feel my heart thudding.

"Leave the wires intact and proceed with caution," I advised. "Look for other traps."

"Hooah," they replied.

JONATHAN MABERRY

I stepped over the wire very carefully and then watched Ghost jump clear. He had been trained to avoid trip wires. Maybe he would have found it had he gone a few more yards into the forest. Or maybe he and I would be scattered across this whole slope. These are the things soldiers base their superstitions on. A lucky break? Maybe. Something felt deeply weird about all this. Why hadn't Ghost seen the man? And where had the guy gone?

Two questions for which I had no answers.

We moved on with infinite care. The uneasy feeling lingered, following me like a shadow.

The trail took us up to a small ridge, beyond which was the main house, with a few smaller outbuildings scattered in a large clearing. Some work had been done to landscape the property, but apart from a few shade trees and trenches dug for hedges, it was bare. Mitrović had filed construction permits to erect a modest mansion, but Bug had picked apart shipping records and determined that more materials had been imported onto the island than were needed to make a twenty-room home. There were corresponding labor records for a construction crew roughly five times larger than needed. Add that to geological surveys from satellite flyovers that showed a radical change in the offshore seabed consistent with the dumping of dirt and rocks far in excess of preconstruction estimates, and you have us all going, "Hmmmm . . . what on earth could he be building?"

I mean, it was either a secret base or a secret base. Possibly even a secret base. One of those things.

Thermal scans also pinged four different heat signatures consistent with industrial generators. So I'm thinking secret base with some kind of laboratory concocting god only knew what horror. Hey, I'm not being paranoid here—or at least not more than usual. Since going to work for Mr. Church a few years back, I've actually seen secret labs that would make comic book super-villains weep with envy. Real-world stuff. Not as much fun as what you see in the movies. Because, yeah, there are actually that many brilliant maniacs in the world being funded by rich assholes, rich governments, rich corporations who do not give a limping fuck for human beings. Except when they can exploit them, marginalize them, or remove them as an inconvenience. Like so many of the bastards I've gone after as part of the old Department of Military Sciences and now with Rogue Team International.

Like Kuga and Santoro, who blew my world apart a few months ago.

Like those monsters.

So Mitrović was probably living like a king in his mini-mansion while down in the basement unspeakable horrors were being cooked up. Brewed or cultured, assembled or uploaded. However he was doing it, I was coming for him.

Ghost and I inched up to the ridge top and surveyed the approach. The house was three stories tall and built of gray stone. Nice-looking place, with a retro Eastern European manor house vibe. Lots of windows, only two of them showing weak lights. Probably hallway lights. There was no fence around it, but when I checked the video feeds from Andrea's bird drones, I saw foot patrols. Two men with Kalashnikovs slung walked slowly around the building, accompanied by a Doberman. They all looked bored, but that was something that could change in a heartbeat. A second pair were stationed in a guard shack built to look like a gazebo. They had another Doberman.

"Havoc Actual to Havoc Team," I murmured. "I'm at the east corner. Count four security and two dogs." I gave the locations of each and the direction of the foot patrol.

"Got them," said Belle.

"Two more each in the towers."

I switched the Scout glasses to low-light enhancement but otherwise normal vision. That made it easy to spot one of the two towers. They were really elevated platforms with camouflage canopies. They wouldn't have dogs up there. Which gave us eight armed sentries but just the two dogs.

The challenge in situations like this is to decide where we fell on the force continuum. These guards might be bad guys, or they might be rent-a-thugs who merely worked for a bad guy. Killing them was not immediately justified. And I hate to kill a dog.

I slipped down from the ridgetop to study the video images in my tac-com. The little high-def computer screen was divided into different feeds, one from each bird, but I selected the overhead view from the bird circling the building at a hundred feet. What I was looking for was a blind spot where I could get close enough to ambush the foot patrol and attempt to take them and their dog out using a long-barreled, high-compression Snellig dart gun.

"Sandman only," I told my team. "Verify my order."

They did, and if I heard some reluctance in their voices, that was fine. I wasn't feeling entirely charitable myself. Mercy and compassion had taken a lot of really bad hits lately. There was a cloud of darkness boiling inside me that took real effort to keep from filling my head with the kind of hatred that could erase all sentiment and humanity.

The order to use Sandman actually stuck in my throat.

It was, however, what I said. It was the only mercy I'd brought with me to Trstenik Island.

Not that Sandman is especially kind. It is a cocktail of chemicals built around the veterinary drug ketamine. It also has a little bit of BZ—3-Quinuclidinyl benzilate—to cause intense and immediate confusion, and DMHP—Dimethylheptylpyran, a derivative of THC—for muscle failure. And it has some benzodiazepines and chloral hydrate and some other goodies. We call it *Sandman* because if you get one hit from it, you go right down right now. No bulling your way through. You drop. Everyone does. And for the next couple of hours, you have intensely strange, disturbing, and—I've been told—weirdly erotic dreams. And by weird, I mean that one of the members of Havoc Team—the big kid from Orange County, Bunny—dreamed he was being seduced by penguins. And liked it. Says he has fond memories of that dream. Most people, though, have what can best be described as a bad trip. Monsters come out of the walls, memories warped into nightmares.

The person on our team—apart from me—who would be least happy about using the darts would be Belle. Calling her Mother Mercy was a dark joke because when it came to bad guys, she didn't have so much as a flicker of pity or forgiveness. And it meant that she had to use her backup rifle, a Stoeger XM1 Air Rifle. It's a precharged pneumatic weapon that has an integrated tank filled to 2,900 psi, which allows it to deliver special loads of Sandman darts at 1,200 feet per second before refilling. The .22 version of the XM1 loses a little velocity in trade for a harder-hitting pellet, with speeds around 1,000 fps. Hers was mounted with a superb scope, which mattered to a degree, because although the darts can penetrate ordinary clothing, they couldn't punch through any kind of body armor. The ideal shot was to skin.

I took my Snellig in a two-handed grip, resting my elbow on the ridge.

"Take them," I said and immediately fired nine very fast shots at the two men and their dog. My distance was about forty yards— tough range even for a specialized gun like the one I was using. The dog and one man went right down, but the other turned, grabbing for his gun with one hand and reaching for the Send key on his coms headset with the other. So, I hosed him. He staggered and sat down hard, then keeled over sideways.

Ghost and I were up and moving, sticking to the shadows until we reached the side of the house. There we paused as I waited for the rest of the team to check in.

"Guard tower two down," said Top. "Wait, guard tower one is also down."

I smiled. I wondered if Top had needed to fire a single shot. Yeah, Belle was that good.

"Second patrol down," reported Bunny. "Men and dog."

"Mother Mercy," I said, "take position in tower one. Jackpot, secure the perimeter. Pappy and Donnie Darko, on me."

INTERLUDE 2
THE PLAYROOM
UNDISCLOSED LOCATION
NEAR VANCOUVER, BRITISH COLUMBIA, CANADA
SIX MONTHS AGO

"You look like someone pissed in your coffee, ol' buddy," said Kuga.

"You brought *him* in?" His mouth had gone totally dry, and he gripped the arms of the chair so tightly the wood creaked. "Are you *insane*?"

"Plenty of shrinks seem to think so." Kuga laughed. "But in this case? Nah. This is me making the kind of executive decision that will move our two biggest projects forward."

"This . . . *man* . . . has gone up against Church and Ledger three times that I know of. And three times, he's failed."

"Failed? No, not really. Think of the amount of damage he's done. He nearly destroyed the DMS. He goddamned nearly helped Hugo destroy the oil supplies in the Middle East, which would have hit the stock market like a tsunami. I know Vox had hundreds of his people poised to profit from that, the same way he had buyers ready to grab stock when the planes hit the towers. Hell, he advised me to have my people ready when COVID hit."

"Are you saying that the coronavirus was of his design?"

"What? Oh, hell no. That was an actual natural disaster, but our friend was very savvy about how certain world leaders would react and when to have cash ready to buy stocks during flights to safety. Mr. Sunday advised me to snap up stock in companies making hand sanitizer, bleach, surgical masks, and ventilators. I did and, fuck, Rafael, I banked a couple of billion on COVID-19. I think we made more money on that than I would have if it was something one of our labs cooked up."

"Yes, and that's excellent in itself, but *he* isn't the only person who could advise on such things."

"Maybe not, but he's the best at it. He understands human nature. He reads presidents and prime ministers very well and can go from a press briefing or Twitter post to a buying frenzy faster than anyone I've ever known. And not only will he handle sales for us, he said that he has some ideas for how to mindfuck your boy Ledger. That boy's already on the edge, and Mr. Sunday says all it'll take is the tiniest of pushes."

Santoro set his coffee cup down hard enough to splash half of it onto the table. "He is a monster. He is the most dangerous person I've ever met. His motives are always his own. He was never really on Vox's leash. Never. He always has a personal agenda."

"*Second* most dangerous," corrected Kuga. "Let's keep perspective. Church is the real Big Bad. But Mr. Sunday is the scariest cocksucker on *our* side. And he *is* on our side, Rafael. Make no mistake."

"He was on Hugo Vox's side, too, and Vox is dead," said Santoro coldly. "He was on Zephyr Bain's side, too, and *she's* dead. Same with Grigor and the Upierczy."

"Sure, but I can name a dozen other people he worked for, going way back, too, who *weren't* killed during a shared operation. Point is, the deaths of some of his employers were not his doing or his fault. If anything, it was the excesses of people like Vox and the rampant insanity of Zephyr Bain that led to them being killed. Do you really want to tell me that if Hugo Vox was not at war with his own goddamned mother, he would be alive today? The Kings would still be out there making the world unsafe for widows and orphans, and you, my friend, would never have spent years in a black site prison."

Santoro glared at Kuga but then settled back in his chair, composing his features through sheer strength of will. "We do not need him," insisted Santoro. "We have the American Operation. We have the K-series exosuits, and we have R-33. And we have all of the formulae and technologies that are by-products of those things. We need a salesman, Kuga, not a monster. That man is too dangerous."

"No," said Kuga, "he's just exactly dangerous enough."

CHAPTER 5
TRSTENIK ISLAND
CROATIA

Top and Bunny found me and earned a wag of Ghost's tail.

They were my closest friends on the job and had been with me since Church shanghaied me into joining. Top was a Black former army ranger from Georgia who had a tight salt-and-pepper goatee and eyes that could be fatherly and kind or cold and dangerous depending on the moment. Though right now, his face was hidden by the Scouts and a balaclava.

"What about the hostile you saw?" asked Top.

"I must have been mistaken," I said. "No sign of him, no prints, and Ghost didn't see him."

Top looked at me. I couldn't read his expression through the glasses and the gloom. He tapped out of the team channel and pulled down his balaclava.

"Not like you to jump at shadows, Outlaw," he said quietly.

"Didn't jump, Pappy," I said. "Thought I saw something, checked it out, and I was wrong."

"But you found the trip wire."

"Yes. Right where the guy was standing."

Bunny loomed over us. He was a huge slab of white boy from Orange County. Six feet six, with more muscles than is reasonable on any human being. He was a former top amateur volleyball player turned marine Force Recon turned SpecOps cave troll. Good-natured, but only to a point. The three of us had walked through the Valley of the Shadow too many times to count, and there is no one on God's green earth I trusted as much.

"Are we talking a guard?" he asked.

"Wasn't wearing a uniform," I said. "No weapons that I could see. No kit or body armor."

"Maybe he was a tech checking on the booby traps?" Bunny suggested.

"Sure, Farm Boy," said Top, "because technicians routinely do that at night without lights or backup."

"Hey, old man," Bunny replied, "Outlaw says he saw someone. How many times has he been wrong?"

I cut in. "I was wrong this time."

Top kept looking at me. "But you thought you saw him."

I avoided his eyes. "I was wrong."

When he said nothing else, I knew that it wasn't actually over. Top had been keeping a close eye on me since we rolled out. This was my second field op since coming back to the job. I'd lost some months recovering from injuries sustained in the Christmas Eve blast that killed my family. Top is way too sharp to assume that a healed body is the same as a healed mind or soul. He's a wise and insightful man—qualities that make him an absolutely peerless command sergeant. And a peerless friend.

But now wasn't the time for a heart-to-heart.

"Let's go," I said, and I headed across the lawn to the back door. Ghost was at my heels, with Top and Bunny close behind.

"What do we got, boss?" asked Bunny as he came to crouch beside me.

There was a standard key card reader set into the wall near the knob. "It's all you," I told him.

Bunny reached into a pocket and produced a gizmo about the size of a nickel, removed the adhesive backing, then placed it on the underside of the key card box that was mounted to the right of the door. He then took a blank magnetic key card and swiped it slowly through the reader. On the first pass, nothing obvious happened, which was fine. That meant that the MindReader Q1 tac-com strapped to his left forearm was infiltrating the security software. When he swiped it again, even more slowly, the pass code data was imprinted on his card. A third and faster swipe unlocked the door. But here's the fun part: MindReader is shy and prefers not to be noticed, so it rewrites the host software so that—for all intents and purposes—that door was never opened. There would be nothing recorded on any security log. Nifty.

Bunny pulled the door open as Top and I positioned ourselves for a cross fire. But we were looking into an empty mudroom. I clicked my tongue for Ghost, who stepped inside with great delicacy, as if he were walking onto a thinly iced lake. I followed, with Top behind and Bunny on our six.

The mudroom was large, with pegs for jackets and slots under bench seats for boots. Big metal bowls filled with water and dog kibble. There were photos on all the walls showing Mitrović and a variety of blond women in sailboats, on water skis, on Jet Skis, and walking on beaches. Four different women, was were what Europeans like to call *American blondes*—meaning long-legged, deeply tanned, with sun-streaked hair, expensive smiles, and improbably large and firm boobs. The photos could just as easily have been ads for a cosmetic surgeon, and they were just about as genuine. In every photo, Mitrović wore exactly the same kind of plastic smile.

He was a good-looking guy in his middle forties. Very fit, glowing with health, with a tropical tan over naturally olive skin, lots of curly black hair, piercing blue eyes, and a smile that went about one millimeter deep.

Not entirely sure who the photos were meant to fool. Casual visitors? Government inspectors?

Bunny produced an Anteater from his pack and turned the gain to high. It's a device for detecting various kinds of electronics. He held it up so Top and I could see the screen. There were all kinds of electronics in the building, though the system registered no active alarms or motion sensors. Mitrović placed a lot of faith in his eight-man, two-dog security force. Dumbass.

Top leaned close and said, "Don't mean he doesn't have something tricky on the door to the basement. There's got to be something to let them know if we go waltzing down to Frankenstein's lab."

"Hoo-the-hell-ah," agreed Bunny.

The satellite scans of the heat signatures gave a 93 percent likelihood that there was at least one floor's worth—and possibly two—of machinery below the one we were on. Basement and maybe a sub-basement.

"So we'll be real damned careful," I said.

Unfortunately, the thermal scans couldn't pick out human signatures with all the heat from the generators. However, shipping manifests included forty beds, eight shower and toilet sets, and enough food to feed a hundred people for six months. No way to work out exact numbers, but it sounded like a party to me.

We moved out of the mudroom into a kitchen big enough for a Manhattan restaurant, and then throughout the first floor. There were the embers of a fire in the living room hearth, but no one around. We went up a big flight of stairs in a quick, quiet single file, then took turns checking and clearing the rooms, providing cover for one another. Doing it all very quietly. The four on the left side of the stairs turned out to be two empty bedrooms, a home gym with every kind of trendy device in the catalog, and a bathroom bigger than my whole apartment. No one there.

It wasn't until we checked the rooms on the right side of the stairs. Top and Bunny moved down the hall to take the second bedroom, leaving the first for me. I scanned the door with an Anteater but detected no alarms. So I reached for the knob.

But before my fingers closed around it, a voice behind me said, "Be careful, Joe. This is a bad place for you."

I whirled, bringing up my barrel.

But the hallway behind me was empty.

Ghost whipped his head around and stared. Not at the hall, but at me. There was confusion in his dark eyes. Down the hall, I saw Top watching me. My movement had alerted him, and he looked at me and past me down the empty hall, then back to me again.

I waved him off. He lingered for a moment and then shifted back to the job at hand. Bunny had been scanning the door and did not appear to notice.

Be careful, Joe. This is a bad place for you.

I'd heard those words clear as day.

But the voice.

Fuck me.

That voice was impossible. Achingly so.

Those words had been spoken in the voice of my brother, Sean.

Sean, who was three months in the cold ground of a Maryland cemetery, along with everyone else I was related to by blood.

The shivers kept wanting to take mastery over me. My knees wanted to buckle. There were tears burning in the corners of my eyes.

Was that who I saw in the forest?

No.

No, that man was older. He was . . .

Oh, Christ. I knew who the man in the woods had been. My height. My basic build, but thirty years older.

"Dad," I breathed.

Top and Bunny stopped, and this time, they both turned to me. I'd whispered the word, but the team channel was live. Which meant Andrea and Belle had heard it, too.

I'm losing my shit, I thought, and no voice—living or dead—spoke out in contradiction.

Ghost pushed against my leg with his nose. I thought he was just concerned for his master going around the bend, until I noticed that all the fur on his back was standing straight up.

Top began moving down the hall toward me, but I waved him back. Again there was that lingering look. He did not like what he was seeing. They all knew the emotional stress I was under and how that was built on a fragile framework of a psychological makeup that could best be described as *shaky*. Or, less charitably, that I was deeply damaged goods.

I made myself turn back to the bedroom door. Forced my body into an attitude of alert professionalism. At least that was the façade I was trying to sell. Top wasn't fooled for one damned second, but we were too deep in the badlands here to back up and give me a time-out and maybe some Zyprexa or Seroquel. Personally, I wanted to drink a whole bottle of Knob Creek 100 and listen to the blues. Ideally with no working firearms on the premises.

Lot of things I wanted, but none were likely.

Ghost watched me with unblinking intensity. I tried to telepathically tell him I was just fine and dandy. And his expression told me I was full of shit.

But . . . had he heard the voice, too? That's how I read the situation.

So, did that make us both crazy?

Or . . .

Not now, asshole, I snarled inside my head. *Do your damned job.*

And so I squared my shoulders, girded my loins, chased the ghosts from my head, and turned the handle.

INTERLUDE 3
THE PLAYROOM
UNDISCLOSED LOCATION
NEAR VANCOUVER, BRITISH COLUMBIA, CANADA
FIVE MONTHS AGO

"He's here."

The two words sent a thrill of unfiltered terror through Rafael Santoro.

He's here.

He.

The man who called himself Mr. Sunday.

Kuga lingered in the doorway, smiling that nasty smile of his. A knowing look in his bright eyes, too many white teeth in that grin.

He would have made a good torturer, he mused darkly. *Not professionally, but as a hobby.*

"His chopper just landed," said Kuga. "I'll bring him in."

The door closed with a soft click. An attempt at subtlety? Probably. Santoro rose quickly from the couch on which he had been sprawled while reading field reports. He straightened his clothes and ran fingers through his curly hair. He glanced around, deciding on what image he wanted to convey when the guest entered the room, and decided on the desk. A physical barrier that created a subjective one. The leather guest chairs had slightly shorter legs than the desk chair, which meant that once Kuga and Mr. Sunday sat, they would be looking slightly up at Santoro. Sometimes it made the guests uncomfortable, putting them at a positional disadvantage; sometimes it made Santoro, who was below-average height, feel more powerful in the moment. Today, he wanted both effects.

He went and sat behind the desk and spent a few quick moments tidying some things up, but also staging it to look like this visit was in the middle of a hardworking day. He dug a few files out of a drawer and scattered them artfully on one edge of the desk, placing them at an angle where the tabs could be read. One was on the exoskeleton production, another was R&D on a new eugeroic drug therapy that showed real promise for increasing factory worker man-hours with existing staff.

The door swung open, and Kuga came right in, saying, "Knock-knock."

Santoro, who now had his reading glasses perched on the bridge of his nose and a thick folder open in front of him, finished reading a sentence before looking up. More theater, but that was how the game was played.

Then he leaned back in his chair and watched the two men walk toward him. Kuga strolled with his usual insolent panther grace, but Mr. Sunday moved like a dancer. Very light on his feet, with a springiness that was at odds with his nature. Santoro closed the folder, took off his glasses, tossed them onto the desk, and extended his hand. He'd shaken this man's hand once before and had been deeply repelled then.

As he was now.

Sunday's grip was cool, moist, and utterly slack; and it left Santoro with a desire to wipe his own palm on the seat of his pants. Or maybe go and wash with lye soap.

"Rafael," said Sunday in a faux Southern drawl, "so good to see you after all this time."

"A genuine pleasure," lied Santoro.

They smiled at each other with all the warmth and sincerity of a snake meeting a mongoose.

"Please, have a seat." Santoro placed his fingers lightly on the phone. "Would you like coffee or something?"

"Thank you, no," said Sunday as he settled down into his chair. He wore a tropical-weight white suit with a coral shirt and tie that blended various shades of pale reds and blues. He had gold rings on most of his fingers and an absurdly expensive wristwatch. Sunday's fingers were unusual in that the index and ring fingers were nearly as long as the forefinger, and the pinkies on each hand were oddly thick. There was also a dusting of red hair on the backs of each phalange, and it was very thick on the back of each hand, and some of it even seemed to inch around toward the palm. Sunday had a full, sensual mouth and eyes that seemed to be a slightly different shade of green or perhaps brown, depending on how the light hit them.

But Santoro had seen those eyes change before. Literally change. And the memory haunted him.

"I have to say," began Sunday as he crossed his legs and smoothed his hand along the top of his thigh, "it was a real pleasure to get a call from you fellows."

"Yes," murmured Santoro. "Kuga was very pleased that you agreed to provide your services to us."

"Services," said Sunday, tasting the word. "Yes."

"We're in a nice position for growth," said Kuga. "The Rage thing helped us make our mark. It got us a lot of attention."

"No doubt."

"Mostly *good* attention," continued Kuga. "People got to see what we were capable of and how far a reach we had."

"And what do you think they learned about you?" asked Sunday.

"That we have the science and are willing to use it. That we have a massive network—because there was no part of that operation that didn't require a lot of people working efficiently at different levels. That we have big brass, clanking balls, because—let's face it—we tried to take out the leaders of all nine nuclear powers. Who the fuck's ever even thought about that before?"

"All very true," agreed Sunday, "and I admire the ambition. But I suspect it came with some challenges as well . . . ?"

"Well . . . ," said Kuga, glancing briefly at Santoro, "sure."

"You are the most wanted man on five continents, I believe? That has to be stressful."

"Sure, maybe. Kind of cool, though, too."

Sunday smiled at that. "Ah yes. Cool. Though it did put you on the radar of our mutual friend."

"Church," said Santoro softly.

Sunday's head swiveled around toward him. It was like looking at a praying mantis. "That's his current name, yes. He's had so many others over so many years. Almost as many as I've had. I wonder if either of you, even with your sophisticated intelligence networks, have any clue as to who he really is. Or, more to the point, *what* he is."

"He's human, and he bleeds," said Kuga. "Rafael here shot him in Oslo."

"To what effect? Did he die? It's my understanding that he was shot multiple times and was out of the hospital in under a week. A week," said Sunday mildly. "That should tell you something."

"It tells me Church was wearing body armor. Maybe one of those new spider-silk and graphene rigs, similar to what we're designing for Fixers. Hard to see under a suitcoat, but they'll stop most rounds and reduce damage from the rest. My opinion is that Rafael should have gone for a head shot."

"Or maybe try silver bullets next time," said Sunday, though with him it was always hard to tell if he was being serious or making a deliberately arcane joke. Santoro knew that Hugo Vox liked using him but was also afraid of this man. Very deeply afraid.

Santoro said, "There are rumors that you are equally difficult to kill."

"Clearly," said Sunday, spreading his hands.

"There was a specific rumor going around for a couple of years that Mr. Church killed you in California."

"And yet . . . ," Sunday said, leaving the rest to hang.

"Okay, okay, enough with the *Twilight Zone* bullshit," said Kuga.

　　　　　　　　　　　　　　　　　　　　JONATHAN MABERRY

"Church is a spooky bastard, and so are you. I don't know the details and, frankly, couldn't give a naked mole rat's hairless nutsack about that. What Rafael and I need is someone who has the talent, the charisma, and the cojones to be the face of our organization."

"A spokesman?" mused Sunday.

"Yup. Spokesman and salesman," said Kuga. "We're setting up a kind of virtual sales floor. Think Zoom but built for the dark web. No possibility of being hacked, even by Bug and the MindReader system."

"Bug," said Sunday and looked at his palm, miming the action of turning the pages of a notepad. "Yes . . . he's on my list for special attention one of these days."

"I'd be okay with that," said Kuga. "He's a nosy little prick, and we'd all sleep better at night if he were found dead in a ditch."

Sunday studied him. "Is that something you would like me to handle?"

"No," said Santoro. "That is mine to do."

Kuga cleared his throat and looked a bit uncomfortable. "Rafael here's got a hard-on for everyone who works with Church."

"An animus shared by many," said Sunday. "Though there are names higher on the list than Bug."

"Like Ledger?"

"Yes. I think we'd all like to see him slip over the edge into the shadows." Sunday uncrossed and recrossed his legs. "I was highly entertained by what happened at the Ledger family farm on Christmas Eve. Highly entertained. However, you killed the supporting cast and missed the marquee star."

"If my intention had been to kill Ledger," said Santoro coldly, "he would already be dead."

"So you say, and I love that confidence. It's very sexy."

"It is a fact," countered Santoro.

"And if you weren't defensive about it, I'd thoroughly believe you." Sunday paused and glanced from Santoro to Kuga. "Killing Ledger's family was fun, don't get me wrong. Big applause from all of us in the cheap seats. But it was a half measure. You should have left him a trail to follow and then set up some traps. I have some people who would have been happy to do that for you on a contractor basis. Michael Augustus Stafford comes to mind. And that, my friend, would have kept you out of it. You're on the administrative level now, as I understand it. You shouldn't be getting your hands dirty delivering novelty Christmas gifts."

"I wanted to see his face," said Santoro belligerently. "Or do you lack enough human emotion to understand that?"

"And that is my point, Rafael, old friend. Since when were you *ever* driven by an emotional need?"

The room went quiet.

"You were always the ice man. The most efficient torturer and extortionist, king of your kind. Subtle and forward thinking. Careful, leaving nothing to chance. And yet you went out there to feed off pain because Ledger handed you your ass."

"We fought to a draw," said Santoro.

"And now you're being defensive as well."

Santoro felt his face burning. If he dared, he would have leaped across the table and buried a knife in this man's throat. From the amusement he saw in Sunday's eyes, he knew the man was aware of that desire.

"May I be frank?" Sunday asked of them both.

"Sure, why not?" said Kuga.

"Why not, indeed?" Sunday's smile was unctuous. "You did not, I suspect, bring me in to flatter either of you, and—let's face it—handholding isn't quite my thing."

Santoro said nothing and placed his palms flat on the desk in a deliberate attempt to trick his muscles into relaxing.

"Both of you made your bones with big-ticket gambits. Sure, sure, I know you want to move product, and I know that you've built one heck of an R&D network. Making all sorts of mad scientist goodies. I'm a fan, believe me. But . . . I suspect all of that is wrapped around something that will be very big and ugly, and the good guys won't ever see it coming. Not asking what it is now, but I look forward to when you decide to tell me. It won't be another bioweapon drop on some who-cares Korean island. And I think you're going to want to put a clear win on the books. Oslo showed what you *could* do. You got within shooting distance of nine world leaders. I bet you're thinking you need a state funeral at some point. Something your competitors would never have the balls to attempt. And something that will tell any nervous buyers that Oslo didn't end in that kind of a bloodbath because that was never the point. It was an infomercial about potential. I mean, that's how I'd sell it."

Santoro and Kuga were both listening now. Both leaning forward.

Sunday said, "Look, fellows, you're both rightly proud of the level of your audacity. The Rage matter made headlines in every country on earth. The twenty-four-hour news cycles mention it to this day. You nearly caused a shooting war between China and the United States, and even if you didn't put any world leaders in body bags, you *did* kill the D9 denuclearization conference. That's very nice. It's big. It's doubtful it will be restaged anytime in the next decade. Which means that there will continue to be scrambles for selling any kind of products or services even remotely related to big-ticket arms sales. So, in those two areas, you have been completely successful."

"Hell yes," said Kuga, but before he could say more, Sunday held up a finger.

"Let me finish my thought," said Sunday smoothly. "Had you been better positioned when Kuga began trending on social media, you would have profited significantly more than you have. I'm not saying you didn't get a nice bump in sales via the dark web. Of course you did. There are plenty of people prone to impulse purchases. And lots of small, angry groups with stolen funds burning holes in their pockets. However, have you really seen a sales jump commensurate with the grandeur of what you accomplished? No, gentlemen, I am willing to bet the whole farm that you haven't."

Santoro saw Kuga go pale and then slowly flush with anger and embarrassment.

"And I'm guessing that's why you fellows called me in," said a beaming Sunday. "Am I right, or am I right?"

CHAPTER 6

PHOENIX HOUSE
HEADQUARTERS OF ROGUE TEAM INTERNATIONAL
OMFORI ISLAND, GREECE

The TOC—the Tactical Operations Center—was fully staffed by the best and the brightest. Mr. Church did not hire second-string players.

Fifty-six people sat at computer workstations of varying complexity and function, each of them set in concentric half circles, arranged to face a wall of high-def screens. There was a massive central screen that ran from floor to ceiling and displayed images with astounding clarity and detail. Dozens of smaller screens ringed it, and pop-up windows appeared here and there. Data crawls ran across the bottom and top of the big screen. The sheer amount of information presented at any given moment was extraordinary, but each technician, specialist, and scientist in the TOC was able to process their part without confusion or overload.

Mr. Church stood apart from all the others. He was bigger than everyone else in the room; broad-shouldered and barrel-chested, giving him a blocky presence. His suit was a superbly cut Kiton two-piece with a light gray check over dark blue wool, and an Ermenegildo Zegna Quindici silk tie. Church's hair was dark but streaked with gray, and he wore tinted glasses. He also wore very thin black silk gloves over hands that had been badly damaged on a case some years before.

As the team worked, compiling and sharing data, talking into mics or tapping away at keyboards, Church seemed to be a calm eye in the storm of activity. He stood with his hands clasped lightly behind his back, eyes hidden behind the glasses, features composed and unreadable.

On the screen, thermal imaging, video feeds from bird drones, and data from RFID chips composed a picture of Havoc Team in play. Belle in a tower, covering the front and side of the house with her rifle hidden in shadows. Andrea walking the perimeter, moving from one patch of darkness to another with deceptive ease. While inside four red dots indicated that Top and Bunny were in a hallway on the same floor as Joe Ledger and Ghost.

JONATHAN MABERRY

The team channel was not synced into the TOC, but Church was listening nonetheless. He had access to every channel and listened quietly to what had just happened. First there was the false sighting of a man in the woods; and now the pause outside the master bedroom.

Something was wrong, and Church had the feeling it was going to get worse. He wasn't sure what was going to happen, but his instincts—grown sharp over many years—were telling him to pull Ledger out now.

He almost did.

Almost.

But he did not.

He wondered if he was being efficient or cruel.

Or, perhaps, both.

CHAPTER 7
TRSTENIK ISLAND
CROATIA

I turned the knob and stepped very quietly into what was clearly the master bedroom.

Mislav Mitrović, naked and hairy, lay on an acre of bed. A huge four-poster draped with expensive hand-painted silks and brocades with gold lace. A woman lay curled into a fetal position on the side of the bed, as far from him as was possible, her bent knees and elbows hanging inches over the side. There were candles guttering on a table, and the room stank of wine, roast meat, sweat, and sex. Clothing was scattered everywhere, and most of the feminine garments looked torn.

I positioned Ghost at the door as I crept over to the bed, coming up at an angle so that one of the thick, ornately carved wooden posts provided cover.

The closer I got, the more I could read the scene. The woman was not a woman. She was a girl. Young teen, maybe thirteen or fourteen, with a premature heft of breast and curves from lingering baby fat. There were bruises and suck marks on her shoulders and thighs. But the face was a child's, though painted like a B-movie stripper. Tears had streaked the mascara, and the mouth was puffy from hard use. She was deep inside a dream that made her body tremble and twitch. It did not look like a happy dream.

I shot the young woman. No choice. If she woke up and screamed, then things would go straight into the crapper. Worst-case scenario was that we took her with us when we left. She was clearly underage and had been abused. Scott Wilson, the COO of RTI, had contacts everywhere, and he'd be able to make sure she was properly treated and cared for. Scott had a wife and three daughters, the oldest of whom was about this kid's age.

The Sandman dart hit her on the hip, and her twitching immediately stopped as she dropped deeper into the well of dreams.

That left Mitrović. He didn't stir when I darted the girl. Good.

I holstered the pistol and drew my Wilson Rapid Response knife, snapped the blade into place, clamped my hand over Mitrović's mouth, and laid the edge of the blade against his throat. That woke him right up.

"Make a sound and I'll kill you," I said in Croatian. Not one of my best languages, but I'd brushed up during mission prep.

His eyes popped open, and every muscle in his body went rigid. I clicked my tongue, and Ghost jumped up onto the bed and bared his teeth. Six of them are made of titanium—souvenirs from having lost the original teeth in combat. Ghost loves showing those fangs. He straddled Mitrović's thighs and lowered his head so those teeth were inches from a quickly shriveling penis.

Not surprisingly, Mitrović did not make a sound.

"I'm going to remove my hand," I said and then switched to English because I knew he was a polyglot. I spoke clearly and slowly, watching his eyes to make sure he understood. There was no confusion, only fear. "If you yell or call for help, my dog is going to bite your dick off. Blink once if you believe me. Good. Now blink once if you promise not to do something very, very stupid. Okay, good. Now we're communicating."

I took my hand away but left the knife in place.

"Tell me what you're doing downstairs," I said. "Lie to me and chomp-chomp."

He stared at me in horror. Up close, his face looked different from that of his pictures. His eyes were slightly out of alignment, one tilted and more deeply set than the other. There were some old acne scars, and the caps on his front teeth did not precisely match the adjoining natural ones. Those details made him look more human and more vulnerable. However, it didn't stir any sympathy from me.

Mitrović stared at me, and I could see, even beneath the terror, a calculator brain assessing the situation, reviewing the odds, and evaluating his options. I was not wearing the uniform of any government military or law enforcement agency. I wore no insignias or patches of any kind. My gear was high end, but of a kind he would not have seen before. Church doesn't buy off the rack. The Scout glasses were also unknown to him. I wondered if he was mentally labeling me as a PMC—private military contractor—and wondering what it would cost to buy the pink slip on my soul.

"Don't make me ask again," I said.

"They'll kill me," he said.

"So will I, and I'm right here."

"So are they," he said.

It was a jolt and made me want to turn and look over my shoulder. But if there had been someone hiding in a secret compartment in the wall, Ghost would have sniffed it and given me a signal.

"Is the room bugged?" I asked.

"I . . . don't know," said Mitrović. "They always seem to know."

I used my free hand to tap into the team channel. "Outlaw to Pappy, report."

"Donnie Darko and I just finished a sweep of the rest of this floor," said Top. "All clear."

"I'm in the master bedroom. Find me."

"Copy that."

And a moment later, the door opened and the two of them came in. Bunny lingered in the doorway to watch the hall. Top came over and looked down at the naked girl. Unlike me, Top is a father, and that makes him a different kind of person. He touched the small, raised lump on her hip where I'd darted her, nodded to himself, took a sheet, and pulled it over her. Then he removed one glove and pressed fingers into her carotid and nodded again.

When he raised his head, I could almost hear his neck muscles creak.

"What's the play?" he asked in a totally arctic voice.

"Sweep the room for bugs."

Top produced his device and carefully ran it over all the walls, cabinets, bedposts, and chairs. He flipped over a heavy leather recliner and pointed to a very small and sophisticated bug hidden behind a strut. He left it in place and finished his search, finding another in the wall nearest to an open laptop on a desk. He used a knife to gouge the device out of its hiding place. It had been placed in a tiny pocket of drywall and then lightly plastered and painted over. Wires trailed down to the baseboard, where they were threaded into the power cord for an ornate clock.

"Call it," he said. "If they're listening, then they already know we're here."

"No alarms going off," I said.

"Doesn't mean they don't know." He looked at the sleeping girl. "There is no part of this that doesn't feel hinky. I think we ought to wrap this up and get gone sooner than later."

"You got that shit right," I muttered.

I bent over Mitrović. And then I froze. His eyes had changed. Before, they were dark and intense, filled with fear and calculations; now they were different. They seemed to be too wide, for one thing, and although he was looking directly at me, there was an unfocused quality about his stare.

And then he screamed.

To hell with my knife, to hell with a big dog ready to bite his junk off, Mitrović let loose with a massive, high-pitched shriek of total, blind, mad rage. Then he came up off the bed with such astounding speed and power it knocked my knife away and set Ghost tumbling to the floor. There was no preparatory tensing of muscles, no sign that he was going to move. He was suddenly and totally in motion. He leaped from the bed and flung himself at me, driving me backward with astonishing force.

His mouth lunged forward, and his teeth snapped shut on the corner of my Scout glasses, tearing them sideways, obscuring my vision.

I pivoted as he drove me backward and clopped him hard on the side of the head, sending him crashing into a bureau. He hit really hard, and although it had to be painful, he spun off the impact and dove at me again, this time trying to bite my throat.

Which was when Ghost hit him like a cruise missile, metal teeth clamping onto Mitrović's thigh, high near the groin. Impossible to ever tell if it was a deliberate attack to the femoral artery or an unlucky accident, but suddenly blood geysered up. I grabbed Ghost and hauled him back, ordering him to release his bite. He did, but he took a chunk of meat with him.

Mitrović did not scream in pain. Instead, even with a mangled leg, he drove at me again, howling like a demon from the pit. My hand moved, and my knife moved with it, slapping across the man's throat, opening a second fire hydrant of blood.

He dropped right there.

All of this happened in the time—call it a second?—that it took Top to run around the big bed and bring his Snellig up. He looked at me, and I shook my head.

"The fuck was that?" demanded Bunny, coming in from the hall.

But I think we all knew what it was.

And when we heard the wild screams from downstairs, it confirmed it. File it under worst-case scenario.

Mitrović—and maybe everyone else on the staff—had been dosed with a designer bioweapon Kuga had used on civilians in both North and South Korea and on a mass of dignitaries, security people, politicians, and the press at the D9 denuclearization summit in Oslo, Norway. A bioengineered neurotoxin made from the *Loligo beta-microseminoprotein* found in the longfin inshore squid. Once dosed, it drove everyone exposed to it into a state of total murderous fury.

We called it Rage.

There was no cure except time. No way to manage it except Sandman, and it was too late for that. Mitrović was bleeding out, and even if I'd wanted to save his life, that ship had sailed right off the edge of the planet.

I whirled.

"The lab!" I yelled, and we ran from the room and thundered down the stairs, following the shrieks. They were coming from the same mudroom we'd used, except they stabbed outward through the very walls. I knew that it meant there was a hidden entrance, but damn if it didn't make me feel like we were in a haunted house. Or a haunted asylum.

INTERLUDE 4
SALES PRESENTATION VIA SHOWROOM
SIX MONTHS AGO

"Please pardon the odd nature of this conference," said Mr. Sunday. "With the global pandemic, we're all forced to make adjustments. But also, let me assure you that our proprietary ShowRoom video conferencing technology is bleeding edge. No one can participate without codes, such as those sent to you. Anyone who tries will discover how disheartening malware, ransomware, and computer tapeworms can be."

The man was smiling as he said it. He even exuded warmth. A charm that twinkled in his green eyes, sparkled from his white teeth, and glowed from his palpable and potent persona.

Mr. Sunday wore a Brioni suit, dark blue with the faintest hint of a plaid in varying shades of thread on similar blues. A cream-white shirt and exceptional Stefano Ricci formal crystal silk tie. His shoes were Louis Vuitton Manhattan Richelieu made from waxed alligator leather. He wore a Richard Mille RM 022 Carbon Tourbillon Aerodyne Dual Time Zone Watch that retailed at just under $700,000. The diamond in his pinkie ring was 2.7 carats set into white gold with sixty-six tiny emerald chips orbiting the great central stone.

It was difficult to gauge his age on the video screen—he could have been forty or sixty, depending on the angle and where the colored lights hit him as he moved across the improvised stage. In blue light, he looked cadaverous, like a movie vampire. In green light, he became sinister, and those tones seemed to make his irises swirl with different shades of green and brown. But in the other shades, he was handsome and affable and looked like a monied entrepreneur and salesman. It was clear from this—and previous ShowRoom events—that Mr. Sunday seemed to be enjoying the effect, and he often moved into unflattering or distortive lights when making certain points.

The audience—sixteen men and women scattered around the world on six continents—were riveted.

"For the benefit of the two newbies to our little chat, I'd like to remind you that everyone can see me," said Mr. Sunday, "but for the sake of privacy—and, well, security and discretion—none of you can see one another. I can hear you all, but when you speak, the others will only see your questions or comments as text. Is everyone comfortable? No need for a fresh cup of coffee or a bathroom break? No? Excellent. Let's begin, shall we? Are you with me? Good."

He paused to smile at each of the sixteen faces on the high-def screens. It amused him that they were about as racially mixed as was likely in a meeting of high-roller industrialists and military buyers. It was all one big happy world to him. The more the merrier. Life was a goddamned peach if you knew how to pick the right fruit from the right tree.

Instead of a standard clicker, Mr. Sunday had two tiny sensors on the thumb and ring fingers of his left hand. He tapped the sensors to send a video file to each of the participants. The same video played on a big screen behind him.

"Our first item today is a little crowd-pleaser of a bioweapon intended for strategic population control," he said. "It is volatile but, used correctly, is self-limiting. Unlike viral or bacterial bioweapons, this does not spread. There is no risk of a resulting pandemic because, let's face it, we're not trying to destroy the world." His laugh was rich and warm and knowing. "There is a very specific delivery system for this, and after a certain amount of time, the substance itself becomes inert. Let's see how this works, shall we? It's highly entertaining."

The video showed a group of four people—three men and a woman—seated on wooden chairs at a metal table in a room with very little furniture. There was a framed painting on the wall of a banal seascape, a generic sofa, and a small table with a coffee maker and fixings. The people were busy filling out forms using yellow Number 2 pencils.

One of them suddenly looked up at a vent set high into the wall above them. He frowned at it, and over the speakers, there was a faint hissing sound.

"*Inch' e da?*" he said, and the video provided translation from Armenian. *What is that?*

The others looked up. There was no obvious cause for alarm. No gas poured out of the vent, nothing but cool air with a few droplets of what appeared to be condensation.

When nothing appeared to be amiss, they lost interest and returned to filling out what they believed were job applications.

The man who'd first looked up was actually sitting farthest from the vent and was now fully engrossed in the form. The woman was almost directly under the vent, and she had stopped writing. None of the three men seemed to notice, or if they did, they didn't much care. People often paused when filling out forms—deciding on what to say, how to phrase it, or fishing for information. The image shifted, proof that there were several cameras in the room. It showed the woman's face. Her eyes seemed to become gradually glazed, as if she were day-dreaming and lost deep in thought. One eye twitched, though. As did her fingers. She looked down at her pencil and studied it as if it were something she'd never seen before. The woman turned it over, apparently fascinated by the graphite point.

Then she turned and drove the pencil deep into the eye socket of the man closest to her. It was a very fast and very powerful blow, and the point exploded the man's eyeball. The man shrieked in absolute agony and absolute surprise.

The other two men leaped up and back, staring in horror.

"*Astvats im!*" cried one man. "*Inch' yes arel?*"

My god! What have you done?

Those were the words that came out of his mouth, but as he spoke them, he grabbed the other uninjured man by the ears and slammed him face-forward onto the table. Once. Twice. Again and again and again. He did not stop, even as the other man's face broke apart and blood splattered everywhere. He did not stop as the front of the man's skull cracked like an egg. He did not stop even when one of the man's ears tore off. He did not stop even as the woman got up and rushed around to his side of the table and drove her pencil into his thighs and buttocks and lower back.

He only stopped when she stabbed him in the back of the neck, and then he released the dying man and whirled, grabbed her by the throat, and strangled her. Her last act before his fingers crushed her windpipe was to drive the now broken point of the pencil into his throat just below the Adam's apple, punching a hole through the hyoid bone.

The man drowned in his own blood, but he dragged the woman's corpse down to the floor with him.

The first man, whose eye was destroyed and who should have been incapacitated by the sheer pain and trauma, got sloppily to his feet and began stomping the two figures on the floor. He stomped and stomped and stomped until they no longer resembled human beings. Then he spun toward the door and tried to jerk open the handle, which was locked. The man howled with inhuman fury and began pounding on the door. With his fists—which disintegrated into pulp—with his feet and knees, and with his own face. He smashed his face repeatedly against the reinforced safety glass. He continued with unrelenting intensity until there was not enough left of his skull and brains. His knees buckled, and he sank down to the floor and flopped over. Dead. Ruined.

The door opened, and a guard had to shove hard to move the slumped body. Then two men with AK-47 machine guns entered and carefully shot all four of the people in the head. Even the dead ones.

The video file ended.

Mr. Sunday was smiling as he looked down at his watch.

"From the first onset of symptoms," he said, "to the elimination of all infected . . . fifty-one seconds. And, in case anyone still has a lingering doubt—yes, this is the party favor used on the island of Gaeguli Seom in North Korea, on Yeonpyeong Island in *South* Korea, and at the D9 conference in Oslo. It has a 100 percent effectiveness. No possible immunity. In practical application, this can be delivered via microdrones, introduced to drinking water, or sprayed in water vapor. Because it's not a bacterium or virus, it doesn't require special storage and can't infect the user. Are you with me still?"

He watched the faces on all the screens. Saw the interest and the repulsion. He was fine with either because it helped him select the best potential customers.

"This bioweapon is available in limited quantities," he continued. "Introduce it to any contained target—a village of an inconvenient ethnic group, a military base, the offices of a corporate rival, even on an individual basis. It's much better than, say, a polonium pellet whose radiation and gas chromatograph signatures allow it to be traced. Better than the clumsy neurotoxins used by some of our colleagues. This weapon is unique and is tied to no specific country of origin. We call it *Rage* for obvious reasons." He paused and dialed up the wattage on his smile. "Now . . . who would like to start the bidding at one billion euros?"

CHAPTER 8
TRSTENIK ISLAND
CROATIA

Top placed his palm flat on the wall through which we could hear the screams most clearly.

"Sounds like inside and maybe down," he said. "I'm thinking basement here."

I called Andrea in from outside but told Belle to hold position. Then I tapped into the TOC channel and very quickly explained the situation. About Mitrović, the bugs we'd found, the girl, and the Rage.

"We're going to need evac for the girl," I said. "Maybe other friendlies here."

"Chopper is inbound," said Wilson. "ETA fourteen minutes."

"Tell them not to stop for coffee."

Andrea came in through the back door, his rifle ready, but he shifted the barrel away from us and pointed it at the wall. Fists were pounding on it with savage intensity.

"Dimmi che questo non è quello che penso che sia," he breathed.

Tell me this isn't what I think it is.

"Rage," said Bunny. "Freaking Rage. I thought we were done with that shit."

"Why's that, Farm Boy?" asked Top in his voice-of-reason tone.

"Just 'cause we spanked them in Oslo doesn't mean they threw away all their toys. We've got to always be ready for them to use this."

"Which means," I said, "if any of us gets dosed, then someone else darts us. And if you get dosed and there's no one around, try to dart yourself before you lose your shit."

"Hooah," they said, though without enthusiasm. Oslo—and the horrors we'd encountered on Gaeguli Seom and Yeonpyeong Island in Korea—were still recent and vivid in our minds.

I punched the wall with the side of my fist. "We need to get in. Rage or not, we need to know what's down there. No need to keep it quiet."

"If we don't need to stay quiet," said Andrea, "then let me get out some toys." He unslung his pack and began pulling stuff out. Bunny knelt to help him.

Andrea Bianchi was on loan to RTI from the Gruppo di Intervento Speciale, an elite division of Italy's Carabinieri, which was a branch of their armed forces responsible for both military and civil policing. He was able to rig a bomb, cut a throat, or pick a lock with equal nonchalance. A lean man who looked like he worked in an office somewhere doing something unimportant but who had become a critical part of Havoc Team.

He took a blaster-plaster from the bag and unrolled it. It looked like one of those gel packs used to ice a strained back, except that it was clear and thin. There was a network of wires through it, and tiny little blisters of chemicals. He scanned the wall and found the probable doorway, then tore the adhesive off one side and pressed it in place.

"*Sta per diventare rumoroso qui!*" he shouted as he backpedaled and then ran into the kitchen. *It's about to get loud in here.*

We ducked down behind the big island as Andrea thumbed a small device.

The explosion was massive, shaking the entire building. We crept back in and discovered that the entire wall was gone—obliterated by the blast. The heavy steel security door had been punched inward and lay drunkenly on the top steps of a metal stairway. Parts of the mudroom ceiling had come down, and the blast had blown the door to the outside and all the windows out.

"Holy monkey balls!" gasped Andrea.

"Think you used enough?" asked Bunny.

Andrea shrugged. "Didn't want to have to ask twice."

I had my Snellig in my hands and leaned into the stairway. There were three bodies on the steps, each badly mangled by the blast. One was dressed in the same nondescript clothes as the guards outside. One was in a lab coat. The third was a woman wearing white capri pants and a scarlet blouse. Except the blouse wasn't supposed to be that color. The blast had torn her arm and head off.

At the bottom of the staircase were a few other people, mostly technicians in white coats. They looked dazed, and most were bleeding. I trained my gun on them, and Top leaned in and did the same with his Snellig rifle. We watched the people get to their feet, shaking heads like befuddled dogs.

"Give me a happy ending," I murmured.

"Day ends with a *Y*," said Top sourly.

The people down there suddenly all looked up. Whether drawn by the sound of our voices or driven by some chemical force, it was hard to say. They glared at us. They bared their teeth.

And with a mingled howl of murderous joy, they charged up the stairs.

CHAPTER 9
THE PLAYROOM
UNDISCLOSED LOCATION
NEAR VANCOUVER, BRITISH COLUMBIA, CANADA
SIX DAYS AGO

"Do you have it?"

Mr. Sunday stood beside his car, his face in dense shadows thrown by a massive old pine tree. The sunlight was so bright and the shadows so dark that the dividing line between made the salesman look as if he were cut in half.

Kuga did not offer to shake hands. Neither did Sunday. It wasn't that kind of moment.

"I got it," said Kuga, holding up a thick padded envelope.

"Blood and hair?"

"Took some doing. We had to get it from an Oslo evidence locker. Not easy and not cheap."

"The effort will be worth it," said Sunday.

Kuga did not immediately hand over the envelope. "You know, man, this is some real spooky shit right here. This whole thing . . . ?"

"Yes?"

"How do I know you're not just running some kind of weird psycho head trip on me?"

"You can't know either way," said Sunday. Although Kuga couldn't see the big smile, with all that darkness, he could *feel* it. That awareness gave him the creeps.

"Shit."

"There's still time to back out," said Sunday. "Just throw that envelope away and forget we ever had this meeting."

Kuga looked at the envelope, at the shadows, and up into the sky. It was blue overhead, but a storm front was troubling the horizon and there were flocks of black birds—ragged-looking crows or starlings—flying toward those clouds. He didn't like the way that made him feel.

He sighed heavily and held out the envelope. A pale hand reached out of the shadows and plucked it from his fingers. The envelope vanished into the shadows, and Kuga heard the seal rip open.

"This will be fun," said Mr. Sunday, though for just a moment his voice sounded different. Rougher, stranger, with a different accent—not Southern but foreign. Italian? And it was a much, much older voice.

Sunday got into his car, keeping his face turned away from Kuga, who stood watching as the car backed up, turned, and drove in the same direction as the black birds.

CHAPTER 10
TRSTENIK ISLAND
CROATIA

Top and I opened fire as we began walking down the stairs. Sandman did its work, dropping them one after another. I heard Bunny's heavy steps on the stairs behind me, and Andrea's lighter footfalls. Ghost stood on the stairs and barked. Had I told him to stay back? I couldn't remember. Or maybe he had been in enough biohazardous situations by now to follow his own wisdom.

We reached the floor and immediately formed a half circle around the base of the stairs, each of us firing. There were maybe twenty people down there. They came at us with bare hands and snapping teeth. Others grabbed whatever they could to use as weapons to smash us. A chair, a piece of pipe, a screwdriver, a mop. The choice of weapon didn't matter. All that filled their minds was an unbearable need to hurt, to kill.

I understood that need. I'd felt it in Oslo when I'd been sprayed with Rage and tried my best to kill everyone, including my own team. I went after Belle, and she'd shot me with Sandman. But . . . damn . . . that rage was real. It was an emotion so real, so pure that it crowded everything else out. It was genuine, it defined me in that moment. I would have killed her and Top and Bunny and anyone else I could have gotten my hands on. Or my teeth. In those few moments, nothing else mattered to me. The rage was my life, my heart, and my god.

As it was to these poor bastards.

I felt a flicker of empathy for them, and with it came that insidious compassion infused with rationalization. Maybe they didn't know they worked for Kuga. Maybe they didn't understand the uses to which whatever they were doing down here would be put. Maybe they didn't know that their boss, Mitrović, was a pedophile who raped and abused young girls.

Maybe, maybe, maybe.

None of that stopped my finger from pulling the pistol. Not sure it would have stopped me if I was pulling the trigger on a more lethal weapon. The three aspects of my fractured personality were all engaged in this. The Modern Man—that normal aspect—was yelling that this was merciful, that once subdued they could be treated, helped, rehabilitated. The Cop was being his pragmatic self, arguing that dropping all these people would allow us access to the physical assets of machinery, computers, samples. And reminding me that if there were bioweapons of any kind here, they'd be sealed in safety containers and flown out to where Dr. John Cmar and his Bug Hunter team were waiting on a biohazard containment barge forty miles off the coast. And the Killer, the savage hunter in my head, just wanted to eliminate the enemy and maybe look for whomever might be down here. More girls like the one upstairs, or test subjects for Rage or other dreadful concoctions.

So my finger pulled and pulled, and the bodies dropped.

There was another presence inside my head. Not a voice per se, though it did sometimes whisper to me. Usually at night when I was deep in a nightmare re-creation of Christmas Eve. Watching Santoro, dressed in a Santa hat and beard, deliver a box to my brother, Sean. Handing it to him. Smiling as he drove away in his stolen FedEx truck. The memory of my brother carrying the box inside, likely to set it down so his hands would be free for hugs with me and Junie Flynn. And then my realization that the port-wine stain on the FedEx driver's face was not that at all but a healing bruise from the fight we'd had in Norway. The package exploded, killing everyone inside the house, nearly killing Junie, and Ghost, and me. And in the weeks of recovery that followed, I became aware of that new presence. Not another facet of my splintered personality. Nothing as sane as that. No, this was like a sentient and lightless cloud of dark energy that was trying to take possession of me, body, mind, and soul. A pernicious shadow thing born of a loss so deep that I could not and cannot process it. In the lexicon of my own damage, I called it the Darkness.

As the screaming people closed around us and we fired the tranquilizer darts at them, the Darkness kept trying to pull my hand down, to make me holster or drop the Snellig and reach for the Sig Sauer with its full magazine of copper-jacketed hollow-points.

That ache, that temptation, that *need* was so damned strong, and so much of me wanted to give in to it. Out of a weariness of fighting it. And out of a desire to *be* it.

The last of the technicians fell, and there was a moment of an awful silence. We were surrounded by a wall of bodies. There was no haze of gun smoke or shuddering gasps of the dying. The people lay in heaps, each of them sleeping.

Almost all of them were bloody, though, just not from us.

Rage is not targeted. It doesn't direct the infected toward an enemy. All humans were the enemy, and so before we'd entered the scene, they had been attacking one another. Beyond the ring of unconscious people were a half dozen corpses, some badly dismembered. One man had almost no head, and from the shape of the pulped mass of what was left, someone had stomped his head to jelly. A woman lay against a row of filing cabinets, her skirt pushed up and her legs spread so wide they'd clearly become dislocated. She had been violated with a long-barreled flashlight. A man had dozens of pencils shoved into each of his eye sockets.

"Psycho wombat balls," breathed Andrea.

Bunny shook his head. "Fuck me sideways."

I looked around. We were in what looked like a computer center. Dozens of workstations, supercomputers off to one side behind glass in a cooled room, and rows of file cabinets of various sizes.

"Spread out and search this place," I said as Ghost crept down to stand beside me. He was quivering with nervous energy. "Jackpot, disconnect the computers from any power source, cable, or landline. Pappy and Donnie Darko, assess the tech and bag anything we need to take."

"Too much to take," said Bunny.

"Prioritize," I told him.

There was a corridor leading off the room, and I thought I heard some muffled sounds coming from there. "Ghost and I will check that out," I said.

Once I rounded the bend, I saw that the corridor ran forty feet to a big door on rails, like a barn door, and made out of oak planks. Very sturdy, and with a big industrial dead bolt lock. No way to tell if it was locked from the outside or inside. I had a blaster-plaster with me, but I didn't want to injure anyone if there were prisoners or test subjects incarcerated there. However, there was a glass case inset into the wall near where I stood that had a red fire extinguisher bracketed in between a heavy flathead fire ax.

I paused to reload the Snellig, then used the butt of the pistol to smash the glass, then holstered the dart gun. I pulled the ax from the aluminum clips. Like the extinguisher, it was painted a vivid red to make it easier to see in smoky situations, with the blade coated in clear rust-resistant lacquer. It had a bright yellow thirty-six-inch fiberglass handle and felt solid and sturdy in my hands as I approached the door.

The muffled sounds I'd heard earlier were definitely coming from there. I leaned close, but the sounds were odd and indistinct. No screams, though. None of the Rage-infused mania.

"Get back," I said to Ghost. "Watch."

He walked backward fifteen feet and sat, eyes alert, ears swiveling, nose sniffing the air.

I braced my feet, grasped the neck of the handle a few inches below the ax's head, with my palm facing away, making sure my grip was firm but not tense. Then, as I swung it down, using muscle, posture, and gravity to accelerate and gather force, my top hand slid down to meet the other, creating a nice fulcrum to deliver that power. The way my father had taught me to split logs on his brother's farm. The farm where they all died. The blade bit deeply into the wood, and splinters flew into the air.

I kept swinging, feeling my muscles flow through the movement, accepting the jolt of each impact, allowing the shock to travel up and out through unresisting tissue, before tugging the blade free again. And again. The wood was thick and did not want to break apart, but the ax and my own brand of personal rage offered a more compelling argument.

Suddenly, the whole lock assembly toppled onto the floor, and the door swung inward. I shifted the ax to my left hand and drew the Snellig with my right, then kicked the door open and stepped in, fading to one side, sweeping the room with eyes and gun barrel tracking together.

I have long ago stopped requiring proof that you don't need to die to enter hell.

What I saw was out of something by Dante or maybe Bosch. Or maybe this was what the U.S. Seventh Army's Forty-Fifth Infantry Division saw and felt when they liberated Dachau. The people were chained to the beds with leg irons and bound with leather belts across waist and chest, wrists secured by cuffs. Many were naked, their bodies punctured by wires and IV lines and electrodes surgically drilled into their skulls and sternums. They were a cross section of humanity with no apparent bias toward one race. More than half were. The room stank of urine, feces, blood, sweat, antiseptic, and human misery. Stepping into that room was like being punched in the soul, and that blow was damned near crippling.

Eyes turned toward me with fresh horror, seeing a big man dressed for combat, armed with an ax and a gun and a combat dog with blood on his muzzle. Those who could scream, did. A few begged for mercy from God or cried out for their mothers. The little ones merely screamed.

And behind the beds were a dozen technicians in stained lab coats. They cringed back against the far wall as if they could distance themselves from my awareness of what they were doing here. As if holding up hands was all that they'd need to escape punishment for their crimes. As if trying to look weak and helpless and pitiable would be effective.

I heard Bunny calling my name, asking about my status. The Snellig slipped from my fingers and clattered to the concrete floor. I tore the coms unit from my ear and ground it underfoot. I slammed the door through which I'd just entered and pulled a heavy steel worktable in front of it. Then I began walking toward the cringing technicians. I passed between rows of children covered in surgical scars, some still with stitches from god only knew what kind of obscene experimentation.

I don't know why these technicians, nurses, and doctors were not infected by Rage when the facility fail-safe was triggered. Maybe they were too senior, too valuable to what was going on. To what Kuga and Santoro had intended for this place.

I also didn't care. I kept walking, trying not to let the horrors on either side of me cripple my progress. The overhead fluorescents threw my shadow across the faces of the cowering.

They screamed for mercy.

They begged for mercy.

But I hadn't brought any mercy with me.

I stood in the doorway, chest heaving, sweat running down my body inside my clothes. The room was far too bright, and every sound was terribly loud.

I looked down at the ax in my hands.

I could hear Bunny yelling from outside the room. Top, too. Ghost stood at the door and barked at them. My team were all outside.

Kuga's people were inside with me.

Here with me and my ax.

In my heart and head, the Darkness roiled and twisted and finally broke free.

CHAPTER 11
FREETECH RESEARCH AND DEVELOPMENT OFFICE
SAN DIEGO, CALIFORNIA

Junie Flynn was in the act of lifting a glass of wine to her lips when she suddenly shuddered with such unexpected violence that the wine sloshed and the glass slipped from her twitching fingers. It struck the side of the worktable and exploded, showering her and her companion with tiny glittering fragments.

Then Junie staggered back, a hand going to her throat.

"What's wrong?" cried Toys, a young man whose normally stern face twisted into a look of mingled shock and concern.

"I—" she began, and then her eyes rolled high and she puddled down to the floor.

Toys caught her under the neck and back, inches from the floor. He squatted, grunted, and picked her up. She was a tall woman, and he was a man below middle height, but he was wiry and much stronger than he looked. Toys carried her quickly to the adjoining staff lounge, kicking the door open and laying her down on a leather couch. Junie was totally out, and he quickly took her pulse. Finding the steady heartbeat was not entirely comforting because it fluttered like hummingbird wings on a window of a house in which it had gotten trapped. He felt her head, but there was no sign of a fever.

Toys pulled a cell phone from his jeans pocket and punched 9-1-1. When the call was answered, he said, "I need an ambulance at—"

"No," said Junie sharply. "No, please, Toys, don't . . . I'm okay."

He glanced down at her. "You sodding well aren't. You dropped into a dead faint."

"Please," she said, gesturing weakly to the phone. "No ambulance."

Toys explored the inside of his mouth with his tongue—a habit he had when he was trying to decide something on the fly. Then said, "Sorry, my mistake." And disconnected the call. He dropped to his knees beside the couch and took her hand. "To quote your beefcake boyfriend, what in the wide blue fuck was that?"

Clouds of doubt passed across her features. Junie was a little older than Toys but normally exuded youthful energy and strength. Anyone who didn't know her and didn't look too closely merely saw a woman with masses of wavy blond hair, sky-blue eyes, and a wholesome smile that was so infectious it made other people smile without knowing why or even being aware they were doing it. But when they looked closely, they saw small lines of care around her mouth and at the corners of her eyes. Lines that may have been born as laugh lines but that had been deepened by stress, awareness, and pain. Life had been unkind to Junie in ways none of the other employees at Free-Tech knew about. Toys did, because they were friends on that special level where there are no secrets.

Just as Junie knew about Toys and his very checkered past.

Their life paths had made them freakish by any normal standards, but there was a bonding in that. They both were from what Junie's lover, Joe Ledger, called the *storm lands*. It gave the refugees from life's more troubled places a shared understanding that ran deeper than mere empathy. It taught them a language that often did not require words and whose aspects seldom had appropriate adjectives.

"What's going on with you?" he asked. His accent, though refined by education and world travel, easily echoed the Essex town of Purfleet, where he'd grown up hard in a bad neighborhood and a worse home. This was long before the local government changed it to the more upscale-sounding *Purfleet-on-Thames* as part of an intended gentrification. "Since when do you get the vapors, you silly cow?"

"It wasn't that," she began, but paused. "I . . . I . . ."

"Finish a sentence for me. There's a good lass."

Junie pushed herself up to a sitting position while Toys watched,

JONATHAN MABERRY

studying her eyes and complexion to look for a drop in blood pressure. She seemed fine, though, if a bit pale.

"It was so weird," she said. "I mean . . . I never faint."

"Because you're not an ingénue from a Victorian drawing room novel," he said. "So why *did* you faint? You feeling sick?"

"No, it's not that."

"Then what?" asked Toys.

"I . . . I think it was Joe."

Toys made a moue of disapproval. "What about him?"

Junie rubbed her face with her hands and looked around the room as if she'd never seen it before. When she looked back at Toys, he saw tears glittering like small diamonds in the corners of her eyes. They broke and fell down her cheeks. The sight touched him, softening his natural antagonism every time Ledger's name was mentioned. The dislike they shared of each other was rooted in just cause and had memories of hurt and harm heaped over it.

He waited for Junie to find the words to say what disturbed her so deeply.

"I think he's in trouble," she said.

Toys smiled. "Oh, honey, he's always in trouble. That man could get into trouble alone in an empty room."

But Junie shook her head, and her ashen skin went paler still.

"No . . . I mean in real trouble. I mean . . . I'm not talking him being in physical danger. He lives for that stuff. No, Toys, I think Joe is in *real* trouble."

As she said that, her fingers brushed her forehead and then fell down to touch the spot on her chest over her heart.

CHAPTER 12
NOWHERE

He sat in near-total darkness. A single votive candle burned, and it cast a circle of pale, trembling light. None of that light touched the man who sat cross-legged on the floor. He was naked, his pale body veined with twisted lines of black and red, as if every part of him was rife with disease, and those diseases warred within him. That was unseen—always—by any eyes but his own and the few unfortunate women who made the mistake of falling for his smile and his charm. Women whose bodies were seldom recovered, and never whole.

The room was quiet except for the faint buzz of insect wings. Flies crawled across the floor and around the rim of the hammered copper bowl. One snuck down into the bowl and lapped at the stinking red liquid. It had been left to rot in this room, and that excited the flies. They, like the man, found the smell to be quite exquisitely exciting.

The man picked up a box of Lucifer matches and struck one, enjoying the flare of heat. He was always cold. Always.

He let the match burn for a moment, then picked up the photograph and studied it.

It was a picture of a man printed from surveillance camera footage. Good quality, though a bit blurred since the man was in motion. A tall, powerful, fierce man with pale eyes and paler hair.

He did not hate this man. He only hated one person on earth, but that one was beyond the reach of a ceremony like this. No, he rather loved this blond man with the icy blue killer's eyes. A man like this was a child of chaos, and every child of chaos was the conjurer's brother. He loved them all.

The light of the match brightened the room, allowing the yellow glow to reach as far as the clothes and jewelry and skin he had removed.

Then he touched the flame to the corner of the photograph and watched as the golden fingers reached up the face, blackening the paper, charring the grim countenance of the killer. When only the small corner he held was unburnt, he dropped it into the bowl of putrefying blood and strands of hair.

It flashed and flared and burned with such lovely colors. Green and brown in all their baser shades.

He sat there, naked, reeking, smiling, and watched it all burn until there was nothing left in the bowl but a smear of darkness.

CHAPTER 13
TRSTENIK ISLAND
CROATIA

"Mary mother of God . . ."

I heard Bunny's voice behind me, but I didn't turn. I was afraid of what he'd see in my eyes. The ax was heavy in my hands, the handle slick. The stink of copper was sharp in my nose despite the balaclava I still wore.

Behind me, the people in the beds had all fallen silent. They'd screamed for a while. Awful screams that I'd only been able to hear distantly, as if they were on the other side of a thick curtain. Or in another world.

"Top . . . is it Rage? Is Outlaw infected?"

I shook my head but could not speak.

"Outlaw . . . ," said another voice. Top.

I looked down at my hand, which was red to the wrist. My knuckles were tight against my skin, my fingers clutching the ax handle so tightly it hurt. The pain felt good, though.

Footsteps a little closer. Then a hand on my forearm. Strong. Steady. Top's hand. For some reason, he'd taken off his glove, and I saw his brown fingers curl around mine. Felt the pressure as he coaxed my hand to release the tool. The ax slipped, and Top caught it. He tossed it away. We both watched it hit the concrete, striking sparks before it went slithering and rasping across the floor and vanished under a bed. The inmate of that bed was a man in his forties who lay staring at the ceiling with eyes that appeared to see everything or nothing at all.

Ghost whined softly, the sound as heart-piercing as a troubled child trying to punch his way out of a nightmare.

"It's not Rage," murmured Top. "This is . . ."

He let the rest hang. I still said nothing.

Top took my arm, turning me to face him. He'd removed his goggles and balaclava. His face looked ten years older than it should have. Seamed and sad, his eyes filled with concern.

I looked past him to where Bunny, a big key ring in his hands, was working to unlock the prisoners. Andrea stood in the doorway, goggles and hood still on, but tension written in his body language. Bunny glanced at Top and me, and then his eyes slid away.

I was covered in blood. It was all over my clothes, glistening darkly like oil. It was on my hands and splashed across the lenses of the Scout glasses.

Top stood in front of me, the heel of his hand resting on the butt of his Snellig dart gun. "Do I need to get you out?"

I said, "What? Oh. No."

His eyes seemed to drill into mine. I saw concern, doubt, something else. My perceptions were so warped. I don't know what emotions I was really seeing.

"Why don't you go upstairs and wait on the chopper," Top said gently. "You don't need to be down here. You've done your part. We can handle the rest."

I looked at him for a long time. Five seconds? Ten?

Then I nodded and shambled to the door. Ghost followed me along the hall and upstairs to the entrance foyer. I was about to reach for the door handle, then paused and turned to look up the stairs. I thought about the young girl in Mitrović's bed. No matter how much medical and psychological help we provided her, she would always remember what he'd done to her. It made me think of Helen; about how her body healed but her heart and mind never did. Some women can come a long way back from the horror and violence of rape, but is it possible to come all the way? I didn't think so.

Those thoughts banged around in the haunted house of my head, and I almost didn't realize that I was climbing the stairs. There were moments when I saw myself doing that, and moments that seemed lost. Then I was in the master bedroom.

Mitrović and the girl were both on the bed, separated by five feet, each of them wrapped in individual cocoons of nightmare because of Sandman. So, yeah, we'd done that. To keep a rape victim from screaming, I'd shot her with a drug that would fill her mind with awful hallucinations. What kind of a total piece of shit was I? How had I even managed to pull the trigger of the dart gun?

How?

How?

I looked down at my hand and saw that I was holding my gun. Not the Snellig. No. It was the Sig Sauer. I watched my left hand reach across to rack the slide. It was like watching a movie. I saw it, but didn't feel it.

Nor did I feel the gun buck as it fired.

And fired.

And fired.

The shell casings glittered as they arced away from the weapon.

I blinked, looking at the utter ruin of Mitrović's face and head.

I blinked again, and I was downstairs. My gun was holstered.

Had I fired it? Had I even been upstairs?

To save my own soul, I could not say.

Ghost was watching me, his eyes dark and intense. I could feel his gaze penetrate all my defenses and see deep inside. I knew he was seeing more than I was.

I reached for the doorknob, and we stepped out into the night.

I pulled off the Scout glasses and let them fall. Did the same with the balaclava and the tactical computer on my forearm. Limb pads next. Rifle. All of it except for my clothes.

Ghost followed me, stepping over the items I discarded.

Belle was still in her tower, so we took a route that was out of her line of sight. In the distance, I could hear the heavy thropping sound of helicopter rotors. At least three or four of them. At least one big Chinook with a medical team to take care of the people down in that room.

With each step away from that building, I felt another piece of myself fall away. The voices inside my head—the Modern Man, the Cop, and the Killer—had all fallen silent, and the default now was silence wrapped around some purely objective thoughts. Step this way. Avoid that trip wire.

Then Ghost and I were down on the beach. When the choppers passed over, I stepped back beneath the shade of a massive oak. Ghost crouched beside me. The helos landed on the lawn, and I went the other way, moving along the beach, past the place where we'd buried the MotorKites, around to the western side of the island, where a pier ran a hundred and fifty feet into the black waters of the Adriatic. There was a big Lürssen super-yacht moored at the end of the pier, which told me there had to be deep water out there. And four small craft—including a pair of Scout 355 LXF fishing boats and a German Cigarette 59 Tirranna with six matched Mercury outboard racing engines and a hull built for speed. Sixty-five feet long, with nearly fourteen feet of beam.

Once again, I heard a rustling sound like dry leaves and turned to see more of the night birds. They were everywhere. On the nearby trees, in the grass, on the dock, and on every flat surface of the moored boats. Hundreds of them. Maybe thousands. And every set of beady black eyes was turned in my direction. Ghost made a small sound that was somewhere between discomfort and a warning. His bushy white tail was tucked between his legs.

"It's okay, boy," I said, and it felt like a lie.

The birds fluttered their wings.

I undid the lines, climbed aboard, and slid into the pilot seat. Ghost lay down on the other seat. The keys were in the ignition. The tanks were three-quarters full, which would give me a range of about six hundred nautical miles, even running at a top speed of seventy-two knots. Italy was a hell of a lot closer than that. From there, I could go anywhere on earth.

The engine started with a growl, and it was loud enough to smother any wandering thoughts. I could feel the Darkness coiling inside me, wrapped around my windpipe, trying to choke me. Cold, like a snake.

Before I hit the gas, though, I caught something out of the corner of my eye. There was a group of people standing on the dock. A tall, middle-aged man. A younger man who had the same posture, the same eyes as the older man. A pretty woman, and a couple of kids. They stood watching me, their faces pale as candles, their eyes filled with horror at what I had done.

I wanted to tell my family I was sorry.

But the thing is . . . I *wasn't* sorry. Not at all.

I pressed down slowly on the gas, and the boat moved away from the pier.

I aimed it toward the darkest part of the western horizon.

INTERLUDE 5
BLUE DIAMOND ELITE TRAINING CENTER
STEVENS COUNTY, WASHINGTON
FIVE MONTHS AGO

Rafael Santoro and Kuga climbed out of the Escalade into dappled sunlight.

It had been nearly two months since either of them had been to this place, and they took a few minutes to look around and admire the work. Quonset huts painted in camouflage greens, browns, and blacks; heavy canopies over everything to reduce surveillance from satellites, planes, or drones; and lots of activity.

"How many people do we have here now?" asked Kuga.

"Forty-seven support staff and four hundred and eleven soldiers under training," said Santoro. "Add thirty in the science and research staff."

"Nice."

Kuga turned back toward the car. "Hey, Barbie, move your ass."

"I don't want to," came the petulant voice of Eve from the shadows of the back seat.

"Come here regardless, my girl," snapped Santoro. "It was not a suggestion."

There was a comically loud put-upon sigh, and then Eve emerged from the Escalade. She wore a tight camo T-shirt and loose pants, with a sidearm hanging low like a Western movie gunslinger.

"Why are we even here?"

Santoro snapped his fingers and pointed to the ground next to where the two men stood. Eve huffed and trudged over.

"Ask your question again with manners this time," said the Spaniard.

Eve started to say something, then caught the look in Santoro's eyes. She took a beat and then tried again. "You never said why we were coming out here except that it would be *educational*." She leaned on the word as if it were a side dish of brussels sprouts. "So, please tell me why we came all the way out here. Is this about that dumb G-55 American thing?"

"Yes," said Santoro, "and other things."

If Eve had any additional comments, she kept them to herself because a woman with a pretty face and a bright smile came walking briskly over. She had her hair in a comfortable bun and clutched a clipboard to her chest. Her smile was large and infectious, and even Santoro found himself smiling.

"My dears," she said brightly, extending a hand to Kuga and a cheek to be kissed; then repeated that with Santoro. "And who's your little friend?"

Santoro placed his hand on Eve's lower back and pushed her gently forward.

"This is my protégé, Eve," he said smoothly. "Eve, this is Jill Hamilton-Krawczyk, the director of our recruitment and training program."

"*This* is Eve?" The woman looked interested. "You never told me she was such a beauty."

Eve colored and offered a hand and was uncharacteristically shy about it. Santoro was amused. Eve was never shy around men, but with powerful women, the girl had a tendency toward deference.

"Hello, Ms. Hamilton-Kray-*chick*." She stumbled a bit over the name.

"It's a mouthful," said the woman. "Call me HK. Everyone does."

"Okay, Ms. HK, I . . . I mean . . ." She colored a deeper shade of red and stopped talking. HK leaned close and kissed her cheek.

Then, to the three of them, she said, "Your timing couldn't be better. I can give you a full tour later, but there's something going on in building 36 I believe you'll really enjoy."

"Let's do it," said Kuga, and they followed HK through the camp to the largest of the Quonset huts, nestled back beneath the furry arms of four massive pine trees. A sentry in full body armor and black fatigues snapped to attention as they walked inside.

The hut was crammed with people. Hundreds sat on bleachers, many with notebooks open on their laps and pens scribbling busily. Others were on the floor, working in teams. Some of these were shirtless—wearing only pants and boots; others were in full combat kit. A few wore bulky body armor of a kind Eve had never seen. They were paired up, going through combat drills at dangerously high

　　　　　　　　　　　　　　　　　JONATHAN MABERRY

speeds. Both combatants in each team held knives, and although the blades were not sharp, they weren't exactly dull, either. Quite a few of the soldiers bled from cuts, and a few of those injuries were deep. The training mats on which they worked were spackled with sweat and blood.

But Eve's gaze was soon jerked away from the bloody drill as she saw what was playing out on a large movie screen that hung down at the back of the hut. On it, two other men were fighting, and it was no drill. One man was a total stranger and wore some kind of security company uniform that Eve was unfamiliar with. The other man was tall, very fit, lean, with blond hair and icy blue eyes. He moved with an oiled grace that was deceptive because his movements were so economical. There was nothing wasted, no obvious concession to style. He simply moved at the right time and was never there when the attacker's blade came at him. Not that the man evaded every attack, but when he was cut, there was no flinch, no facial reaction, and no hesitation at all. He responded to each attack as a direct counterattack, often cutting the attacking arm during the attack, or shadowing it back to cut during the withdraw. The opponent was a mass of blood, and as soon as he began to tire, the big blond man moved in like a blur and in less than a second slashed his blade across his opponent's inner thigh, the biceps, and the throat.

Eve felt herself floating, as if somehow a cloud of burning rage was lifting her off the ground. There *he* was. Forty feet tall, right in front of her. With at least sixty soldiers training to mimic and beat the man's ruthlessly efficient fighting style. Eve wanted to cry. She wanted to scream. She wanted a knife so she could stab someone to death. If not *him,* then anyone close. She wanted to stab someone in the eyes, in the balls, in the heart.

A hand closed around her shoulder, and Eve spun, trying to slap away the grip, throwing a punch with all her speed and fury and hurt. But Rafael Santoro's grip was iron, and with his other hand, he parried the blow.

"Calm yourself, child," he said softly.

Kuga and HK watched with surprise and amusement.

Tears sprang into Eve's eyes. They burned, hotter than acid.

"*Ledger*," she snarled, and there was so much pure and unfiltered hatred in that one word, in that name, that several of the closest people on the bleachers turned in surprise.

"Ledger," agreed Santoro. "And this, my daughter, is how we'll destroy him."

CHAPTER 14
TRSTENIK ISLAND
CROATIA

Top Sims stood on the pier and stared at the black water. The ripples were limned with faint red from a reluctant dawn.

He was alone but spoke aloud in a normal tone of voice. Normal in volume, but twisted with doubt and fear and sorrow.

"He took a boat," he said. "Don't know how long ago. Pretty sure he took the cigarette boat we saw in the satellite photos. And you're telling me you can't find a fifty-nine-foot racing boat on a sea as small as the Adriatic? It's what? Only five hundred miles long and one-twenty wide? How's that even possible?"

"Satellites aren't in geostationary orbit, Pappy," said Scott Wilson, speaking from the TOC five hundred miles away. "We retasked a CIA eye in the sky to sync up with your infiltration, but it's necessarily moved on."

"All due respect, Grendel," said Top, using Wilson's call sign, "but you can shove that answer where the sun don't shine. Outlaw's on a boat in the Adriatic. You telling me we have no assets that can find him? I don't want to hear that bullshit."

"Calm down," began Wilson, but Top cut him off.

"Don't you fucking tell me to calm down," snarled Top. "Tell me you can *find* him. The man has an RFID chip, for god's sake. So does his dog."

"Those chips went inactive thirty-seven minutes after Havoc Team entered the mansion," said Scott, his tone patient but not contrite. "Unknown yet whether he removed the chips or is using a Faraday wrap on them."

Faraday wraps—like Faraday cages and bags—were sophisticated tech that nullified all electronic signals. Each member of the team carried them to secure devices taken from targets. The wraps were used to blank out RFID chips implanted in hostiles they apprehended. RTI policy forbade any team member from using them to shield their own telemetry. Those chips sent a continuous signal even if the host died.

"Or," continued Wilson, his tone as dour as an undertaker's, "Bug thinks there's even a chance Ledger may have used a Lightning Bug. Some of the island's perimeter security and electronics went out shortly after Ledger left the building. And I'm not talking about the stuff Andrea took out during the mission. Ledger may have deliberately killed his own RFID. I've told the cleanup team to look for evidence."

Top looked up at the sky for a long moment, then rubbed his eyes. "Then how do we find him?" he asked wearily.

Instead of a direct answer from Wilson, a new voice came on the line.

"Pappy," said Mr. Church, "we're on a confidential line, just the two of us."

"Sir," said Top.

"Tell me exactly what happened. Be as detailed and precise as you can."

Top took a breath and then gave his report. He left nothing out and included his conjectures about Joe Ledger's crumbling mental state. He mentioned that Ledger had reported seeing someone in the woods, and then mentioned "Dad" later on. Church listened without interruption.

"We thought it was Rage," said Top. "With Outlaw, I mean. He didn't go after us, though. But . . . even so, maybe I should have hit him with Sandman just to be safe. This is on me."

"You can secure that line of thinking right now, Pappy," said Church sternly. "This is not on you. On any of you. End of discussion. Now . . . did Outlaw say anything before he left?"

"No, sir. I told him to go outside and get some air, and he did."

"And you think he went straight to the pier and took a boat?"

"Yes, sir. Followed his footprints here. His and Ghost's. I'll retrace those steps to see if there's a spent Dragonfly. Either way, he's gone. My guess is he used the sound of the choppers to cover the boat's engine noise."

Church was silent for a long time, but Top knew him well enough to understand that the big man was thinking things through. So he waited as the sun clawed its way over the horizon and turned the black waters to a sea of blood.

"Pappy," said Church, "I need you to listen very closely to what I have to say. You may not like it and doubtless won't agree that this is the right play, but it's what I feel is best."

"Already don't like the sound of it," Top admitted glumly.

"Let him go," said Church.

"Say again?"

"You heard me. You and the rest of Havoc finish processing the island and then turn all materials over to the crew now on the ground. Come back here and write your after-action reports. I do not want you or any member of your team to go looking for Outlaw. I don't want to make it an order, however. I am asking for you to trust my judgment."

"That's a big ask."

"I know it is."

Top closed his eyes and contemplated putting his fist through the first really solid wall he could find.

"Outlaw is way the hell out on the edge," he said. "You didn't see what he did in there. Those people on the medical staff were monsters, no doubt, but they were unarmed. He chopped them into dogmeat and pissed on their corpses. That's not the Outlaw we both know. He's crossed a line, and I don't know if leaving him alone out there is in his best interests. Have you run this past the docs?"

By that, he meant Dr. Rudy Sanchez, Joe Ledger's best friend and psychiatrist; and Dr. Jane Holliday, the head of the RTI integrated sciences division. Both of them had argued against Ledger being cleared for this mission. The arguments had gotten heated, but Church won because Church tended to win. And now this.

"This is my call," said Church. "Mine alone."

Top sighed and sat down on a piling. "You're a religious man, aren't you?"

Church paused again. "In my own way."

"So am I, though it's getting harder and harder to hold on to that."

"What's your point, Pappy?"

"My point is that we're maybe compounding a sin," said Top. "Maybe committing another sin by doing nothing to help Outlaw."

"I believe this is the best way to help him."

"Then if he continues to go down this road, may God have mercy on our souls, because any drop of innocent blood he spills is on us."

He waited for Church to answer, but when he tapped the coms, it was clear the line had gone dead.

INTERLUDE 6
SALES PRESENTATION VIA SHOWROOM
FIVE MONTHS AGO

"One of the optional extras in this package is what we like to call a self-cleaning oven," said Mr. Sunday, beaming a great smile. "Exfiltration after a highly dangerous operation is always the challenge, isn't it? If the assets are captured, then there is a risk of them becoming chatty during enhanced interrogation. That leads to way too many complications, not the least of which is creating a cause for your enemies to rally around and to garner international support. And, frankly, who needs that? It's expensive, embarrassing, and unnecessary."

He took a small computer chip from an inner pocket and placed it on a wooden stool, then walked over and stood behind a sheet of three-inch-thick lead hung by chains from the ceiling. The audience could see him and the chair on split screen. Mr. Sunday removed his cell phone.

"We call it 3B, which is short for a nickname given to it by a pop culture–obsessed senior tech on our team. It stands for *Burn, baby, burn.*" He paused and grinned. "We should probably give that particular tech a vacation somewhere with nice, quiet scenery."

Mr. Sunday chuckled at his own joke and made sure the laugh was only three short beats. Fun, but not silly. Jovial, without losing the edge.

"The chemical compound in that chip is proprietary," he said, "and is not for sale at any price. And I highly recommend you *not* trying to remove one of these chips from any PMC you lease or purchase from us. Resist all temptation to analyze the compound. Each chip is synced to the heartbeat of the operative, and if that pulse rate goes below twenty beats per minute, the chip detonates. Allow me to demonstrate."

He pressed a button on his phone, and the chip exploded.

The blast was immediate and massive, far beyond what any of the audience could possibly have expected. It obliterated the wooden stool and a good portion of the floor and left smoking pits all across the surface of the lead shield.

"Burn, baby, burn," said Mr. Sunday, waving smoke away.

A very pretty young woman dressed in a short skirt and an extremely low-cut top stretched across improbably large and firm breasts came mincing out from backstage with a bright yellow fire extinguisher. She flashed a lot of white teeth at the people on the screens, then doused the fire, gave the hole in the floor a final playful blast, gave the audience a saucy little curtsy, and pranced off.

Mr. Sunday came out from behind the lead barrier and blew a kiss at her retreating back. The woman turned, pretended to catch the kiss, and placed it daintily on her left cheek.

"The chemical compound is, as you can see, quite a corker," said Mr. Sunday. "It is designed to burn at such a high temperature and at such an accelerated rate of speed that it leaves no traces of itself and very few of whatever is in its blast radius. The weapons, uniform, and equipment used by the PMCs are likewise prepped with chips keyed to that specific operative. That means any forensic analysis will have a hard darn time making sense of anything. And, let's not forget, even if they are somehow able to salvage pieces of the device, nothing is traceable. The weapons, equipment, and even the clothes are all manufactured by us under controlled situations. There is no trail to follow."

He used his clicker to bring images onto his screen and those of the people watching from their private spaces around the globe. A graphic of data streams appeared, showing heart rate, blood pressure, respiration, and other details.

"The telemetry sent by the chip is constantly monitored—and you would have access to the data feeds. You would have access to the detonation code, and the purchase price gives you the option of using that code whenever you want. Or . . . not. Just remember, though, it is much more cost effective to purchase a few *new* PMCs for new missions than to repurpose the old ones. No muss, no fuss. Like, say, walking into the middle of a crowd of political dissidents or protesters with the wrong slogans on their signs. Oh, heck, folks, you could have a couple of these lads take a tour of a statehouse or presidential palace and—poof! Suddenly, there *is* no opposition leader, and no one to be arrested, interrogated, or tried. Now how's that for making a political statement? Oh, *hell* yes."

His eyes swirled with color as he stepped forward, passing through a downspill of green light. For a moment, even the whites of his eyes vanished as sickly greens and toxic yellow browns eddied. Then he took another half step forward, and his eyes were normal. His smile was broad and affable. A kindly, slightly corny old uncle, or a clichéd storekeeper from some old episode of *Gunsmoke* or *Leave It to Beaver*.

"Now," he said, "let's see if we can get us a yummy little bidding war going on here."

DAYS OF
DARKNESS
PART 2

Revenge is a confession of pain.

—LATIN PROVERB

But if there is any further injury,
then you shall appoint as a penalty life for life,
eye for eye, tooth for tooth, hand for hand,
foot for foot, burn for burn,
wound for wound, bruise for bruise.

—EXODUS 21:23—25

CHAPTER 15

PHOENIX HOUSE
OMFORI ISLAND, GREECE

Scott Wilson stood under a canopy outside the security office, watching the big helicopter land. It was a huge Boeing Ch-47 Chinook; nearly a hundred feet long, with twin propellers spun by a pair of powerful Lycoming turboshaft engines. It had come out of the dawn like some mythic beast but landed as softly as a butterfly on the tarmac behind Phoenix House.

The noise diminished, and the massive blades began to slow. The rear hatch eased down with a soft hydraulic whine, revealing a knot of shadowed figures within. Wilson walked out to meet Havoc Team as they descended from the bird. They all wore black trousers and tank tops. No other gear or weapons, except for Belle, who had a rifle case slung across her back. No one ever handled her guns but her.

Bunny, Andrea, and Belle walked past Wilson with barely a nod. Only Top paused to talk with the chief of operations. The soldier looked older by ten years than he had when he'd set out with Havoc Team for the mission. Top's face was more deeply lined, his eyes red-rimmed, and his posture stooped with a weariness that ran miles deeper than mere physical exhaustion.

Wilson offered his hand, and Top looked at it for a moment before taking it.

"The medical teams are still triaging the prisoners you liberated," Wilson said. "The Chinook is going to refuel and head back as soon as they're ready for transport. Our doctor on the ground there says that all but one of them is likely to recover. Sad that we'll lose *any* of them, but . . ."

Top took a toothpick from his pocket and put it between his teeth. He chewed on the pointy end for a few silent seconds, working it from one corner of his mouth to the other. His dark eyes were completely unreadable.

"You did good work tonight," said Wilson.

Top shook his head. "Did we? Well, sorry, boss, but I'm not putting this one in the win column. No *damned* way."

He started to walk away, but Wilson hurried to catch up.

"We *will* find Colonel Ledger."

Top snorted. "You'll find him exactly when and where he wants to be found."

"We have considerable resources, or have you forgotten?"

Top stopped and turned to him. "How do I put this? Scott, if Joe wants to be found, you'll find him. If he doesn't, then you probably won't. But if he doesn't want to be found and you *do* ping him, you'd better make sure you only send operators you don't care about, because they may not come back in one piece."

"I—" began Wilson, but Top cut him off.

"I have to write my after-action report, get fed, get some rack time, and then Farm Boy and I are out of here in the morning. I'd rather cancel this other thing, the gig in the States, because I'd rather be here. But, like I said . . . hunting Colonel Ledger isn't going to move the needle on what we're trying to do. Appreciate you trying to be cheerleader for the team, Scott, but stop trying it on me."

He walked away.

Wilson stood on the tarmac for quite a while, staring at the door Top Sims had closed behind him when he'd entered the building.

INTERLUDE 7
THE PAVILION
BLUE DIAMOND ELITE TRAINING CENTER
STEVENS COUNTY, WASHINGTON
FIVE MONTHS AGO

Rafael Santoro, Kuga, and Eve stood in a little cluster with HK as the trainees filed out. Two of them required stretchers; six others had to be helped by their comrades. Everyone who'd participated in the drill was marked in one way or another.

"That was a good session," said Kuga. "Those sons of bitches can fight."

"You should know," said HK.

"Flatterer," laughed Kuga, and he gave her a pat on the back.

"Telling the truth. These men and women have studied videos of you, too. And Rafael, of course." She glanced at Eve. "I don't suppose there are any of you . . . ?"

Eve said nothing, and HK shrugged.

"We are fortunate to have collected so many. The tapes from Oslo, of course, but also some hacked from the servers from the DMS raid on the Dragon Factory and elsewhere."

"The Dragon *what*?" asked Eve.

"It was a genetics development facility on Dogfish Cay in the Bahamas. The Jakoby twins ran it."

"Oh," Eve said slowly, "yeah. I read about them in one of the files. Freaky albinos, right? Brother and sister who fucked each other? Wasn't their father some kind of Nazi?"

"How well you summarize it," said Santoro.

"She's not wrong, though," said Kuga. "Paris and Hecate were freaks, no matter from which angle you looked at them. Brilliant, but weird on a level that even gives me the wiggins."

Eve echoed the word *wiggins,* enjoying it.

"Point is," said HK, "we have enough good real combat footage of Joe Ledger to make sure our training supervisors can use them effectively. There are some truly outstanding fighters in our team, and that's *before* the enhancements. Later this afternoon, we'll have a chance to see what our next-generation Fixers can do."

"Next generation?" echoed Eve, posing it as a question. "Are you talking that exoskeleton stuff?"

HK shared a brief secret smile with Kuga and Santoro. "Exo-suits, to be sure," she said, "but we have some other surprises that I can truly guarantee will raise a smile on all your faces. I think it's fair to say that the American Operation is going to be quite the event."

"Now that," said Kuga, "is what I like to hear."

"Yeah," said Eve, more to herself than anyone, "me, too."

CHAPTER 16
IL POMODORO BEACH
LUNGOMARE MARINA ITALIANA
GIOVINAZZO, PUGLIA, ITALY

The two young men came out of the restaurant, exiting through a staff door, which they closed and locked. The place was closed for the night, and they were exhausted from hours of cleaning, restocking, and prework for the next day. Enea was the short, fat one, a deputy chef and shift manager; Federico—known to all his friends as Spike because he looked vaguely like the character from the old American TV show *Buffy the Vampire Slayer*—was the tall, skinny one. Spike had started bleaching his hair white and spiking it after having met the actor who played Spike at the big comic convention in Lucca. It didn't matter that the waitstaff, all of whom were at least a decade younger, had no idea who Buffy or Spike were. They liked the nickname, though. Most women he met thought it was a euphemism for how well he was hung.

They were best friends and had worked at this restaurant, and two previous ones, since high school. Whenever possible, they worked the same shifts—Enea running the kitchen on the evening shifts whenever the head chef was on days; and Spike doing prep work and cleanup after the last customer was gone. They cranked up the sound system and blasted old Italian punk, with a heavy bias toward Derozer and Punkreas. The screaming vocals rattled the glassware and made the whole cleanup process fun and fast.

Their post-work ritual was to go down to the big rocks by the water, smoke some good Turkish weed if there were no *polizia* around, or smoke their way through three or four Benson & Hedges Reds while talking about politics and watching the stars. Tonight was a *canapa* night, and the joints were fresh and potent, spiked with something special that brought them quickly to a nice level and softened the edges of reality.

They sat on their favorite rocks and felt the day slough off. They were aware of the many dark birds—ravens and crows and cormorants—clustered on the surrounding rocks, in the trees, or on the hoods of cars—but neither much cared. There were always birds by the water's edge, and so what if these were black instead of white? The only thought either gave was Spike briefly wishing he'd brought a bag of table scraps with him, and he filed it away to do some other night.

Enea talked about owning his own restaurant one day. Spike talked about how he'd like to ask out Gioia, the hostess, if her damned divorce ever went through. A lot of their conversations were retreads, but they didn't care. They were doing okay in their lives, still young enough to enjoy the world, and content to be in each other's company after another long, good day.

The structure of the night changed dramatically, though, when they saw the boat.

It came out of the night, pushing a bow wave, showing no lights at all. Like something emerging from a dream. Mysterious and a bit spooky. Only the muted growl of its engines—idling low as the boat moved toward the rocks—gave it any sense of reality.

Spike tapped Enea and pointed. They'd lived on the coast all their lives and knew boats, but this . . .

This was something special. A German-built Cigarette 59 Tirranna. A sleek black hull with red interior and seats—the color visible in the starlight. A monster racing boat that had to run two or three million euros. It looked brand-new.

"*Accidenti!*" breathed Enea.

"*Dio santo,*" agreed Spike.

Then for a moment, they froze because the unreality of such a boat appearing out of the night was suddenly made nightmarish as they caught a glimpse of the pilot.

It was not a man at all. The creature they saw had a huge, shaggy head covered entirely in white fur flecked with a red deeper than the boat's interior. That red was smeared all over the thing's elongated muzzle.

"*Licantropo!*" cried Enea.

They were practical young men who did not believe in werewolves, but here was a gigantic wolf piloting a ghostly boat. They were also very seriously stoned. Their mellow high turned to terror in a heartbeat, and as the boat slowed and ground onto the rocky sand below where they were sitting, they leaped to their feet and fled, shrieking about werewolves.

The boat came to a softly rocking stop. The monstrous white dog stood up, then climbed over the windscreen and onto the bow. His pale fur glowed like silver in the cold starlight.

The man, who had been in the other pilot's chair, killed the engine, plunging the small stretch of coast into silence except for the fading footfalls of the two restaurant employees. Their continual yelps, prayers, and curses lingered long after they vanished down a side street. Then the man clambered out of the boat and onto the rocks. His clothes were dark, and the angle of approach had hidden him behind the dog. He clicked his tongue for the dog, who leaped from the bow to the rocks and then followed the man up to the street.

They lingered for only a moment as the man oriented himself.

Then they faded into darkness and were gone long before anyone came to investigate. The night birds watched them go and then one by one lifted off the sea-soaked rocks and followed.

CHAPTER 17
INTEGRATED SCIENCES DIVISION
PHOENIX HOUSE
OMFORI ISLAND, GREECE

Dr. Jane Holliday sat perched on a stool sipping tea from a delicate china cup, the saucer held between thumb and index finger of her other hand. She was the calm center of a storm of activity as handlers brought in dozens of boxes of paper printouts, crates of laptops, cell phones, and hard drives. Another team, dressed in lemon-yellow biohazard suits, carried special metal boxes boldly stenciled with the distinctive symbol, the four stylized circles of which representing the infection chain of agent, host, source, and transmission. These boxes went into a cold room guarded by two stone-faced guards with automatic rifles at port arms.

"Wow," said Isaac Breslau, Doc Holliday's senior research assistant, "that's a lot of stuff."

"Yeppers," said Doc happily. "They got it all, soup to nuts. No one at that site had the presence of mind to delete the data or toss a lit cigarette butt into the file cabinets. Might as well be Christmas morning."

"Sure, but only if there's something of use in there," said Isaac. He was a very short man, barely above five feet tall, which made him quite a comical companion to Doc, who was over a foot taller. And while Isaac was slim as a sword blade, Doc was what her Jewish aunt used to call *zaftig*—curves upon curves. The running joke was that Doc looked like a younger Dolly Parton on growth hormones, which was not entirely inaccurate, even down to the embroidered cowboy shirts and hand-tooled boots. Doc, who had endured being a figure of fun as a girl—having grown to double-D cups by tenth grade—decided to stop trying to hide and instead use her body as both a distraction and a challenge. People too dim to look past the bustline, wildly coiffed blond curls, and oversized hourglass figure did so at their peril. It meant they didn't bother to look into Doc's eyes and see the scathing humor and bottomless intellect. While most of the kids in high school were trying to get laid, she was filing her first dozen patents. She was born poor, graduated high school three years early, and with $4 million in a new trust account. She blew through the corporate world, racking up more patents and more millions, then fell in with the Defense Department eggheads at DARPA until they started to bore her. When Mr. Church offered her carte blanche to do any side research she wanted while also overseeing the Integrated Sciences Division—first with the DMS and then in an even more expanded capacity with RTI—she jumped at it. It was refreshing to work for someone who was not her intellectual inferior.

Isaac Breslau was not on the same level as Doc, though he wasn't that many floors below. A professor of biological engineering from MIT, with a handful of master's degrees in chemistry, materials science, and health sciences. They'd met at a conference in Zurich and fell in together thick as thieves, because they were in a room of brilliant minds but were clearly—in terms of intellect—the big dogs in that room.

Doc had hired Isaac, and when he saw the sophistication of the RTI science labs, he nearly wept.

"There'll be something we can use, lamb chop," she said. Doc was fond of diminutives with everyone except Church—at least not to the boss's face. Not often, anyway. "We'll pick all the meat off it and suck out the marrow."

"First . . . ewww," said Isaac. "And second . . . I agree."

They watched the workers move in a constant line like ants going out to forage, bringing back goodies, and heading out for another load.

"How much of this *is* there?"

Doc looked at a clipboard, flipped over a few pages. "Three tons of paper, two tons of computers, including several Fujitsu Fugaku supercomputers."

Isaac sniffed. "*Last* year's models."

Doc grinned. "Yeah, once we strip 'em out, we can sell 'em for a nickel at a yard sale."

"They're mine," said a voice. "Calling dibs."

They turned to see a slim young Black man come hustling into the room. He wore an open bathrobe over pajama bottoms and a T-shirt with the big red Superman symbol on the chest.

"Well, hell," said Doc, "we've gone and woke li'l Bug from his beauty sleep. And aren't you cute in your little blue PJs."

"They told me they were bringing back hardware," said Bug, stopping by the two scientists, "but this is kind of a jackpot."

"Again," said Isaac, "only if there's something worth finding."

Bug cocked an eyebrow at Doc. "He's cheerful tonight."

"He needs a foot rub and some hot cocoa," said Doc.

"Stop it," said Isaac, but she ignored him.

A lab tech came over with paper cups of coffee for the three of them, and they sipped and watched. After several minutes, during which the incoming crates and boxes grew to resemble the Grand Tetons around them, Isaac sighed and said, "Are we going to drink bad coffee, make jokes, and *not* talk about the elephant in the room?"

Doc sipped and shook her head.

Bug set his cup down and rubbed his eyes. "I keep telling myself Joe's going to be okay."

"Joe," said Doc slowly, "has never been okay since I met him. He is, by any clinical interpretation of psychology, a bag of rabid hamsters. What he went through at Christmas messed that boy up so bad that he should never—and I mean never, *ever*—have been allowed anywhere near a field op."

"Rudy Sanchez might disagree," said Isaac.

"Rudy Sanchez is at home with his son and very pregnant wife in Corfu," said Doc. "Besides, ever since our boy got out of the hospital, Rudy has been lobbying for Joe to step down from fieldwork. He's badgered Mr. Church just about every damned day."

"And yet Church sent Ledger out on this mission," said Isaac. "Granted, I haven't been around Church as long as you two have, but this feels like it's out of character for the big man, too."

Bug picked up his coffee cup, stared into it, and set it down again. "No comment," he said.

Isaac shook his head. "We don't even know where Ledger's gone. It's been hours now. God only knows what intel he got from those people he . . . he . . ."

"*Butchered* is the word you're looking for," said Doc. "Let's not be imprecise."

"Fine," said Isaac, though he didn't actually repeat the word. "We don't know where Ledger's off to. He has no resources, no backup. I heard that Top Sims wasn't even sure if Ledger took any weapons or equipment with him."

"Oh, honey bear," said Doc, "that's one thing you don't ever have to worry about. Joltin' Joe's trained for this kind of thing. He knows how to acquire money, equipment, and other resources. He might even ask nicely for some of it, but—let's face it—for a man as skilled and resourceful as he is, do you really think for one blessed moment that he's going to let anything get in his way?"

Bug sighed. "What I'm really afraid of is Joe finding a quiet place to stick one of those gun barrels up under his chin and see if that stops the pain."

It was such a cold, frank, and plausible statement that it sucked all the warmth out of the room.

CHAPTER 18
BARI KAROL WOJTYŁA AIRPORT
VIALE ENZO FERRARI
BARI, ITALY

The fat old man with the emotional support dog waited nearly forty minutes for the pay phone to be free. Coin phones were harder to come by lately, and this one seemed very popular. He watched a nun use it, then a teenage boy wearing a Pro Italia Galatina football jersey, and then a woman with a baby. Why none of them had cell phones this far into the twenty-first century was a mystery.

The old man waited until there was no one around to observe him, and then he waddled over to the wall-mounted phone and thumbed in some coins. The fact that he wore gloves to do this also went unobserved. He let the phone ring while he stood there, eyes closed, one hand clutched tightly around the handset, the other balled into a fist at his side.

When the woman answered, the man sagged against the wall as if he'd been punched. There were tears in his eyes, and his breath was a ragged wheeze.

"Hello?"

The woman's voice was soft, tentative, and uncertain. Almost as if she suspected but did not believe who was calling.

The fat old man said nothing.

"Hello, who's calling?" asked the woman.

He did not reply.

Then she said, "Joe?"

That one word. Soft, scared, hopeful.

It took so much of what he had left inside to speak. "I . . . I love you, Junie."

And then he hung up, whirled, and fled. The dog followed as the man hurried toward the closest trash can, and it stood guard while the man vomited.

CHAPTER 19
PHOENIX HOUSE
OMFORI ISLAND, GREECE

Church woke in the lightless depths of the night with a name on his lips. It tasted like blood and bile.

He reached for Lilith, but her side of the bed was empty. Then he saw her by the window. Standing so still, her naked silhouette a study in tension. He could read that in every line, from the rigidity of her back muscles to the fist clenched tightly beneath her chin. Without turning, she said, "He is alive in the world again."

He.

She didn't need to say the name. They both knew.

And they were both afraid.

INTERLUDE 8
THE PAVILION
BLUE DIAMOND ELITE TRAINING CENTER
STEVENS COUNTY, WASHINGTON
FOUR MONTHS AGO

Eve was alone even though she had company.

That was how things were since Adam died. Men came and went, through her life, in and out of her bed, coasting on the far edge of her awareness. She kissed them, had sex with them, sometimes made them have sex with one another. She used them hard. She even killed one of them once just to see if that would make her feel anything.

It didn't. And it was messy and a bit disgusting. Two of her other men had to clean things up. HK tried to scold her, but Eve walked away and locked herself in her bedroom. That had been . . . when? Two weeks before? A bit longer? She couldn't tell. Time, like so many other things, had lost its meaning.

The only highlights of her day—the only thing that gave her any joy and brought her to a sharp focus—were the visits. Daddy came and sat with her, telling her things he wanted her to learn, filling her mind with plans about how they were going to find Joe Ledger. Find him, capture him, and spend days—*weeks*—ruining him. Breaking his will and his heart. Turning his body into a cage of broken pieces. Feeding him on pain and making sure the doctors did not let him die. Eve wasn't even sure she *wanted* him to die. No. It would be so much better if Ledger were turned into a cripple. Maybe with no feet and just a few fingers on each hand. He'd only really need one eye. He wouldn't need his cock or balls. Daddy said that a man could be reduced to something barely recognizable as having been human and still survive. A person like that could live for years. Kept in a cage or given a little dolly to push himself around on. No teeth, no nose. No hope.

And together they would drive him to the very edge of madness, but not push him over. No. She wouldn't want that. She—and Daddy—wanted him alive so he could be aware, every single day, of what he'd become and to live with the knowledge that everyone he loved was either dead or being similarly destroyed.

Whom, then, should they remove from Ledger's life first? Always a delicious speculation. Church, of course. Both Daddy and Kuga wanted that spooky prick dead and run through a wood chipper.

Junie Flynn. Yeah, she had to go. Eve wanted to hand her over to a dozen—no, *two* dozen of the biggest, ugliest, meanest Fixers—and then tape every moment of their fun and games with her.

The others, too. The big stupid white guy with all the muscles? Dead. The Black man who looked too old to be a soldier? Dead. The bitch with the sniper rifle and the gay Italian guy? Dead, dead.

All of them dead. Not quickly, and not all at once, but dead in the end. And their deaths shown on movie screens ten times bigger than life, so Joe Ledger could watch. Every. Single. Day.

The very thought of that made her *feel*.

It made her weep.

It made her scream.

It kept her completely alive.

CHAPTER 20
INTEGRATED SCIENCES DIVISION
PHOENIX HOUSE
OMFORI ISLAND, GREECE

Doc and Isaac stood side by side, looking at the material brought from the island.

Folding tables had been brought in and arranged like spokes on a wheel radiating outward from where they stood. Each table represented a specific branch of science. Scott Wilson found them and threaded his way through boxes of additional materials that littered the floor, creating a labyrinth.

"Good lord," Wilson said when he reached the center and stood by the two scientists. "What is all this?"

"It's the haul from Mislav Mitrović's lab," said Doc.

Wilson glanced from one table to the next. "Is there a method to this madness?"

"Well," Doc said, "a couple of hours ago, I'd have said that it was just a mishmash of records from a bunch of unrelated lines of research." She tapped one table with a bright blue fingernail. "For example, here we have some pretty advanced work on neural memory chips, including some off-market studies on closed-loop neural prosthetics clearly purposed for military use."

Tap.

"Here we have what are clearly stolen documents from DARPA focusing on human-machine fusion—that's cyborgs to you, Scottie sweetie. A well-funded and long-range program to determine how best to integrate machine parts to human combat soldiers, with an eye to having a cybernetic ground force by 2050. But there's also a lot of material here, including very sophisticated schematics, that leads me to believe that actual development is much further along. Some that seems like it's in-house development by Kuga's group of Frankensteins because those newer reports aren't written in the DoD-friendly military doublespeak."

Tap.

"Here we jump into biochemistry, specifically eugeroics," Doc said. "And before you embarrass yourself by telling me you don't know what that big word means, it's the science of developing wakefulness-promoting drugs. Ostensibly for dealing with a raft of sleep disorders from narcolepsy to idiopathic hypersomnia, with some very specific train stops in between. But Isaac here—who, I should tell you, is more than just a hobbit-size stud muffin—thinks that some of this research ties into a case that Church started a bunch of years ago and Ledger wrapped while on a gig in Paris with Violin. The bulk of this research is new stuff, and it's not the kind of thing that's going to play well with labor unions. There are reports in there for use in factory workers to permit them to work shifts of forty to sixty continuous hours—and that's like combining a sweatshop with the Boston Marathon. And references to research lines with military applications. Think about that—soldiers on a specific mission who don't need to sleep and don't tire even with constant movement and exertion."

Tap.

"Then this stack is science straight out stolen from us, and I think it was back before my time, during that time MindReader was being bent over a barrel and rogered. Before Bug gave her a big ol' makeover. There's data here that I know for sure we took from the Jakobys—from the Dragon Factory run by Paris and Hecate, and from their father, Cyrus. There are extracts from Zephyr Bain, from Sebastian Gault, from the Seven Kings, from maybe twenty of the cases the DMS worked on. And all of it is coded. Bug thinks the codes are a cross-indexing system, and he put someone on it to figure out how it works."

She tapped another, but then hesitated.

"I could go on," she said. "Bottom line is that this is both a jackpot and a big ol' ball of confusion."

"How so?" asked Wilson.

"Well, on one hand, it's a treasure trove that will, I hope, give us a clearer peek inside Kuga's research and development process. Given enough time, we might be able to determine what they've been working on and the likely applications of the same."

"Except that it may not be as random as it appears," said Isaac.

"Correctamundo," agreed Doc.

Wilson chewed his lip as he wandered around, looking at the mountains of material. Without turning, he said, "The manifests

JONATHAN MABERRY

say that there were biological samples. Is there anything there that might explain this?"

"Oh, hell, sugar bear," said Doc, "there's forty *kinds* of bioweapons. We have full specs on some—and, Rage is in there, by the way—and then there are some that all we have are samples, but no specs. Those are in a hot room, and I have people studying them."

"What about the people? The, um, test subjects?"

"We turned them over to my big Wooly Bear and his team. The patients are in quarantine."

Wooly Bear was Dr. Ronald Coleman. He was a molecular biologist who oversaw a Division of Integrated Sciences dealing with the hunt for what he called "disease identity," a radical new field of diagnostics.

"He'll suss out what was done to them," Doc assured him.

"Some of those folks have implants," said Isaac, "and we think that's where a lot of this ties together."

"In what way, exactly?" asked Wilson.

Isaac smiled. His smiles always looked like he was wincing from some mild abdominal pain. "The more we tried to separate out the different fields of science here, the more they seem to want to clump together. I mean, especially if we start with a 'what's the worst that can happen' point of view. And if you start with the idea of cybernetic implants for soldiers and add a cocktail of chemicals to enhance stamina and wakefulness, then what we might be looking at is a very damned scary new kind of super-soldier."

"Or," added Doc, "if you stir in some nasty short-duration, high-effect bioweapons as a possible payload, we could be seeing the birth of the next generation of suicide bomber. A virtually unkillable soldier who is faster, stronger, and able to fight his way into a crowded airport, a major concert, or a sports event and make himself go boom."

Scott Wilson stared at them, and he could feel the blood drain from his face.

"You were right," said Isaac to Doc. "You said he'd look like that."

CHAPTER 21
SALES PRESENTATION VIA SHOWROOM

"Hello, my friends," said Mr. Sunday, "welcome back. How delightful to see all of you, and a big welcome to some new folks who have joined us. I know that several of you are here on the recommendation of regular—and satisfied—customers. Don't forget to ask me about the new customer premiums after the regular presentation."

Mr. Sunday was dressed in a lightweight wool suit with a hand-painted tie and polished oxblood loafers. He looked like he was ready to host a cocktail mixer at a tech conference. All casual smiles and relaxed posture.

"We live in a troubled world," he said. "There are all kinds of problems out there, both foreign and domestic. Access to the internet has allowed for unification of dissident voices, which in turn has led to strikes and walkouts, work slowdowns, and pressure from global watchdog groups. Our police forces are under siege for doing their jobs, and soldiers following sensible orders are being tried as war criminals. It's getting to the point that we are being prevented from running our companies and our countries the way they need to be run. Are you with me still?"

He began pacing slowly, making sure that at any given moment he was making eye contact with one of the potential buyers. He made sure to make such contact with every face on those screens. He would let his eyes linger, forcing contact until he saw a tell—a nod, a tilt of the head, a smile, or even a wince. Everyone had a tell, and what mattered was how they reacted relative to what he was saying, down to key words he used and subtle inflections intended to evoke those reactions.

His pace was slow, but his hands moved at varying speed, each gesticulation giving emphasis to some point, much as a conductor's baton will.

"A corresponding challenge," he said, "is that public pressure growing out of trending social media outrage often results in either stock drops, knee-jerk legislation, the implementation of regulations imposed by whoever is up for election and wants to appeal to key demographics, and also the courts. What was it Shakespeare said? 'First, kill all the lawyers'? I'm for that. Except *our* lawyers, of course."

His laugh was warm and inclusive. A "we all get this" thing.

"The days when we could just send in a *quality control* team seem to be passing." He leaned on those words, casting them as catch-all euphemisms that his customers could apply as needed. "And the resulting lawsuits are obscene. The amounts that juries are awarding these days is beyond absurd. All that class-action attorneys have to do is show ten seconds of footage from a smartphone and the jurors start adding zeros to the amount awarded to the plaintiffs."

He paused and turned toward the full bank of screens and gave three measured seconds of his full presence.

"What if we could control each of those kinds of moments?" he asked calmly. "What if we could control what is—and more to the point, what is *not* recorded, what is not allowed to be shared on Twitter or Instagram or any other social media platform?" He paused. "And what if in those moments of actual privacy, we could completely resolve the situation? Whether that is an arrest in one of the more problematic parts of one of our cities? Or a field operation to resolve a political inconvenience? Or a money-shredding strike at a factory?"

Another pause.

"What if each of us possessed the technology to completely own that moment and to later control any messaging? What if here in the third decade of the twenty-first century we could move and act with the cost-efficient impunity of the 1950s? Yes, I can see that *you* see the potential. But, my friends, let me actually *show* you how this played out for one of our clients. I share this with the full permission of that client, who is a very happy returning customer. Settle back and watch . . ."

CHAPTER 22
REALSPORT FACTORY
MUTIARA VILLAGE
CENTRAL JAVA, INDONESIA

Darmana was a very small woman—under five feet, less than ninety pounds—but she stood tall as the two men approached her. Behind her, forty other women, including several who were barely into their teens, shrank back. However, Darmana stood firm, arms wide as if she could shield the other workers from what was coming.

A few men—employed in the same factory to carry and package the heavy boxes of sneakers, sweatshirts, and other branded items—hung at the fringes of the group. They looked ready to run, and more than half of them had already deserted the protest.

And Darmana held fast.

One of the two men wore a lightweight gray business suit that probably cost as much as she made in a year. He wore a crisp white shirt and striped red-and-gray tie. A very expensive-looking gold wristwatch caught bits of sunlight as his arms moved. He had thinning hair, brushed to conceal the paucity, and gold-rimmed steel glasses. He was smiling in the wrong kind of way for what was happening.

"He's from the corporation," murmured a woman behind her. "He's come to fire us."

That sent a ripple of nervous chatter through the group, but Darmana shushed them.

"He doesn't have police with him," she said. "None of those thugs, either. Let's hear what he has to say."

Her eyes, though, flicked to the other man. The other was not one of the factory managers or supervisors. He was a stranger to her. He did not wear a suit and tie. Or even a sports shirt, which was better suited to the oppressive heat. Instead, he was dressed head to toe in loose-fitting black clothes that looked like something a soldier might wear, except there were no emblems or insignia. No weapons, either.

The men walked slowly toward her. Two more men dressed in the same black clothes leaned against a dark SUV, muscular arms folded across their chests, eyes hidden behind sunglasses.

JONATHAN MABERRY

"Just be calm," said Darmana quietly. "Maybe they've come to talk."

This was day six of the shutdown. Darmana and her supporters had used chains, ropes, even plastic zip ties to seal the doors to the factory. For one glorious day, everyone was behind her. All eighty-eight workers, and even two of the shift supervisors, though they were likely spies sent to learn about the new union's plans.

Now there were forty protesters left. Some of the others stayed home, claiming they were sick. A few went looking for other work, finding it in similar sweatshops. And a dozen had climbed into the factory through a rear window and were actually working—hoping to curry favor with the supervisors once the protest was squashed. As it would certainly be. The government favored the corporations, as it always had. The world press was denied access to the town once the strike started, and only handpicked reporters were allowed to cover the event. What they wrote was mostly cut and pasted from corporate headquarters, the government's public relations office, or from articles from *The Capitalist* and other magazines or news services slanted toward the owners.

Darmana had read a few of those. Articles that said the pay rate of Rp22453.90 was more than enough to live on in both comfort and luxury. Those articles, written for Western readers who would be drawn to the number and not the value. In truth, the rupiah was crumbling, and this factory's pay rate of Rp99379.29 worked out to $6.45 in American dollars. Below even the national minimum wage. Not enough to survive on, what with agriculture production still recovering from COVID-19 and stores raising their prices to maximize profits during shortages. More than 70 percent of Darmana's meager pay went to food, and that was hardly a feast. Many working parents like her were half-starved so that their children and grandparents could eat. Debt mounted, and since the company that owned the factory also controlled the banks, there was nowhere to go but further down the poverty hole.

Darmana had hoped that by forming a small union and blockading the factory, the corporation fat cats would realize it was better to offer sensible—if small—raises rather than lose money from production slowdowns. She'd sent carefully written letters to the executives and foremen, pleading for those raises. Not a lot. The workers did not want to leave their jobs, but was it too much to ask for money to live? To put enough food on the table? To buy clothes for the children? To buy schoolbooks and to have enough for them to visit a clinic every now and then? It was so little to ask. Some of the celebrity-endorsed sneakers made in her factory sold for anywhere from $800 to $6,000 American dollars. Six thousand was three times as much as Darmana earned in a year working fourteen-hour shifts six days a week. Surely, the executives would find it in their hearts to offer a little more. Only a little.

At first, it had been the factory manager yelling at her and the other workers to go back to work, promising to forgive and forget once the machines were running again. When that hadn't worked—mainly because Darmana knew that retaliation would follow and told her coworkers that—the management sent strikebreakers. There were some minor scuffles, but many of her neighbors who'd come to watch the drama had cell phones. The strikebreakers were, too, clearly villains, and if it got onto social media, then corporate stocks would drop.

Darmana was not deeply educated, but she was savvy. She understood the power of social media. She had her cousin's cell phone, and she raised it as the corporate man and the tougher-looking man in black approached her.

They came right up to her and stopped only a few feet away, with the one who looked like a soldier a pace back. The corporate man stopped so close that Darmana could have reached out and touched him. She tried to stop the hand holding the cell phone from trembling, but she was too frightened. It was hard to say who frightened her more—the corporate man who could fire her and everyone else here, or the man in black.

There was something awful about him. He was taller than the well-dressed man and much taller than she was. He looked to be over six feet, with broad shoulders and a powerful build. A white man with maybe a bit of West African blood. Handsome, in his way, except for the eyes. They were as cold and dead as stones.

The corporate man broke the silence. He spoke Indonesian with

JONATHAN MABERRY

an accent that she could not place. Not American. Maybe German? She wasn't sure.

"My name is Michael Augustus Stafford," he said. "Your name is Darmana, right? You are the leader of this little protest."

It wasn't a question, so Darmana merely waited for more.

"What you are doing is hurting business," said Michael Augustus Stafford. "It's hurting your friends and coworkers. Surely, you understand that you've already lost much in wages that you'll never be able to recoup. How is that helping any of you?"

"You're paying starvation wages," she said, trying to keep fear out of her voice.

"No one here is fainting from hunger," said Stafford. He managed a smile that showed very good teeth. His breath, however, stank of cigars and whiskey.

Darmana didn't even bother to reply to that. Everyone who worked at the factory was stick thin. She had two children at home, the oldest of whom would soon leave school at age twelve to work right alongside her mother. Her daughter told her that she dreamed they were all dead and the town was filled with *pecong*—ghosts who were stuck in their shrouds. Only the factory was a big shroud in which all of the ghosts worked forever and ever.

Stafford shook his head. "Darmana, you need to listen to reason. No, let me change that—you need to think about what's best for you and your children. For your elderly mother and your grandparents. You need to think about what's best for all of the people here—and their families. What good can possibly come of you causing trouble and keeping the others—your own friends and neighbors—from earning their pay? You see, it's not the management who are picking your pocket. Hardly. We provide jobs for everyone. No, it's you and people like you who complain even when you're well off. It's people like you who are never satisfied and certainly never grateful."

"Grateful to be slaves?" she fired back. The camera she held above her head felt like it weighed ten tons. Beads of sweat ran down her arm.

"Grateful to have work," corrected Stafford. "Grateful to have steady employment at a time when the whole world is reeling from the global financial meltdown. Hundreds of millions around the world, even in

Europe and America, are still out of work. But *you* have work. And here you are, loitering, idle, causing problems, making false accusations against the people who provide those jobs to you. People you should praise. Instead, you berate them and make false accusations. You concoct blog posts filled with lies, exaggerated claims, and clips from fake news sources."

"It's not fake," snapped Darmana. "I've worked here all my life. I know. Everything I've said in letters and on blog posts is the truth."

"No," he said, shaking his head and smiling like a shark. "Lies. Nothing but lies from an ungrateful slut."

Darmana, long used to insults, didn't flinch, but instead gave him a smile of her own. Angry and triumphant. "Go ahead and insult me," she crowed, shaking the cell phone. "Every word you just said is going out to people all over the world."

"No," said Stafford, "it is not."

It took her a few seconds to process that. "What?"

"Look at your phone," he said. Still a smiling shark.

She did. Instead of a link to a YouTube channel run by a political blogger in Jakarta, the screen read: NO SIGNAL. She glanced around and saw a few other people in her group, and many among the crowd of townsfolk were also frowning at their phones.

"It's called a jammer," said Stafford. "Not a word of what we've said here has gotten out to anyone. And nothing those busybodies in this rabble"—he jerked his head toward the crowd behind him— "has gotten out. Not one word."

Darmana stared at her blank screen and then up at the man.

"It doesn't matter," she said weakly. "We're not going to budge until—"

"Shut the fuck up," said Stafford. The words froze Darmana to the spot.

"Wh-what did you—?"

"Shut your mouth and listen to me," said Stafford in a voice pitched loudly enough for everyone to hear him. "You have one chance left— just one—to stop this bullshit and get back to work."

Darmana looked around and saw the doubt and confusion on everyone's faces. And she saw it transform into alarm and then fear. She turned back to see that the man in black had stepped forward. Behind

JONATHAN MABERRY

him, the other two men pushed off from the SUV. One turned toward the onlookers, and the other came over to stand close to the knot of protesters. These men did not smile. They didn't speak.

Another pair of men got out of the vehicle and produced cell phones. They held them up with the lenses facing the crowd.

"Livestreaming now, sir," said one, and the other said he was as well.

Darmana glanced down at her phone, but it still said NO SIGNAL. That made no sense to her. How could her phone—and all the other phones—be jammed and yet allow the two men to livestream? It was a kind of technology she didn't understand. And a chill began creeping up her spine. Something bad was about to happen, but she couldn't imagine what. Why would these people video anything? It seemed the opposite of what thugs like this would want.

She looked up into the eyes of the tall, silent man standing close to her. At his face. At his eyes. Moments ago, he'd looked calm, detached, uninvolved with the corporate drama being played out, letting Stafford do all the talking. Now the man's eyes were filled with life, with strange lights. His mouth trembled as if he were fighting back laughter, but there was a fever brightness to his eyes. Sweat beaded on his cheeks and upper lip. Once more, Darmana glanced down to see if he had any weapons, but he was unarmed.

The man who called himself Stafford patted the taller man's shoulder. He spoke in a language Darmana didn't recognize. She thought it might have been German, but she met so few foreigners except the upper management, and they were usually French or British. She had no idea what the man said.

What filled her mind was what happened immediately after.

The man in black began trembling. Shuddering. Only a little at first, the way someone would if they felt a *pecong* walk over their grave. But the shudder grew instantly worse, and within moments, the man in black looked like he was being electrocuted. Or having an orgasm. There was a strange and appalling ecstasy on his face, twisting otherwise handsome features into a parody of pain or lust. Or both.

She looked past him and saw that the same thing was happening to the other black-clad men. All three of them were having some kind of fit. Their faces flushed as if their blood pressure were spiking. Foamy spit bubbled out from between the lips of the man in front of her.

Darmana backed up. First a single step, and then more, backpedaling as the fit grew more violent. Then all of a sudden, those tremors stopped, and the whole street in front of the factory went dead silent.

For two full seconds.

The men in black stared at her and through her and at nothing, and she saw to her horror that the tall man's eyes had changed. The whites had turned a dark, vibrant red.

Blood eyes, she thought with the odd clarity of someone in terrible danger. *He is a demon.*

And that was her very last thought. Then, or ever.

The man in black struck her with such shocking, hideous speed that she never saw his arm move. She did not truly feel the blow that caught her on the side of the jaw. Shock buffered her mind from hearing the sounds of her jaw shattering, just as it masked the wetter snap of her neck vertebrae. She was dead before her heart took the next beat.

She crumpled to the ground, unable to hear the high and terrible screams of the rest of the protesters. Of the crowd of townsfolk who'd gathered to watch.

Or of the shrieks of horror and agony that followed as the three men in black moved through the village like a monsoon wind, killing everyone Darmana had ever known.

Stafford stepped over her corpse and walked over to the car, leaned against it, produced a silver cigarette case, and removed a filterless Roth-Händle, which he lit with a gold lighter. He dragged in a deep lungful, held it to feel the bite, and then exhaled. The blue smoke swirled in the air as all around the screams rose and rose.

He glanced at the two men with cell phones and drew a hand across his throat, telling them to cut the feed. They did.

"You get all that?" he asked.

"Every bit," said one of the men.

"Sweet."

Michael Augustus Stafford pulled his cell phone out, punched

JONATHAN MABERRY

a number, and when it was answered, said, "Looked great from my end, boss. I think this'll play well in your next ShowRoom gig."

"Excellent work," said Mr. Sunday. "The buses of replacement workers will be there first thing in the morning."

"Right-o."

Stafford ended the call and smiled. He loved days like this. Made him glad to be alive.

CHAPTER 23
INTEGRATED SCIENCES DIVISION
PHOENIX HOUSE
OMFORI ISLAND, GREECE

Dr. Jane Holliday sat with Church and Bug at a small table in the lab.

The rest of the staff were busy working, but they knew better than to pester the boss and two department heads. There were glances thrown that way, though, and even some unapologetic eavesdropping.

"The problem is," said Doc, "that we know too much and not enough."

Her masses of blond hair had spilled out of the bun and hung unevenly around her face, making her look like she'd just come in from riding a horse on a windy heath.

Bug snorted. He was bleary-eyed and unshaven. "Welcome to Rogue Team International, where that is on everyone's page-a-day calendar for any day ending in a Y."

"You're not wrong," said Church. His only concession to the long hours since Ledger had gone off the radar was that he'd taken his suit jacket off and tugged the knot of his tie loose. He still looked immaculate.

They had cups of coffee and a plate of cookies. Church was nibbling on his fourth vanilla wafer, and no one else seemed interested in cutting into his supply. Doc had a bunch of animal crackers laid out like a parade and was biting off bits of each animal but not eating any whole cookies. Bug sat there, slowly unscrewing double-filled

Oreos and eating the cream. Only when he finished the fillings did he begin eating the cookies.

"Ron Coleman and Isaac are studying the cybernetic implants on the patients we brought from Croatia. Right now, there seem to be several kinds of implants. Some have neuro chips, and there's research suggesting that the chips are designed to interface with add-on gear like a targeting helmet, exoskeleton, or even drones. And there are implants that Coleman is certain will trigger the release of different kinds of chemicals. Some of these chemicals are natural to the body, so the implants regulate those. Dopamine, for example. Or they can sync with a med pack prefilled with drugs. Modifications of modafinil and armodafinil, for sure. They act as selective and atypical dopamine reuptake inhibitors; and then there's adrafinil, which serves as a prodrug for modafinil. And a prodrug is a compound or medication that, once administered and metabolized into a pharmacologically active drug, controls and improves how the drug is absorbed, distributed, metabolized, and excreted. And we also found experiments with other eugeroics—the norepinephrine–dopamine reuptake inhibitor solriamfetol, and pitolisant, which acts as a histamine receptor antagonist and inverse agonist."

"Interesting," said Church.

"And there are other compounds referenced that we haven't found details on yet. One in particular is R-33. There are notes saying that it's promising, that tests are showing it to be stable for field use, though of limited duration. And a list of side effects, including possible heart trauma. But we have a ton of stuff to go through, and there's the encrypted stuff, so maybe it'll be in there."

"So," said Church, "hit me with your most compelling theories. What is it you think we're learning?"

Bug and Doc exchanged a long look, and then shrugged.

Doc said, "These naughty boys are planning something very big and very bad that will involve cybernetically and chemically enhanced PMCs."

"Probably top-tier Fixers," said Bug. "They'd be the ones most solidly under Santoro's control."

"His cult of killers," agreed Doc.

Church tapped crumbs from his cookie onto his plate. "To what end? Enhanced military contractors are hardly a new idea. We've taken down at least nine groups with that agenda."

"We have," said Doc, "and two of those were since I've been your chief mad scientist, but it's remarkable, perhaps significant, that much of the R&D for those older cases is included in what Top brought back."

"Oh yeah," said Bug. "The Jakoby stuff and all?"

"How much of it is material likely stolen from us during the hack a few years ago?" asked Church.

"A bunch," said Bug. "A lot more than I thought had been taken at the time. There's even a good chance—call it 99.9 percent—that some of this was stuff stolen by Artemisia Bliss."

Church chewed for a moment in silence. Bliss had been a protégé of Doc's predecessor, Dr. William Hu. She'd been a brilliant research scientist, analyst, and strategic thinker . . . but she'd gone badly astray. Church had fired her and then had her arrested for theft of data and technologies obtained after the takedowns of some of the more dangerous groups and cartels the DMS faced. Then Bliss faked her death and reinvented herself as a firebrand among the anarchist crowd. This new persona, Mother Night, had done a lot of damage, had broken into one of the most secure bioweapons storage facilities, and tried to release the Seif al Din pathogen—the single most dangerous bioweapon Church's teams had ever faced—at a science fiction convention in Atlanta.

"But don't get me wrong, Mr. Boss Man," said Doc, "there's a lot of new science here, too."

"Some of that's based on stolen R&D, too, though," said Bug. "I'm finding fingerprints—and what amounts to computer watermarks—on lots of the data files. Stuff looted from the Department of Defense and maybe forty other places, including a lot of universities. Their mainframes are so easy to hack they might as well not even try to use encryption. Though there's stuff here from some private corporations . . . stuff that was much better protected, and from companies that I'm pretty sure aren't in any way tied to the Kuga brand."

"What's the rest?" asked Church.

"Totally new stuff," said Doc.

"Without a doubt," said Bug.

"Tell me," Church said.

"There are three areas these bad boys seem to be focusing on. First is surgically implanted technologies. True cybernetics."

"Ah'll be bahk," said Bug in a fair impersonation of Arnold Schwarzenegger.

"Second area," continued Doc, "is a new generation of body armor that's really a kind of exoskeleton. In their notes, they refer to it as a CR, shorthand for *combat rig,* and there are references to several models or perhaps generations of it. K-14, K-57, K-79, and so on. Most recent generation is the K-110."

"I'm guessing the *K* is for *Kuga*?" ventured Bug.

"That'd be my guess, sugar," agreed Doc. "And I have to tell you boys that if these jokers decided to go straight and simply patent this stuff, they'd probably get rich as Croesus selling it to the various official military or private military markets. We're talking billions. Some of this is really freaking awesome."

"Because they have an actual evil master plan," said Bug. It was only partly a joke, and no one laughed. "Besides, some of these innovations are based on stolen science. Sure, the finished product may be new, but anyone can reverse engineer it and see what came out of other labs."

"There's that," conceded Doc. She flipped open a folder and showed a schematic for a bulky exoskeleton. "See this? I ran an image and data search, and what did I find? This is a variation of the Guardian XO full-body exoskeleton by the Sarcos company. It was marketed as the first battery-powered industrial integrated robot, which means it has machinery run by software but integrates with the driver's commands. It augments operator strength but doesn't inhibit freedom of movement. The difference is that the Sarcos one is used mostly for industrial work—lifting and so on. But see here? Those fittings are for machine guns, I'm sure of it. And see these specs handwritten down there? That's for add-ons made from Kevlar and also bullet-resistant clear polymers. Protection and visibility. Kuga's guys took the industrial version and weaponized it. I ran the numbers on the armor, and it will create a protective shell that allows more than two hundred and fifty degrees of visibility while keeping the driver safe from anything up to armor-piercing rounds. My guess is that they'll rig a double-capacity backpack. One side for batteries, the other for belt-fed ammunition. You put a Fixer in one of those and he can walk into any building and do an incredible amount of damage. With a minigun or a grenade launcher? Well, butter my buns and call me a biscuit, but that is some scary, scary stuff right up in there."

"This is adapted to military," said Church. "Did you find anything designed specifically for combat?"

"Oh yes," said Doc. "A lot of that, and it's pretty goldurn scary, too."

She produced another folder, and this one had schematics, pages of materials analysis and other data, and some glossy photos. Church picked one up and studied it. It showed a soldier wearing a series of complex braces around his legs, torso, and arms. There were wires and coaxial cables in bundles running from servos to battery packs.

"This is based on the ONYX system," he observed. "They developed the lower-body exoskeletons to help combat soldiers carry or pull heavy loads."

"They also reduce fatigue," said Doc, nodding. "But see how it's been modified? It's been expanded out to support hips, lower and mid-back, shoulders and arms. The effect is—if their notations are correct—a 320 percent increase in physical strength coupled with far greater endurance. A soldier in that rig could do a fifty-mile hike faster and with less energy drain than a regular soldier could hike fifteen miles on the flat and carrying no battle rattle. We're talking enhanced endurance, especially over uneven terrain and inclines, better handling of heavy weapons, and it guides orthopedic alignment to help evenly distribute weight and maintain skeletal system alignment to avoid overstress and pressure injuries."

Church shuffled through the photos and paused on the last one. This showed the same basic exoskeleton sheathed in sleek black armor that hid the vulnerable materials and kept the bundled cables from being a nuisance to the man in the suit. A notation in the corner indicated that this was a K-110 prototype. And below that the word *Production?* With a question mark.

"This concerns me greatly," he said, setting the photo down and turning it around for them.

"It should," said Doc.

Bug picked it up. "Yeah, this scares me, too. Just the thought of our guys running into even *one* of these . . ."

He didn't finish but shivered, which was eloquent enough.

"And," said Doc, "there are two more things. We found four separate mentions of something called G-55. At first, I thought it was another product line, but it seems to be part of some upcoming project, or perhaps a location. Not really enough to go on, and it may be nothing. Does it mean anything to you, O Mighty Sage?"

"It does not," said Church. "What's the other thing?"

"Well," said Doc, "all through the records, there are references to something called AO. Again, no clue as to what it stands for, and there's little contextual help, since it's usually just a reference like, 'For AO?' and 'AO Parts List.' Like that. But it shows up in almost every document—mostly handwritten on printouts—connected with the exosuits and other potential field combat tech."

"AO," mused Church. "That's not particularly helpful."

"I'll put Nikki on it."

Nikki Bloom ran the pattern recognition team within Bug's department.

"Have to tell you boys," said Doc, "every time I see those two letters, it gives me a nasty little itch right between my shoulder blades. Like someone's out there in the tall grass lining me up nice and proper in the crosshairs."

"I'm quite familiar with that feeling," said Church.

"Are you getting that feeling now?" she asked.

"I am."

With that, he stood and left the lab.

CHAPTER 24
IN FLIGHT OVER THE SOUTH ATLANTIC

The cabin steward, a slim Genoese woman who was a bit older than the others in the flight crew, stood in the galley with the curtain drawn. Her fingers touched the crucifix beneath her uniform as she peeked out through a narrow gap in the blue cloth. The first-class passengers were mostly dozing. Beyond them, most of the overhead lights were off, though a few travelers had their faces lit by whatever screen they were watching. The big 250-seat Airbus A330's engines, running on autopilot, were a constant heavy drone that lulled most people to sleep.

Midway along the aisle, there was a large service dog curled on the floor, partly under the seat, but occasionally leaning his big white head out to look up and down the walkway. Beside him was a blind man. Older, heavyset, wearing sunglasses with very dark lenses. He wore earbuds, but when the cabin steward passed by on her rounds, she noticed that the headphone cable wasn't plugged in. It merely dangled. When she leaned over and asked if he needed help finding the jack for the music, he turned to her and—she was positive—looked at her.

That had been a very odd moment. Over the thousands of flights she'd worked since joining the Alitalia team, she'd encountered countless vision-impaired passengers. She could always tell whether they'd been born blind, had lost sight due to age or injury, or were merely legally blind.

She did not think the man in seat JJ66 was blind at all.

When he'd turned to her and raised his face, even though the glasses—as well as the dimmed ambient light—were too opaque to see his eyes, she could *feel* them.

It was so unnerving.

It wasn't merely that sensation of being watched. No. It was more of being *seen* and seen all the way down to the skin. To the nerves and blood and bone. It was violative, invasive, and made her skin crawl.

Now she watched the aisle, hoping no one near the man and dog needed her.

And, as if hearing her thoughts, she saw the blind man lean out and look in her direction. Those black glasses against his pale skin. The touch of his perception.

It was so . . .

Dark.

That was it, she realized with an abruptness that made cold sweat pop out of her skin over her heart.

It was like the darkness outside the plane was looking at her through that blind man's eyes.

She did not like that feeling. No, not one little bit.

Her fingers pressed the crucifix against her skin.

CHAPTER 25

WORLD-A-WAY SHIPPING AND STORAGE
THE PORT OF HOUSTON, TEXAS

Eve limped down the warehouse aisle, flanked by Cain and Abel. The rest of the Righteous—her special cadre of elite Fixers—were back at the Pavilion in Washington State. These boys, though, had become her constant bodyguards, and they'd passed the intense background checks imposed on them by Daddy.

She wished Rafael Santoro was there, but Daddy preferred to stay in Canada with Kuga. He was always so busy, and she missed him.

"Miss Eve?" called a voice, and a man's head and shoulders popped out from between two stacks of crates. "I think I found them," said the logistic supervisor.

"You think or you have?" she snapped back. It was the kind of thing Kuga said, putting people on the spot, making them jump.

"I . . . well . . . I, um, found the crates with the correct—ah—markings," fumbled the supervisor. "We'll need to actually open them to see."

Eve went over to where he stood and peered at the labels stenciled on the heavy pine boxes. There were four, and each had *AO/G-K*, and then three smaller, narrower crates with *AO/G-C*.

She tapped Cain. "Open them up, and let's look."

"Ma'am," said the Fixer and jogged off, returning quickly with two long-handled crowbars and a smaller pinch bar. The supervisor got a forklift, and soon all the boxes were sitting in a row on the floor. Cain and Abel set to work opening the big crates, while the supervisor used the pinch bar on the smaller ones. The wood was green, and it cried out in protest as the long nails were pulled out.

Once the lids were off and the packing straw tossed away, Eve peered inside to see a device that looked like a hunchbacked robot.

She used a portable scanner to read the bar code on the back of the cowling, and a small light on her device flashed green. She repeated it with the three other units. All green.

"Those are good," she said. "Repack it."

The contents of the smaller crates took longer to inventory because there were many objects—gallons of chemicals, large bottles of capsules, and mechanical devices wrapped in bubble paper. There was no way to hurry the job, because the scanner was uplinked to Wi-Fi and sent the scan results directly to HK at the Pavilion and Daddy in Canada.

Tasks like this were tedious but necessary, and Eve knew that it was part of her training to be an executive within the Kuga organization. Daddy was watching, and so was Kuga himself.

Eve did not disappoint.

She knew she was a different person from what she'd been when she and her late lover, Adam, had been recruited by Rafael Santoro. They had both been smart and dangerous, but Daddy had begun a process of refinement. Eve also knew that her emotional extremes since Adam's death had caused Daddy some embarrassment and a lot of concern. She'd very nearly gone too far, and that was a terrifying thought. More recently, she'd forced herself to be more controlled, less a victim of her own excesses. And so Daddy had begun gradually giving her more tasks—often mundane, things that anyone could do—and watched how she handled them.

This project, the one they all called the American Operation, was big. It was high profile, and any mishandling at any level could be catastrophic. The fact that Daddy was allowing her to oversee this . . . well, maybe it wasn't such a nothing job after all, she mused.

She just hoped she'd get a chance to play when everything began going to shit here in America. That would be worth the wait. That would be fun.

And, who knew, maybe she'd get to shoot Joe Ledger in the process.

CHAPTER 26
PHOENIX HOUSE
OMFORI ISLAND, GREECE

They sat together on a couch in Church's study, which was lined with books and hung with art. They had cups of coffee growing cold on a table, and slices of uneaten quiche neither had an appetite for. The speakers were turned low as Leonard Cohen sang soft, brooding songs about love and loss and the decline of the culture of insight.

Church wore a dark blue robe, and Lilith's was red, a shade darker and more luxuriant than fresh blood. A fire spilled light and warmth into the room, but the shadows clinging to the corners were cold and resisted being chased completely away.

Lilith was a tall woman with very pale skin, intensely dark eyes, and full red lips. Her glossy black hair fell around her shoulders, with tendrils reaching to the tops of her breasts. Like Church, her age was impossible to guess. They were both older than they looked. Sometimes—as with tonight—they each felt every one of their years. And every inch of their scars.

"He's back," she said. It was the first thing either had said for ten minutes.

"He's back," agreed Church.

They watched the fire.

"*How?*" she asked.

Church almost smiled. "Rhetorical question?"

"Only to a degree," said Lilith. "I thought after the Dogs of War case, he would be gone."

"For good? Hardly."

"For a while, I meant. Longer than this."

Church touched her face, gently tracing the curve from high cheekbone to tapered chin. She was inarguably beautiful, but many people over the years had described her as looking cruel, unemotional, queenly in the ways history's more powerful queens sometimes look. Not at all a fairy-tale princess. He loved those qualities about her. Lilith had never once compromised who she was or acted conciliatory to anyone. Certainly never to a man.

He was also aware that people used many of the same adjectives to describe him. Cold, cruel, aloof. Strange.

Fair enough. They were both strange, and their world was infinitely stranger than Scott Wilson or Doc Holliday or Joe Ledger knew.

Lilith touched Church's face as she studied his eyes. The tinted glasses he usually wore were on a table in the other room. He did not wear them in private. Certainly not when he invited this woman to see his unguarded expressions.

She said, "Do you fear him? You've never actually said."

"I fear what he can do," said Church after a long pause.

"That's an evasive answer."

"No," he said, "it's really not."

She laughed and shook her head. "Your *people*," she said, gesturing vaguely in the direction of the floor because the apartment was at the top of a castle and Rogue Team International was based in underground chambers many floors below, "think nothing scares you. That you are incapable of fear. Above it."

"They believe what they want to believe. They believe what comforts them."

"Oh, and you do nothing at all to perpetuate those beliefs."

Church shrugged. "It's useful to be calm when things are catching fire."

"They think you destroyed Nicodemus."

"I have never made that claim," said Church.

Lilith smiled but let the topic go. Instead, she returned to an earlier point. "Nicodemus is a monster."

"He is a disease," said Church. "He never really goes away. And if there is a vaccine for a parasite like him, then I will be the first customer for it."

She picked up her coffee cup and sipped, winced because it was cold, then drank anyway. Her eyes flicked toward his. "He's aligned himself with Kuga."

"Yes," said Church.

"We have to be careful. He delights in revenge."

"Yes."

"He likes to *hurt*," said Lilith. "I've already sent a coded message to Arklight. You should warn some of your people. And, given that he's now tied to a criminal network with tentacles in governments, business, and social media, maybe there are people we should both contact."

"I will be making quite a number of calls," said Church. "Kuga has resources, but so do we. And we have friends we can call."

She nodded. "Some of our friends are no longer in the best position to defend themselves. Aunt Sallie comes to mind."

Aunt Sallie was the former chief of operations from the DMS days and before. Church had met her in Germany when she was a young but highly respected CIA field operator on loan to Interpol, doing elimination and cleanup against the Soviets and other groups. Aunt Sallie had been Church's strong right hand for decades, but during the DMS's last case, she'd suffered a terrible stroke. Now she lived in a very upscale, very private nursing facility in Corfu, where Auntie would likely spend her last years. If she still had years left. Of all the people with whom Church worked closely, Auntie had been with him the longest. She'd known some of his secrets. Some, not all.

"And here I thought you couldn't stand her," he chided.

Lilith gave a small shrug. "There's no love lost between us, but she's family. We both know that family may dislike and even disown you until the chips are down, and then blood tells."

They sat and thought about that for a while.

Blood tells.

Church's daughter, Circe, was estranged from him. Her choice. They had never been close. Or, rather, as soon as she knew what kind of things her father did for a living, and to what lengths he would go to fight the never-ending war, she withdrew from him. He got to visit her and her husband, Rudy Sanchez, only because Rudy insisted that Church be allowed to see his grandson. But the visits were few, they were chilly, and Church always left more brokenhearted than he had been when he arrived. Church visited Aunt Sallie's care facility four times as often as he got to see his grandson, a fact made even more painful because that facility was less than a quarter mile from where Circe and Rudy lived on the island of Corfu.

"Blood tells," he echoed. Lilith gave him a sharp, penetrating look, then set her coffee cup down and pulled him to her for a kiss.

CHAPTER 27

HÔTEL BYBLOS
20 AVENUE PAUL SIGNAC
SAINT-TROPEZ, FRANCE

Michael Augustus Stafford lay poolside, splitting his attention between a flock of exceptionally lovely women sunbathing across from him, an email from his stockbroker, and news stories about a terrible terrorist attack at a sportswear factory in a small village in central Java. What a shame. Total loss of life.

The reporters did not focus on the complete lack of cell phone photos or videos. Of course they didn't. Mr. Sunday and Rafael Santoro would make very sure of that. That deep in the third world, it was easy to buy off anyone who mattered.

It made him happy that his employers were happy.

It made his banker and his financial advisor happy, too. And his broker was all but coming in his pants.

In all, a good week to be a bad guy.

And that's how he saw himself. He had plenty of friends who wrapped themselves in cloaks of rationalizations, ranging from "There's a sucker born every minute" to "They stood in the way of progress," and all the iterations in between. But that wasn't how he rolled. He knew exactly who and what he was, and Stafford liked that guy.

Once, watching an interview with a movie actor who played a famous serial killer, the actor said, "No one is evil in their own minds. No one looks into a mirror and sees a villain. Villains, like everyone else, have to maintain a worldview that paints them as the good guy, or at least not a distinctly bad one."

Stafford found that amusing as hell. And maybe it was true for some people in his line of work. But he thought on the whole it was naive. He was a murderer, a contract killer, an occasional trafficker in very young sex workers, and frequently in cahoots with terrorists. That made him a bad guy, and that was what he always wanted to be.

He was not a product of a bad childhood. His folks were great. So were his two sisters and older brother. All of them, fine people. Gentle, supportive, fun. Nor was he bullied in school. He had no chemical imbalances, no brain tumors, and was not anywhere on the autism spectrum. He was pretty sure he wasn't even a sociopath, though perhaps an argument could be made.

Nope, he was just a bad guy.

A very good-looking, well-hung, and seriously rich bad guy.

And that made him very, very happy.

CHAPTER 28
PHOENIX HOUSE
OMFORI ISLAND, GREECE

The four members of Havoc Team were in a corner of the mess hall. Top and Bunny, Belle and Andrea. There were other people around—operators from the other teams—Bedlam and Chaos; scientists and lab techs, general staff. No one came and sat with the four remaining members of Havoc Team. No one even came over to chat.

They knew.

Everyone knew.

Colonel Joe Ledger had gone off the reservation. That was the expression, and it carried with it a lot of weight, a lot of doubt and uncertainty. A lot of fear.

Ledger was the cornerstone of the field operations division. To everyone who worked for Mr. Church, Ledger was something of a mythological figure. He was the jovial party guy who was everybody's friend when the beer was flowing and the steaks sizzling. He was the operator you wanted coming when you'd been praying for the Seventh Cavalry to ride over the hill. He was the guy people told stories about without having to exaggerate a single detail. He was a warrior who stood between the innocent and harm, preferring to take the shot meant for the good guys. He was the one who'd actually saved the world. Time and again.

And now he was gone.

Just . . . gone.

Andrea stared into the depths of a coffee cup as if it would suddenly become a magician's mirror. "Alligator balls," he murmured.

Many of Andrea's comments focused on the testicles of some animal—real or mythological—or those of various saints.

Bunny grunted. "Why alligator balls?"

"Because it is," said Andrea. Bunny thought about it, nodded, and went back to looking sick and stricken.

"He will come back," said Belle. It was not the first time she'd said this. And, as before, the others nodded without any real optimism.

Top Sims sipped his coffee, which was excellent, but winced as if it caused him physical pain. The wince had nothing to do with the coffee, and his friends knew it. He was in serious pain that had nothing to do with nerve endings or old injuries. Top was not taking this well.

Bunny punched him lightly on the arm. "Not your fault, old man."

"Maybe it's all our faults, Farm Boy," said Top.

"How d'you figure that?"

Top shook his head. "We all knew the colonel was still too busted up from last Christmas. No way he should have been let back into the field. That's on us."

"And were we supposed to stop him?" asked Belle.

"By any means necessary," said Top, "up to and including knee-capping him. Better a limp than him losing his shit and going rogue out in the world."

"He is going after Rafael Santoro and Kuga," said Belle. "Maybe this is a good thing."

Top turned slowly to look at her. "*We* are going after Santoro and Kuga. All of us. Field teams, everyone at the TOC, integrated sciences and computer sciences. The whole RTI machinery. That's what we're here for. The colonel is a force of nature, sure, and I'd walk through hell on Sunday for him, we all would . . . but he can't do this alone. Cannot and damned well should not."

"Hooah," said Bunny softly.

"We're the ones closest to him, and we let him down." Top paused and gave another shake of his head. "*I* let him down. I told him to go out and get some air. That was on me. I should have put one of you with him."

"No," said Bunny, "that's bullshit. If the colonel wanted to slip away, he'd have found a way even if we were babysitting him. This is Joe Ledger we're talking about. No . . . you can secure that shit right now because it's not true. He wanted to go, and he went. If it wasn't on that island, then he'd have found a moment and gone."

"Then we need to find him, Farm Boy, instead of sitting here with our thumbs up our asses. Instead of mounting a full-on hunt, what are we doing? You and me? We're flying all the way the hell to goddamned America for some goddamned undercover mission that might not be worth a goddamned thing."

"Job's a job," said Bunny.

"Colonel Ledger should be our job. We don't know where he is or what he's doing . . . but whatever he's up to, it's not good. This isn't him making sound decisions. That bomb on Christmas Eve blew out all his circuits, and you know it as well as I do. Best-case scenario is he's in some bar god knows where drinking himself to death. Worst-case scenario . . . well, you all saw what he did in Croatia. Those lab techs . . . then executing Mitrović in cold blood. While the man was unconscious and helpless. Find him? Find him in *time*? Shit. How?"

"Bug's looking," said Bunny. "Scott Wilson's looking. And you can bet Mr. Church has put out calls to everyone he knows. Arklight, Barrier, Sigma Force, Kingdom, SEAL Team 666, the whole damned network. Someone's going to find him."

"If he wants to be found," said Belle. "Only if he wants to be found."

They fell silent.

A few moments later, Andrea repeated, "Alligator balls."

"Yeah," agreed Bunny. "Absolutely."

CHAPTER 29
O. R. TAMBO INTERNATIONAL AIRPORT
KEMPTON PARK
JOHANNESBURG, SOUTH AFRICA

The fat old blind man with the service dog deplaned with the rest of the passengers and headed to the men's room. Not the first one, or the second, but the third lavatory in the terminal.

He loitered at the sink, washing his hands until everyone was

JONATHAN MABERRY

gone, and then slipped quickly into a stall. More travelers came in, but if any of them took particular notice of a tall, middle-aged businessman with salt-and-pepper dark brown hair, bushy eyebrows, and a neat mustache, no comments were made. One exception was when a child in the terminal went to pet the man's seeing-eye dog; a young mother scolded him and then apologized to the dog's master.

"Quite all right," said the blind man. His accent was a local one, and the woman took her child away.

The blind man and his dog went outside, caught a cab, and took it first to an electronics store, then to a pharmacy, a clothing store, and finally to the Reef Hotel on Anderson Street in the Marshalltown area of the city. He paid the driver and tipped well enough to pay for the man's patience.

Once settled into the room, the man showered and changed into new clothes. Then he sat on the edge of the bed and set up the new burner phone he'd bought. He made several short phone calls, and then lay back on his bed and closed his eyes. The dog jumped up and sprawled next to him.

They both fell asleep at once.

They both dreamed.

Both twitched and moaned softly as dreams took them down and took them deep.

They woke when there was a discreet tap on the door.

The man padded barefoot to the door, peered through the peephole, and then opened it. The dog stood on the other side of the door. Ready. Always ready.

The deliveryman spoke only one word. A question.

"Paladin?"

"Charlemagne," answered the man.

The courier brought in two large suitcases, set them down, and left without comment.

When the door was closed and locked, the man took the cases to the bed and opened them. He stood looking at the contents for a long time. At the equipment, the weapons, the sets of papers, and the laptop, each snugged into a special foam slot.

Then he took a pillow from the bed, opened the closet door, crawled inside, pressed the pillow to his face, wrapped his arms around it, and screamed.

He screamed for a very long time.

The dog sat vigil outside, whining softly, the hairs on his back standing straight and stiff, his brown eyes filled with pain.

CHAPTER 30
FREETECH RESEARCH AND DEVELOPMENT OFFICE
SAN DIEGO, CALIFORNIA

Junie sat in her office, looking out at the California night.

Starlight sparkled on the waves as they rolled onto the sand. Beyond that silver luminescence, the ocean became totally black. So intensely black that it seemed as if she were looking at nothing, just an empty vastness in the world. Or like looking into the deep darkness between stars.

She turned away from the window, forcing herself not to look at that nothingness. Afraid that it was some kind of omen.

Her cell phone was on the desk, and she picked it up but did not immediately make a call. After all, it was nearly dawn in Greece. Would anyone over there still be awake? She'd already tried to call Church, but it went to voice mail each time. Rudy and Circe had a young child, and Circe was having some complications with her pregnancy; Junie could not be heartless enough to wake them up.

Bug? No. He hated talking on the phone at the best of times.

And if Joe was on a mission, as she believed, then Top and Bunny wouldn't be taking calls. She didn't have Scott Wilson's cell number, nor did she have much of a relationship with the RTI chief of operations.

Toys was gone. After her fainting spell, he'd lingered for hours playing nurse, but he was dead on his feet, and she finally called his driver, Mad Max, and had her take Toys home.

Who did that leave?

She could wait until it was morning in Greece and then call *all* of them. That was only a few hours away.

Movement drew her eye, and she turned to see a bird land on the windowsill. It was a raven. Common to California, though she was more used to crows. The bird was about two feet from beak to tail feathers and looked like he'd been freshly rinsed in gleaming oil. Black on black on black. The starlight traced the contours of his feathers and sparkled in the small black eyes.

Junie touched a finger to the pane. "Nevermore," she said and immediately regretted the joke. It was the wrong word to use. "Pretty bird," she said, trying to fix the moment and cancel any accidental jinx.

Then she picked up the phone and punched in a number. It rang five times, and just when Junie expected it to go to voice mail, a woman answered.

"Well, I guess I'm not the only night owl drinking too much coffee and burning the midnight oil," said Doc Holliday. "How are you doing, sugar lumps?"

"Jane," said Junie, "I'm just about going crazy here."

Doc sighed. Long and heavy and dramatic. "Oh, honey, if you're calling in the hopes that this ol' gal has some news about your honeybunny, then I have to be the bad guy. I don't know where Joseph is, and that is the God's honest."

"Is he alive?" begged Junie.

"I'd bet my whole stack of original Dolly Parton albums on vinyl he's alive."

"Is he safe?"

There was a pause, and when Doc spoke again, there was much less of her country girl affectation. "If you were someone else, I'd spin a big pack of lies, but I know you have enough sawdust for the straight truth, Junie-girl. The plain truth is that I don't know. *We* don't know. But that's also the nature of the job."

"I know, but—"

"But nothing. Look, I shouldn't be telling you this, but Mr. Church can fire me if he wants to—which he won't. Joe's out in the field, and for reasons that he hasn't shared, he's gone off on his own. And before you ask, that is all I know."

Junie covered her mouth with her hand.

"God . . . ," she breathed.

Outside the window, the raven opened his mouth and uttered a high, soft, sad cry.

CHAPTER 31
HÔTEL BYBLOS
20 AVENUE PAUL SIGNAC
SAINT-TROPEZ, FRANCE

Michael Augustus Stafford sprawled on the bed and watched her walk naked across the room.

Angelique was tall, slender, beautifully made, with lean muscles and good curves accentuated by skin that took an excellent deep-honey tan. And that tan was flawless except for a tiny white triangle around her shaved crotch. Everything about her was luxuriant. Masses of curly dark hair that fell like smoke around her shoulders. Green eyes filled with both questions and information. A smart woman who had the good genetic luck to also be exceptionally beautiful, even by the exacting standards of the South of France.

Stafford studied her as she moved around the suite. She was as unselfconscious as a child, but wickedly aware. Every now and then, she'd throw a tiny, knowing smile his way. She liked being watched.

"This was a lovely oasis," Angelique said as she bent to fish for a lacy thong that had somehow made its way under the foot of the bed.

"Very," he agreed.

He was satiated, tired, and happy. He'd met the woman at Gaïo, a posh restaurant-club on Rue du 11 Novembre 1918. They'd danced, dined, had a lot of very good drinks, and then went back to his hotel rather than hers because he was alone, and she had a roommate. The fact that her roommate was also her fiancé did not seem to matter much to Angelique, and it didn't matter at all to Stafford. They'd made love on the bed, on the balcony, and in the shower; then napped for an hour and made love again. And it felt like that to him—making love, more so than merely having sex.

Angelique was, he discovered to his delight, as much of a sensualist as he was. She liked all the little things—the slow process of discovering each other, the attention to small details of the landscape of their bodies. There was a mutual generosity, empathy, and creativity. Each of their four bouts of passion was on a different frequency, which resulted in a different kind of orgasm. When it became apparent that they both shared the dedication of sensualism, the whole evening had transformed from the potential of good sex between two healthy adults, and instead achieved beauty. Her first orgasm had been a screaming frenzy, but the subsequent ones had grown quieter, more internal as she focused on small details instead of grand gestures or a gallop to the finish line.

And there had been quiet moments of holding, of talking, and of a shared and companionable silence.

He was very glad he wasn't on a job. He was very glad he wouldn't have to kill her.

Stafford did not look like a killer, but that's what he was. And he knew that among the right kind of people—men and women whose judgment and opinions mattered—he was considered one of the very best killers alive. Several other people who would have been on that list were dead. He had crossed many names off himself. Not as a vendetta or through an insecure need to be number one but because they had been given to him as targets.

Angelique was not a target. She was, for five delicious hours, his lover.

She thought he was an investor who'd gotten rich trading currencies.

The people who knew him back during his college days agreed that he looked like either a third baseman from one of the better teams or a tennis pro. Fit but not in any overdeveloped way. He moved like an athlete, one of the fast kinds. A springy step and easy grace. And he smiled like a sports star. Lots of white teeth, brown hair with natural blond highlights, and a tan nearly as good as Angelique's.

He was considering whether he had the stamina for another round when his cell phone buzzed. Stafford picked up the device, looked at the screen display, and got out of bed immediately.

"I have to take this," he said. "Business call."

Without waiting for an answer, he went into the bathroom, turned on the shower, and sat on the closed lid of the toilet. He used a cable to attach the cell to a tiny device no larger than a cigarette lighter. A small red light glowed, flickered, and then turned green, letting him know that the scrambler was engaged. It used a sophisticated 128-byte cyclical encryption that was virtually impossible to crack. The device was specifically designed to foil the MindReader computer system. Satisfied that his end of the call was secure, he cupped a hand over his other ear and spoke one word.

"Line?"

"Clear," said the caller. "What is on your business agenda for today?"

It was the right phrase, and he recognized the voice. All the screen display had shown was a number he didn't know. A burner, a disposable phone. Very few people had his current cell number. Had the caller used any wording other than those nine words, Stafford would have hung up and fled the hotel, leaving most of his possessions behind, along with Angelique's corpse. The fact that the right phrase was used told him he hadn't been compromised.

However, it was not a phrase he particularly wanted to hear. Nor did he want to hear it from this man. Kuga. It was hard as hell to tell him to go piss up a rope. But he gave it a try.

"I'm enjoying my vacation," he said, meaning it. Letting a bit of resentment flavor his tone.

Kuga snorted. "Yeah, well life's a bitch, and then you die."

"Nice. You should put that on a coffee mug and sell it thirty years ago. Look, boss, I haven't had a full week off in three years. Three," he insisted. "Years. And you promised me that my phone would not ring once until I checked back in. So, tell me why I'm talking with you right now?"

"Joe Ledger," said Kuga.

Stafford closed his eyes for a moment.

"Ah. Of course," sighed Stafford. "I suppose this was inevitable."

"It's become necessary. He is doing considerable damage to our network."

"What kind of damage?"

"Do you remember Mislav Mitrović?"

"What do you mean, do I remember? Of *course* I do."

Which was true enough. After Stafford and his small team handled the labor dispute in Java, the new staff he brought in to fill the sudden vacancies had all juiced up on a super eugeroic cocktail cooked up by Mitrović's team of mad scientists. Even the laziest of them was now able to work thirty-six-hour shifts without sleep.

"Did you know Mitrović was dead?" asked Kuga.

　　　　　　　　　　　　　　　JONATHAN MABERRY

Stafford sat up straight. "*What?* How . . . ?"

"That's what I'm trying to tell you," said Kuga. "Ever since Java, you've been off the fucking radar. Ledger and his goon squad hit the island. Staff was wiped out, and we lost a shit ton of key research data for the next phase of the factory workers project. Unless we can get back up to speed, we stand to lose twenty billion in the next fiscal year because we might not be able to fill the orders that our friend Mr. Sunday is taking. Twenty billion. That's billion with a *B*."

"Holy shit."

"Oh, there's more," said Kuga. "That cocksucker hit Van der Veer in Johannesburg. Gerald Engelbrecht is dead, along with all eleven of his staff. And god only knows what Mitrović and Engelbrecht might have told him before he put them down. We are in serious trouble here."

"So put a team of Fixers at every lab we have. Your boy Santoro has enough of them trained by now. More than enough. He could invade a small country. No, let me correct that; if he gives them all the special upgrades, he could invade a *large* country. I don't care how tough Ledger is, he can't duke it out with those next-gen Fixers. Christ, did you see the footage from Java? It was like the police station scene from *The Terminator*. Those boys went through the crowd like shit through a goose."

Kuga made a small sound of disgust and annoyance. "Yeah, well, that spooky bastard Church and psycho Ledger have a habit of winning against high odds. Ask the Jakobys, ask the Seven goddamn Kings."

"You sound like you're afraid of them."

There was a beat. "Be real careful in your choice of words, buddy boy."

"My point," said Stafford, ignoring the implied threat, "is that they're just a couple of guys. Tough or not, scary or not, they're just guys. And their new group, that Rogue Team International? It's not even a tenth the size of the old DMS, and besides, they don't even have the protection of the U.S. government anymore. They're freelance busybodies."

"Which is why I'm calling you," said Kuga, his tone harsh. "I want you to go find Joe Ledger, and I want him dead in a big way. Pieces all over the place. I want it to make the news. I want it to trend on Twitter. I want it so big, so ugly, and so outrageous that Eli Roth makes a movie about it."

"I can do that," said Stafford.

"Show me," said Kuga. "I'm sending you a shit ton of data from our field analysis team and some notes Sunday put together specially for you. We think he's in Italy now, but he's likely to go to either Romania or Germany next. What we can't allow—and I cannot stress this enough—is for Ledger to go back to the United States. We're ramping up for the big play there, but there are a lot of moving pieces, and it's very delicate. I need Ledger off the board."

"What if he's already in America?"

"Then pick up his trail. I've wired expense money to your account in the Seychelles. Kill him and anyone he even looks at over there."

"You're really hot about this," said Stafford.

"You're damn right. Kill that bastard Joe Ledger, and I will quadruple your usual rate. Take out Church, too . . . and I'll wire transfer five hundred million into your account."

"Very funny."

"I'm not joking," said Kuga.

And the line went dead.

CHAPTER 32
PHOENIX HOUSE
OMFORI ISLAND, GREECE

Bug shoved a handful of Cheez-Its into his mouth and crunched loudly. The latest H.E.R. disc was playing on twelve high-end speakers, with the bass turned high enough to make the various laptops, external drives, monitors, and a complete set of Wakanda Funko POP bobbleheads tremble. A row of alternating Red Bull and Monster cans was close at hand. The empties were in or near the blue recycling can. The door to his office was locked and the security system activated, ensuring that no one could walk in.

Bug brushed orange crumbs from his fingers before placing his hands on the keyboard. He was invariably messy.

With Joe Ledger missing in action and Rogue Team International engaged in the search for him and Santoro, there were very few actual field ops even in the planning stages. That gave Bug time to play.

The Kuga organization was vast. It was like an octopus with a thousand tentacles that stretched across oceans, across borders, and into so many sections of world governments, the private research and development sector, and criminal organizations. Kuga was also rich enough to hire the very best black hat computer pirates. Some gray hats, too, and, Bug suspected, some white hats who did some dirty work when no one was looking.

"Two can play at that game," he said aloud.

They had the numbers, and they had some radical tech. That was the challenge. Kuga not only hired some of the very best, he gave them money and other incentives to encourage innovative thinking.

Bug was able to see some of this rippling across the entire internet. New software, reports of impossible intrusions into systems guaranteed to be unbeatable, all manner of cybercrimes. A lot of it appeared random, but Nikki Bloom, the head of the pattern search team, had already built a case to the contrary.

"If it were just one or two, or even six or ten, random big-profile hacks, I'd say it was just . . . random," Nikki had told him the other day. "But then there have been some serious intrusions to government computers, university labs at MIT and Princeton, and even a military base in Germany. Radically different targets when viewed from one perspective, but when you look closer and see how their cybersecurity was configured and how it was bypassed, well . . . it's obvious."

Obvious to Nikki or to Bug was not obvious to most. Even some of the members of the computer team needed some handholding through the explanation. As did Scott Wilson, who was more diplomat than operative at heart, despite some years pulling triggers for the SAS and MI6. Church, of course, grasped it at once.

When that briefing had concluded, Church took Bug aside.

"I think it's fair to say that Kuga has a bunch of real hitters on his bench," he said when they were alone.

"He does," agreed Bug, "and they're doing some damage. Weirdly, though, they're not doing a lot of measurable harm to what Nikki calls the 'true targets.' Mind you, they could have left spyware, malware, and viruses inside Trojan horses that aren't easy to find unless they're activated. The real damage is kind of a smash-and-grab attitude toward the test targets. The ones they experiment on before hitting the true targets. Some of those groups were hit bad. Doctors Without Borders lost an entire year of Ebola field research. They removed dozens of key world heritage sites from the UNESCO mainframes. They blanked out the donor emails and contact information for the World Food Programme—you know, those guys who won the Nobel Prize a while ago. That's vandalism for vandalism's sake because none of that helps Kuga sell weapons and crap on the black market. These assholes are doing it because they can, and the bigger asshole paying their bills probably thinks it's fun."

"No argument," said Church. "That vandalism is also hurting a lot of people."

"Tell you the truth, boss, but that really pisses me off."

Church had looked at him for a long moment. "Then perhaps you should direct that anger in useful directions."

"What do you mean?"

Church smiled. Not a big smile, and certainly not a warm one. "I'm certain something will occur to you. Oh, and Bug?"

"Yeah?"

"Make it hurt."

INTERLUDE 9
THE PAVILION
BLUE DIAMOND ELITE TRAINING CENTER
STEVENS COUNTY, WASHINGTON
FOUR MONTHS AGO

Eve sat on a chair and watched the nerd herd—her name for the technicians here at the Pavilion—finish their work on the Fixer.

The man, Spiro, was a volunteer, but they'd strapped him to a chair anyway, and the chair was bolted to the floor. Six armed guards stood around in a large circle, rifles in their hands, barrels pointed down but ready to snap up if things went south.

As they had several times before. The bloodstains were still there, somehow locked into the surface of the concrete floor. She idly wondered why they hadn't used poured linoleum for the floor. Much easier to clean. Adam had taught her that.

And Daddy would have used a tarp. He was very neat and tidy. Always was. He could cut someone to pieces and not get a drop on him. He wasn't like her. She *liked* getting bloody, but Eve understood that her appetites were not the same as Rafael Santoro's. He was not crazy, and Eve was absolutely certain she was. She liked being crazy. There were clinical names for it, but who cared? When she and Adam were working their way through the convention circuits before Daddy recruited them, she'd become aware that her mind was wired entirely differently from anyone else's. Except Adam's, of course. They were two sides of the same coin.

"We're ready, HK," said the tech, stepping back. Even with the test subject restrained and under guard, the technician was sweating heavily. Eve could smell the fear stink on him.

Pussy, she thought.

Spiro did not look particularly threatening. He was fit, sure, but not particularly brawny. Pale skin that hadn't seen enough sun, buzz-cut black hair, lifeless brown eyes, and the beginnings of a beard. If she passed him on the street or in a club, she wouldn't give him a second look, and not even much of a first glance, either.

But everyone in the room was terrified of him.

Well, not *of* him. They were scared of what he would become.

HK, in a pencil skirt and electric-blue blouse, stood with a clipboard pressed to her chest as if it were a suit of armor. Her glasses were perched on her nose, and Eve saw a sheen of perspiration glistening on her forehead and upper lip.

She wished she had popcorn.

"Everyone on their marks," said HK crisply. The six rifle barrels rose and pointed at the Fixer in the chair. "Bryan, you may begin."

The tech—Bryan—nodded and walked over to a small portable computer console. Beside the console was a cart laden with a device whose name Eve could never quite remember. One of those long technical names. She'd nicknamed it "the juicer," and everyone else, even HK, picked that up.

Thin tubes ran from the base of the juicer across the floor and up to IV ports in Spiro's wrists and throat. Bryan bent over his computer, and for a few moments, the only sounds in the room were the tappity-tap-tap of his fingers on the keys and the test subject's labored breathing. Then something went *click* inside the machine, and Eve saw liquid follow through the tubes. Two lines were clear, two were a pale amber. Spiro's eyes clicked toward the tubes, and his fingers gripped the arms of the chair. Eve saw his muscles tighten as he braced for whatever was coming.

"This will work," said Bryan.

"Oh, it had better," said HK coldly. "You made a lot of promises, and I passed them up the line. We will all be disappointed if anything goes wrong. Again."

Spiro was sweating worse than Bryan now, though the tech had gone gray pale.

Then the fluids reached the IV ports and entered Spiro's bloodstream.

For a moment, nothing happened.

"Bryan?" queried HK, a note of warning, even of threat in her voice.

"Give it another second," whispered the tech. Other scientists were grouped behind him, but since Bryan began the process, they'd inched back. Either afraid of Spiro or afraid to stand too close to Bryan if this was another failure.

The scream was so sudden. So loud and shocking that it seemed to punch Eve in the brain. Spiro didn't even have time to throw back his head—the scream just ripped its way out of his chest with such force that blood flecked the Fixer's lips. The sound was so enormous that everyone shrank back. Even the guards flinched. Had they been less professional and had their fingers on their triggers rather than laid along the sides, Spiro would have been riddled with bullets.

The scream rose and rose . . .

Then it stopped.

Spiro clamped his jaws shut as every muscle in his body went into a spasm of such tight rigidity that even his goggling eyes seemed to swell. His lips were curled back from bloody teeth. Veins stood out everywhere, and Spiro's pale skin was flushed a dangerous purple red. Red veins whipsawed across the whites of his eyes.

JONATHAN MABERRY

"Talk to me, Bryan," growled HK.

"I . . . ," he began, but then bent over the computer again, typing furiously. Then Eve heard his tap-taps slow. "Wait . . ."

HK snapped her head around to look at him. "What?"

"Look," whispered Bryan, pointing.

HK turned back and stared. Spiro's color was fading from the violent flush to a paler, humaner tone. The veins still popped on his arms and neck, but now they looked like a bodybuilder's after some heavy sets. Nothing looked like it was going to explode. And the man was breathing. Panting, but not in a labored way. Eve thought there was a sense of exhilaration to it. His eyes were still strange, though, with the sclera now an even shade of scarlet.

"How are his vitals?" asked HK.

"Leveling out," said Bryan with a sense of wonder in his voice. "My god, HK . . . he's leveling out."

Everyone stared. Eve even found herself leaning forward, her breath held, fists balled.

HK took a tentative step forward, and one of the armed Fixers moved up to stand beside her, rifle stock tucked into his shoulder.

"I got you, HK," he said quietly, though clearly loudly enough for Spiro to hear. If he could hear. The last test subject had stroked out by this point. And the one before that kept screaming and screaming until something in his heart ruptured. A valve, Eve thought.

HK spoke very calmly and slowly.

"Spiro?" she said. "Can you hear me?"

The Fixer blinked several times and looked momentarily confused. Then he gave a single jerky nod.

"Do you know who I am?"

Spiro licked his lips, either unaware of the salty blood on his lips or past the point of caring.

"Y-yes . . ."

"That's good," she said. "That's very good. Tell me your name. Can you do that?"

The confused expression came and went, came and went. His lips formed the words several times before he finally managed to put sound to them.

"Spiro . . . Spiro Frangopoulos."

It began as a gasp but firmed up quickly. He repeated his name several times, nodding, as if it were a returning memory.

"And who am I?"

"You're HK," he said immediately. "You're the boss lady."

"Excellent," said HK, throwing a radiant smile in Bryan's direction. "Now, Spiro, tell me what it is we're doing. Tell me what you volunteered for."

"I . . ." Spiro paused and licked his lips. "I'm a . . ."

"Go on . . . say it."

Spiro took a big breath. "I'm a god," he said.

"Yessss," said HK.

Eve jumped to her feet and ran over to the Fixer.

"No, wait!" cried HK, but it was too late. Eve began unbuckling the straps that held Spiro in place. When one proved resistant, she whipped a knife from the sheath on her left thigh and slashed the straps. It did not matter to her—or to Spiro, it seemed—that the blade sliced into him, too. The Fixers with the rifles threw worried, questioning looks at HK, but she held up a hand, telling them to wait.

Eve cut the last of the straps and then viciously jerked the IV tubes from Spiro's veins. He began to slide out of the chair, but Eve grabbed him and pulled him forward and up, making him stand. He held on to her, swaying dangerously for a moment, but then mastered his balance.

Eve looked up into his blazing red eyes.

"Say it," she growled. "Say it again. *Say it.*"

He towered over her, his body swollen and immensely powerful. His hands on her shoulders, inches from her throat. His fingers twitched and pressed into her skin, but Eve didn't care.

"Say it again," she snarled.

"I'm a god," declared Spiro.

And Eve pulled his head down and kissed him.

CHAPTER 33
VAN DER VYVER BIOMEDICAL ASSOCIATES
JOHANNESBURG, SOUTH AFRICA

His name was Dr. Gerald Engelbrecht, and he lay dying in darkness.

It startled him. He spent so much of his life studying the phenomenon of human mortality but had never really considered his own. He was aware that he had lived forty-two years, many of them good years, and expected to live at least as long yet, then he would be gone. He had no will, no living trust, no thoughts about how he might die—heart attack, cancer. Something natural. Something distant.

Now Engelbrecht was abundantly aware of the concept of personal mortality. Nothing else was as real or as present to him. Not the lab he'd spent eight years designing, building, running. Not his work, which had been everything to him—biomechanical engineering, biomedical implants, microminiaturization, and the fascinating related science. Not the money in his offshore accounts in the Seychelles. Not the bonuses that fattened those accounts whenever his team made a breakthrough, as they had five times in the last two years. Not even his wife and grown twin daughters. None of that mattered. All of it was at a distance now, blurred as if behind frosted glass.

All that mattered now was that he was dying. That he *could* die. That death would come looking for him. Not with some discovered malignancy in colon or prostate in his golden years. Not a drunk driver punching through a red light thirty miles an hour above the posted speed limit. Not sudden pain in his left arm on the seventh hole, two under par and an easy line from his ball to the cup.

Despite what he did for a living, and who he did it for, death of a violent and immediate kind was never something he ever considered—not for one moment—as something that could be focused on him. *Aimed* at him.

Now it was impossible to think of anything else.

Engelbrecht was dying there in the darkness.

He couldn't understand why it was so damned dark. There were fires burning in the lab. He could feel the heat.

Pain was a monster that seemed to crouch on his chest, crushing the air from him, feeding on his pain and his astonishment. The heat of the fires was getting closer. The smoke was cloying, but when he coughed, the pain spiked into impossibility. Engelbrecht wanted to scream, but he didn't have the breath for it, so the pain stayed trapped in his chest, charring the walls of his lungs in its frustration.

Two words managed to sneak past the stricture, though. Not as screams but in a strangely conversational tone.

"I'm dying," he said.

And a voice said, "That could change."

It was a man's voice, reaching him through the walls of his pain and the veils of utter blackness that clouded Engelbrecht's eyes.

It was *he*. The killer. The one who smashed the world apart with his guns and knife and that dreadful white dog. He was still here. And . . . close, too.

"I . . . I don't want to die," said Engelbrecht, his voice still reasonable. "I'm not ready."

"I don't care," said the killer. Was he closer now?

Engelbrecht licked his lips. "Will you help me?"

He knew it was a stupid question, but it came out anyway and in a different tone of voice. Plaintive, but not in a good way. Childish, almost wheedling. He had a vague desire to apologize.

"I asked you a question," said the killer. "Clock's running out for you to answer."

"I don't remember the question," said Engelbrecht vaguely. *Had* he, in fact, been asked a question? If so, was it in this lifetime or some other distant incarnation? Perhaps in a dream? Or was this the dream and soon he would wake up? He distantly wondered what dreams of violence and fire meant.

"I'll ask one last time," said the killer slowly. He had an American accent, but there was something odd about his voice. The timbre had a quality that Engelbrecht could not define. It felt somehow darker than it should, though he had no idea how such a thing was possible. "Two questions, really. Where is Kuga? Where is Santoro?"

"But I . . . I don't know where they are."

"Are you lying to me?"

"No! I've never even met them. Everything goes through . . . goes through an intermediary!" cried Engelbrecht. "I have no idea where to find—"

JONATHAN MABERRY

"Who is the intermediary?" asked the killer. "Lie to me and I'll know."

Engelbrecht's mouth was so dry and the heat from the fires was so intense. Terror filled his soul, crowding out any chance he would ever think of lying to this man.

"His name is Fong. Alexander Fong," he said hoarsely. "Chinese, but from Italy, I think. His accent is Italian."

"How do you contact him?"

"He contacts me."

"No . . . there has to be a way to contact him if there is a problem. You're running out of time. Tell me right damn now."

"Email," blurted Engelbrecht. "It's in my sent messages on my phone."

"What's your password?"

Engelbrecht told him.

There was a silence filled by the sound of the fire devouring the room.

"Please," croaked Engelbrecht, "will you help me? I don't want to burn."

But there was no answer from the man. Not a whisper, not a word. Not even a growl from that white devil of a dog.

And in his personal darkness, Dr. Gerald Engelbrecht burned.

CHAPTER 34
PHOENIX HOUSE
OMFORI ISLAND, GREECE

Church was back in his apartment, but he was alone now. Lilith was gone, taking with her all that unique and complex energy, her grace, her insights, and her magic. Although theirs was a relationship that could never be normal by any metric, it mattered very deeply to him. It mattered to love, and be loved, by someone who understood him. Someone of equal power and who was a complete individual. Neither defined themselves by the other, nor needed approval or validation.

The love, though. That mattered. It amused him to think that so many of the people who knew him, good and bad, enemies and allies, past and present, regarded Church as a cold and unemotional person. A machine. A freak.

He'd switched the music to Miles Davis. *Blue Moods*. He'd met Aunt Sallie at a jazz club in Berlin, where Davis was test-driving the songs that would eventually make up that album. Charlie Mingus had invited Church to the date, and they'd sat together through three full sets. That was the night Aunt Sallie walked into his life. She'd never been a particularly pretty woman, but her level of personal power and integrity made her beautiful. Now Auntie was old and dying, and Church endured.

It was all the proof he ever needed that the world was mad.

Even so, the memory of that night was a calm place for him to put his emotions. Even Mingus—the legendary "Angry Man of Jazz"— had been in a mellow mood, even when between-set table conversation turned to politics. During the sets, of course, no one spoke. Church and Mingus shared the view that if you went to hear someone play, then you should be quiet and experience it. Church remembered another night, at the Five Spot in New York, when Mingus had been so angry at a heckler that he picked up his bass, an instrument worth $20,000, and destroyed it in front of a shocked crowd.

He opened his top desk drawer and removed a package of vanilla wafers, carefully opened the package, selected a cookie, took a small bite, and munched quietly.

Then he began making calls. It was a long list, and not all the people he called were the ones he needed to warn. For some, it was easier to call one of his many friends in the industry—in various industries—to ask if they could help watchdog the innocent. With others, however, particularly those with whom he had once worked, it was more direct to call them. They had the skills to take care of themselves; however, Church told them to expect couriers who would deliver credit cards with no spending limits, passports in several different names, and other documents that would allow them to shelter in place, or bolt and run.

He was at that desk for hours. Going through the papers recovered in Croatia, scrolling through decrypted computer files. Seeing frequent mentions of AO but never with enough context to give it meaning. So far, even Nikki Bloom couldn't find enough to build a supposition. And yet everything in him made him believe this was something of great importance.

The feeling that he was not seeing the forest for the trees.

Outside, the world sank into the deepest part of the night. Starlight painted everything—the forest, the other buildings, the beach, the moored boats, and the rolling waves. It also traced the outlines of dozens of black birds huddled in the branches of the trees. Hundreds of them, and of at least eight species. Church had noticed them beginning to gather shortly after Christmas. Some were migratory birds that should long ago have flown south. It was Church's habit most mornings to go outside with a bag of bread and toss it around so the birds could eat. But that would be hours from now. The night birds were in their trees, pretending to sleep but not selling the lie. He could feel them watching.

As he worked, Church wondered where Joe Ledger was at that moment. He had a general sense of location, but no specifics. Those details would be scraped off the ground in Ledger's wake.

He wondered what was going on in Ledger's broken heart and in his furnace of a head.

He wondered how much damage all this was doing to an already dangerously compromised individual.

He wondered what the price tag would be when it was all over. And how big an amount he'd be adding to the deep debt already stacked against his own immortal soul.

CHAPTER 35
VAN DER VYVER BIOMEDICAL ASSOCIATES
JOHANNESBURG, SOUTH AFRICA

The man staggered away from the burning building.

He tripped and fell twice. Again. And finally stopped trying and sank slowly to his knees. Everything in front of him was darkness.

Everything behind him was hell itself. Long fingers of bright orange flame clawed at the sky, tearing apart the midnight clouds.

The man knelt there, panting, gasping for clean air in a soiled world. A big white dog stood nearby, his coat speckled with blood, eyes bright, muscles trembling. All around them both, in every tree, the night birds watched with black and unreadable eyes.

The man looked down at his hands and for a twisted moment thought he was wearing red gloves. But then the truth punched him in the face, in the heart.

The blood-spattered dog came over slowly, cautiously, and stopped beside the man. Then pushed at him with its muzzle as if urging him to get up. To run.

The man shook his head and began furiously scrubbing at his hands, but one bloody hand could not clean the other. He caved slowly forward until his forehead touched the dirt.

"God," he begged, "*help me . . .*"

But it was not a divine hand that pulled him up, forced him to stand, made him run when the banshee sirens filled the air. It was no clean hand at all that saved him.

It was the colder hand of darkness. Sure, and steady, and inexorable.

The man and the dog vanished into that endless black of night.

WHERE NIGHT BIRDS FLY
PART 3

Before you embark on a journey of revenge,
Dig two graves.

—CONFUCIUS

Life being what it is, one dreams of revenge.

—PAUL GAUGUIN

CHAPTER 36
FREETECH RESEARCH AND DEVELOPMENT OFFICE
SAN DIEGO, CALIFORNIA

Junie Flynn did not expect the call to go through. It hadn't the last dozen times she'd phoned, and it was becoming apparent to her that Mr. Church was dodging her calls. That annoyed her. Partly because it seemed beneath the man's dignity, and partly because it was unkind. If it had been anyone but Church, she'd have thought he was being cowardly.

But Church surprised her by answering on the third ring.

"Miss Flynn," he said, then corrected it. "Junie."

She didn't ask him how he was or what was new. This wasn't social, and she got straight to it.

"Have you heard from Joe?"

"Junie . . ."

"I'm using the scrambler," she said.

"My answer would be the same regardless," said Church. "No. He has not been in touch."

"It's been so *long*," she said, trying to keep both heartbreak and fury from her voice, and aware that she was failing in both cases. "It's been weeks."

"Yes," said Church, "it has."

"What are you doing to find him?"

"Everything that we can."

"Can I have a real answer instead of a pat one?"

"Junie, listen to me. I know you're scared. Terrified. So are all his friends."

"But—"

"Let me finish," said Church gently. "We *are* looking. We have many of our allies looking. I have my entire network on the alert."

"How do you even know he's alive?" she demanded.

There was a pause. "For the same reason you know that he is. We would know."

Junie closed her eyes against the tears that wanted to fall. The tears that fell regardless.

"Please," she said, "find him. Help him."

"Yes," said Church. "Yes . . ."

CHAPTER 37
LAKE PALESTINE
TEN MILES SOUTHWEST OF NOONDAY, TEXAS

The two men who sat on the top of the picnic table looked like truckers. The taller of the two was a huge slab of a white guy with the sleeves cut off a threadbare denim jacket. His arms were packed with corded muscle and covered with Marine Corps tattoos. He wore jeans, scuffed work boots, and had a pair of mirrored sunglasses pushed high on his short blond hair. He had a long scar slanting downward from above his left eyebrow, across the bridge of his nose, and down to his right cheek. Both his canine teeth were gold, and the beer bottle clinked against one of them each time he took a sip.

His companion was shorter and older, but no less rough-looking. A Black man in his late forties, with a heavy silver chain around his neck, handcuff earrings, and a mouth that looked like he never smiled. His head was shaved, and he sported a Vandyke style of goatee, with the salt-and-pepper chin hair coming to a sharp point. He wore a Dallas Cowboys cap pulled low to shade his eyes and slowly chewed on an old kitchen match.

Their fishing skiff was pulled up on the bank, rods sprouting like antennae, an old blue Coleman cooler resting in the boat. There were only a few fishermen left on the water. The news had said the bass were jumping, but no one seemed to be pulling many in. The February sun was hotter than it was supposed to be, and there wasn't a cloud in the sky.

"I ever tell you I hate fishing?" asked the white man.

The Black man scratched his cheek. "Today or ever?"

"Ever."

"Yeah. About a thousand damned times."

"Well, it's true."

"So you keep saying."

They drank beer and watched the boats.

"It's boring as fuck."

"So is NASCAR," said the Black man.

"I never said I liked NASCAR."

"Wasn't asking if you did, Farm Boy. I was adding it to the list of boring sports."

"Golf, too, then," said the white man.

"Golf's okay. At least you get to walk. NASCAR's sitting on plastic chairs and drinking flat beer. Fishing is sitting in a boat and drinking warm beer."

"I like beer."

"Beer isn't the point."

They watched the boats.

"Volleyball's fun to watch," said the white man.

"You just like to watch girls playing volleyball."

"Women," corrected the younger man.

"Women," agreed the older man.

"And, sure, what's not to like? All those buff women. Tall, too. Jumping around in bikinis."

"That's some grade-A sexist shit right there."

The white man thought about it. "I guess. Don't know that I care. I mean about that part. If they were just women jumping around, it'd be all about boobs and buns. But that's a tough sport. I like the serious players."

"Uh-huh. And boobs and buns got nothing to do with it, is that what you're trying to tell me?"

The white man shrugged. "I'm not going to lie and say they don't, but if there's no skill, then it's just a meat rack."

"Uh-huh."

"No, I . . . oh, wait," said the white man, interrupting himself, "I think this is our guy."

They both turned to watch a blocky man walk toward them. He had Popeye forearms and a face like an eroded wall, and he wore jeans, boots, and a gray nylon windbreaker with a blue diamond symbol on the chest. A billed cap with the same symbol was perched on his wiry red hair. He walked with purpose, his chest thrust out as if with a desire to smash the air itself out of his way. Then he slowed to a stop ten feet away and studied the two fishermen with cold appraising eyes.

He pointed a finger at the younger man. "Are you Redfield?"

"I'm Buck Redfield," said the white man, putting just a touch of belligerence in it. "Who's asking?"

The red-haired man smiled thinly. "I'm the guy who needs you to tell me two little words."

That was the right signal, the opening of a code phrase exchange. The big man named Buck looked at his friend, who nodded.

"I'm Spartacus," said Buck, giving the proper response.

"I'm Spartacus," said the Black man.

"And what's the other thing?" asked the redhead.

"Azure carbon," said the Black man, completing the code.

The red-haired man's smile broadened, and some of the tension went out of his shoulders. He glanced at the older man. "You're Guidry?"

"Marcus Guidry," agreed the Black man. "People call me Guidry or G. And you are . . . ?"

"Randall Flagg."

"Real name?"

Flagg snorted but didn't answer. Instead, he glanced at the boat pulled up on the dirt. "You catch anything?"

Buck shrugged. "A light beer buzz and ten million motherfucking mosquito bites."

Flagg nodded. "We checked you out. Interesting service records. Good in a fight, the right training, lots of experience, but a little trouble here and there. Buck, you got kicked out of the Marines. Got caught running a sideline in military gear. And, Guidry, you retired from the army before they could retire you for fucking the wrong officer's daughter."

"She was of age," said Guidry, and he punctuated it by spitting over the far end of the picnic table, getting good distance and velocity and without losing his kitchen match.

"What about it?" asked Buck. "You going to lecture us on good behavior?"

JONATHAN MABERRY

Flagg's smile remained in place, but there was a calculating look in his eyes.

"You're here because you're looking to sign on with the people I represent," he said. "We're a bit more—and I hate to use this word—*liberal* in our views about what a man does in his free time. Same for when a man sees an opportunity and wants to make a buck off it."

They said nothing.

"But here's the thing," said Flagg, "all of that is okay when you're *off* the clock. But when you're *on* the clock, then you don't break any of the house rules. You keep it zipped, and you don't so much as pick up a tarnished penny that isn't yours. That has to be understood and agreed to, or you fellows can go back to fishing."

Guidry took the matchstick out and considered the gnawed end, then put it into the other corner of his mouth. "I really fucking hate fishing," he said.

Flagg glanced at Buck.

"Hell, I hate *bass* fishing most of all," said the big man.

They all grinned at that. Flagg looked around at the thirty or so pickup trucks parked behind them. "Which one's yours?"

"Piece-of-shit blue old Ford yonder," said Guidry.

"You gassed up?"

"Mostly," said Buck. "Three-quarters of a tank."

"That'll do," said Flagg. He pointed to a sleek black GMC Terrain, the current year's model. "That's mine. Follow me."

"Where we going?" asked Guidry.

"Just follow."

With that, Randall Flagg walked back to his car, got in, started the engine, and waited. Buck and Guidry exchanged a look, picked up their gear, returned the rental boat, and climbed into their truck. Buck drove, following the SUV onto Route 49 heading north.

Once they were on the road, Guidry tapped a small mole near his left ear.

"You get all that, Bug?" he asked.

"Got all of it, Pappy," said a younger voice. Both men wore similar tiny earbuds that were designed to fade into the landscape of their complexion and skin type.

"You get a read on him?"

"Well," said Bug, "he sure isn't Randall Flagg. That's the bad guy from *The Stand*. Old Stephen King book about—"

"I read it. Who's the guy?"

"I pulled his image from the cameras in your shirt button and ran it through facial recognition. Someone tried real hard to erase him from the net."

"But . . . ?"

"But, this is me."

"Stop bragging, Bug," said Guidry. "Who is he?"

"John Andrew Saxon," said Bug. "He was a lieutenant in the air force. Opted out in 2012. Minor-league asshole. Four ex-wives and several domestic violence complaints. No charges because the women seemed unwilling to testify. Might have been involved in a gang rape in Iraq, but there's a reference to a written statement that isn't uploaded to any military database. Whatever it was, they squashed the charges and expunged most of Saxon's computer records. MindReader Q1's able to gather scraps from fragments left online, and some data scars. It's not much. Bottom line is that he's a total prick, and that makes him the poster boy for what he does now. Talent scout for the PMC biz. Been on the Blue Diamond Security payroll for nine years."

"And . . . ?" prompted Guidry.

"And he's on our list as a possible recruiter for Kuga."

"He's a Fixer?" asked Buck.

"Nah, just a scout. He's exactly who we needed to find, though, and my guess is he's taking you to either a meeting with someone higher up the food chain, or maybe to a camp. I've got buzzard drones in the air tracking you. Just ease back and enjoy the ride."

"Copy that." The blond young man flipped his sunglasses down and cruised along fifty feet behind the SUV.

"Bug," asked Bunny, "we have *any* word on Outlaw?"

There was a lag before Bug answered, "He's still out there. We're still looking."

That was all he'd say, but it was enough.

"Copy that," said Top.

They settled back as the miles burned away under their tires.

CHAPTER 38
FLORENCE, ITALY

The man came awake while walking.

That's how it felt. He had been lost in a nightmare of flight and pursuit, and in that dream, he had been both predator and prey. Now he was awake. Walking down a street.

He looked around, completely unsure of where he was.

The street signs and store names were in Italian.

But . . . how?

He fought for memories, found a few swimming away from him in the darkness of his thoughts, grabbed at them. Caught one or two.

His last clear memory was of the burning building in Johannesburg.

Was that a real memory? Were the things he remembered true?

"God help me," he whispered, choking on the words. Praying that none of those memories belonged to him.

Knowing, though, that they did.

There were too many details for it to be something borrowed from a movie or book, and too vivid—with all five senses horribly engaged—for them to be residue from a dream.

Dr. Gerald Engelbrecht.

The guards and the staff.

The fires.

He looked down at his hands, surprised to realize that they were gripping suitcases. Heavy ones. Cases he did not recognize.

Saw his dog looking up at him. Ghost looked strange. Wrong. Older, thinner. Hungrier in bad ways. The emotional support animal vest he wore was like a bad joke. How could any animal support him emotionally? He was miles past being a train wreck on any emotional level. And . . . as for his soul . . .

He looked around, saw a bench across the street, and carried the cases over, laid them on the seat, opened each. Both were crammed with file folders, flash drives, cell phones, and hard drives. Some of the papers were singed. Some were spattered with blood.

How the hell did he ever get them through customs?

He fished for that knowledge, but there was nothing there. Just a vast black wall without window or door. Impenetrable. Immutable.

"Please . . . ," he said. But to whom? And for what?

Beside him, the dog whined.

He closed the cases and sat down, patting his pockets for something to feed the animal. Found nothing. There was a wallet, though. Stuffed with currency from four different countries. Plenty of euros.

The photo ID was his face, but the name was different. Kurt Grobler.

The man stood up slowly, took several long breaths, and then picked up the cases. He walked and walked until he found a convenience store. In there, on a local paper, he discovered that he was in Florence.

There were cans of dog food on a shelf, and he bought a dozen, as well as every kind of treat he could find. He paid for it, asked where he could find a cab, and took the taxi to the Hotel Bernini Palace on the Piazza di San Firenze. Big hotels were easier to become lost in. Fewer people noticed. And they allowed service animals.

Once he was inside his room, he fed Ghost, ordered room service, went into the bathroom to shower.

And was gone again before the water even hit his skin.

CHAPTER 39
PHOENIX HOUSE
OMFORI ISLAND, GREECE

"Explain to me what it is you're doing."

Scott Wilson pulled up a chair and sat next to Bug. He'd brought a peace offering of a quadruple-shot espresso with four Red Bull pumps and topped with chocolate whip and mocha sprinkles made special by the RTI barista, Mustapha. Wilson had winced while watching the drink being made because there was enough caffeine in there to give a coronary to a bronze statue of Atlas. It was known around Phoenix House as Bug's Chug.

Wilson watched Bug sip—and sigh. The RTI's chief of operations sipped from a cup of green tea with a drop of alfalfa honey.

"Which *part* of what I'm doing do you need explained?" asked Bug, dabbing at foam on his upper lip.

"You know what I mean," said Wilson mildly. He was a short and very thin man who—to a casual stranger—looked like someone wasted by sickness. That was deceptive, though, because he was actually very fit, slender, and wiry. With his quiet business suits, striped club tie, pocket square, and thinning medium brown hair brushed straight back, he looked like a merchant banker or perhaps an estate lawyer for old money. Wilson had exceptionally pale skin and ice-blue eyes, both of which gave him a somewhat washed-out look. His Eton accent was precise and clipped, and his smile often looked more like a wince.

Bug, although about the same height and only a few pounds heavier, was his polar opposite. He had medium brown skin, black hair in dozens of braids, very thick glasses with heavy purple frames, a rather hopeful attempt at a beard that refused to look authoritative, and an earring fashioned to look like a hatchet stuck in the lobe. He wore a Wakanda Olympic Bobsled Team T-shirt, jeans that were so ancient it was impossible to tell the brand or original color, and flip-flops. The walls of his office were lined with shelves on which were hundreds of very rare and lovingly preserved superhero action figures, most in their original unopened packaging. The newest additions of which were the Marvel Legends: Silver-Shirt Luke Cage and Crimson Dawn Psylocke. There were also framed photos of Bug with Chadwick Boseman, Stan Lee, Lupita Nyong'o, and Danai Gurira.

Wilson, a very patient man, waited for Bug to decide how to answer.

"It's authorized by the Big Man," said Bug.

"Fair enough," said Wilson. "But what *is* it?"

Bug grinned. "I'm doing to Kuga's online presence what the Visigoths did to Rome."

"I rather assumed that. Please give me some details."

"You ask Church about this?"

Wilson smiled. "He said to ask you."

"Ah."

"Ah, indeed."

Bug looked at the specialty drink, smiled, picked up a blue Sharpie, and wrote *Attempted Bribery* on the cup, sipped, and set it down with the words turned toward Wilson.

"Okay," he said, "so we know Joe is out there doing some damage to the Kuga labs, right?"

"We do."

"He's hurting their R&D and taking some very bad people off the checkerboard."

"Apparently," agreed Wilson.

"I can't help with that," said Bug. "Not directly anyway. So, instead of sitting here doing nothing and going slowly out of my mind, I decided to see what kind of fun I could have with Kuga's network online."

"And by fun, you mean . . . ?"

"Maybe it's better if you *don't* know."

Wilson's smile looked like thin plastic. "Tell me anyway," he said.

"You won't like it," said Bug.

"Would you like a comprehensive list of all the things I haven't liked recently?"

"Not really."

"Just tell me," said Wilson.

"With details or the highlights?"

"Let's start with the highlights."

"Sure. Well, we know that Kuga has some hotshots on the cyber warfare team, cyber espionage team, and cyberterrorism team."

"You think they're separate teams?"

"Sure. Maybe with some crossovers, but it's easy enough to see that their online strategies operate according to different philosophies. Maybe there's one or two guys overseeing it, but the actual attacks are all over the place. You see, they've been going after their competitors with sophisticated attacks going back a few years. I mean before Harcourt Bolton was sprung from that black site prison, which means he had infrastructure in place to run that part of things. That means Kuga not only had people already in place, but whoever was in charge of that division knew how to pick top talent. When I realized that I put some of my people on it, mostly looking for known or suspected top-tier black hat or black-leaning gray hat hackers who have either vanished recently or who've gotten rich."

"Did you find any?"

"Sure. The one thing about the kind of hacker who specializes in this stuff is that a lot of them are young, and they have egos. They want to be known for what they've done. They tag it, usually by working some kind of smart-ass code into whatever software they wrote to do the intended damage."

"What kind of damage?" asked Wilson. "And who are the targets?"

"Well, before Ohan was killed, his network had been thoroughly hacked. Dissected, really. We've acquired enough of his laptops, external drives, and even one mainframe—thanks to Arklight—and those files are riddled with malware. Those are applications designed to perform a variety of very malicious tasks. All kinds, too, and my bug-hunter guys were able to isolate each. There were malware strains designed to create persistent access to a network, which allowed Kuga to spy on Ohan's day-to-day business operations. Other malware was planted to clone IDs, passwords, and the kind of encryption coding used to hide numbered bank accounts. We found these little bits of code left in the system, hidden inside Trojan horses, that pinged Kuga every time a transaction was made above a certain dollar amount. Kuga was able to review the purchases, which is how—I'm guessing—he was able to know which products and product lines were selling for top dollar, what the swings in sales numbers were, and who was buying the stuff."

"Clever."

"Very, and that code is a real bitch to find. Maybe two or three of the world's top cybersecurity companies or groups could have found it, but then again, maybe not."

"But *you* found it," said Wilson. Not quite making it a question.

Bug sipped his drink and didn't comment on that.

"We also found spyware that was so thoroughly wired into Ohan's personnel records and business contacts that it gave Kuga a great laundry list for recruitment. Kuga's team was siphoning off people from Ohan even before Arklight killed him; and within two hours of Ohan's body being discovered by police, Kuga had his human resources people out there scooping up the rest of the top talent. Very smooth, which tells me that it was something set in place for just such an event."

"How is this you being a Visigoth?"

"I'm getting there," said Bug. "Kuga's people also did a massive amount of phishing attacks—using all kinds of tricks to get Ohan's customers to hand over valuable information, such as passwords, credit card details, intellectual property, and so on. That worked so well because no one but Ohan was ever supposed to have the email addresses used in that level of black market sales. The fact that they were receiving emails at all made them appear legit. Which, by the way, is stupid. People are stupid. Most people should never be allowed anywhere near a computer or email *or* the internet."

"You're preaching rather than explaining," said Wilson, sipping his tea and privately regretting having asked. He wished it were cognac in the cup instead.

But Bug was clearly getting into gear. He went through a whole slate of other kinds of attacks.

"There's the MITM stuff," said Bug with real enthusiasm. "That stands for *man in the middle,* which is where the attacker intercepts communications between two parties in an attempt to spy on the victims, steal personal information or credentials, or perhaps alter the conversation in some way. Now, you might try to tell me that MITM is old stuff and that end-to-end email and chat encryption prevents that kind of thing, but you'd be wrong."

"I wouldn't dare suggest such a thing," said Wilson faintly.

"MITM has undergone a lot of upgrades and—at worst—looks like tech-support messages from the internet or email provider."

"I see," said Wilson, who barely did.

"What's a bit more dangerous are DDoS attacks, where the bad guys flood a target server with traffic in an attempt to disrupt and perhaps even bring down the target. And I'm not talking some pansy denial-of-service attacks here—because most sophisticated firewalls kick their asses pretty easily these days—but superprograms that can hit multiple compromised devices belonging to the target and bombard them with traffic. We're talking tens of thousands of emails, robocalls, text messages, and even social media posts. The target is buried and has to abandon their email addresses, domain names, and stuff like that. Kuga's people usually hit them with political stuff from the opposing parties or, using the go-to they all like, filling the in-boxes and chats with kiddie porn. Then dropping dimes to whichever law enforcement agency has jurisdiction. It's almost impossible to prove that the kiddie porn was planted, and by then, reputations are shot, jobs lost, security clearances removed, and lives destroyed."

"Ugly, but I can see how it would be effective."

"One of Kuga's favorite tricks is zero-day exploiting. They are clearly following R&D on the latest business and e-commerce software, like when a new software-driven product launches, they slip in code to screw it up or totally hijack it. That's bad enough for the good guys, but when they hit a major company doing some off-book shady stuff, like maybe doing backdoor deals with bad actors among the more negative foreign governments—then that company has to pay up or they'll lose more than business. Or, if Kuga wants to screw up the flow of business, he has his people look for some vulnerability in the software—and there's usually something—and then do as much damage as possible until a fix is found."

"That sounds nasty but useful."

Bug sniffed. "It's okay. Not enough companies and organizations monitor for this, and done right, it creates a tunnel through a firewall. That's a nice pipeline for introducing malware or other fun stuff."

Wilson sat back and listened as Bug went on and on about the different types of cyberattacks, including business email compromises, cryptojacking, drive-by attacks, cross-site scripting attacks, password attacks, eavesdropping attacks, AI-powered attacks, and IoT-based attacks.

By the time Bug was finished, the chief of operations was somewhat dazed. He got to his feet, patted Bug on the back, mumbled, "Jolly good, keep up the good work," and shambled out. He was back in his own office before he realized Bug never actually answered his question about what he was doing.

But Wilson did not dare go back downstairs for another round.

CHAPTER 40
CIVITELLA IN VAL DI CHIANA
AREZZO, TUSCANY, ITALY

Alexander Fong crouched behind his desk and listened to the gunfire. And the screams.

So much gunfire, so many screams.

But now . . . less of each.

He had a gun of his own, but it was a little .25 automatic that he'd only ever fired once, and then badly, missing the paper target with four of the six bullets in the magazine. The two that hit the paper missed anything of value. As for screams, he had plenty of those; they were still bottled up inside him. Ready to be let out if whoever was killing his people got through his office door.

That seemed likely.

Fong wondered if he should simply put the barrel of the little Raven Arms pistol under his chin and pull the trigger.

Would it work, though? He'd heard stories about people missing. Or maybe that wasn't the right way to phrase it. Missing the right part of the brain—the part that would switch the brain off forever. Last thing Fong wanted was to be a cripple or a vegetable.

The gunfire paused for a moment.

Fong listened, praying that his people had managed to cut the invaders down. He had no idea how many there were. He'd only caught a glimpse of one man—big, dressed in body armor and wearing a helmet and balaclava. A man who moved like a soldier. There was a dog, too. Also armored. They had torn into a group of Fong's administrative assistants. In the four seconds he'd watched, the carnage was terrible. Like nothing he'd ever seen. Fong was so far removed from anything his employers did that all he ever got to see was the sanitized versions on the news. Sure, he'd heard stories, and some of them were extreme to the point of grotesque absurdity, but that was different from actually *seeing* it. Those stories were abstractions. What he'd seen in the foyer of the administrative suite was brutally real.

He was aware of the historical irony of what was happening. His direct supervisor, Rafael Santoro, had chosen this building because it was in the square outside where Hermann Göring's Nazis massacred 244 civilians from this town in retaliation for the killing of two German soldiers. Except the townsfolk were innocent—the killings had been done by partisans. The slaughter in the town square, way back in June of 1944, had had the opposite effect of what Göring intended. Instead of cowing the civilians, it had sparked an increase in guerrilla activity and gave the Germans no real peace. When the war ended, any surviving Germans were hunted and torn apart. Santoro held that up as an example of how *not* to manipulate people into cooperation. Fear of what might happen was always more effective than having martyrs to rally the passion of resistance.

Was *irony* the right word? Maybe it was karma. Or something. It was hard to structure his thoughts.

The pistol felt like a toy in his hand. Stupid little gun. Weren't these things supposed to make him feel strong?

The silence outside seemed to stretch. All he could hear now were the cries of crows and ravens. The birds seemed to be everywhere these days. He hated them. They touched some unspecified and atavistic dread buried deep beneath the surface of his introspection.

But . . . why wasn't anyone yelling anymore?

Fong hid where he was, not daring to even peek out from behind his desk. His hands were sweaty, and he was afraid that if he had to shoot, the gun would just slip out.

Then there was a sound.

Not a scream. Not a gunshot. Not the creak of an opening door.

It was a growl.

And it was right above him.

Fong raised his head slowly and stared up. Amazed. Dumbfounded. Terrified.

There, crouched on top of the very desk behind which he cowered, was the dog. Big. White, except for its muzzle, which glistened with an awful, dreadful crimson. The animal bared its teeth.

Those teeth.

Some were dog teeth. The others . . . ?

They were metal. Pasted with red. Twenty inches from his face.

Fong fumbled with the pistol, trying to bring it up. Uncertain if he'd racked the slide. Was there even a bullet in the chamber? God, he couldn't remember.

A shadow fell across him, and he turned to see that the man was here, too. Both of them had come into his office without making a sound. The gun in the man's hand was big and ugly, and it was pointed at him.

CHAPTER 41
BLUE DIAMOND TRAINING CAMP
CADDO MILLS, TEXAS

They called it a camp, but it was really a gymnasium, part of a middle school that had been closed due to redistricting and budget short-falls. The windows were all sealed and blocked, and there was a stout metal security fence around the perimeter, with a guard station at the entrance and regular foot patrols.

Bunny pulled the old Ford into a slot next to the GMC, and they got out, waiting as Saxon finished a call inside his car. Then he got out, still smiling. He was a smiler, that one, and Top Sims didn't like the smile at all. It was the kind of smile alligators wore right up until they took a bite out of you. There was nothing at all trust-worthy in that grin, as if he knew no one trusted him and wanted to assure them that they shouldn't. Top thought about how much fun it would be to bust out every one of Saxon's flawless teeth and maybe knock the lantern firmness out of his jaw. Maybe kick his balls up into his chest cavity for good measure.

But all that was unlikely, since Saxon was a low-level talent scout, and messing him up would endanger the mission. Fun to think about, though.

"So what's the play here, Flagg?" he asked Saxon.

"Let's go see," said Saxon vaguely. He paused. "You boys carry-ing?"

Top and Bunny hesitated as if surprised by the question. Bunny gestured to his ankle.

"Got a Colt Mustang XSP," he said.

Top half turned and raised his shirt to reveal a Glock 9 mm in a belt holster.

"You'll need to check those at the door," said Saxon. "Rules."

"Not a big fan of giving my gun up to anyone," said Bunny, putting some bluster into it.

"And you can drive your ass out of here whenever you want, son," said Saxon. "No one stopping you. But if you want to come in and talk to the man, then you got to check your guns at the door. Your choice."

Top contrived to look pained and then nodded. "It's cool, Buck. House rules."

"House rules," agreed Saxon.

"Fuck," said Bunny, but he bent and removed the holstered piece. Instead of handing it over, he went around and unlocked a heavy steel box in the bed of the Ford and stowed his pistol in there. "This work for you, hoss?" he asked.

"That's fine," said Saxon.

Top pulled the holstered Glock from his belt and handed it to Bunny, who locked the box.

"And neither of you boys will object to a metal detector and a patdown," said Saxon, not really making it a question.

"Yeah, sure, whatever," said Bunny.

They followed Saxon into the gymnasium, which was a huge cinder block structure attached to the back of the school building. There were armed guards at the door, and another pair inside, flanking a good-quality metal detector.

"New recruits, Mr. Saxon?" asked one guard.

Top contrived to look surprised. "Saxon?"

The talent scout spread his hands. "Yeah, well. John Saxon in here, Randall Flagg out there, capisce?"

"It's copacetic," said Bunny. "Flagg's like your combat call sign."

"Sure," said Saxon. "Like that." He gestured to the metal detector. "Shall we?"

It beeped once, requiring that Bunny remove his belt, which had a heavy steel buckle, and once inside, a moonfaced guard patted them down. He was very thorough.

"You done stroking my dick?" asked Bunny.

"Nah, couldn't find it," said the guard, which knocked a genuine laugh from Top. The guard straightened. "They're clean."

Top and Bunny followed Saxon toward the building. They were

unarmed and greatly outnumbered. It was not the first time they'd been in something this tight, but previous experience and the memory of how some of those other situations played out did not inspire a single ounce of confidence that they were either safe or secure.

CHAPTER 42
PHOENIX HOUSE
OMFORI ISLAND, GREECE

Church and Lilith sat together, though they were not on the same continent.

She was in an Arklight safe house in a quiet suburb of Johannesburg, and he was in his office at the RTI headquarters. The illusion was created by the ORB—the Operational Resource Bay—which was one of Doc Holliday's inventions. Dozens of small cameras worked in sync to use a proprietary imaging tech to put holograms of them both into a shared space. It looked like they were seated together on a bench in Döbrentei Square in Budapest on a quiet evening. The ORB even added ambient noise of nearby traffic, birdsong, and laughter—but muted.

Lilith was amused. "Here, of all places? Since when are you sentimental?"

He smiled faintly. "I often come here."

"Not really," she chided.

"Not really, but the ORB allows me to mix business with pleasure."

She smiled and shook her head. "St. Germaine mooning over where we had our first kiss."

"Behave," he said.

They smiled at each other, and he saw the small movement as she very nearly reached out to try and take his hand but stopped herself because that was beyond even the ORB's capabilities.

Then she asked, "Do they know?"

"Bug knows, of course. He's known since the beginning."

"Who else?"

"Scott Wilson suspects, and as long as it's only a suspicion, I'm not burdened by the weight of his disapproval."

"What about Rudy Sanchez?"

"We've . . . had talks about Ledger. Diagnosis and prognosis. I shared with him the psych eval from the profiler Wilson put on it. Rudy's conclusion was that it was a very well-written, well-considered piece of garbage."

"I read it, too, and Sanchez is quite correct."

"It's not entirely without merit," said Church, though he didn't push the issue. In truth, he found it to be pedestrian. Wilson had wanted an objective opinion from a top forensic psychologist, but applying standard models—even models of known psychological deviations—to Joe Ledger was a waste of time and resources. But Wilson was as concerned and as frustrated as everyone else, and approving the report was something he could at least do.

"Will you tell Junie?"

"No," he said. "Not until we know more. Right now, all we've been able to do is lift the crime scene reports from whichever agency has jurisdiction. And we've received uploads of data, but all the data transfer is from sites like internet cafés, or coffee shops with no camera surveillance. Some materials were left in airport lockers. No collectable forensics of any kind."

"Ledger knows his tradecraft, I'll give him that," said Lilith.

"Bug has done a lot of searching for real estate rentals and hotels, and he believes Ledger is using the Bucharest model."

"Smart," she said.

The Bucharest model was a technique established during the Cold War but greatly refined since. A person with the right resources would use several different credit cards to book different rooms in the same hotel. He would check in to each using a variety of disguises. Sometimes confederates were employed for this purpose, but Ledger was almost certainly acting alone. Each room would serve a different purpose—equipment storage, bolt-hole, or actual lodging. Since modern hotels no longer required returning key cards to the desk, there was little way to track the movements of guests until the cleaning staff knocked on the door after checkout time. It was complicated, but the extra steps made it virtually impossible to find someone. And the upper-tier pros often went the extra mile to check into more than one hotel. With Ledger's high-end talent for languages and regional accents, becoming invisible was easy. The complication for him was Ghost, but somehow Ledger managed. Bug had logged eight different combinations of tall men with large dogs—though the color of the dog's hair and the stated purpose—guide dog or different levels of emotional support—raised no particular eyebrows. Except to Bug.

And there were also safe houses attached to various organizations, some of which were left empty. Someone with RTI-level equipment could game any monitoring devices, however.

"Ledger used two sets of identities to obtain field kits from two different in-country resources," said Church. "With those, he can stay off the grid for as long as he wants. And we've determined that he used a Lightning Bug to kill his and Ghost's RFID chips."

Lilith grunted. "He and his dog are both ghosts."

"Yes," said Church. "Which is why I asked you to meet me. What have your people found?"

"We may be getting close," she said, "or at least closer. After the first few hits here in South Africa, we were able to make an educated guess as to who he was going to target next. We know he's been going after people of two kinds—scientists who have been on lists of people with possible or likely ties to Kuga operations, and people in the technologies and terrorism arms of the black market who used to work for Ohan."

"Ledger was very familiar with Ohan's operation," said Church. "We were building a mission profile to go after him, but . . ."

"But Arklight got there first. No apologies, St. Germaine."

"None needed. My point is that Ledger is well versed on those names."

"There are people on both of my lists—tech and sales—who are in morgues all over this part of the country. We got to one in the hospital, though. Well, let me rephrase that. We hijacked the ambulance taking him to a hospital. He's now in a landfill."

"He talked?" asked Church.

"Oh yes. He gave us a very accurate physical description—though the attacker wore a balaclava. Right size and build. Right description of how he moved. And the attacker had a white combat dog in next-gen body armor. The dog had metal teeth."

"Ah. And what did this unfortunate person have to say?"

"He admitted that he gave Ledger some names. We're staking out those places now."

"What was this man involved in?"

"That's the odd part," said Lilith, "he was rambling a bit. Screaming, really. And he kept referring to two things. Some kind of drug or drug treatment called R-33, and some upcoming event he knew only as the 'American Operation.'"

"Did he have any details about what this American Operation might be?"

"Nothing specific, alas," she said, "but he said it was—and I quote— 'what we're all working on.' We've been wondering what Kuga's next big play is going to be, and I think this is our first true whiff."

CHAPTER 43
CIVITELLA IN VAL DI CHIANA
AREZZO, TUSCANY, ITALY

The man sat on a bench in a park on a street he couldn't name.

The park was in shadows except for a few lights along the wandering stone pathway. The man's dog lay on the bench with his head on the man's lap. They'd been like that for more than two hours.

The man watched nothing. His eyes were out of focus. The world was a gray-green blur of inconsequential colors. His fingers flexed open and closed, massaging the ruff of the dog's neck. He did not remember washing the blood off his hand. Or off the dog's coat, for that matter. He didn't remember changing back into civilian clothes. So many things lately were blurred out of his consciousness.

He knew he should be afraid of that.

Of that he was certain.

When a voice spoke behind him, the man snapped to full awareness. But he did not turn around.

"I have to say, Joey," said the voice, "I'm getting worried about how you're handling things."

The voice was warm, mature, and familiar. So familiar.

"You're leaning way out over that edge, son."

"Go away," said the man.

"I already went away. You know that, Joey."

"Don't call me that."

"It's your name."

"That's what you called me when I was a little kid."

The man chuckled softly. "Well, you're always going to be my little boy, Joey. Always and forever."

"You're not real."

"And yet here you are talking to me."

"I'm . . . I . . ."

"Go ahead, take your time. Say what you need to say."

"There's something wrong with me."

"Joey, there's been something wrong with you since you were fourteen. After what happened to you and that poor girl? Of course there's something wrong with you. They broke you, son. They broke your bones and they broke your heart and they broke your head."

"Why are you doing this?" the man demanded, though he still did not turn around.

"Because I love you, Joey. Always have, always will. And I'm scared for you. You're not right, and I think you know that."

"Leave me alone," begged the man. "Please."

The big white shepherd woke up and raised his head. He looked over the back of the bench, and for a moment, his bushy tail wagged back and forth.

Then the man felt a breath on his ear as if the person behind him had leaned close. He squeezed his eyes shut. The breath was cold and damp and smelled of rotting things.

"The darkness never forgives," said the voice, "and it never forgets. It has almost all of you now, and if you're not careful, son, it's going to swallow you whole."

The man got to his feet and turned.

"Dad, please . . ."

But there was no one standing behind him.

The trees in the park were crowded with night birds, though. Thousands of them like a cloud of shadows. Watching with their bottomless black eyes.

The man sank slowly down onto the bench and put his face in his hands.

CHAPTER 44
PHOENIX HOUSE
OMFORI ISLAND, GREECE

Bug was not naturally a vindictive person. It took some effort for him to be mean. But he could get into gear when he tried.

When Mr. Church suggested that he go after the hackers working for Kuga and to "make it hurt," that came with a great deal of license and a tremendous reach. And MindReader Q1 gave that reach a lot of punch.

He locked his office, turned on some late-1990s dubstep, dragged his cooler of Red Bull to within easy grabbing range, tore open a one-pound bag of Twizzlers, and set to work.

The first thing he did was dive into some bookmarks he'd created especially for darknet market sites that were supposed to be access-only by special encrypted invitation. Over the years, Bug had created scores of online personalities, including one as the highly respected and highly feared hacker Coal Tiger, named for Stan Lee and Jack Kirby's original—and unfortunate—name for the comic book character who later became the Black Panther.

As Coal Tiger, he was admitted to chat rooms that would otherwise have been sealed shut against him. In those chats, computer experts who worked for the black marketeers using the darknet got together to—among other things—brag. Hackers loved to brag, though they typically hid behind obfuscatory walls, false identities, and location rerouters. They were by nature and necessity an exceptionally paranoid bunch. One error and they could invite their own competition inside their online Fortresses of Solitude.

There were several hundred of these chat rooms, though most were poseurs who wanted to be seen as top-level black hats without actually having the chops. But the key players—a group of less than a hundred worldwide—were the kings of the matrix. Most of their chat rooms were located on Tor or I2P, premier darknets for black market vendors selling or brokering large quantities of drugs, weapons, all manner of physical and cryptocurrencies, unlicensed pharmaceuticals, hijacked credit card information, passwords, weapons of every kind, old Soviet-era military technology, and slaves. Sex trafficking was huge on the darknet, and because the sites could not be found via any kind of standard search engine, the flow of business was seldom interrupted. The hackers remained aloof and apart, like an extended family of trickster gods—Loki, Coyote, raven spirits, Wakdjunga, Anansi, and others.

Bug had variations on his darknet identities. He was Coal Tiger and the Fisher King; he was BigBadBoi and Punji. And others. Identities he created, cultivated, and left on the net, touching them up every now and then to keep them fresh and active. Some of his online avatars were actually repurposed from hackers the DMS and RTI had taken down.

It was as the Fisher King, though, that he went on a buying spree.

He put feelers out that he was looking for cybernetic implants, neuro chips, and cutting-edge eugeroics for wakefulness. Bug was very careful reaching out, making sure he did it from obscure angles and never—never, *ever*—appearing too eager or too desperate. He found that the B and B approach worked best. Bitching and Bargaining. Complaining about the sale price for something and then haggling like a carpet merchant. Eagerness was either the sign of a rookie or, most often on the darknet, an indication that he was a cop of some kind.

It took weeks to get into the right position, and each day, he'd repeat the same ritual of ultra-caffeination and sugar rush, which brought him to that elevated state of hyperawareness and quickness of thought. The trick was to intersperse the sugars with proteins and fats so that he didn't crash.

Each time he made contact with someone promising, Bug used MindReader Q1 to send a Trojan horse back to whomever emailed or messaged him a quote. Most of the very top hackers believed that they were immune to those kinds of intrusions, and they had software to review every line of code in the metadata of that email. Except

JONATHAN MABERRY

MindReader's quantum speed was too fast to be caught. As soon as a connection was made by receiving the email or message, it attacked without using a reply message at all. This was something Bug developed years ago for Mr. Church. The super-intrusion software swept into the sender's system via their own email and positioned itself to make the target unable to read any of the Trojan horse code. It wouldn't even see that it was there, no matter which kind of cyber-security tools were used.

Long ago, Bug and Church had discussed sharing this software. The pro side of the argument was that it would greatly protect the military, universities, hospitals, and the computers running the power grids. Though while that was true, sharing it was greatly outweighed by the cons of it simply being too dangerous. If the tech got out, then there would be no protection for anyone.

The compromise was that Bug went into the systems running nuclear power, electrical grids, and a few key places and planted a different set of Trojan horses. A set of analytical and reactive programs designed to prevent the most sophisticated and dangerous kinds of black hat hacking. They called it Operation Counterpunch, and only the two of them were aware that it existed.

Bug was not in a mood to send benign protective viruses out there, however. He was hunting for links in the Kuga chain of black market experts. And although he had not yet found the main Kuga online presence, he had a serious in. A bit less than two years ago, one of Lilith's Arklight teams had captured, interrogated, and executed the man who had been, to that point, the most successful and powerful black marketeer of all time, the Turk named Ohan. Before he died—and he died very badly—Lilith's team extracted a great deal of information from him. They were on the hunt for key players in the sex-trafficking world, and they found many. Found and removed in very ugly ways. However, the by-products of all that were what Lilith considered "scraps." Names, email addresses, passwords, and darknet sites for nearly forty of Ohan's top people who had been recruited by Kuga.

In a sane and smart world, all those people would have erased their previous online identities and created new and antiseptic ones. However, as most cops in the world know, few criminals are masterminds. Even those who hired brilliant black hats to advise them still did profoundly stupid things, like keep old email accounts to communicate with friends. Or maintain back-channel lines of communication thinking that those were, by their nature, safe.

Bug loved that kind of thing. A window only needed to be opened a crack for him to get in.

And each day he worked at Mr. Church's project, he did more damage. He shared crucial information with competitors and outright enemies; he planted unbreakable ransomware on banking systems working with these people; he outed them as pedophiles—even when they weren't—to the right media sources; he stole billions in funds and donated it to charities; he crashed expensive systems on exactly the wrong days; he leaked corporate secrets just as the opening bell sounded on the world's various stock exchanges; he created compromising pictures, texts, and emails and sent it to girlfriends, boyfriends, spouses, and the law; and he made social media posts that—he was certain—would embarrass them in the eyes of their new employer. Some of those people vanished, and Bug figured that was the result of those posts coming to the attention of Rafael Santoro.

He did a lot of damage. He ended careers, businesses, fortunes, and lives.

He made it hurt.

But he did not find Rafael Santoro or Kuga.

Not yet.

Not yet.

CHAPTER 45
FORESTED AREA
APPROXIMATELY 3,800 YARDS FROM THE BLUE DIAMOND TRAINING CAMP
CADDO MILLS, TEXAS

The sniper was invisible. An angel of death hidden within the shadows of a massive pine tree, lost in the great ocean that was the forest.

The rifle rested on a sturdy limb, and the sniper was covered in cut pine boughs and wore a camouflage hood and balaclava, with grease paint over any inch of exposed skin. Unseen and silent.

The rifle's scope moved without hurry from one face to the next. The crosshairs drifted over the recruiter's smiling face, then the man doing the pat-downs. It moved on to the sentries and then to the two big men. First the tall white man and last the older Black man. Each time, the crosshairs froze over their hearts. At that distance, head shots were possible for a sniper of this skill level, but with the sheer destructive power of the copper-jacketed rounds, a center-mass body shot would be both lethal and easier to guarantee.

A voice spoke quietly in the sniper's ear.

"Do you have them?"

"Yes," murmured Belle. "I have them."

CHAPTER 46
JAPANESE ICEBREAKER *NOBU SHIRASE* (AGB-5003)
NEAR EAST ONGUL ISLAND
QUEEN MAUD LAND, ANTARCTICA

The ship punched through a crust of ice that was far thinner than it should have been. That had become the routine, even here at the bottom of the world.

Captain Hanzo sipped his tea and peered gloomily out at the brilliant blue sky, the flawless blue-white ice, the calm waves, and hated it all. He was old enough to remember first coming to these waters back in the late 1990s, when the ice sheets seemed too vast, too dense, too ancient to be vulnerable to the stupidity and careless cruelty of man.

Now he was watching a continent die, seeing it melt away as the waters rose and the air grew warmer. He personally wished he could get every fool who denied the realities of climate change and force them to work for a full year down here. Force them to see the damage being done to the planet. To *his* cold world down here.

He kept such thoughts to himself. He was eighteen months from retirement and did not want to go out on a psychiatric discharge. His wife was counting on a full pension and the invitations to all those fancy dinners. She also liked the extra money waiting from lecture tours on sailing the Antarctic that would come once he was a civilian. The same had happened to her father, who'd died well off and a very happy man.

Hanzo, however, was not happy.

The *Shirase* was not happy, either. Hanzo knew that ships had souls, had memories. They were alive, and he knew that his ship was grieving for a planet out of balance with its natural order.

Those were his thoughts when one of his crewmen cut through the morning air with a yell. Suddenly, a lot of men were bellowing. Feet thudded up and down ladders and along the deck as a knot of sailors clustered together by a section of the port bow rail, all of them pointing to something in the water.

Before Hanzo could demand an explanation, a petty officer dashed onto the bridge.

"Captain, we've spotted a lifeboat a mile three points off the port bow," said the petty officer excitedly. "There are survivors in it."

"Is it from the *Hakudo Maru*?" demanded the captain.

"I think it is, sir."

Hanzo immediately gave the orders for heave to, and to have a pair of his boats swayed down and lowered.

The *Hakudo Maru* was a scientific vessel that had been sent from Tokyo a few months ago to study the release of ancient bacteria from melting ice. It was part of a joint venture initiated a few years ago after research teams had found—and revived—an eight-million-year-old bacterium that had been dormant in the Mullins and Beacon valleys of the icy continent. Since then, other bacteria had been discovered, and the growing fear was that these prehistoric biologicals could pose a serious threat once ocean currents moved them around the globe. The *Hakudo Maru*'s task was to catch random fish and study them for the presence of unknown bacteria and viruses.

However, ten days ago, the *Hakudo Maru* went missing during a particularly aggressive storm, and the high winds made search efforts difficult. No trace of the ship had yet been found. It was believed that the high winds likely drove the vessel into the path of some massive icebergs that had recently calved from the dwindling ice sheet. One of the new icebergs was estimated to be three-quarters of a trillion tons, nearly as big as A-68, the trillion-ton supergiant that broke from the Larsen C Ice Shelf back in 2020. On a dark night, with a mighty storm blowing and the ocean filled with killer ice islands, a small research vessel would have had no chance.

But now . . . a lifeboat? And hundreds of miles from where the *Hakudo Maru* was believed to have sunk? This was amazing. The thought of it lifted Hanzo's heart. He called for his jacket and ran on deck.

Everyone crowded the rail, watching as two shallow-draft rubber rescue boats zipped across the water at high speed. A lieutenant handed Hanzo a pair of binoculars, and he used them to study the operation. There were three men in the boat, each wearing a heavy coat, gloves, and a balaclava against the cold. The coats were unusually bulky, and Hanzo figured they were wearing more than one. How else could they have survived so long in an open boat down here in the coldest place on Earth?

However, as the rescue team came alongside, the men were able to catch ropes and make them fast to their cleats on their own boat. That was promising.

"They must have been able to bring food with them," said the lieutenant. "They don't move like dying men."

"Let us pray you're correct," said Hanzo.

Twenty minutes later, the boats had returned, and the three survivors were helped aboard. Despite having been able to secure the ropes, it was clear they were in bad shape. Sailors had to support them to keep the men from collapsing on the deck.

"Thank you, sir," said one of them quickly, and he repeated the phrase over and over again. He, like the others, was Japanese. They all looked to be in their thirties. None of them looked much like scientists, but then again, there were a lot of people aboard a vessel. Men as rugged and hardy as these were likely engine room specialists or equipment engineers. The other two seemed incapable of speech and just shivered, heads lolling.

"Take them below," ordered the captain. "Call the doctor."

The crew helped the men down to the sick bay. Hanzo lingered on the deck for a while, watching as his people hooked onto the lifeboat and hauled it, dripping, onto the deck. He lit his pipe and puffed until the tobacco was burning smoothly, then clamped the stem between his teeth, watching his men work. They were a good, reliable crew.

Hardier than most because work in this kind of extreme weather conditions was not for the average seaman. It required toughness of physical and moral fiber. A toughness of spirit. And not merely tough, but practical, uncomplaining, and good-natured. The kind of sailors who took to this work *because* it was so difficult. He loved them all.

"Captain," called his petty officer, "I think you should come and look at this."

The man was leaning over the side, pointing to one of the thwarts. The captain leaned over, too.

"What is it?"

"Well, sir," said the petty officer, "I don't know what this is."

He reached down and picked up something small and round. It resisted his pull for a moment and then came away with a small *pok* sound of parting adhesive. The petty officer frowned at it and then handed what was clearly an electronic device to the captain.

Hanzo frowned, too.

"I think it's a camera, sir," said the petty officer. "See? There is a lens and below that a battery pack. There's a green light. It's still functioning. I think it's on, sir."

The device was about the diameter of a binocular eyepiece and made from hard black plastic. It was heavy for its size, likely owing to the batteries, which were sealed into a case that had no visible means of opening. He held it up to his head and heard a small, steady electronic pulse.

"It sounds like a remote transmitter," he murmured.

"Sir," said the petty officer, "why would they put a camera on a lifeboat? I mean . . . if there was a working camera with a transmitter, then why hasn't anyone picked up the signal?"

Hanzo said nothing, but the questions were curious. No, more than that—they were troubling.

"I'm going below," he said, and he headed for the hatch through which the rescued sailors had been taken.

He went down the companion ladder and through the ship, the little camera clutched in his hand. As he approached the door to the small sick bay, he suddenly stopped.

"What . . . ?" he said aloud.

There, on the outside of the doorframe, was another of the cameras.

JONATHAN MABERRY

It was identical, and when he touched it, his fingers came away wet. He sniffed them and smelled seawater.

This makes no sense, he thought, and stepped into the sick bay.

What he saw made no sense, either.

The doctor, the nurse, and the six sailors who'd helped the rescued men down here lay sprawled inside. Each of them had small black dots on their foreheads or in the centers of their chests. Sometimes more than one.

Hanzo felt his heart judder to a stop in his chest, and his whole body went as cold as the icy seas that slapped against the hull. His mind, sharp as it was, slipped a gear as he tried to navigate through the seas of impossibility. All eight of the people in that room were dead.

They had all been shot.

There hadn't been any noise of gunfire, but there was brass on the floor.

There was so little blood, but Hanzo knew that dead people do not bleed. He also realized that the head shots had not exited. There was no blood spatter.

Only death.

The three survivors were gone. Their heavy coats and gloves were on the floor, but they were gone.

What had been beneath those bulky coats?

He stood where he had stopped, one foot inside the sick bay, one in the hall. Hanzo looked down at the little camera transmitter in his hand.

"God help us," he said.

He did not hear the footfall of the man who stepped up behind him. He barely felt the feather-light pressure of the sound suppressor of the pistol touching the hair over his ear. The shot was a soft *thup*, which he did hear, though only as a fading afterthought as the .22 slug punched through the bone and began ricocheting around inside his skull, expending its foot pound of force by destroying his brain utterly. Lacking the force to exit the skull.

He fell into the sick bay.

Captain Hanzo did not hear the screams and yells as the rest of his crew died.

There were fifty-three scientists and forty-four crew aboard the *Shirase*. There were weapons aboard, but the lockers were never opened, the guns and rifles never handed out. There was no time for that. The three Fixers swept like a storm through the ship, from stem to stern, deck to deck, killing silently, killing efficiently. They disabled the radio room.

Hanzo, who appreciated tough men working at peak efficiency, might had been impressed. He might also have been terrified, because these men moved much too quickly than was reasonable. In instances where a crewman was able to mount some kind of defense, they swept the counterattacks aside. For all the toughness of the sailors aboard, they might as well have been toddlers.

It was a massacre.

A quick, quiet massacre.

In under nine minutes, all ninety-seven people aboard the *Shirase* were dead.

INTERLUDE 10
SALES PRESENTATION VIA SHOWROOM
FOUR MONTHS AGO

Mr. Sunday froze the image on the face of Captain Hanzo. The officer had twisted as he fell so that his face was visible, and there was a look of profound surprise stamped on his features.

"Now *that*," crowed Mr. Sunday, "is entertainment!"

He chuckled as small windows opened on the screen, each one showing the feed from cameras placed throughout the *Shirase* as the Fixers moved through it. Each man had a pouch of the camera transmitters, and they activated as soon as they were pressed to a hard surface. The video feeds showed the slaughter.

"Ninety-seven hostiles taken down," said Mr. Sunday, "by *three* enhanced Fixers. And ladies and gentlemen, that is an average of 32.3 kills per Fixer. No explosives, no air strikes, no booby traps. Small arms only. Oh, and watch this . . . this is really fun."

He cued up one clip where a petty officer tried to rally a group of men on the forward deck of the ship as two of the Fixers emerged.

JONATHAN MABERRY

The sailors had oars, improvised clubs, and knives, and there were enough of them that sheer weight of numbers should have carried the fight.

The Fixers stood back-to-back, each holding two .22 automatic pistols with ten-shot magazines. Forty total shots without reloading. Eighteen men charged at them, circling them, trying to crush them in a brutal rugby scrum.

The Fixers began moving in a slow circle, firing and firing. The attackers came at them, and the Fixers had a target-rich environment. Their hands were rock steady, and they emptied their guns into the ring of sailors. Only one sailor—the chief petty officer—made it all the way through the storm of lead and managed to strike a Fixer across the jaw with a three-foot length of pipe. The blow whipped the Fixer's head to one side, tearing open the balaclava and ripping a red gash along his jawline. Blood splashed out. However, the Fixer neither cried out nor fell. Instead, he walked up to the petty officer, who was about to swing again, buried the pistol in the man's chest, and fired three shots.

The petty officer grunted and sank to his knees, swayed there for a moment, and fell over.

Mr. Sunday turned to the wall of screens showing the faces of sixteen potential customers. Some of those people would have been appalled had they known who else was watching this sales pitch. Some were sworn enemies who had lost loved ones to the attacks of the others. Some were overtly cruel, others merely desperate in fights against enemies they could not hope to defeat in any kind of standard battle.

"These men here are prototypes," said Mr. Sunday. "We expect the first batch of our *enhanced* private military contractors to be ready to board planes to your locations in under six months. Oh, wait, I see we have a question. Let me read it for the group. '*When did this take place?*'" The salesman grinned and looked at his wristwatch. "Just under thirty minutes ago. If this wasn't in the Antarctic, the bodies wouldn't even be cold yet."

He paused and cocked his head as if listening to a surprising thought.

"As you'll all recall from the prospectus I emailed you, there is the 'self-cleaning' option. And the reason we staged an op on the underbelly of the world is to highlight the logistical complications of extracting this team. I mean, it *can* be done, but only at great expense and with great risk. Now . . . since these PMCs are rentals and not heroes of your homeland or cause, why would you want to put your standard military assets at risk to recover them? Once the mission is accomplished—be that taking a ship, securing a military installation, a rival corporation's lab, or a target with significance to your particular idealistic or religious stance—the operatives themselves become liabilities if captured or killed. And we—meaning the Kuga organization—do not want prying eyes to play with our toys."

He walked to a small table and picked up a satellite phone, punched a coded number, and waited. When the call went through, an image— fed by one of the camera-transmitters—showed one of the three Fixers.

"Ichi," said the man.

"Mr. Ichi," said Sunday, "have you launched the surveillance drones?"

"Yes, sir. I will key you into the feed."

Immediately, there appeared an aerial view of the *Shirase* drifting in the ocean current.

"Thank you, Mr. Ichi. Where are Mr. Ni and Mr. San?"

"They are below in the engine room, sir."

"Excellent," said Mr. Sunday. "You have done an excellent job. Please pass along my congratulations on a brilliant performance."

"Thank you, sir," said the Fixer, giving a short, sharp bow toward the camera. "When can we expect extraction?"

Instead of answering, Mr. Sunday looked up from the sat phone, raised a small device so that the audience could see it. Then he pressed a button.

On the screen, the picture of Mr. Ichi vanished. The feed from the drone, however, continued to focus on the ship. The middle section of the *Shirase* suddenly bulged upward as if the whole craft were made of inflatable rubber. The illusion persisted for a full second, and then a massive fireball burst upward from the part of the ship where the engine room had been a moment before. The blast was massive, tearing the icebreaker in half and flinging pieces of metal, wood, and human flesh high into the air. Mr. Sunday let the video play for a full fifteen seconds as debris rained down in what seemed like surreal slow motion. By the time the last bits slapped onto the icy water, both halves of the icebreaker were gone, each slipping beneath the waves to vanish entirely.

Mr. Sunday killed the video feed and allowed for silence to settle over his presentation venue. He spent that time looking from one face to another and another. His smile was exactly the same as a Nile crocodile watching a limping gazelle edge down onto the bank for a sip.

"Now, my friends," he said softly, "I think we can start the bidding at one million dollars per unit. Ooooo, I see we already have some bids. Nice. I like that enthusiasm. Another bidder. And another. Very, very nice . . ."

CHAPTER 47
BLUE DIAMOND TRAINING CAMP
CADDO MILLS, TEXAS

Inside the building, they passed a room with an open door, and Bunny caught a brief glance of a man in what looked like the hydraulic power loader from the movie *Aliens*. A sturdy exoskeleton that gave the man a strange almost crustacean appearance, with enormous arms that had large pincers. Bunny lingered long enough to see the exosuit's driver swing around and point one pincer at a wall. Bunny realized with a start that instead of actual pincers, the two prongs at the end of the arm were, in fact, gun barrels. Large bore, nearly as big as an M242 Bushmaster, but the overall barrel length was shorter. The recoil from a weapon like that would put any soldier, no matter how burly, flat on his ass; and that explained the heavy structure of the exoskeleton. It was, he realized, a short-barreled Bushmaster that could chase opponents.

The sight of it sent a chill through him. He tapped Top's arm and got a nod. He'd seen it, too.

Saxon led them through another doorway into the main gymnasium. The room was big, with a floor painted out for basketball. The paint was faded and scuffed and mostly covered by exercise mats and racks and benches for weights, and a row of speed bags and a dozen heavy bags hung from chains. Along one wall were racks of training weapons—padded pugil sticks, throwing knives, paintball guns for nonlethal close-combat drills, training body armor, various kinds of rubber and wooden weapons, and handheld targets. About thirty men and women were training in pairs, some under an instructor's eye, others—more advanced teams—working out on their own. Top and Bunny followed Saxon between the groups in what was clearly an attempt to impress them. And they were impressed. These were not raw boot camp greenhorns; they were seasoned fighters who knew their trade. Very fast, very dangerous.

They stopped by one square where a fight was ending. The loser was on his hands and knees, goggle-eyed and purple-faced, crawling like a geriatric away from a man who was five and a half feet tall and about four wide, with no visible neck, a bull chest, pig eyes, and a blend of navy and prison tattoos. He also had a stylized *88* over his heart.

"Sergeant Wilkes," said Saxon. "Meet the candidates. Big one is Buck, older one is Guidry."

Wilkes ignored Bunny and looked Top up and down. His expression was one of abject disregard. To Saxon, he said, "Old Black Joe here looks like he's past his sell-by date."

Top said nothing, showed nothing. Bunny couldn't help but laugh.

Wilkes gave him a sharp look. "You got something to say?"

"'Fuck you' comes to mind," said Bunny. That caused a murmur of comments and snickers from the watching crowd.

Wilkes pointed a calloused finger at him. "You're officially on my list."

"Don't give a cold, dried shit."

That made the sergeant grin with ghoulish delight. He clapped Saxon on the shoulder. "I'm calling dibs on these two assholes."

Bunny turned to Saxon. "This how you run your recruitment program? Must have missed that in the sales pitch."

Saxon looked momentarily uncertain, then shrugged. "They're not signed on yet," he said to Wilkes, "but . . . yeah. Run them a bit. See how they shake out. It'll tell me how much work we have to do to get them back in the game. Just don't mess them up too much."

JONATHAN MABERRY

"Yeah, yeah. I'm officially shitting my pants," said Bunny, punctuating it with a yawn.

"Oh, hell," said Wilkes with real delight, "I'm going to saw a good yard off this big cocksucker."

Bunny was six foot six and was easily the tallest man in the gym. "Let's do it, old hoss. Let's rock and roll."

"No," said Top, and everyone looked at him. "I've got some things I'd like to discuss with the sergeant here. You step off, Farm Boy. Let the grown-ups have a chitchat."

Wilkes burst out laughing. "*You* want to go a few rounds with *me*? That's awesome."

"No," said Top. "Just the one round'll do."

That got an even bigger laugh, and Wilkes grinned so hard it looked like his gristly ears would fall off. He cut a look at Saxon. "Arrogant *and* stupid. You sure know how to find them. What's the other one? An autistic faggot?"

Bunny merely smiled and went over to lean against the wall, arms folded across his chest, watching as Top removed his wristwatch, hat, and shirt and placed them neatly on a corner of the mat. Beneath the shirt, he had a faded green, brown, and black camouflage tank top. His dark skin was crisscrossed with scars, old and new, and although he was muscular, he was not a muscle freak like Wilkes. Or like Bunny, for that matter. He was built more like a first baseman— solid, the kind who could block a runner sliding into base. However, his age was apparent in the white salted through his black goatee, and in the lines around his eyes and mouth.

People were joining the crowd from the other training areas, drawn by loud voices and laughter. They looked from Wilkes to Top and elbowed each other, laughing, making bets on how fast the sergeant was going to dismantle the old guy.

Wilkes made a big show of waving Top onto the padded training area, even to the point of giving a small comical bow like a ringleader at a dog circus. He never stopped grinning. When he stepped onto the mat, he looked Top in the eye and tapped the 88 tattoo. The eighth letter of the alphabet was *H,* and *88* was shorthand for *Heil Hitler.* There was a burning cross on the sergeant's stomach.

Top did not take up a stance or even bring his guard up. His only concession to the level of threat was to shift his weight subtly to the balls of his feet. He waited for the brute of a sergeant to make his play.

When it happened, it all happened fast.

Wilkes faked left and then stepped in very fast with an overhand right that was a rock breaker, a bone crusher, a lethal blow. His whole body went into the punch—good stance, the right kind of pivot to torque energy into his monstrous shoulders so that the punch was a blurred whipping loop of gristle and bone. A younger, faster man would have had trouble slipping or evading that punch, and it was very obvious this was Sergeant Wilkes's deal closer, the blow he used when he wanted to prove a point to everyone within visual range. The kind of punch that would be talked about among the Fixers for years.

Top did not evade, did not duck, bob, or weave.

He stepped right into the attack, shifting only a little to the right as he brought his elbow up into the path of the muscular arm, the flats of his curled fingers pressed against his skull. And he used his step to drive a single punch into the narrow gap between one eight and the other. Every ounce of Top's two hundred pounds, forty years of karate, and career as a tier-one special operator went into it. This was *his* deal closer. A tighter, smarter, less obvious punch that channeled all his muscle, mass, and momentum into an impact point no larger than a dime.

The sergeant's entire body folded around the punch. The blow knocked spit from his mouth, drove all the air from his lungs, took all the rigidity from his muscles, turned his legs to overcooked pasta, and sat him down hard on his ass in front of everyone. His eyes bulged, and his face turned an eggplant purple as he tried to suck in even a spoonful of air.

Top knotted his fingers in Wilkes's short hair, jerked his head back so violently there was a wet creaking sound, and then he spat in the sergeant's gasping mouth. Top straightened, started to turn, paused, and shot a back heel kick into the man's right eye socket. Wilkes flopped back, arms and legs splayed like a starfish. The right side of his face no longer held its shape. Blood leaked from nostrils, ears, and mouth.

JONATHAN MABERRY

The room was utterly silent.

Top went over and retrieved his shirt and stood buttoning it very slowly. His eyes were locked on Saxon's. Bunny came and stood next to Top, but facing away, watching the crowd.

"We didn't come here to fuck around," said Top quietly. "I thought we were here to audition for a job."

Saxon looked aghast.

At first.

Then a slow smile blossomed on his face.

CHAPTER 48

PHOENIX HOUSE
HEADQUARTERS OF ROGUE TEAM INTERNATIONAL
OMFORI ISLAND, GREECE

Mr. Church moved through the rooms of his big apartment on the top floor of the ancient castle he'd purchased and had brought—stone by stone—to the island. The gigantic building had once belonged to Francis II Rákóczi, a Hungarian nobleman from the early eighteenth century who had been a prince of Transylvania and a celebrated member of the Order of the Golden Fleece.

As was his habit when deeply troubled, Church lingered in his study, which was lined with bookshelves on which were volumes in scores of languages, books both new and ancient. There was a rack of scrolls, and a row of small and exquisite busts in a case. Church opened the case and looked into the marble faces of Prince Charles of Hesse-Kassel; Gian Gastone de' Medici, last of the Medicis; the Marquis de Créquy; the composer Jean-Philippe Rameau; the occultist Giuseppe Balsamo, who preferred to be called Count Alessandro di Cagliostro; the Italian adventurer Giacomo Casanova; the duc de Belle-Isle; and the theosophist Madame Blavatsky. Other faces watched him from canvases carefully framed and hung so that they leaned slightly forward from the walls as if bending to participate in hushed conversations.

Speakers of superb fidelity in the other room played an aria, Op. 36 XXXII, *Povero cor perche palpito* in G Major, sung by a Japanese soprano whose voice called to mind an angel wreathed in light. It was a necessary change from the improvisational jazz he'd listened to while making all those calls.

Church's cat, a Scottish fold with fur the color of woodsmoke, watched him from his favorite niche between a high-quality bound photocopy of *Inventio Fortunata*, written by a fourteenth-century monk whose name was lost to time, and a pair of George II flintlock brass-barrel militia officers' dueling pistols made by George E. Jones in 1803, with an inscription carefully scrolled onto the brass butt plate of the right-hand gun. The inscription read, "*Post tenebras spero lucem*"—"After darkness, I hope for light"—though the inscriber was not referring to the old Calvinist catchphrase. That phrase had very special meaning for Church and was also chiseled into the first foundation stone when the castle was erected here on this small Greek island.

A discreet bell rang in the foyer, and he walked out to look at the screen mounted beside the door. A young and very muscular man stood there, face lifted to the security camera. His name was Luke Merishi, and he was a moran—a Maasai warrior from Kenya—and a former member of the Lion Guardians. Luke's grandfather had been a close friend of Mr. Church, and together, they'd torn down a huge poaching ring. Luke was one of Church's private guards but was also in training for possible inclusion in an RTI field team. He wore a standard gray patrol uniform but with a red-and-black-checked Maasai sash, ornate multicolored arm bracelets, necklace, and earrings. A pistol was holstered in a nylon shoulder rig, but he carried a twenty-inch *rungu,* the deadly throwing club made of polished ebony wood, in one strong hand.

Church pressed a button. "Yes, Luke, what is it?"

The young warrior stepped aside to reveal a second man standing behind him. This man, though still in his thirties, was ten years older than the Massai. He wore distressed jeans and a dove-gray T-shirt with a French tuck.

"Mr. Chismer is requesting a meeting," said Luke. "He insists it's urgent. Mr. Wilson sent him up."

"Very well," said Church and opened the door.

"My apologies, sir," began Luke, but Church waved it away.

"You were quite correct to bring him up here, Luke," said Church. "Thank you."

The young Maasai frowned and turned to Toys. "Don't make me regret doing this."

"Cheers, mate," said Toys. Then he turned to Church. "We need to talk."

"So it seems. Come in."

He stepped aside and allowed Toys to come inside. Guests in this part of the castle were exceptionally rare, and normally, Church would never have allowed Toys up here. However, Church was intrigued by the young man's urgency. He nodded to Luke and closed the door, then ushered Toys into the study, waving him to one of the big leather chairs positioned before a modest fire. Toys refused a glass of wine and instead flung himself into the chair and spent a few moments staring at the books and art.

Toys frowned and nodded to a manuscript of a play left open inside a Plexiglas case.

"*The History of Cardenio*?" he mused. "Really? I thought that was one of Shakespeare's lost plays. So, what's this? A re-creation? A novelty? Or did someone sell you a high-end phony?"

Church sat back in his chair, crossed his legs, and brushed a tiny piece of lint from his trouser leg. "What can I do for you, Mr. Chismer?"

Toys kept looking around for a few more moments, making occasional grunts. Then he sighed and looked at Church.

"Did Junie Flynn tell you about her premonition the night Ledger went missing?"

"She did. She also discussed it with Dr. Sanchez."

"Did she tell you she passed out when she had it? We were at Free-Tech, celebrating the completion of the water purification system we set up in Botswana, and she dropped her glass and went tits up. I thought she'd had a bloody heart attack. But it was that vision of Joe Ledger being in some kind of trouble. And she hasn't been the same since, and it'll be a month tomorrow."

Church said nothing.

"I know she's been calling here 'round the effing clock, and all Scott Wilson will tell her is that Ledger is on a mission and unavailable.

But I know for a fact that Top and Bunny are in the States working on something else. And that Belle and Andrea are off working on something in the UK. All of which suggests the 'on a mission' thing is tosh."

Church did not ask how Toys knew all this. The young man was notoriously resourceful.

"Given what happened on Christmas Eve," continued Toys, "my guess is that Ledger has gone 'round the twist. Something dodgy like that. Maybe you have him locked up somewhere for his own good, and if so, then all's right in the world and I can go back home. I can even try to sell Junie a story that'll let her get some sleep at night. But . . . I don't think that's it, is it? I think something's happened to Ledger, and on some level somehow, Junie knows it. Feels it. Whatever."

"Is there a point to all this?" asked Church.

Toys leaned forward and rested his elbows on his knees. "I think we both know that I don't give a leper's missing left nut about Ledger, and I'm hardly his favorite bloke. But I care a lot about Junie. Fair to say there's no one I care about as much. She is the best human being I've ever met, and she treats me—a total piece of shit like me—like I'm a person. She has from the jump, even though she knows my past. She knows the things I've done, and she doesn't care about it. She judges me on who I am now, which is something I don't even bloody well know how to process. Are you following me?"

"Get to your point," said Church.

"My point is that if Ledger is in trouble, then I want to help."

Church folded his hands in his lap. "There are a lot of people already positioned to help Colonel Ledger."

"Sure," said Toys, "and so what?"

"Why would I even consider putting you into the field?"

"For the same effing reason you pick up the phone every time you need a throat cut," snapped Toys. "You keep doing it, too. When you're resource poor, you make a call, and I come running. Want to or not, I bloody well take that call because I have a debt outstanding with you we both know I can't ever repay."

"You are doing the work that best suits you."

"With FreeTech? Give me a sodding break. A trained monkey could do what I do. I write checks that allow Junie and her people to do the real work. I sort out logistics, rent offices, and all of that shite, but it's a misuse of who I am, and we both know it."

"And who are you, Mr. Chismer?" asked Church. "In your eyes, who are you?"

Toys looked into Church's eyes. Deeply enough that the ambient temperature of the room seemed to drop.

"I'm a killer," said Toys. "And I'm very damned good at it."

Church pursed his lips for a moment. "You are."

"Know what else I'm good at? Know why Sebastian Gault, the Seven Kings, and Hugo Vox all knew about me? I can find things. I may be out of the game, but my connections are still out there. I used to be wired in everywhere. You have your cronies—Lilith and her Arklight witches, friends in the industry, that lot—but my connections are likely off your radar. Or maybe *below* your radar. Look, I know that you're hunting Kuga. I know that Kuga took over most of Ohan's black market network after Lilith cut his throat. That's fine. But I'll bet Kuga allowed or encouraged a lot of the key players in Ohan's network to come over to *his* team. Why? Because that's the smart way to run a business like that. I have connections on the dark web left over from my time with Gault and Vox. Just because I stepped away from that life doesn't mean I can't work the game if I really wanted to."

"And you would step back into that world for Joe Ledger?"

"No, weren't you listening?" said Toys, shaking his head slowly. "It's not for Ledger. I told you, this is for Junie Flynn."

Church pursed his lips again. "Do you think this is your path to redemption, Mr. Chismer?"

"No," Toys said flatly. "We both know that I'm past any chance of redemption. So, this isn't about me. Not sure why you can't see that. This is all about Junie. She's worth a hundred of Ledger. She's better and cleaner than either of us."

"I won't argue that," said Church.

"I want you to put me into play. Put me back in the game and let me help her by doing what I can for the man she—beyond all common effing sense—loves."

"There is every chance many of your old contacts will never believe you've changed sides."

"So what? Seriously, Church, there is no honor among thieves. It's all about business, about money. I can make deals that will make people money, and that will erase all past sins."

"You might find that some people are less forgiving. There are likely old allies of the Seven Kings who might want to nail your hide to the wall."

Toys gave him a smile that was very much like one of the more poisonous jungle snakes. "Let them try."

Church was silent for a long time. The aria that had been playing ended, and another began. A moody violin piece, an adagio in E-flat major.

"If you do this," he said at length, "there may be no turning back. You escaped this war once. You may not be able to do so again."

"I know the risks. Put me in play."

Church stood up. "Very well, if you want to risk whatever measure of peace you've achieved, then welcome to the war, Mr. Chismer."

The young man stood up, too. His dour face underwent a slow process of change. The lugubrious mask of grief he'd worn for years seemed to fall away, to be replaced by the smallest of smiles. A cold, sly, unpleasant smile.

"Stop calling me that," he said. "My name is Toys."

CHAPTER 49
BLUE DIAMOND TRAINING CAMP
CADDO MILLS, TEXAS

"These are the two men I told you about," said John Saxon.

They were in a classroom that had been repurposed as an executive office. Top and Bunny stood flanking Saxon, all of them facing a woman behind a big oak desk. Everything in the office was high-end, from the imported Turkish carpets to the display case of bronze sculptures. A brass plate on a block of lignum vitae read *Jill Hamilton-Krawczyk*. She was a short brunette with a pretty and intelligent face. Her expression had the kind of apparent brightness of spirit that Top thought looked more like an executive in the music or film business. She did not look like the kind of person to be

　　　　　　　　　　JONATHAN MABERRY

overseeing a training camp for private military contractors. She wore a pendant with an exquisite marquis-cut blue diamond that had to be three carats and was a rich and radiant azure. Small half-carat matching diamonds dangled from her earlobe. Top, who'd once researched that kind of stone when Blue Diamond first came on the DMS radar, estimated that the total value of those gems was north of a million.

She gave them a radiant smile and waved Top and Bunny toward a pair of leather chairs that were soft as butter. Top noted that the chairs were set too low so that the desk was slightly higher than normal, creating a subjective view of the executive being taller and more physically imposing than anyone who came to meet with her. A nice trick. It wasn't all that different from the trick Colonel Ledger often used—slouching slightly to make himself look shorter, smaller, and slower than he actually was, right before he went apeshit over someone.

Saxon introduced the two recruits. "Anything else I can do for you, HK?"

"Thanks, John," said the woman to Saxon. There was a quality of dismissal in her tone, and Saxon nodded and left.

When they were alone, HK spent a few moments studying the two men, and they sat in silence, allowing it.

"Mr. Guidry and Mr. Redfield," she said. "It's a pleasure to meet you. Please call me HK."

"Meetcha," said Bunny.

"You here to give us some shit about what happened last week?" asked Top.

HK raised her eyebrows. "What? With Sergeant Wilkes? Ha! No. He was a racist, sexist, homophobic piece of shit, and from what John Saxon said in his report, you were within your rights."

"Don't sugarcoat it," said Bunny.

She gave them both a sunny smile. "He patted me on the ass once. I was planning on having him kneecapped anyway."

Top made a soft grunting noise and folded his arms.

"Saxon set us up," said Bunny.

"Well, that's his job, isn't it?" she countered. Then she sat back and laced her fingers together on top of the desk. "Look, guys, this isn't the Cub Scouts. You know what Blue Diamond does or you wouldn't be here. One of our field scouts pegged you as likely material, and we did a thorough background check on each of you. All the way back to kindergarten. You, Mr. Redfield—"

"Call me Buck."

"You, Buck, are a bit of a bad boy type," she continued. "Maybe playing to type? Milking the reputation?"

Bunny said nothing.

"And you, Mr. Guidry," said HK, "you make a big show of liking to sit racist pricks down on their ass, but I wonder if what you really like is the fight itself."

"You walking anywhere in the direction of a point?" asked Top.

"Right to it, then . . . sure. That's fine," said HK. "Over the last eight days, you've been tested on a lot of different weapons systems, military tactics, and threat assessment capabilities, and you each demonstrated a remarkably wide range of knowledge and comfort."

"If it goes bang or boom, we know about it," said Bunny.

"And your unarmed combat skills are several cuts above the norm. On a par with Delta. Which makes me wonder why neither of you were ever recruited by them."

"I think you know the answer to that," Top said quietly.

"Because you don't play well with others except when you want to," said HK. "And because neither of you is averse to making some unreported money on the side."

"Times are tough," said Bunny. "Economy's in the toilet."

"Oh, I'm not judging," HK said brightly. "I'm very much in favor of an entrepreneurial spirit. *We* are, to be more precise."

"'We' being Blue Diamond?" asked Top.

Her smile changed, became smaller and a bit secretive. "Consider Blue Diamond—at least this division of it—as a talent agency for very specialized services we offer to a variety of clients."

They said nothing, waiting for the other shoe.

"It's clear that you two are a cut above the usual herd," continued HK. "Your aptitude, resourcefulness, and knowledge are top-shelf and, quite frankly, you're overqualified for the kind of work most of Blue Diamond does."

"Not much I won't do for a paycheck and bennies," said Bunny. "Most employers stop reading when they get to the details of my discharge."

"We are not *most* employers," she said, again flashing that thousand-watt smile. "We are a concierge service that provides top talent to customers who need the very best. And I do mean the best. That is not sales hype, gentlemen. It's a point of fact. To keep you here at this facility would be a waste of your time and ours."

"Wait . . . are you firing us?" asked Bunny.

"Just the opposite. I want to transfer you boys to a different training camp. A place where we work with upper-tier operators like yourselves."

"This some kind of scam?" asked Top.

"No," she said, "it's really not. In fact, I'd like to put you both on a plane this afternoon."

"To where?" asked Top.

"To meet who?" asked Bunny.

"Where isn't important. You both have passports? Good. You may need them. As for who . . . well, let's just say it's someone very special."

CHAPTER 50
IN FLIGHT OVER THE IONIAN SEA

Toys sat on a leather bench seat behind an oak table as the private jet punched through the skies toward Italy.

He had a MindReader Q1 laptop open and was sipping a very good Bloody Mary while reviewing data that Church told him was "eyes only."

"You'll have access to the information Bug has been compiling," Church had told him before the flight. "We have people in the field already looking for Ledger. Violin is out there, along with others from Arklight. And a few of my old friends are keeping their eyes and ears open. Their reports are in the material I'm sharing with you."

"Have to say," Toys had told him while they were on the tarmac behind Phoenix House, "I'm surprised you agreed to letting me do this."

Church had studied him for a long three count before saying, "You've had plenty of opportunities to betray my trust. You haven't. You've had opportunities to refuse some of the wet work jobs I've sent your way. You did not."

"What's that make me? A well-trained spaniel?"

"No," said Church, offering his hand, "it means that you're part of the family."

They shook hands, and Toys had turned away quickly, nearly running to the plane because he absolutely did not want Church to see his expression. To see the shock. To see the tears.

Now he was on his way.

Toys was impressed by how much data had been collected, and he was already seeing some patterns emerge. And it was a rather ugly pattern. Ledger was moving like a plague through the technologies and weapons black markets. Not counting the slaughter in Croatia, Bug estimated that the body count was somewhere around forty.

"Well, mate," he said to the photo of Joe Ledger on his screen, "you're throwing a wobbly and no mistake. Bloody hell."

He finished his drink and hit the bell to call the cabin steward to make another. The steward was a slender young chap with the most beautiful eyes. Toys was the only passenger aboard the jet and liked seeing the way the steward moved. Like a dancer. Very tasty. But, alas, there was no time for recreation. It was a short flight, and once he was on the ground, there would be no time for anything but work.

He gave the lad his very best smile as he accepted the new Bloody Mary, then forced himself to go back to the screen. To the horrors. And to doors Toys was very sure he could open if he applied just the right leverage.

CHAPTER 51
CHAMBLEY-BUSSIÈRES AIR BASE
NEAR METZ, FRANCE
FOUR WEEKS AGO

There are few jobs as deeply tedious as patrol shifts on a military base.

Marcel Chaufour was convinced of that. He'd thought it through over many a long night as he paced along the geometry of his prescribed route. Sometimes he was with another airman, often the lout Anton, who seldom used two words when one would serve, and who smelled of bean farts and cigarettes. Marcel preferred his particular friend, Gerard, who was chatty and funny and actually read, which allowed the two mates to have long, involved conversations about politics—they were both centrists, Marcel leaning left and Gerard tilting right; and books—Gerard preferred contemporary crime writers like Antonin Varenne and Pierre Lemaitre, while Marcel liked the nineteenth-century horror authors such as Petrus Borel, Théophile Gautier, and Guy de Maupassant. They liked the same music— mid-twentieth-century American jazz—but could never agree on poetry, which allowed for some truly satisfying arguments.

Tonight, though, Marcel was walking alone, patrolling in the new captain's staggered pattern. That meant the sentries were spaced out so that, while there was always someone in line of sight, fewer men could walk a larger grid. More cost-cutting. Which meant hours trapped in his own thoughts. Well-formed opinions are a burden when there is no one to share them with.

The base was a large one and had once been used by the United States Air Force and as a front-line installation during the Cold War. But the Soviets had never tried to march into France, and the Americans left in 1967, the year Marcel's father was born. Since then, it had been the sole property of the Armée de l'Air, and more recently, much of the base had been redeveloped as a commercial business park. Military staff were reduced constantly, though the place was still technically a military airfield. Sort of. The most exciting thing that happened on the base was the Lorraine Mondial Air Ballons,

Europe's grandest hot air balloon festival. That was only every other year, though, and this wasn't the year.

And so, Marcel Chaufour was profoundly bored.

What would have been nice would be a transfer to the *other* team, to the mixed group of airmen and soldiers working underground. One hundred meters below the groundskeeper's barn and under part of the biomedical research center was the *lab*. A very secret lab that had no official name and did not, according to the detailed maps of the air base, exist at all.

One of those oh-so-clever hide-in-plain-sight facilities in which the government does all sorts of unspeakable stuff. This one, a close friend had confided in him five pints into a Friday night, had been built by the Agence de l'Innovation de Défense. France's answer to the American DARPA—Defense Advanced Research Projects Agency. The people who invented things like the bloody internet, Siri, and GPS. He knew that the French, being much smarter than the Yanks, must be doing something on the level of *Star Trek*. Not the original series, but something like *Discovery* or *Picard*. Sleek and sophisticated, where function is in harmony with form.

That thought pleased him, because it was proof the three semesters at university were not, as his father so often said, wasted.

But he wasn't on that detail. A place like that was not patrolled by regular airmen like he was. He was not supposed to even be aware of it, and the fact that he did was probably a capital crime.

Even so, it must be interesting to work there, he thought. Just to stroll around and look here, or there, or in there. It would be so great.

But . . .

It was such a long evening that he actually prayed for an interruption. A truck delivery, perhaps. That would be nice, because verifying papers and inspecting cargo could nicely chew up half an hour. More if it was a small convoy bringing supplies in for one of the commercial properties. And there was a redhead who drove one of those trucks, and Marcel was sure he could get her number or email address given another opportunity.

He was on his third circuit and wondering if he could get leave to go take a piss—the third cup of coffee was probably a poor decision before patrol—when he saw headlights bumping over the road.

JONATHAN MABERRY

"Yes," he said aloud.

He headed over to the gate, which was part of his patrol zone, and stood close to the corporal working the booth. Paul was not a friend, but friendly enough. One of those older fellows who joined the military after a failed marriage, with the simple plan of letting someone else run his life henceforth. A bit dull, but always up on the latest football scores.

"What's coming in?" asked Marcel as he leaned on the rail by the open booth door.

The corporal frowned down at a clipboard. "Mmmm, says here 'decorative foliage.'"

"For whom?"

"I think for the little common area they're building. Goes in the barn."

"Odd," said Marcel, "they've not even finished the hardscaping on that. Isn't it too soon for plants?"

"The hell should I know?" groused Paul. "I grew up in Paris. I don't think I ever saw a tree or shrub until I enlisted."

He stepped past Marcel and made that hand-patting gesture that told a driver to slow down and stop. The lorry was a big one, and Marcel wondered how many damned shrubs they had ordered. Or did someone screw up and send a big lorry like this instead of a more appropriately sized van?

The driver was a very pretty woman, and Marcel perked up. She was petite, blond, very nice to look at. A bit like that actress from the comic book movie. The one with the baseball bat and too much lipstick. Marcel could not fish her name out of his head. His knowledge of American cinema was only marginally better than what he knew about British film. He was okay with the Italians, but mostly the retro stuff. This driver, though, could have fit into the old sixties and seventies *giallo* films. Or maybe a young Catherine Deneuve, but with a punk finish.

Marcel watched the woman hand an ID card to Paul, give only a slight uptilt of her nose at Paul's leering smile, pop chewing gum very loudly, take her card back, and drive in through the gate.

Marcel smoked a cigarette with Paul, then continued his patrol. He kept thinking of the driver mostly because he could not remember the name of the actress who played in that superhero movie. The sentries were not allowed to use their cell phones on patrol, so he couldn't do a search. And, eventually, he forgot about the actress, the driver, and the truck.

His memory was triggered when the truck drove out ninety-four minutes later, and then it vanished again.

What really made every detail of that woman and that truck was when all the lights on the base flashed on, a dozen sirens blared, and military police swarmed through in riot gear. For the next three days, Marcel—along with Paul and everyone on patrol or guard duty that night—sat in rooms while teams of investigators screamed questions at him.

They did not actually explain things outright, but over time, by piecing together bits of different questions, he worked it out. The truck drove in using false ID. It parked behind the biomedical research center. A gate was lowered, and two forklifts were offloaded—and later found abandoned—and then used to remove tons of vital and highly classified machines, computer mainframes, and other unspecified materials.

INTERLUDE 11
SALES PRESENTATION VIA SHOWROOM
TWO MONTHS AGO

Mr. Sunday had a somewhat larger group of buyers online today. So many that he had his team bring in two mobile racks of monitors so that he was able to give a sales pitch to faces on eighty-four screens. The key was to make sure none of them could see the others, and all mics were muted.

It was a rare day when there were no women among the potential clients. He found that disappointing. He was an equal-opportunity vendor.

"Gentlemen, so delighted that you could join us. And . . . so many. You can't see all the smiling faces, but I can. Well . . . maybe not smiling yet, but I can guar-un-teee that I'll have you all grinning by the time I'm done."

A few of the faces were smiling. Most were a mix of first-time buyers who were either scowling, frowning in uncertainty, or wearing their best poker faces. Sunday was not fooled. He could read their eyes and none of them would have accepted his invitation had it not been for the teasers in the auto-deleted sales prospectus he'd sent along with the invitation.

That had been a fun piece of work, and Sunday used a top music video editor to make the blink-or-you-miss-it peeks at the exosuits and other goodies that were fast and sexy. He wondered what most of these men would say if they knew that film editor was Black. Sunday loved his little jokes.

Not that every face on the screens was white. There were Black and brown faces, too. Not as many, but they were every bit as radicalized, every bit as committed to their causes. When viewed from any objective distance all these men were cut from the same essential cloth. Us, not them. Our way, not anyone else's.

Zealotry was Sunday's oldest friend.

"I'm here to offer you a chance to get in on the ground floor of what will—without any *chance* of a doubt—be the biggest damned thing that's ever happened in the U.S. of A. Something that will change the political landscape and return power to the people—to *your* people. Now, my fellow patriots," he said, "let's talk about how to take back America."

CHAPTER 52
BLUE DIAMOND TRAINING CAMP
CADDO MILLS, TEXAS

The window in HK's office looked out on green trees standing like a wall around a training area. Men and women wearing full gear and backpacks filled with rocks jogged by. Some puffed and sweated and lagged, but most moved with the oiled efficiency of machines. Even among those, there were a handful who seemed to be untouched by the exertions of a ten-mile run with over a hundred pounds of weight, and over uneven and treacherous terrain.

Each of the fittest and most elite of the Fixers, and the men all wore beards, though some were still new and scraggly. Growing beards was required for this operation, and the length and cut would be determined later. Nearly all of them had tattoos of various kinds—military, patriotic, some prison ink, and a lot of symbology ranging from a dozen variations of *Don't Tread on Me* to KKK images, Nazi party images and codes, and flags tied to different political ideologies. Some of the skin art had been in place long before the recruiters like John Saxon scouted them, but a lot was new. It made for a strange mix, because a white man with a Klan tattoo of a burning cross jogged next to a Black man with an Antifa symbol. They joked as they ran. In one of the tents, a group of tattoo artists were at work, day and night.

They ran past the repurposed middle school, directly beneath HK's window, and then along a series of trails that took them outside the compound and through the woods.

They passed under thousands of pine trees. But as alert and trained as they all were, and as sharp as the drill sergeants were, not one of them saw the shrouded figure high in the boughs. None of them felt the invisible crosshairs touching them over the hearts or between the shoulder blades.

The group ran past a crumbling old shack that had been abandoned by a failed logging company thirty years ago. A row of birds stood on the eaves, their heads turning as the men and women went by. None of the soldiers peeled off to check the shack, and even if they had, they would have needed to lift a section of rotted floor to find where Andrea crouched, covered in a tarp, head bowed over a MindReader screen on which the video feeds from two of the birds played out. Each time a face came into focus, Andrea took a screenshot and fed it to the facial recognition software.

The Fixers ran on.

Belle and Andrea might not have even existed for all they were aware of them.

JONATHAN MABERRY

CHAPTER 53
FREETECH RESEARCH AND DEVELOPMENT OFFICE
SAN DIEGO, CALIFORNIA

"This feels weird."

Junie Flynn sat on a park bench with Rudy Sanchez. Birds by the hundred chattered in the trees. Sunlight filtered through the canopy of softly shifting leaves, dappling everything with lemon drops. Across from the bench was a big field where crews were inflating gorgeously colored hot air balloons. A dozen were already lifting off the ground, their colors almost glowing against a flawless canvas of blue sky.

"I agree," said Rudy. "Would you like a different background? Here, let me see if I can change it."

"I don't want anything, Rudy," said Junie. "Just us talking is fine."

The park, the trees, the birds, the sunlight, and the blue sky shimmered and then winked out. Junie was immediately back in her office at FreeTech. Rudy was still there, sitting now on a chair that seemed to fade out at the edges so that it had no legs and an incomplete back. He shimmered, too, but otherwise remained.

"ORB technology," he said with a disdainful sniff. "Everyone else seems to love it, but I guess I'm like you. It disturbs my sense of order."

"Rudy," said Junie, diving right in, "I've called Mr. Church I don't know how many times, and I always get the same answer. 'Colonel Ledger is on an extended field op and has gone dark for security reasons.' Or some variation on that."

"Yes, I know," said Rudy with a sigh.

"And now Toys is gone."

"Gone?"

"He said he wanted to look into something and then, *poof*, he vanishes from the face of the earth. I tried to get in touch with Top and Bunny, but apparently, they're on an operation, too. God, Rudy, you have to give me *something*. Like . . . since you're there, can you talk to Church? I thought I was in the inner circle, but he, Scott Wilson, and the others have closed me out. It's not right, and it's not fair. I don't need to know every detail, but at least someone should be able to tell me if Joe is all right." Junie paused and looked into Rudy's eyes. "Can *you* tell me something?"

Rudy looked uncomfortable, even pained.

"I can tell you some things I discussed with Church before I set up this call. And, quite frankly, I read him the riot act for closing you out like this. Church, as you know, is a man more concerned with fighting the war than dealing with the human emotions of the people on the field and—more to your point—on the sidelines."

Junie leaned forward, her fists knotted together in her lap. "Rudy . . . is Joe alive?"

"Yes," said Rudy, managing what looked like a careful smile. "He is alive."

Junie closed her eyes for a long moment, taking very slow and very deep breaths.

"Is he hurt?" she asked, looking once more at him. "Is that what this is? Is Joe in some hospital somewhere with half his face torn off or a bullet in him? What is it this time? I can tell something's wrong."

"As far as I know, he is not injured. Not physically."

"What's that supposed to mean?" Then she paused. Two vertical lines appeared between her brows. "This is about Christmas Eve, isn't it?"

"Yes, I'm afraid it is."

"*What* is it, though? Some kind of PTSD because of what happened?"

"PTSD is the very least of it," said Rudy, his rich baritone voice filled with cracks. "Listen to me, Junie, you know that Joe is who he is because of trauma. The horrors inflicted on him and his girlfriend, Helen, when they were fourteen destroyed much of the person he'd been before that. You know that this trauma created fractures in his psyche that resulted in the emergences of a number of limited-dimension shadow personalities. Many of them at first, and since he and I began our therapy, that number was reduced to three."

"Yes, the Modern Man, the Cop, and the Warrior."

"Correct. The Modern Man is the closest to who Joe might have become had his life not been so profoundly overshadowed by what

JONATHAN MABERRY

happened at age fourteen and then again later when he found Helen after her suicide."

Junie nodded. She knew that the suicide had also done considerable damage to Rudy, because Helen was the first of his patients to take her own life.

"The Cop shadow self is the one that gives him the balance, the pragmatism that allows him to function in day-to-day life but that collects and refines his acquired skills in ways that made him an excellent police officer and later detective. He tries to be the Cop every minute of every day of his professional life. You've seen that aspect of him, but I suspect you are most in love with the affable, somewhat goofy Modern Man—that lover of rare steaks, craft beer, Hawaiian shirts, and baseball."

Junie smiled despite the stress, and she nodded, then added, "But I love *all* of him."

"Is that really true, though? You mentioned his third shadow self, the Killer, but you used the older nickname Joe had for that aspect when you called him the Warrior. In truth, I believe the Warrior part of him was really an extension of the Cop self, in the same way that a pragmatic policeman who tries to prevent or investigate crimes might be required to draw his weapon and even take a life. The Cop is the true Warrior—a person who studies the art and science of warfare and is sophisticated in his understanding of the often ugly things such a person is forced to do in defense of those incapable of their own protection. However, since joining the old Department of Military Sciences, his third shadow self has had cause to become far more aggressive than before. Less a warrior and more of a primal savage. Not mindless or heartless—rather the reverse; possessed of a deep and unshakable need to protect the weaker members of the tribe. In that defense, there is no limit to what the Killer would do. I have heard the slang that it is 'going to war under a black flag.'"

"Yes," she said, "Joe's tried to explain that to me. I try to correct him when he calls that self the Killer. He pretends he doesn't hear me."

"He hears you," said Rudy. "We've talked about it in therapy."

Junie thought about that, then nodded. "So what are you trying to tell me? That the Killer has gotten off the chain? That it's become his dominant personality?"

"Junie, please," said Rudy, "let's be clear . . . Joe does not suffer from multiple personality disorder. Not in any clinical sense of that diagnosis. His blend of shadow selves is unique in my experience. Joe perpetuates the three-personality verbiage, but they are really aspects of a central personality that is in great turmoil. He is plagued by self-doubts when he is not on the job and is almost inflexible when in combat. His inner certainty of right and wrong is uniquely structured, and it gives him one particular skill set that makes every other quality he possesses function with an unnatural efficiency."

"You're talking about his lack of hesitation? Isn't that one of the reasons Mr. Church hired him?"

"Yes. It's more than merely being quick-brained and having superb reflexes. Joe does not hesitate at all in combat."

"He's like that a lot," said Junie wistfully. "Ever gone shopping with him? He doesn't browse. He goes right for what he wants. And if you offer him a choice—like when we were browsing online at that place in Eureka, California, he likes—Big Fun Shirt Company—he'll go through their catalog and then straight to checkout. No thinking about it, no waffling."

"Yes, I suppose he does that."

"He's only slow and picky when buying beer. He'll spend an hour in the cold aisle at Vons or Trader Joe's." She cocked her head to one side. "But this is off point. Where are you going with all this? *Has* the Warrior or Killer or whatever taken over?"

"If it had," said Rudy, "I'd be able to sleep at night."

"Oh my god. What are you saying?"

"When his family was killed on Christmas Eve, when you were so badly injured and nearly died, I believe we witnessed the birth of a new shadow self. A *true* shadow. Not a personality with dimension, possibly not even with morals or a mission beyond revenge. Junie, he calls it 'the Darkness,' and it is so large, so powerful, so potentially dangerous to him that he begged me to find a way to get rid of it for him."

"Can you?"

Rudy shook his head. "I don't even know. We talked about it during his convalescence, and because he was unable to access this new shadow self in any meaningful way that would allow him to evaluate it or even properly describe it . . . we made very little headway."

"What do you know about it?"

Rudy paused for a long time, clearly weighing his words with care. "It is very dangerous, Junie. To Joe and to anyone—and I do mean anyone—who might get between Joe and his goal of finding and killing Rafael Santoro and Kuga."

"*And you let him go into the field?*" roared Junie.

"No, no, please," pleaded Rudy, holding his hands up, palms out. "I did everything I could to stop him. I spoke to Jane Holliday, Scott Wilson, and Church and—"

"And they all agreed?"

"No," said Rudy quickly. "Jane and Scott were totally opposed to the idea of Joe returning to active duty. Not merely in the short term but ever."

Junie stared at him, her fists clenching so tightly that her knuckles ached. "Church let him go?"

"Yes," said Rudy.

"*Why?*"

"I've asked him that question a hundred times, and I always get the same answer."

"Which is what?"

"He tells me that this is war. And that's all he'll say."

CHAPTER 54
HOTEL EDEN
ROME, ITALY

The burly fellow with the bushy mustache never saw the other man come out of the stairwell. He did not hear him come up behind him. He was entirely unaware of the man's presence until he felt the cold steel of a gun barrel press against the nape of his neck.

"Easy does it, Luigi," said the man.

"Who . . . ?"

"An old friend. Here, let me have that key card. Jolly good." The man with the gun swiped the card, turned the handle with his free hand, and then nudged the door open with the toe of his shoe. "Inside. There you go. And don't try any of your stunts on me, Luigi. You didn't take enough karate to help last time, either."

Luigi stepped inside, frowning, trying to connect the voice to a face, a name.

"Face the wall," said the man with the gun as he closed the door. "I'm going to pat you down. You know how this works. Good. Spread your feet wider. Brilliant."

The pat-down was quick but thorough, and it was very professional. The gunman removed a small Beretta from a belt clip and a switchblade from a pocket. Then he stepped back.

"You can turn around now, old son," said the gunman.

Luigi turned, and when he saw who it was, he gave a small, sharp cry. A *yip*, like a kicked poodle. He gaped, sputtered, stammered, and finally choked out a name.

"*Toys?*"

"Surprise, surprise, old chum."

Toys held his little automatic with the comfort of a professional, keeping it low and out of reach, the barrel pointed center mass.

"What the hell are you doing here?" demanded Luigi. "I thought you were dead."

"I get that a lot," said Toys. "But, no. Still a bad penny."

"What is this? Why come after me with a gun? What have I ever done to you? Are you an assassin now? Is that it?"

"Oh, settle down, Luigi," Toys said, stepping back and waving the man toward a pair of comfortable chairs by the window. "If I'd wanted you dead, you be on your way to the morgue right now. Now sit down and stop pissing your pants."

Luigi sat. Toys pulled the other chair to a safe distance and lowered himself into it.

"I need information," he said.

"I . . . I don't do that anymore," said Luigi quickly. "I'm out of that business. I swear."

Toys crossed his legs and rested the hand holding the pistol on his thigh. "I have a sound suppressor in my pocket," he said. "Shall I

JONATHAN MABERRY

screw it in place and see how many kneecaps I need to blow off before you stop telling lies?"

"No—*no!*"

"Then let's try this again. I need information. You *have* information because you always have information. You're no more out of the game than I am."

Luigi licked his lips and clutched the arms of the chair with nervous fingers.

"What kind of information?"

"Ah, there we go," said Toys, smiling. "I'm looking for a few people. Now, you're going to want to take the piss and pretend you've never heard of them. I understand why. They're scary people, and if they ever found out you were telling me anything, they would do very bad things to you. Very bad indeed. You're already starting to sweat. You never did have the stomach for this. God only knows how you got into the information trade."

Luigi stared at him.

"I will say three names," continued Toys. "You can give me a price for information. I'm willing to negotiate, and if things go well, there's a bonus on top of it. But . . . if you lie to me, or if you tell anyone I was here . . . well, really, do I need to be explicit with what those consequences might be?"

"No . . . ," whispered Luigi. Sweat really was bursting from his pores and running down his cheeks.

"Here are the names," said Toys. "Try not to shit your pants. Neither of us needs that."

Luigi wiped sweat from his eyes.

"Kuga. Otherwise known as Harcourt Bolton Sr."

Luigi stiffened as if ten thousand volts shot through him.

"Rafael Santoro."

Tears broke from Luigi's eyes.

"Joe Ledger."

Luigi put his face in his hands.

"Good," said Toys. "Clearly you know them. Now, let's have a nice little chat."

CHAPTER 55
PHOENIX HOUSE
OMFORI ISLAND, GREECE

Bug popped the top on his sixth Red Bull, tilted back, and drank a third of the can. The first five had just about helped him reboot his brain and get his mental circuits back online. Maybe the sixth would ignite some optimism, though he rather doubted it.

This was day thirty-four of what he thought of as the Big Silence. He did not like to use the nickname Doc Holliday hung on it—Days of Darkness. That made him too sad and too stressed.

It had been thirty-four days since Joe Ledger walked away from the slaughter on the small Croatian island. Thirty-four very long days.

His absence—and the events precipitating it—had spread a cloud of gloom over the entire organization. People spoke more quietly, sometimes in actual hushed voices. There was a pervasive sense of sadness. And of dread. Not specifically for the actual life of RTI's legendary senior field team leader, but because if the war could damage Ledger that badly, then who was really safe? This was an extreme form of post-traumatic stress that now seemed inevitable for all of them. The effect was evident in the lack of laughter in the mess halls, the drop in combat range scores, the overall sense of hesitancy that hadn't been there before. And it didn't help any that Top and Bunny were away on some secret mission.

Only Church seemed unmoved, though Bug doubted the boss's famous calm was genuine. Bug had been with Church longer than anyone in Rogue Team. Only Aunt Sallie knew him better, and she was retired, still going through extensive physical and occupational therapy at an ultra-high-end facility on Corfu, next to where Rudy Sanchez lived with his wife, Circe O'Tree, and their son.

There were plenty of people who loved Joe, too. Maybe not Circe, who still held him—and her father—responsible for the harm that had come to Rudy. Her husband had lost an eye and a knee because of his involvement with the old Department of Military Sciences. Injuries he would not have sustained had he not followed Joe into the group or let himself hook his star to Church's never-ending war. It was sad and disturbing.

Joe had Junie, who had also been injured badly because of her association with him. An assassin's bullet had destroyed her uterus during the Code Zero case, and she'd been impaled by flying debris when Rafael Santoro blew up the Ledger farmhouse. She still loved Joe with an intensity that often made Bug want to cry. He'd never been loved that much by a woman. Well, except his mom, but she was another casualty of the war—murdered by Sebastian Gault for the crime of being blood kin to a person working for Church.

"Ashes, ashes, we all fall down," he murmured.

Bug was alone in his office, which was a very messy anteroom to the spotless clean room in which the MindReader mainframe and supercomputers hummed relentlessly. Bug swiveled around and looked at two figures inside the room, both of them in protective white garments and safety goggles. One was the slightly hunched and emaciated figure of Yoda, his number two. The other was a woman he'd met in South Korea. A top-of-the-line super hacker named Annie Han. Originally an operative in the NIS—National Intelligence Agency's computer counterespionage or cybersecurity divisions. That was a front, though, a functional cover for her real job, which was that of cyber warfare expert for Arklight, the militant arm of the Mothers of the Fallen. A group of intensely fierce women who waged a private war against human trafficking, sex slavery, and other crimes against women and children. Now Annie was a member of RTI and of Bug's team.

She was also his girlfriend.

Not quite a lover in the truest sense of that word, though she was that in a deliciously physical way. But although Bug had fallen pretty heavily for Annie, she was more reserved and guarded with her emotions. The result, she said, of a string of truly disastrous relationships that ended very badly.

Bug had hopes, though. He hadn't had a real girlfriend in years. He knew that everyone he worked with thought he was a sexless worker bee who was secretly in love with MindReader. And Bug had encouraged that viewpoint because sharing his sadness and loneliness with his friends never felt right. Just the thought of it made him feel like a bit of a freak.

He was very much in love now, though.

But if Annie was going to fall in love with him, then she was playing a very subtle long game.

She and Yoda were in the middle of a very finicky process of stripping the Calpurnia AI system out of MindReader Q1 so that a much more efficient and intuitive system could be uploaded. It was painstaking work requiring long days. And Annie so often said how tired she was when she headed to her apartment. No accompanying invitation.

Bug sipped more of the Red Bull as data flowed across his screen. He did not hear the office door open. He heard no footfalls.

"Bug," said Mr. Church.

Bug jumped halfway out of his chair, spilling the energy drink down the front of his University of Wakanda T-shirt.

"Jesus H. T. Mortimer Christ." Bug coughed, grabbing for tissues to dab his shirt.

Church made no apology. He never did. Instead, he went around and sat down on an empty chair. He waited while Bug sopped up the spill, tossed the tissues away, and grabbed another can of Red Bull.

"Tell me where we are," said Church. "But before you answer, lock the room."

Bug tapped some keys to send a security command to his system, locking his office and engaging anti-intrusion devices built into the walls. He trusted everyone at Phoenix House, but when it came to conversations like this, Bug tended to err on the side of caution.

"Okay," he said, "where are we? Nowhere, really. Joe killed his RFID chip, which means we can't track him. And, let's face it, he knows a lot of ways to get lost."

"Give me more than what I already know."

"Okay," said Bug. "After Joe abandoned the cigarette boat in Giovinazzo, Scott thinks he went to ground somewhere in Italy. And he supports that because of the hit the other day at Civitella in Val di Chiana, Tuscany."

"And you don't buy that?" asked Church. "Even though there was an eyewitness who said they saw a tall man with a white dog near that location?"

"Yes and no. I mean, sure, I think Joe hit that place, and we can tie Alexander Fong to the Kuga group, but I think that was something Joe did when he got *back* to Italy."

"Explain."

Bug gave Church details about the hit on Van der Vyver Biomedical Associates in Johannesburg, South Africa.

"That's another place that has ties to Kuga. Now, before you tell me that a *lot* of independent labs have ties to Kuga through X number of removes, let me explain. Dr. Gerald Engelbrecht ran that lab, and he—more so than the rest of the staff—has, or rather *had*, a bunch of skeletons in his closet. He farmed out a lot of product manufacturing to sweatshops all through Malaysia and Java and a few other places. One standout is that sports equipment factory where there was that riot just recently. And by *riot*, I mean the highly suspicious one where there was *zero* cell phone footage or at-the-moment news coverage. Engelbrecht had contracts with them for what the computer records call 'orthopedic overgarments.' No idea what that is, but I'm looking into it."

"Now isn't that interesting?"

"I think so."

"And you think Ledger hit Engelbrecht in Johannesburg?"

"I do. And then he went *back* to Italy and took out Alexander Fong and his team. Left Fong alive, though. Not sure why. Killed just about everyone and everything else, up to and including the ficus trees in the damned lobby."

"You believe this despite Scott Wilson being completely convinced that Ledger was holed up in Italy, perhaps gathering intel before finally making Fong his first move."

"I'd bet a lot on it."

"So would I," said Church.

"Then we come to something I haven't shared with Scott yet. I haven't told anyone about it at all, not even you, because I wanted to dig around a little and make some educated guesses."

"Tell me now," said Church mildly.

"So, I got a heavily encrypted email from our old friend Oskar Freund."

Captain Freund was the son of one of Church's old friends from the pre-DMS days. Freund worked for the GSG 9 der Bundespolizei, a very effective police tactical unit of the German Federal Police. Officially, GSG 9 is only deployed for hostage situations, kidnapping, terrorism, and similar threats. However, there was a more elite and much more covert counterterrorism strike force within the group that had a much more flexible charter than the public thought. Freund was an investigator for them, and one who was at the top of the game. He was also an ally of Mr. Church. Another friend in the industry.

"Oh?" said Church mildly.

"Oskar received a package delivered by courier. The contents slip said, '*Kontenbuch*,' which translates as—"

"'Accounts ledger,'" finished Church, leaning a bit on the second word. "Very interesting indeed. What was in it?"

"Six four-terabyte external hard drives. The kind that can be bought at any electronics store in any of the bigger cities in South Africa. There was a Post-it note on top. Let me pull it up. You'll like this."

Bug hit some keys, and a JPEG filled the screen, showing a cell phone photo of the note. There were two simple line drawings—one of a church steeple and the other of a six-legged insect. The words *to share* written in ballpoint and clearly using a ruler to prevent any chance of handwriting analysis.

Bug grinned. "A church and a bug."

"Eloquent," murmured Church. "What's on the drives?"

"A lot. Looks like Ledger prepped it for us. There's one drive that has logistics, employee lists, and other stuff that I think he intended for Scott. There's one with a crap-ton of encrypted computer files, and I have Nikki Bloom working on it now. The rest are more of the biomechanical stuff and copies of records that I'm now positive are copies of stuff Artemisia Bliss stole from the Jakobys and the Kings. But there's some CIA stuff, too, and a bunch of DARPA research, mostly on military exoskeletons and neural chips for soldier-equipment interfaces."

"Who else knows about this?"

"Well, like I said, I have Yoda and Nikki on the encrypted files, but that's it. I wanted to talk with you first because—unless I'm reading this all wrong—you seem to be coy about who and what you're saying about Ledger since he's gone off the radar."

"Yes," said Church. He sat there, drawing slow circles on the desktop with his left index finger. "Don't misunderstand me about this, Bug," he said after a while. "There is no mistrust with anyone here at the RTI. No one is under suspicion, and they all have my highest confidence in all critical matters."

"You have 'but' face."

"Consider rephrasing that for future use," said Church, "*but* . . . I know how much resentment there is among some of the staff about my letting Ledger back into the field at all."

"Yeah, Junie tells me you're dodging her calls."

He sighed. "I am. And I've shut down discussions with Scott, Top, and some others because I don't care to explain my motivations. Rudy has already read me the comprehensive riot act for endangering Joe's mental and physical health. And he's not wrong. I am doing exactly that, but not from a lack of compassion."

"No," said Bug. "I get it. Even though we're not really answerable to the UN or any world government, ever since Oslo, we're pretty high profile. They're expecting us to be the white knights here. We can't put a foot wrong, because that ruins our credibility with governments from whom we'll need to get permissions to operate within their borders. If they know that we let Joe bugfuck nuts Ledger off the leash deliberately, every door will be shut. And we won't get stuff like this." He pointed to the screen.

Church smiled faintly. "You understand me very well, Bug."

"We've been family a long time."

"We have."

They sat in silence for a few moments. Church reached over and picked up a can of Red Bull, read the ingredients, and put it back.

"Share the data," he said. "Tell Doc and Scott that it came from me via one of my contacts. They'll know not to ask. Make sure Yoda and Nikki get the same story."

"Will do."

Church lingered. "What's your theory on this?"

"Well, I'm still leaning toward this being Kuga and Santoro giving their Fixers a serious tech upgrade. Those cats, with bleeding-edge cybernetics and exoskeletons? And maybe some drug therapy to get them all juiced? Shit, boss, I think we're in real trouble here."

Church stood. "I think we've been in real trouble for some time and are only now beginning to see the shape and scope of it."

He gave Bug's shoulder a squeeze and went out.

CHAPTER 56

THE PAVILION
BLUE DIAMOND ELITE TRAINING CENTER
STEVENS COUNTY, WASHINGTON

Top and Bunny were taken to a commercial airport in Texas where John Saxon greeted them with travel documents and first-class seats for a direct flight to Washington State.

"If we're going to Washington, why'd we need our passports?" asked Bunny.

Saxon smiled. "You're going to Washington today. Other trips are possible, and we don't want to waste time fussing over papers."

Top nodded. "Yeah, okay . . . that makes sense."

"You coming with us?" asked Bunny.

"Nah, I don't think you fellows need me to hold your hands."

He shook their hands, grinned, waved, and walked away out of the terminal building.

"Okay, then," said Bunny. Forty minutes later, they were in the air.

They had no idea if anyone else on the flight was a spook for Blue Diamond, so the two of them kept their conversation to ordinary stuff. They talked sports and old movies, but mostly they slept. Conserving energy the way professionals in their line of work do. They had one beer each but nursed them.

In Spokane, they were met at baggage claim by a thirtysomething man in a crisp white shirt buttoned to the throat and blue jeans with severely ironed creases. He held a sign that showed only the Blue Diamond logo.

"You gentlemen should hit the head because it'll be a long drive," he said. That was his only comment from the moment they met him until he dropped them off at a checkpoint in the middle of nowhere, deep in Stevens County. The checkpoint was manned by two men dressed in military-style forest-pattern camo uniforms. The drive had taken more than three hours, and from the route, it was clear the driver was deliberately changing roads and even backtracking. Wary of surveillance.

At the gate, both guards wore masks that covered their features, and carried Sig Sauer MCX Rattler assault weapons.

　　　　　　　　　　　　　　　　　　　　　　　JONATHAN MABERRY

The gate was set in a forest clearing and was the only part of the fence that was easily visible. From what they could see, the fence was high and wrapped in razor wire. A road led from the checkpoint, and it curved out of sight within a dozen yards. No other buildings were visible from where they stood.

Top and Bunny were asked to get out of the car, show their IDs, and to log in to a terminal using thumbprints and retina scans. This didn't bother either of them, because Bug and MindReader had long since gamed the system. Their false identities were unbreakable, and all traces of who they had been were long since erased entirely from hospital, school, military, and other databases. The tapeworm search-and-destroy programs Bug wrote were hungry and thorough.

However, Top acted as if he didn't understand how the thumbprint scanner worked. He kept putting the wrong finger on the pad or missed the pad entirely.

Bunny laughed. "How old *are* you, dude? You just put your freaking thumb on the freaking pad. It's not rocket science."

"I don't like gadgets," complained Top.

The guard overseeing the scan looked amused and gave Bunny a knowing wink, more or less saying, *Old guys.*

Once the scan was complete, Top and Bunny were told to wait near the guard shack. No one bothered to check the scanner housing, and even if they had, they might not have noticed anything odd. Only a very close examination would reveal a very small dot of plastic stuck to the underside of the machine. The dot had been on the pad of Top's left forefinger, and when he touched it to the device while bending over to frown and cuss at the machine, the reactive chemicals scanned and mimicked the exact color of the housing. When he held on to the scanner while finally placing his thumb in the right place, Top transferred the chameleon scanner to the housing. It was a bit of sleight of hand he'd done many times before. The scanner was a marvel of design, developed years ago by Dr. Hu and updated by techs working for Doc Holliday and Bug.

Within six seconds, the microcircuitry in the wafer-thin dot was opening a door to allow MindReader to waltz in. The super-intrusion software around which MindReader was built instantly picked all the encryption locks built into the Blue Diamond security system. At the same time, it rewrote the target software to erase all traces of the intrusion and its lingering presence. No one at the camp would raise an alarm because nothing within the security system recognized the intrusion.

While they waited, Top and Bunny glanced briefly around. The camp looked rustic, but their security was not. The guards wore a slightly different uniform from the ones they'd seen in Texas. Camo with a slightly darker color scheme, appropriate for the denser woodlands here in Washington State. No insignias except for small blue diamond-shaped patches on the shoulders. The cut was better, suggesting individual tailoring rather than off the rack, and these men had sharper eyes and unsmiling mouths. Observant professionals. And yet Top's tomfoolery with the scanner had tricked them. That suggested a bit of arrogance over the professionalism. Top and Bunny both thought it was useful to know.

Colonel Ledger had a theory about that. Or, perhaps, an observation. He called it the "arrogance of power"—when the strong and abusive assume the weaker potential prey were inarguably easy targets *because* they were weaker. It was the assumption used by so many rapists, child abusers, muggers, and similar predatory monsters. Gangs often made the same assumptions. And, in the absence of training, natural or acquired confidence, or preparedness, they were often right. But—just as the larger male lions learn to their peril when trying to bully the lionesses with cubs—underestimation can backfire quickly.

It also led to habits of inattention, and that's what Top and Bunny both hoped would be at work here. This was, after all, an elite camp. Lots of testosterone, lots of predators thinking with their biceps, sidearms, and contempt.

Bunny caught Top's eye, and they shared a tiny, knowing smile.

A golf cart came whisking silently up, and they climbed into the back. The driver was every bit as chatty as a potted plant. As soon as they were seated, he set off along the road. They made sure to look around at everything, partly to collect intel for themselves and partly to make sure the tiny body cams they wore picked up useful data for Bug.

As they drove, Scott Wilson began speaking quietly in their ears, his voice as clear as if he were in the cart with them rather than on an island six thousand miles away.

"This is rather exciting," said Wilson. "We had no idea this camp even existed. None of the Fixers we, ah, *interviewed* ever mentioned or even hinted about it. Be aware, lads, that it will take a bit of time to arrange for drone flyovers, so try not to get into trouble."

Top casually tapped the lowest button on his shirt, signaling the affirmative.

"Jackpot and Mother Mercy are inbound and will be on station within three hours. Jackpot has his whole bag of tricks with him, including bird drones appropriate to that region."

Another tap.

"And if you're asked to change clothes," continued Wilson, "we can attune the drones to your RFID chips. We won't lose *you* chaps." Leaning a little on that, another of the thousand subtle ways each of them was reminded of Joe Ledger.

Top gave another tap.

The path through the woods was not long but was made up of deliberate switchbacks so that screens of old-growth trees foiled any chance of visual surveillance from the ground. The dense canopy of pine needles hid the road from the air. Smart and effective. A camp like this *couldn't* be found by accident or even through normal flyover surveillance. You had to know it was there.

Their silent driver passed through another checkpoint with an even sturdier gate and then entered a compound made up of many small one-story buildings draped with camouflage netting. Even the outside areas used for drills were under a canopy. No smoke from cooking fires or heaters, which meant they probably used electric or propane. And, as they got out of the cart, they saw a row of industrial generators chugging away.

"Nice place," Bunny said to the driver, but got no response. "You're a regular Chatty Cathy."

The man stared into the middle distance, still behind the wheel. When they stepped away from the cart, he drove off. That left the two of them standing a dozen yards inside the gate. They dropped their bags and waited for the next play.

CHAPTER 57
HAMLET OF ARBATAX
TORTOLÌ, PROVINCE OF NUORO
SARDINIA, ITALY

Bruno Melis was one hundred and three years old and still had most of his teeth, his eyesight, and a memory that stretched back to before his days as a pilot in World War II. His wife of eighty years, Maria, was fourteen months in her grave, bless the Virgin Mary. Angelo, Bruno's youngest son, was seventy-seven and still walked with his father two miles every afternoon to split their daily bottle of wine in Enoteca Mirai, which had been in his wife's family since the days when Catalan conquerors ruled the entire island of Sardinia. Bruno had seen a century's worth of history.

But he had never seen anything like what happened at the house of the banker who lived on the hill overlooking the Tyrrhenian Sea. Bruno's own house—much more modest than the banker's, though large by the standards of Arbatax—was on a promontory and offered a view over a part of the southern wall into the banker's rear garden. On many an evening, Bruno had seen the banker—a man known only by the surname of Otranto—receive guests after banking hours. He knew they were guests and not friends because there were handshakes but no embraces, no laughter, no bottles of wine drunk as the sun set and the stars above ignited like God's party lights.

People spoke in whispers about those guests because they nearly always arrived by boat around twilight and left in the dead of night. Few ever stayed the night at Otranto's house, and none ever stayed in the town. They came quietly and left quietly, and no one ever knew their names. They were unusual visitors. Most were clearly not Sardinian or even Italian. There were Asian and African visitors, and others dressed in clothes more like what people wore on TV shows from England or America. Or Russia.

To Bruno and his small circle of friends, it was clear these visitors were there to do business, and business of a kind not conducted at the bank offices or in bistros or *enoteche* like normal and respectable people did.

But Otranto never caused a problem, nor did his guests. They came, they did whatever business they did, and they left. Always quiet, always discreet. And life went on.

Then the man arrived on a small boat. A man dressed all in black and accompanied by a very large white dog. Bruno saw the boat come motoring to a deserted section of beach just as the last of the day's light was dying like embers on the wave tops. Despite his age, Bruno saw very well, and besides, his great-great-grandson had sent him a very fine telescope four Christmases ago. For bird-watching and star-gazing, the boy had said; though everyone in the family knew that Bruno was a little bit of a snoop. That was not how he saw himself, of course. He considered himself a people-watcher, a perpetual student of human activity. Otranto was merely one of the people he watched, because Bruno was intrigued by the clandestine nature of those secret backyard meetings.

He spotted the man nearly by accident, and had he gone inside a few minutes sooner to use the bathroom, he would not have seen him at all. However, one of the benefits of being very old was that he didn't need to use the bathroom with any real urgency anymore. When he got there, it would be time enough.

So, he saw the big man and the big dog get out of the black boat. Bruno watched him through his Kowa spotting scope as the man unzipped a duffel bag and removed a kind of suit of armor that looked like what the Nucleo Operativo Centrale di Sicurezza wore on news stories about dangerous police raids. Body armor. The man also put on a helmet and a strange pair of oversize goggles. Then he removed weapons from the bag. Handguns and a rifle, but Bruno did not know modern makes and models. After the war—*his* war of more than seventy-five years ago—Bruno had only ever used a shotgun, and that was for rabbits. He could not remember the last time he'd even held a firearm—1970, perhaps, or a few years later. The guns he saw through his telescope looked like something from TV or one of those movies about Special Forces. Ugly things, lacking any aesthetics.

Bruno watched him attach some of the armor around the dog's body and even a kind of skullcap over the dog's head, but which left the animal's eyes, ears, and snout free. It was a strange thing to watch. Very much like television. And nearly as entertaining, though it also filled him with a growing sense of unease. There were no movie cameras down there on the beach.

His unease grew as the man left the beach and hiked, with his dog, up a sheep path into the hills toward Otranto's compound. For nearly five full minutes, Bruno argued with himself about whether to call the police. But a voice—very much that of his late wife—spoke in his head and told him not to get involved.

"Ad Arbatax è arrivata l'oscurità," the ghost of his wife seemed to whisper.

A darkness has come to Arbatax.

He thought about that for a long time as the man and dog climbed the steep hill.

A darkness.

The echo of those words through his mind seemed to pull the lingering heat of the day out of his world, leaving Bruno Melis cold and frightened.

So he watched and made no call. Not even to his son, who lived not half a kilometer from where he sat.

The shadows of night swallowed the man entirely, and for nearly twenty minutes, there was nothing to see. Bruno even began wondering if senility was finally, after all these years, catching up with him. He was the fifth-oldest person currently living in Arbatax, a town known for centenarians, and there were seventeen people over a hundred who were younger than he was. Some had lost their faculties, but he had not. A fact he ascribed to his daily walks, his daily crossword puzzles, and the wine he shared with his son.

He sat on his little stool and peered into the scope and tried to calculate the rate of climb for the man and where he might reappear among the rocks and shrubs.

Bruno's estimate was correct nearly to the minute. The dog emerged from the broom shrubs forty meters from Otranto's garden wall. By now, it was full dark, and the patio lights were burning behind the big house. Otranto himself was smoking a cigar as he strolled along the flagstones in his yard, speaking on a cell phone while two of his men—Bruno assumed they were bodyguards of some kind—stood watching, silent as statues.

The flash of gunfire sparked through the night, but Bruno did

JONATHAN MABERRY

not hear the echo of shots. Through the excellent lens of his scope, he saw that the pistol the big man held had some kind of silencer on it. Fire spat from the barrel, but even as the two bodyguards fell, Otranto—looking the other way as he talked on his phone—did not appear to hear.

Then the dog rushed past the man and dragged Otranto down, savaging his arm. Not trying to kill him, though, that much was clear. The big man went into the house while the dog stood guard like Cerberus over the bleeding Otranto. There were many flashes inside the house, and the reports of guns—not silenced ones—bounced up the hills toward Bruno. Then a window exploded outward, and another burly man went flying out and landed badly on the flagstones. After a while—was it thirty seconds or a full minute?—silence and stillness fell over the house of Otranto.

Soon the big man came back out of the house carrying an armful of computer laptops, which he placed on the patio. He waved his dog away and knelt by the banker. Bruno was not sure whether he wished he could have heard the conversation that followed or not. Maybe not. He watched, though, riveted to his seat, unable to look away.

Until the knife came out.

After that, Bruno turned away, appalled, sickened. He pressed one hand to his chest, sure that his old heart was going to burst. With the other, he crossed himself and said a prayer to the Madonna. Over and over again, as sweat beaded his face and the world seemed to swim around him.

Then, finally, he summoned the courage to turn back to his telescope and look down at the patio.

And this time, his heart nearly did freeze.

The big man stood above a red ruin of a thing that had once been Otranto. The man was not looking at the dead banker. Nor at the fallen guards or even the house. No . . . the big man was looking up the hill, toward the promontory on which Bruno Melis sat. The goggles were off and the balaclava, too. The big man had blond hair that was soaked with sweat and plastered to his scalp. He was unshaven and hollow-eyed.

But he was looking directly at Bruno.

There was no way he could see that far without at least binoculars, and Bruno sat in the utter blackness of his unlighted backyard. He had not even gone inside to turn on the kitchen light.

The man, though, seemed to see him anyway.

There was something wrong about the way he stood, about the way he looked. It was as if Bruno were seeing a cutout of a man pasted badly onto the moment. Shadows seemed to cling to the man, though he was not near enough to the house or the garden wall for any shadow to fall across him.

The man looked at Bruno and gave a single, slow nod.

And then he turned, picked up the stack of laptops, stuffed them into an empty backpack, slung the pack, gestured to his dog, and left.

Bruno did not watch them go back down the hill.

No. By then, he was in his house, the doors locked and windows closed. Bruno sat by the cold hearth clutching his wife's crucifix to his chest. Praying.

What surprised him, though, was that he was not praying for his own immortal soul, nor the souls of the people he had just watched die.

For some reason he could never thereafter explain to himself, his son, his friends, or the police, he prayed for the soul of that stranger. He prayed far into that night.

INTERLUDE 12
THE PAVILION
BLUE DIAMOND ELITE TRAINING CENTER
STEVENS COUNTY, WASHINGTON
FOUR MONTHS AGO

"This is the target," said Eve.

The twelve Fixers—known around the Pavilion as the Righteous—stood in a loose half circle around Eve. Behind where she stood was a trifold set of portable monitors, each seven feet high and capable of 4096 × 2160 pixel density, giving the images incredible clarity. The images being shown were also manipulated by a program that made sure that the central figure on each screen remained exactly the same height—actual height for the star of those video files. At first, watching that was a bit jarring, but the eye and the mind adjusted quickly.

All three monitors featured the same person. A bit over six feet tall, blond-haired, and blue-eyed. Very fit and, as the file display speed was not in any way adjusted, clearly very fast. Whether fighting with a blade, a gun, or his hands, he seemed to blur at times.

One of the Fixers raised a hand.

"Miss Eve," he said, "is that Mr. Stafford?"

Michael Augustus Stafford had been a lecturer briefly there at the Pavilion a few months back.

Eve blinked in surprise and turned to look at the image.

"Huh," she said, "you know, I never noticed the similarities before but . . . damn, you're right. They could almost be brothers. But Stafford's better-looking."

A few of the men chuckled, the rest did not.

"No, campers," she continued, stabbing a finger toward the center screen, "this is Colonel Joe Ledger. Some of you know him, but mostly by reputation. Or going to funerals of friends of yours he killed."

That got a few nods and some glares.

"He is the number-one pain in the ass of Kuga and Daddy . . . I mean, Rafael Santoro. He and his team have been fucking with them since long before they put this new organization together."

She rattled off what amounted to Joe Ledger's greatest hits, giving them the official case code names lifted a couple of years ago during a hack of the DMS records. Patient Zero and the Seif al Din pathogen. The Jakobys and the Dragon Factory. The Seven Kings and the Sea of Hope. The Assassin's Code and the Red Knights.

On and on.

"And then last year, they barged into our Rage operation and nearly spoiled everything."

One of the Fixers said, "I heard that he messed up Mr. Santoro pretty bad."

Eve turned toward him very slowly, and the look in her eyes was so venomous that he actually recoiled a step.

"Daddy *won* that fight," she snarled.

"Hey, I didn't mean nothing; I was just—"

"You were just sticking your dick in your own mouth is what you were doing." But then Eve caught sight of HK across the room, watching the session. It was like a cup of cold water on a burn. Eve took a breath and made herself focus. As Daddy so often said, *When emotions rule your thoughts and words and actions, then you are their slave.*

She forced a smile onto her face. Cold, and fragile, but it held.

"Do you want to know what else Ledger did?" she asked, impressed at how reasonable her voice now sounded. She reached down and tapped the knee brace she wore. "He put his gun to my knee while I was helpless and shot me. I'm going to have the entire knee replaced, and at my age, that means it'll wear out in maybe ten years and I'll have to get another, and another, another. So it'll be like him shooting me over and over again."

One of the men—Spiro—breathed, "Damn."

The Fixer who'd made the comment about Santoro straightened. "Tell you what, Miss Eve, you point me in his direction, and I'll cut his balls off and have them put in one of those acrylic paperweights and give that to you gift wrapped. How's that?"

She walked over to him. The man was easily eleven inches taller than she was, so she had to reach up to pat his cheek. One pat, another, and then a sharp crack of a slap. But she smiled as she slapped him, and he understood. He grinned down at her.

Eve turned to look at them all.

"We have a lot of footage of Joe Ledger in combat. We know what kinds of martial arts he's studied. We know he prefers a Wilson Rapid Release folding knife, and we know he's a much better shot with a handgun than a long gun. We know that one of his most dangerous skills is a rare and complete lack of hesitation. We know he isn't fancy, no moves that are there for style rather than effect. That makes him an apex predator in our line of work." She paused. "You twelve were picked because you have similar backgrounds and skill sets. However, you need to up the game and tilt the odds in your favor by becoming completely familiar with him. His body, his movements, his speed and power. *Know* him. Become him so that if

JONATHAN MABERRY

you ever meet him, he'll be facing his own skill set *and* yours. That, boys, is the edge."

They nodded. One or two looked mildly apprehensive or skeptical, and Eve took note of that. The rest looked merely ready to learn.

"One last thing," she said. "From this moment on, you're going to stop being who you were, and you'll become *my* team. I'll give you new combat call signs, and you'll use them 24–7 from now on. Spiro, you're Cain. Bobby, you're Abel." She gave them each a biblical first name. "You answer to me and only me. Is that understood?"

"Yes, ma'am!" they shouted.

"That means you'll do whatever I say whenever I say it. No arguments, no complaints, no questions. Is *that* understood?"

"Yes, ma'am!"

"You'll still be Fixers, but you are *my* Fixers. You're the Righteous. Let me hear you say that and mean it."

"We are the Righteous," they said, tripping only slightly on that.

"No, boys, say it like you mean it," said Eve, giving them a dazzling smile. "Say it like you *love* me."

"We are the *Righteous*!" they roared.

And each and every one of them said it like they loved her.

CHAPTER 58
VAN DIJK BIOMECHANICA
ROTTERDAM, THE NETHERLANDS

The barking dog woke him.

And nearly killed him.

The man saw the headlights coming toward him without any understanding of where he was or why he was driving.

Reflexes took over. No hesitation, no panic.

His hands moved on the wheel, one foot on the brake, the other on the gas. Adjusting, compensating, avoiding by inches. The Doppler wail of the truck horn scolding him as the semi blew past, rocking the car.

Then the road ahead was clear. No oncoming nights. Nothing at all except a wash of pale moonlight over the asphalt and headlights on road signs.

They were all in Dutch. Well . . . Dutch and English.

That made no sense. Why were Italian road signs in Dutch?

He slowed to a stop and looked around. He was on a country road. Two lanes. The billboard beside advertised a Burger King four kilometers away, but the street address was in Rotterdam.

"What the fuck?" he whispered.

In the back seat, the dog barked again. Just once. A hungry bark.

The man realized that he was hungry, too. Starving, actually.

With only that as a destination, he stepped on the gas and drove.

He remembered ordering food. Remembered opening three burgers for Ghost. Remembered eating while sitting in a darkened parking lot of a closed factory.

Thoughts drifted out of the shadows, and he grabbed at them, hoping to puzzle them together, to form some kind of picture. Hoping for coherence and cohesion, for insight.

He remembered faces and names. Some of them. Engelbrecht, Bishlow, Fong, Orlando, Barbaneagra, Kaschak, Jones. Others.

Names belonging to dead faces. No. Not all. Some, he was certain, were still alive. Had that been circumstance or mercy? He couldn't be sure. Not on any level of his awareness.

And information. So much of it. Cybernetics, chemical therapies, something called a K-110, militia groups, explosives, implants, chips. Something else, too. He spoke that last thing aloud.

"The American Operation."

Hearing it aloud triggered something, but not the right thing. No details. Merely dread.

"The American Operation," he said again and looked at Ghost as if the dog were able to fill in the details. Ghost looked up from a burger that he was eating with great delicacy, and for a moment, those dark brown eyes softened. Became wet. Which made his own eyes burn with unshed tears.

"What's happening to me?" asked the man. "What's happening to us?"

Suddenly, there was nothing else in the conscious part of his mind as the darkness inside overwhelmed the darkness outside the car.

He did not notice the hundreds of night birds lined up along the edges of the building's roof or strung out along the telephone lines.

CHAPTER 59
HAMLET OF ARBATAX
TORTOLÌ, PROVINCE OF NUORO

Michael Augustus Stafford walked slowly through the ruins of the mansion on the cliff.

Everything that could break appeared to have been deliberately and viciously smashed. The furniture was slashed, as were the expensive paintings on the wall. He paused in front of a rather nice modernist painting by Dino Basaldella that had to have sold for north of fifty thousand. Now it was tatters. Worthless to anyone. And a number of Auguste Moreau bronzes, each of them signed, were broken or bent out of shape. Clearly, they had been used to do some of the damage in the room. And some of the damage to the staff.

The bodies of the victims were all gone now, but Stafford had photos on his cell phone to match against the dried bloodstains on the carpet, tiles, and walls. Hundreds of shell casings still littered the floor, and bullet holes pocked every possible surface. One round had punched a neat hole through a blue-and-white Yuan dynasty vase without shattering the whole thing. A low-caliber, high-powered round, he judged. He had a couple of boxes of Stinger 22 LR rounds at home that could have done that. It was interesting, though. He was a collector of art and felt a twinge for the lost treasures. But he was more impressed with the amount of damage and the skill insinuated by it.

According to the police report, there had been one intruder and a dog.

"You're a madman, Ledger," he said aloud. "Can't wait to meet you."

He walked through the place, following the logical path of destruction. Even with sound suppressors and the element of surprise, Ledger must have been moving at incredible speed. Sure, the guards probably thought this place too inaccessible and too tough a nut to crack, and maybe that made them a little lazy, but once the shooting started, they'd have gotten up to speed quickly enough. They were pros.

And Ledger had killed them all.

In the military, that's called having a John Wayne day. But even so . . . even with the breaks going his way, the sheer enormity of all this was incredible.

He wondered if he could have done it. This would be at the upper range of anyone's skill set.

When he reached the master suite at the top of the house, he stopped in the doorway and stared. It looked as if someone had attached a fire hose to a tank full of dark red paint and then cut loose. Stafford tried to do the math on the blood spatter and still came up short.

What *had* happened here?

Stafford knew that Ledger had been pushed all the way to the edge by what Santoro had done to his family. Okay, there was the edge, but this was past that. And that called to mind a whole raft of Nietzsche quotes, and as he walked into the room, he spoke them aloud, fitting each like puzzle pieces to Ledger's fractured psyche.

"That which does not kill us makes us stronger."

That was often not true, as Stafford knew. Santoro proved that with virtually everyone he went to work on. Most people crumble under a certain level of pressure. And even if they survive, they're crippled by their own immutable awareness of how fragile and powerless they truly are.

But when that statement was true, in those rare cases, then it was a cosmic verity.

Santoro had tried to break Ledger's heart and mind and will, but instead, he'd made him into this. Into a monster.

Maybe Santoro didn't understand that. He'd won so often with people, broken the unbreakable, that he'd lost perspective.

"And those who were seen dancing were thought to be insane by those who could not hear the music."

Santoro—and possibly Kuga—were drinking their own Kool-

Aid, believing the hype that was scaring the piss out of the tourists in the business.

He walked through the room, seeing the blood, matching it to the bodies in his photos. This was where the last stand had been.

"Whoever fights monsters should see to it that in the process he does not become a monster. And if you gaze long enough into an abyss, the abyss will gaze back into you."

The Christmas Eve slaughter had been Ledger's abyss, and he'd looked way too close. He'd become a monster. An actual monster.

Stafford stopped by the wall over the bed. It was smeared with thick blood that had now dried to the color of bricks. He studied it in exactly the same way he studied the brushstrokes of Van Gogh, Paul Wright, and Philippe Pasqua. There was so much to learn from the way an artist applied his brush, or knife, or fingers.

This was artwork.

Of a kind.

There were strokes within it. Fingers had played on this wall, moving through the red, running blood even as the corpses lay cooling around the room. Even as the smell of death permeated the air.

"There is always some madness in love," he said. One of Nietzsche's less frequently quoted insights. "But there is also always some reason in madness."

So, what then, was the reason in this madness? What was Ledger saying to himself, or about himself?

He did not believe that it was a cry for help. Nothing as weak as that, or as pedestrian. And yet there was a message here. He could *feel* it.

Stafford walked around the room, looking at the big smear from a dozen angles. Finally, he turned out the lights and used his cell to shine a bright blue-white beam at the swirls from several different angles.

And that's when he saw them.

Two words were smashed together, written in a fit of rage, the letters colliding, violating one another, bursting through each other.

Umbra.

Tenebris.

Two Latin words.

Each casting a different meaning but inextricably linked. Bound together by the *intended* meaning here.

He spoke the translated word aloud.

"Darkness."

It made him shiver.

It made him smile.

CHAPTER 60
PHOENIX HOUSE
OMFORI ISLAND, GREECE

Church tapped on the open door of Bug's office.

"Word is that you have something for me," he said.

"Maybe I do."

Church closed the door, and Bug activated the lockout system.

"Still no *actual* sightings of Joe," said Bug, "but what I'm calling discovery via circumstantial evidence."

Church sat. Bug opened a drawer and removed a package of vanilla wafers and handed it to him. Church smiled and opened it, selected one, and bit off a piece. He brushed crumbs from his tie.

"Enlighten me," he said.

"Last night someone broke into a sport boat rental company in Singita Miracle Beach in Malta and stole something called a *gommoni*."

Church nodded. "That's a commercial version of the RHIB." The rigid-hull inflatable boats were used by both military and private sportsmen because they were fast, light, and extremely durable. "And you think this was our missing friend?"

"Yup. All their security cameras seemed to malfunction at the same time."

"Funny how that keeps happening." Church took another bite, chewed, then asked, "Where is Mrs. Gondek?"

Peggy Ann Gondek was a semiretired field agent who had worked with Church and Aunt Sallie in the days before the DMS. She was part of a network of associates whom Church trusted and occasionally employed.

"Her flight touched down in Rome three hours ago. I've sent her the relevant information. She said she'll try to work up a list of possible targets. Her horseback guess is that Joe got a lead on some black market stuff right there in Rome and may have swiped the boat to go out to someone's yacht, or maybe a freighter taking whatever Kuga's selling. Second guess would be one of the biotech labs in either Rome or Naples. There are five on our watch list. And then there's the bioweapons broker in Sardinia, but his place is a fortress, so Joe might leave that to us or the Crociati. It would take a small army for that gig."

The Crociati—Crusaders—were an Italian rapid response team modeled after the UK's Barrier and Church's former group, the DMS.

"So, my money's on one of the targets right there in Rome."

"One more thing," said Church. "Have you made any progress on whatever Kuga might be planning in America?"

"*Progress* is an ugly word," said Bug. "I've been noodling around on some dark web sites, and all I can find so far is that one of Kuga's black market crews moved some weapons into the U.S. via trucking routes from Canada. Don't have manifests, but it's a fair amount. And, before you ask, I had MindReader poke around in surveillance logs from the CIA, DoD, and Homeland, but there's no indication of any nuclear materials. My guess is it's guns and ammo."

"Being sold to whom?"

Bug fished around in the mess of papers on his desk, found a pair of stapled pages, and handed them to Church.

The big man scanned the lists. "These are mostly militia groups. Some very far out on the political fringe."

"All with avowed nationalistic politics. Bunch of 'em are white supremacists, too."

"But not all," mused Church.

"No. Doesn't mean much except they're buying from the same vendor. Kuga's undercutting everyone else's prices."

"Put Nikki Bloom on this," said Church. "Her whole team. There's a pattern in here, and we're not yet seeing it."

Bug glanced up at him. "You think there really *is* something big brewing?"

"I do."

"Any idea what?"

"No. That's why I want Nikki on it. Nobody finds a pattern better than she does."

"Agreed. I'll go over this with her right away." He paused. "Is this on the same level of hush-hush as tracking Joe?"

"No. Brief Scott on it as well."

"Okeydokey."

"This is all very good work, Bug." Church stood up. "You know that I appreciate all that you do."

Bug smiled faintly. "You don't need to say it."

"I do," said Church, "and should probably say it more often."

With that, he left the office.

CHAPTER 61
VAN DIJK BIOMECHANICA
ROTTERDAM, THE NETHERLANDS

"Tell me about the American Operation," said the man. "I won't ask again."

The scientist backed away, his feet slipping in the blood. He wanted to turn, to run, but the dog stood there by the exit to the stairs, and the big man with the knife was between him and the main door. The scientist's name was De Vries. He was corrupt, and willingly so. He was bought and owned and content with that. He was also trapped.

"Please . . . ," he mewled.

"I can make you tell me," warned the big man. "You know I can."

The knife was red, and the hand holding it was scarlet to the wrist. All around the room was evidence of what the knife could do and what the man was willing to do.

If this man was really a man at all.

There was something wrong about him.

He seemed to be darker than anyone should be, given the bright fluorescent lights. And there was something in his face, in his eyes. They seemed to burn, to give off real heat.

I'm going mad, thought De Vries.

"If you tell me," said the man, "I may let you live."

The scientist's back thumped against the wall. "Wh-what?"

"You heard me. It's the one chance you have. The only chance."

The man was so close now. De Vries held his hands up in a gesture of surrender, a plea for mercy. He knew who this man was. Everybody in the network was talking about him, yelling about him, screaming about him. The insane American and his dog. Colonel Joe Ledger and Ghost. Monsters, both of them.

Ledger stepped very close now and placed the blade of the knife against De Vries's cheek. The flat, not the edge. It was almost a caress, almost tender, but in the worst possible way.

"You're *him*," gasped De Vries. "You're Ledger."

That made the American smile.

But it was not a good smile. No, not at all. There was death in that smile. There was hell in it.

"Joe Ledger isn't here right now," said the man. "*I* am."

"I . . . I don't understand . . ."

"Tell me while you still have a tongue."

De Vries felt his bladder go. A moment later, his sphincter failed as well. Then his knees. He thumped down to the floor, his trousers filled with piss and shit.

He could not look at Ledger. He dared not look away. So De Vries closed his eyes, squeezing them shut. He jammed his balled fists against his head.

And he told the monster everything he knew.

He talked for a long, long time.

When he was finished, when there were no more follow-up questions, De Vries toppled over and curled into a ball on the floor. Waiting for the knife.

Waiting for the pain.

He lay there for a very long time.

So long. He felt as if his mind and body—perhaps even his soul—were shutting down. Preparing to be ended. Preparing to meet God. Or the devil. He prayed to saints whose names he had thought he'd forgotten. To a god he had abandoned before he'd entered university. He wept, and he prayed.

Perhaps he even slept.

When he finally summoned the courage to open his eyes, he was alone.

Completely alone.

With the awareness of having soiled himself. With the knowledge of how deep his betrayal had run.

Alone with the bodies of everyone he worked with.

Alone.

But alive.

CHAPTER 62
THE PAVILION
BLUE DIAMOND ELITE TRAINING CENTER
STEVENS COUNTY, WASHINGTON

Top and Bunny didn't have long to wait.

A door opened in the closest of the small buildings, and two women came out. It surprised the men to see that one of the women was Jill Hamilton-Krawczyk—HK—and from her broad smile, it was obvious she enjoyed the surprise. She wore a different blue diamond, this one a pear-shaped cut of at least four carats, and half-carat stud earrings. She wore a billed cap in the same shade as her diamonds.

"Well, fellows," she said, coming over and shaking their hands, "welcome to the Pavilion."

"Happy to be aboard, ma'am," said Top.

"Yeah. This place looks tight," agreed Bunny. "Love the layout. Done right."

"Oh, we do our best," said HK, "and I think you'll be even more impressed once you see what we have under the hood." She gave them a broad conspiratorial wink.

"Who's your friend?" asked Top, nodding to the younger woman at her side.

The other woman was a slender blonde in her early twenties. Very fit, very pretty, but not at all nice to look at. There was a reptilian coldness in her eyes, and her lips were compressed into a tight red line. She wore camo pants, an olive drab T-shirt, no jewelry, and had a leg brace around her right knee. A Glock 19 was tucked into a low-slung holster, and she had a leather sheath strapped to her left leg from which the handles of three slim throwing knifes protruded. Her pale hair was pulled back into a ponytail so severe it looked painful. And although there were no lines at all on her face, there was an ancient glower in her eyes.

Top and Bunny had to fight to keep all reaction from their expressions. They *knew* her. They'd seen her in surveillance photos and videos.

"This," said HK, "is Eve."

Bunny offered his hand, but Eve stared at him as if he were doing something rude and inappropriate. He withdrew his hand without comment.

In his ear, Top heard Scott Wilson say a couple of very crude four-letter words. Then Doc Holliday said, "It's a good thing our dear Outlaw can't see this. He'd have a goldurn coronary."

Top tapped his button.

"Eve is here overseeing one of our projects," said HK, beaming with pride and good humor.

"Oh?" asked Top.

But HK did not elaborate. Eve stood beside her as if she'd been cut and pasted into the moment. She ignored the two big men and mostly ignored HK and instead seemed to look inward into her own thoughts. The energy she radiated was odd and unpleasant. She fidgeted, and her hand kept absently touching the handle of her pistol.

Bunny nudged his suitcase. "Is there someplace we can put this stuff? Maybe take a shower and get a hot meal?"

"Oh, of course," said HK. "Where are my manners?"

She led them to one of the buildings used as a bunkhouse. Eve came with them but remained aloof and apart, not even bothering to look at either of them and clearly tuning HK out completely. They were put in a large, nicely appointed two-bedroom suite, with king beds, soaker tubs and showers, a small dinner table, a big couch, and a massive wide-screen TV.

"No cable out here," she said, "but there are a few thousand DVDs in the rec hall. And if there's something playing in the theaters you like, just ask and we can get a screener."

"Cool," said Bunny.

"Not that you'll have much time for watching movies," laughed HK. "We have a lot in store for you fellows."

"Like what?"

"Drop your bags, and I'll give you a quick taste before dinner. How's that?"

"That," said Bunny, "would rock."

They went outside, found a golf cart, and HK drove the four of them to the far side of the compound—an area that proved much larger than they had first thought. There was a cluster of buildings that were actually linked to a larger central structure. Top noticed that Eve began to brighten and become more visibly focused as they entered the building. This, for whatever reason, was clearly important to her.

Once they went inside, Top and Bunny found out why.

Despite the rather mundane exterior and the rustic setting, the interior was at the bleeding edge of advanced technology. There were racks upon racks of combat exoskeletons, and unlike the stripped-down model Top glimpsed in Texas, these were complete, with structural armor to protect the drivers, belt-fed machine guns, rocket launchers, and other gadgetry that was so exotic Top didn't know what it was.

"Pappy," said a very excited Doc, "do a slow turn and let me see everything."

There were dozens of the exosuits, each hung on a rack that approximated the dimensions of a person. And, Top saw, each rack was different, suggesting that these machines were designed to the specs of individual users. That was not good. Not at all.

Along another wall were racks of rifles and handguns, some of which were augmented with different kinds of high-end scopes, personalized trigger mechanisms, and variations on standard designs. On the opposite wall were racks of backpacks. Top recognized some as a new generation of flamethrower, but the others looked like they were built to deliver other payloads. Perhaps RPGs or other heavy explosives.

"Oh, lordy, lordy," said Doc. "We are way up the brown smelly river, and not one of us has a paddle."

No joke, thought Top.

This was not any kind of mercenary training camp. This was a base for staging an all-out war.

Staging, and maybe winning it.

Beside him, Eve was smiling like a little kid on Christmas morning.

CHAPTER 63
THE DARKNESS

I came back to myself.

Slowly.

As if from a far-off place.

No, not *as* if. No. That's wrong. I came back from a far place, no doubt.

Very goddamned far.

One minute, I was lost inside the darkness, inside my broken head.

Then I was sitting with my back to a wall.

Covered in mud.

Blood everywhere. On my hands, on my clothes, in my hair, in my mouth. I looked over at Ghost, and he was soaked with it, too. I had to look for a long time to assure myself he was breathing. Then he twitched and whined softly, the way he does when he's dreaming of pain.

I turned and spat my mouth clear and kept spitting until the spit had no lingering traces of pink. My knuckles were torn, and I had aches in places I couldn't connect with incidents that might have caused damage.

Blood smells like copper and tastes salty. It tastes wrong. I've walked through lakes of it since joining up with Church's goddamned crusade, before enlisting in this endless damned war. Professionally, I was indifferent to the smell and the sight of it. Personally, though?

I'd never enjoyed spilling it, touching it, smelling it, or tasting it.

Until recently.

A shiver chopped its way through me.

I wondered if this was how vampires were born. Not from a bite or a curse but out of some maniacal need to assure oneself of complete domination over the enemy to the point where the blood in their veins is the wine of victory.

Was I becoming that kind of monster?

I was bathed in blood. I knew that I'd swallowed some—there was that nausea in the stomach you get from nosebleeds, when you swallow your own blood against your will. I'd swallowed it . . . why? I couldn't remember. Was it an accident of being in physical line with the hydrostatic release of an artery I'd opened with bullet or blade? Or had I gone even deeper into the arms of the Darkness and actually drunk it? Was it some kind of ritual undertaken by my deepest need for revenge—to not only end the lives of my enemies but devour their essence and by doing so tie their damnation to my own?

I closed my eyes for a moment and tried to convince myself that there was still more of me in here than there was that new aspect. It was another round in a fight that'd begun in that basement lab in Croatia.

The room around me was unfamiliar. An office in a building somewhere. I did not at that moment know where. Not the building, not the town, not the country. My memories of the last several weeks were in my head, but there were chains looped through the door handles and big shiny locks. I kept telling myself that it was a good thing that I lacked a key and could not remove those chains and open those doors until this was done. Until it was Santoro's blood boiling in the pit of my stomach. His and Kuga's.

But that was a lie. I'd put those chains there, I clicked the padlocks into place, and somewhere in my fractured soul, I had the key.

CHAPTER 64
TWILIGHT

I wandered through the building.

It was a laboratory. And that poked a stick into a beehive of memories. But it wasn't until I found a desk with preprinted envelopes that I realized where I was. Van Dijk Biomechanica in Rotterdam.

I stumbled around until I found a bathroom and stood looking at myself in the mirror. If someone had used a hose and sprayed me with red paint, that's how I'd look. Except this wasn't paint.

There was a sound, and I turned to see Ghost standing behind me. Nearly as soaked as I was. His eyes were wild, and he bared his teeth.

At me.

Flash images of things we had both done exploded in my mind.

"Ghost," I said, and my voice was not my own.

I staggered to the sink, turned on the spigot, and washed my face and then my mouth, gargled with the water, spat it out, did it again, and again. Then I drank handfuls of it.

I turned back to my dog. He'd inched closer, and the primal wolf still glared out at me from his eyes.

"Ghost," I said again. This time, I recognized my own voice.

So did he.

Ghost rushed at me, whining piteously, jumping up, pushing me back against the wall, pushing his head at my hand, needing me to pet him. Needing me to be *me*.

I sank down onto the floor and pulled him close. He kept licking my face. The only part of me not painted with blood.

"It's okay," I said softly, kissing his head over and over again. "It's okay."

I'd lied to him so many times before, so many times recently. Right now, though, I felt as if I meant it. I hoped it was true.

CHAPTER 65
THE PAVILION
BLUE DIAMOND ELITE TRAINING CENTER
STEVENS COUNTY, WASHINGTON

Top and Bunny sat with a dozen other new recruits and watched something straight out of a science fiction movie. It was no comfort at all that the two of them had seen earlier prototypes of the exoskeleton tech. Rather the reverse, because most of what they'd known coming into this was the pervasive belief that this level of sophistication was five to ten years down the road.

Not right now.

And not rolling out with a major nation's flag stenciled on the hood. This was true radical combat science. Top wished he could actually have a conversation with Bunny, and another with Wilson and Church. Doc, too. And the content of that conversation would likely include calling in an air strike.

One end of the hall was clear of all spectators and was set up as a target range. Though it was an odd one. There were targets of various sizes, each done as a cutout of people—singly and in groups, and vehicles ranging from police cars to armored personnel carriers and even a tank. All fashioned from metal and wood, but with stacks of lumber and cinder blocks behind them to give the targets resistance. There were also a few dozen pepper-poppers—metal silhouettes lying on the floor but attached to high-tension springs that would cause them to stand up very quickly. From where he was sitting, Top couldn't quite make out what the pepper-poppers were intended to represent. As for the standing targets, most were stationary, but several were on wheeled platforms that were in turn attached to a complex pulley system rigged at floor level. A small group of technicians with laptops sat off to one side, close to the targets but behind thick bulletproof polymer shields.

In all, Top counted 18 vehicles and 110 simulated human targets.

Very pretty young women, all wearing abbreviated versions of Pavilion uniforms that showed off long legs, deep cleavage, and muscular rumps, walked around the room handing out gun-range ear defenders. Top accepted one from a woman young enough to be his daughter. Her smile was bright, but there was a glazed, drugged look in her eyes. She also had a lot of makeup caked on her cheek beneath one eye, and Top thought it might be hiding a bruise.

HK walked out onto the training floor. She wore a wire mic headset and beamed a great smile, clearly as happy about all this as was Eve. For her part, the younger woman sat on a nicely padded chair—one of a pair—someone had brought in for her. The other chair was empty.

The rest of the hall was crammed with more seasoned trainees as well as forty or more Fixers in full Pavilion uniforms. Everyone was armed except the people in the bleachers with Top and Bunny.

Excitement rippled through the packed house, and Top saw some of the spectators grinning and nudging one another. Apparently, they knew what was coming and were totally into the moment.

"Ladies and gentlemen," said HK, affecting the big voice and grand gestures of a circus ringmaster. "Welcome to another edition of Blue Diamond *Battle Zone*."

It was meant as some kind of inside joke, and it got the expected laugh from the regulars. Eve clapped her hands and stamped her feet on the mat.

"Oh boy," said Bunny under his breath. "This is going to get weird."

"Hush now, Farm Boy," murmured Top.

"We have a full house today," continued HK. "That's marvelous. So many of you have been with Blue Diamond since it was acquired by our new benefactors."

She didn't give a name, but Top didn't need one. Everything about this was on a grand scale, and with massive money and tech savvy behind it. Kuga's name might as well have been in neon lights at the gate. And Top's heart sank at the thought that this was just one camp. Were there others? Here and elsewhere around the world? If so . . . how many and where?

"And we have some new members to the Blue Diamond family," said HK. "Come on, boys and girls, stand up so everyone can give you a proper hello."

She waved in the direction of the new recruits, and after a moment's surprised hesitation, the people in Top's section got to their feet amid thunderous applause. Top felt like a fool, and he felt incredibly exposed. Bunny, for his part, played to the crowd and raised both hands over his head, making the heavy metal horns hand sign and sticking his tongue out like Gene Simmons from Kiss. That amped the applause up a notch, and the other recruits turned and held fists out for Bunny to bump.

When they were all seated again, Top leaned toward Bunny to say something, but the big young man cut him off.

"Don't even, old man."

HK pulled the audience's attention back to her.

"As *most* of you know," she said, "we're ticking down to game time—"

Applause drowned her out for a moment.

"—and that means we are going to light things up like nobody's ever seen."

More applause. Actual screams and yells.

HK held up her hand, and the room settled.

"For those of you who haven't yet seen the K-110s in action, you are in for a real treat."

"K-110?" asked Bunny, but Top shook his head. They both got their answer a moment later. There was a soft whine of hydraulics, and everyone turned to see one of the exosuits come walking out onto the floor. It had an oddly mincing and delicate gait, almost like the velociraptors from *Jurassic Park*. But it moved quickly, with only the slightest perceptible lag between the leg movements of the driver and the servo reactions that made the legs move.

The exoskeleton—clearly a K-110, and probably named for Kuga—stepped out onto the floor and turned in a slow, complete circle, allowing everyone to see how well protected the driver was and how fully loaded was the machine itself. Then the K-110 turned another 180 degrees so that it was facing away from the targets. The driver hit a button, and the internal motors immediately powered down, rendering the suit inert.

Immediately, six Fixers wearing a kind of body armor Top had only seen in DARPA reports trotted out onto the floor. They were heavily armed with rifles, handguns, and grenade launchers. The people seated nearest to the K-110 became restive and started to shift away, but HK held up her hand.

"Don't worry, don't worry," she said, patting the air placatingly. "Have a little faith that we didn't bring you all here to kill you."

That got a laugh from everyone except those at the wrong end of the room. But then the soldiers trotted toward the K-110 and formed two tight lines behind the exosuit's bulk, the way soldiers did when going into battle on foot behind a tank.

"Everyone take your seats, please," HK called, and when the crowd was settled, she once more raised a hand. "Danny, give me twenty seconds on the clock."

A large digital clock flared to life over where Eve sat. Twenty seconds.

"Wonder how many it'll get," mused Bunny. "I've got a five-spot that says he gets a full third of them."

HK stepped off the floor and, in a voice filled with joy, yelled, "Let the games begin!"

What happened next was not a game at all.

It was a horror show.

CHAPTER 66
DAWN'S EARLY LIGHT

It took me a long time to get cleaned up. There was a shower adjacent to one of the hot rooms where dangerous biological items were kept. I stripped naked and washed my body until my skin was raw, and washed Ghost until he was a white dog again. The idiot dog liked it. Kept wagging his tail.

Then I had to find clothes.

The only choices were between a dead security guard and a scientist. The scientist's pants fit; the guard's shirt almost fit. I covered it with a white lab coat from a closet. My shoes were leather, and they rinsed clean enough.

I put my weapons and equipment into a gym bag and the data files I'd stolen into a briefcase. Wearing dead men's clothes, I left the building. On the way out, a man crawled out of a side room on his hands and knees, his clothes stinking of urine and feces. He saw me and screamed, then scuttled back into the room.

I fished for his name. De Vries.

A sudden crushing desire to kill him punched its way through me. The Darkness did not want to let go. Ghost began barking furiously, and I forced myself to turn away and continue making my way toward the front door. The Darkness faded. Maybe for once it was glutted. Or maybe the spell was broken. I didn't know and was afraid to even think too much about it.

Outside, there were no sirens, no cadre of police or Fixers or anyone waiting to ambush me. Dawn was breaking on the horizon. As red and bloody as I'd been half an hour ago.

I had the scientist's car keys in my pocket and used the fob to locate it with a honk. A blue Saab. Last year's model.

We drove away.

CHAPTER 67
THE PAVILION
BLUE DIAMOND ELITE TRAINING CENTER
STEVENS COUNTY, WASHINGTON

As soon as HK dropped her hand, the lights dimmed, and floods splashed bright illumination onto the demonstration floor. A siren began howling, and the pulleys started moving the targets. The lights began to strobe, making it nearly impossible to understand what was happening at that end of the hall. And the digital clock began ticking down.

Instantly, the K-110 came back online, the contraption seeming to wake up around its driver. The fighting machine turned with surprising and—to Top—disheartening agility, swinging around toward the madness. The driver brought the arms up, and even under all the noise, Top could hear a faint whirring noise.

Then the back door of hell broke open.

The K-110 began stalking forward as the driver opened up with both guns. Shell casings arced through the air as hundreds of rounds chunked into the moving targets, punched holes through the metal, and tunneled through the wood and cinder block. Those rounds chewed up the rear wall of the structure. The standing targets were obliterated in moments even though the pulleys tried to yank them away at high rates of speed. Top realized that the exosuit had some kind of persistent aiming system that locked onto targets, chased them, got ahead of them, and chewed them to pieces.

Pepper-poppers sprang up from the floor, and now Top could see that some were civilians of four distinct kinds—official-looking men and women in good suits, wearing American flag pins on their lapels and broad photo-op smiles; other men and women wearing the dark suits, white shirts, dark ties of Secret Service agents, all the way down to sunglasses and wires behind their ears; people wearing T-shirts or hats with various political party slogans—both right and left wing; and more of the Fixers in the fancy body armor.

The K-110's machine guns fired continuously, cutting every single member of the first three groups to pieces but somehow—despite noise, movement, strobes, and gun smoke—selectively ignoring the Fixers. As the field was cleared, the K-110's left machine gun stopped firing and swung around and down on a hidden track, allowing a weapon with a bigger mouth to roll up and lock in place. A grenade launcher. It fired eight rounds, and each one struck one of the bigger target vehicles with enough destructive force to blow them to pieces. Debris filled the air and rained down, but none of it fell on the spectators.

The six Fixers behind the fighting machine now spread out and ran forward, using their weapons to guarantee that any target with a wound was given a kill shot. The K-110 still fired with its right-arm machine gun, but even with the Fixers moving all over the floor, not one round so much as scratched them.

And then it was over.

Just like that.

The echo of the gunfire banged off the walls for a few seconds but died away into a ghastly silence. Even the Fixers in the Pavilion uniforms seemed surprised, dazed. Perhaps they had never seen a demonstration of this magnitude before.

Then someone began clapping.

All heads turned toward a small man standing by an open door. He was dressed in a brown suit with a European cut. A swarthy man with glittering dark eyes.

A few Fixers joined in the applause, and as if that was the last thing holding back a collapsing dam, everyone in the hall began applauding. The entire crowd leaped to their feet, clapping, yelling, roaring out, slapping one another on the back, grinning with overwhelming joy. Eve jumped to her feet and ran over to the small man, threw her hands around his neck, and kissed him on the cheek. The way a daughter would kiss her much-loved father.

Top and Bunny were the last to start clapping, but they joined in, forcing enthusiasm past the walls of their horror and shock. Not just at the level of destruction they'd witnessed—a degree of deadly combat efficiency beyond anything they'd ever seen—but because of that man.

Because of him.

In his ear, Top heard Scott Wilson hiss as if burned. He heard Doc Holliday say, "Oh my god," over and over again.

And, nearly buried beneath the weight of that crushing adulation, he heard Mr. Church speak the name.

"Rafael Santoro . . ."

CHAPTER 68
THE PAVILION
BLUE DIAMOND ELITE TRAINING CENTER
STEVENS COUNTY, WASHINGTON

The crowd surged forward around Rafael Santoro, Eve, and HK. Everyone seemed eager to elbow their fellows out of the way to shake hands with the small Spaniard. And, to a lesser degree, HK. No one offered a hand to Eve, and she seemed okay with that.

Santoro was ebullient, smiling broadly, accepting the offered hands and shaking briskly, pausing to speak to specific individuals, even hugging a few. He exchanged cheek kisses with HK and leaned closely to speak quietly into her ear, and the executive blushed a bright red, her eyes twinkling with happiness.

Top and Bunny lingered near the very back of the crowd. With Bunny's height and mass, it was tough to remain inconspicuous, but they managed. Shifts in body posture change height and alter physical presence.

Staying out of Santoro's line of sight was key because even though they'd never met, there was no chance at all that their faces were unknown to the man.

"Never thought that fucker would be here," said Bunny quietly.

"Uh-huh," agreed Top, putting a lot of meaning into those two syllables.

In their ears, Wilson said, "Chaps, you really need to get the hell out of that room."

Bunny turned toward Top's button camera and pretended to scratch his chin with his extended forefinger. Leaving was not an option, because it would draw too much attention. This was their first day at the Pavilion, and any unusual movements would be dangerous, if not fatal.

So, instead, they drifted over to where a couple of techs were helping the K-110's driver out of the fighting machine. There were a series of snap releases, but it still took assistance to disengage. As Top saw it, that was one of very damned few design flaws.

The driver was sweating and accepted a towel and a bottle of water from a friend.

"That's one hell of a show," said Top, coming over to shake the driver's hand.

"Thanks, man," said the driver. He glanced at Top and Bunny's street clothes. "You boys new?"

"New kids in school, brah," said Bunny.

"Welcome to the monkey house," said the driver, grinning broadly. He stripped off his sweat-sodden shirt and tied it around his waist. Top noticed that there was a small, barely healed scar on his upper chest, about the size and placement typical of a pacemaker. It was the fifth or sixth time he'd seen a Fixer here with the same scar, but now wasn't the time to ask. The driver looked at his machine with obvious genuine affection. "What d'you think?"

"It's fucking awesome," said Bunny, and Top thought that the big man didn't need to feign his enthusiasm. As frightening as the demonstration was, the level of technology was so superior that it was, undeniably, impressive as hell.

Top tapped the K-110's shell. "Can you run in this thing?"

"Yeah," said the driver, "but she's a pig. Turns fast, fires fast, runs like a cow. But hey, after all that shit, I can just *stroll* away."

"I *heard* that," said Bunny. "Totally badass. Like . . . serious next-level *Star Wars* badass."

"You got that right."

"How much of your ammo did you burn through?" asked Top.

"All of it except two grenades," said the driver. "Once it's spent, the weight is cut in half, but it's still slow getting out of Dodge."

"That why you have the ground troops?" asked Top. "Cover your back for exfil?"

"I guess," said the driver. "We haven't really gone into exfiltration logistics yet. That's coming up, I hear." He was about to say more and then indicated something with an uptick of his chin. "Here comes the man."

Top and Bunny glanced across the room and saw that Santoro was heading their way, flanked by Eve and HK.

"Gonna peel back and let you get your kudos," said Top.

"Totally awesome demo, man," said Bunny. They swapped fist bumps with the driver and then melted into the thickest part of the crowd, angling away from Santoro's path.

They saw the Spaniard embrace the driver and then link arms with him and walk the Fixer toward the door. They vanished into the sunlight outside.

A supervisor came over and herded the new recruits into a bunch, told them to go back to their rooms and get some rest. Armed Fixers accompanied the recruits, and once inside, Top and Bunny heard the locks click from outside.

That left them in their shared suite. There was no chance at all that the rooms were not being monitored, so they did not fall into conversation about what they'd seen. Instead, they took turns using the bathroom, made some food in the kitchen, and while eating had a conversation of exactly the kind men like they were pretending to be would have. Then they went to bed.

Top lay awake for a long time, replaying every detail about what happened. There were so many things about all this that scared the living hell out of him. And so few things on which he could hang the thin garment of his hope.

Sleep came reluctantly, and it was filled with very bad dreams.

CHAPTER 69
MARIA BEATRICE HOSPITAL
FLORENCE, ITALY

When the door to his private room opened and the man stepped in, Alexander Fong nearly screamed. The shriek got as far as his throat when he realized that this was not the same man.

This was not the monster.

But the similarities. Same height, similar coloring, blue eyes and blond hair, and the same muscular build and pantherish walk.

But it was not the man who'd nearly killed him. It was not the maniac who'd murdered all of Fong's colleagues and destroyed their research. It was not the cruel bastard who'd forced him to betray the organization. This man wore a lab coat and carried a clipboard, and he had a stethoscope looped around his neck.

"Dr. Fong?" asked the man, smiling disarmingly. "I'm Dr. Bianchi."

His name was northern Italian, but the accent . . . ? Was it genuine? Fong wasn't sure. He'd grown up in Tuscany, but his own accent had Cantonese overtones because his parents had always spoken it at home.

"Yes," said Fong uncertainly.

Bianchi came into the room, closed the door, and walked over to the bed.

"Just want to check your vitals and ask a few questions."

"Sure," said Fong. "Okay."

The doctor smiled and came close. He put the earpieces in and listened to Fong's heart, front, and back, asking him to take deep breaths at the right time. Nothing unusual there. Then he took a pulse and glanced at his watch.

As he did that, Bianchi said, "So, you were caught up in that awful terrorist attack at the lab?"

"What? Oh . . . yes."

"Such a shocker. A tragedy. Did you lose many friends?"

"They . . . they were all killed."

"But not you?"

Fong shook his head. "No. Thank god."

Without looking at him, Bianchi asked, "Why not you?"

That took a moment to register. "Wh-what?"

"Why were you spared, Alexander, and all the others killed?"

Those blue eyes turned to him. Looked down at him. Into him. And the grip on his wrist tightened.

"Owww . . . Let me go . . . You're hurting me . . ."

Dr. Bianchi smiled. "Hurting you? No. Not yet. But we can explore that if you'd like."

Fong opened his mouth to scream, but Bianchi whipped the pillow out from under his head and thrust it against the doctor's mouth.

"Shhhhhh," warned Bianchi. "I'm not here *to* hurt you, Alexander. I just want some information. If you cooperate, then everything's going to be just fine." Fong was thrashing against the smothering pillow. Bianchi leaned close. "Fuck with me and we'll both find out just how badly I *can* hurt you. Trust me when I say that you don't want to know the answer to that. Now . . . if you want this to be a nice, friendly chat, then stop struggling."

After a moment, Fong did that, though his body was shuddering with terror. Bianchi eased the pressure but kept the pillow in place.

"I'm going to move this away from your mouth," he said. "If you start to scream, well . . . I don't really see the need to spell it all out, do you?"

Fong waved his hands back and forth, the closest he could manage to a headshake.

The fake doctor removed the pillow, and Fong stared up with horrified eyes at the man who stood over him. Another blond-haired, blue-eyed monster. It was the smile that was the worst. There was something in there. Not the same thing he'd seen in the killer's eyes— that had been a darkness of soul. No . . . this man smiled like he had no soul at all.

"Now," said Bianchi, "we both work for the same man, the same organization. We won't say his name, but I want you to understand me. Good, I see you do. That's lovely. Now, I want you to tell me everything that happened when Joe Ledger came to your lab. I want to know what he said, what he did, and—this is really the most important part here, Alexander—what *you* said to *him*."

CHAPTER 70
THE PAVILION
BLUE DIAMOND ELITE TRAINING CENTER
STEVENS COUNTY, WASHINGTON

Her name was Mia Kleeve, and she was a very efficient killer.

It was something she accepted about herself. She'd known it since her first active tour as a Green Beret. She'd been one of the first women to join the Army Special Forces even though it had been open as a possibility since the Pentagon opened all combat jobs to women. At five foot two, though, she was a tough sell to that distinguished and elite group. But Mia earned her place.

Her family had emigrated from South Korea, where her ancestors had served with the military going back centuries. Those, of course, had been male ancestors, since that was one of many nations reluctant to let women participate in actual combat. Mia had been in the army for six years before she applied for Special Forces, and she'd fought her way through layers of resistance, sexism, and abuse. What her stubborner male comrades discovered, however, was just how powerful and determined women can actually be. Some of those soldiers had learned this lesson in extremely painful ways.

But her time in the army had not turned into the lifelong career she'd intended. Four years ago, while in Iraq, a noncombat field exercise had turned into a firefight when her platoon encountered a Taliban group of three times their number. The encounter took place in an area supposedly free of Taliban presence, but the bullet that punched through the sergeant's throat had changed that math forever. The lieutenant was the next to fall, and in under six minutes, more than half of her fellow soldiers were down, dead or wounded. It left Mia, a newly minted corporal, in charge, and she rallied her remaining men, found good cover in a cluster of tall rocks, and engaged the enemy. By then, night was falling, and as soon as it was too dark to see, she'd put on her night vision goggles, told the others to hold fast, and went searching for survivors. She dragged three soldiers back to the rocks, and on her fourth sally encountered a group of four Taliban who were sneaking up on her position. They were spread in a wide line, attempting to encircle the rocks.

Mia slung her rifle, drew her knife, and went hunting in the dark.

She was terrified and had not, until that night, ever drawn blood in a fight.

When dawn came and helos came whipping in over the mountains, the rescue team found five American dead, several wounded, and seven Taliban with their throats cut. In that long, hellish night, Mia had avenged her five fallen brothers-in-arms, and then took two more as punishment. She earned the Silver Star and the nickname Little Devil. It was notable that none of the soldiers tried to minimize that as Little *She*-Devil.

One month later, an older, middle-aged Black woman who looked remarkably like Whoopi Goldberg was waiting for her in the colonel's office at the base. The woman introduced herself as Aunt Sallie and said she worked for a domestic counterterrorism rapid response group called the Department of Military Sciences. And she was there to offer Mia Kleeve a job.

Mia ultimately joined Manitou Team, a DMS team based in Colorado Springs. From there she rolled out on missions on six continents and became a personal favorite of Aunt Sallie's.

Then two things happened. First, Aunt Sallie had a terrible stroke and was forced to retire. It broke Mia's heart. Auntie had been like a real aunt to her.

And shortly after, the DMS closed up shop in the United States and re-formed in Greece as Rogue Team International. Everyone who worked for the DMS was given a choice of retirement with full pay and benefits package, or they could travel the world and kick more terrorist ass. For Mia, it was not even a question.

Now she was officially part of Chaos Team, though Mr. Church tended to send her out on solo missions. Mia was fiercely independent and liked the autonomy.

And all of that brought her to Stevens County, Washington, where she currently crouched in the shelter of shrubbery, a pair of high-powered binoculars pressed to her face, watching Top and Bunny train with a group of Fixers. All the time waiting for the call from Phoenix House to send her in, knife in hand, for some fun and games.

JONATHAN MABERRY

CHAPTER 71
ROTTERDAM MARRIOTT HOTEL
ROTTERDAM, THE NETHERLANDS

More and more of my memory came back as I was driving to my hotel.

Like where the hell my hotel was. And that the room key was in my soiled pants in the gym bag. I'd have to use the lavatory off the lobby to get it, then wash my hands again before heading to the elevators. Logistical thoughts like that.

At first.

As I drove, though, more and more of it was filtering back. It wasn't like I had true blackouts. More like some kind of fugue state like what happens when the Cop or the Killer take over and drive my mental bus. More extreme than that, though, because I'd never had to fish for exact memories before. This was more insidious, as if the Darkness wanted to keep things from me. And maybe that was still happening. It wasn't like being possessed by a demon or anything silly like that. My personality was never canceled out but merely overridden.

And I'd liked it. I'd accepted it. Yielded to it.

No exorcist was going to declare me clean, because I wasn't. Even in the worst moments of excess, I was still holding the gun or the knife. I couldn't take the coward's excuse of saying it was temporary insanity. It wasn't temporary, and—let's face it—I've been insane by one metric or another since I was fourteen.

No, this was me. The question was whether the Darkness was off the clock for good, or if he would join my cadre of personalities from now on.

If that was the case, then . . .

Well, once this was all over, I might decide that I needed to be all over, too. I knew exactly how to do it.

Immediately, Junie's face came into my thoughts. I could feel her out there, hurt by my silence, aching to know how I was. What was worse was that I knew she'd forgive me. Somehow, she would.

And I was not worth her forgiveness. I wasn't worth anyone's kindness or generosity of spirit.

When this was over, even if the Darkness was somehow excised,

I knew I was done with RTI. No way they'd ever let me back in the field. No way they ever should.

We made our way through the streets, me taking a complexer route than was necessary because the habit of checking for—and foiling—tails was too deeply ingrained. Not sure how long it took to get there. Hadn't looked at the car's digital clock. That worried me, because it meant that, although some safety habits were working, others were not. I'd have to watch that.

I parked four blocks from the hotel and walked the rest of the way, carrying the bags, with Ghost beside me. I'd taken a few minutes to thoroughly wipe down the car before abandoning it. Kept the keys, though, just in case I needed to make a fast exit. If things were cool, I'd toss the keys into a culvert. Wasn't sure how quickly the deaths at the lab would be discovered or how fast things would be investigated. A scientist with his pants missing would logically and ultimately lead the cops to check the cars in the lot. There would be one missing, and it would eventually be found. If I had time later, maybe I'd go out and swap the plates. But not now.

At the hotel, I went straight to the elevator, which was located between the twin reception desks, and rode up to the tenth floor. I had a room with two queen beds. One for me, one for Ghost. All I could think about was getting out of dead men's clothes and taking another shower. Maybe order some room service and upload the information I got from De Vries and send it via a rerouting system to Church.

In my more lucid moments, that's what I'd been doing.

My brain was still sorting through what De Vries had said about the American Operation. It seemed improbable. Definitely ambitious, even grandiose. Which made me wonder if it was legit. Had the terrified scientist lied to me?

No, whispered a dark and ugly voice from way down deep inside my head.

We reached my room, and I swiped the key card.

Suddenly, Ghost went tense, sniffing at the door before I even opened it. He's trained to give me clear signals so that I immediately understood if there was a threat, and if so, what level of threat.

But he just stood there, sniffing. Damned near frowning. He looked up at me with quizzical brown dog eyes.

I had no weapons except in the bag, and they were covered with drying blood. If I got one out, it would leave bloodstains on the carpet right outside my room.

I began to back away. There was still time to run, to get to one of my other rooms here in the hotel. There were weapons in each, hidden where even room maids wouldn't find them.

Before I got very far, the door opened.

A man stood there. Shorter than me. Slim and fit. He had a pistol in his hand, but the barrel was pointing at the floor.

"It's your own damned room, Ledger," said Toys. "Might as well come in."

MOVING PIECES
PART 4

There are some sordid minds, formed of slime
   and filth,
to whom interest and gain are what glory and
   virtue are to superior souls;
they feel no other pleasure but to acquire
   money.

   —*LES CARACTERES* BY JEAN DE LA BRUYERE

If you prick us do we not bleed?
If you tickle us do we not laugh?
If you poison us do we not die?
And if you wrong us shall we not revenge?

—*THE MERCHANT OF VENICE* BY WILLIAM SHAKESPEARE

CHAPTER 72
ROTTERDAM MARRIOTT HOTEL
ROTTERDAM, THE NETHERLANDS

I pushed him back and kicked the door shut. He didn't like being pushed, but he didn't resist, either. Ghost, who—despite everything—liked Toys, gave me a strange look but didn't interfere. I pointed to a chair by a small table near the window.

"Sit," I ordered, and Toys sat. So, too, did Ghost.

"What in the wide blue fuck are you doing here?" I demanded.

"Looking for you," he said. "As are half of the covert operations groups around the bloody world."

"But you found me," I said. "Not thrilled."

"Try to imagine how much I care."

"Two things," I said. "How did you find me, and why are *you* even looking?"

"Finding you was easy. I had a good idea of what you're hunting for, and maybe even a better idea than you have for who to ask. I still have contacts. What our friend Mr. Church would call 'friends in the industry.'"

"You mean terrorists and psychopaths."

"In a word." He smiled a faint, condescending smile. "You've been blundering through Ohan's old network. People have noticed, and patterns have emerged. The only difficult thing in all this was trying to make sense of why you're not dead already. Kuga and Santoro want your head on a pike. Surprised they haven't set a trap."

"They have."

He looked at me, waiting for more, but I hoped his seat was comfortable because he'd be waiting a long time for that.

"As to the why," he said after a small shrug, "I think you know why."

"Is this some kind of penance thing?"

"First, fuck you. Second, try again."

As the implication of that sank in, I felt my knees getting weak. I sat down on the edge of the bed and looked past him, out the window. Seeing nothing, not even the curtains.

"How is she?" I asked after a long time.

Toys took a minute with that. I could feel him studying me. Could almost hear the wheels turning in his head.

We have a complicated relationship. Basically, we hate each other. When I first met him, he was the personal assistant cum attack dog for Sebastian Gault, the rich pharmaceuticals mogul who was trying to game the system by creating a bioweapon so terrifying that the whole drug industry would have to go into high gear to try to create a counteragent. His company, not one of the biggest in the field, would make billions, and the relatively small size of his firm when compared to Merck, Pfizer, and the others would be useful camouflage. The problem was that the pathogen, a weaponized prion-based disease form, was actually too good. It had a 100 percent infection rate, a 100 percent kill ratio, and was highly communicable. For all intents and purposes, it was an honest-to-god practical zombie plague. Had it gotten off the leash, planet Earth would likely be Disneyland for the living dead. And it was that case that resulted in my being drafted by Mr. Church.

Then Toys and Gault resurfaced when his boss was hired to be the King of Plagues by Hugo Vox. Once again, Gault concocted a deadly pathogen—in that instance, it was an airborne version of Ebola.

And the third time, he was more or less Vox's houseboy during a gig in Iran where a group of genetically engineered freaks were planning on detonating nukes in the Middle East oil fields.

Now, granted, during all that, Toys was gradually edging away from what Gault and Vox were doing, and he ultimately betrayed both men, but that didn't change the fact that Toys had a lot of blood on his hands. Innocent blood, as well as that of his employers' competitors.

But then Church surprised the hell out of all of us by offering Toys a very weird deal. One I struggle to understand to this day. He gave Toys a chance to change his life path and do measurable good in the world by giving him a massive amount of money to invest in projects and programs of a beneficial nature. Toys founded FreeTech, with the intention of taking the really nasty technologies that guys like me took away from people like his former employers and repurposing them to benefit humanity. Junie came to work for him, and although it's true that Junie is the primary driving force behind FreeTech, it was Toys's idea.

Also, in the years since, Toys has several times put his life on the line to protect Junie when the enemies Church and I have made tried to damage our efficiency by hurting those we love. Toys even saved the lives of Rudy and Circe and their first baby.

I told Toys a little while back—after one of those incidents—that although we'll never be friends and that I didn't forgive what he'd done in the past, he and I were no longer at war. However, that doesn't mean we bonded.

Now, of course, the world had changed. Santoro slaughtered my family, nearly killed Junie and me, and I have become so comprehensively fucked in the head that maybe I have no stones left to throw at Toys. I cannot say with any real certainty that every life I've taken over these last weeks has been a justified kill. I'd love to say that, but I really don't know. There are too many blacked-out spaces in my memory that could be my fragile brain trying to hide the truth from me.

We sat there in our silence. I wondered if he was going through the same process of thought that I was, and when I looked at him, I knew he had been. His eyes were hard as marble, and there was no smirk. For a moment, I saw behind the veil of his practiced defenses, and there was the real man. Hurt, ashamed, angry, filled with the kind of refined self-loathing that comes from deep self-awareness.

Then he saw me looking, and the shutters dropped behind his eyes and that sly, nasty little smirk of his reappeared.

"How's Junie?" he asked, raising his eyebrows. "Oh, she's effing wonderful. Skips along singing tra-la all day long. How do you bloody think she is, you dreary git? You lose your damned mind and vanish from the radar without so much as a postcard to let her know you haven't been turned into fish chum. She was hurt, too, remember. Or are you so self-involved that you forget she lost family, too? Maybe not blood relations, but she—for some unfathomable reason—loves you with her whole heart. She doesn't have a family, and so yours became hers. She watched them die. She lost them, too. And she nearly died. So, sure, she's the happiest girl in the world, you dick."

God, how I wanted to punch him.

God, how I wished he'd just shoot me.

Fuck.

Junie.

God help me.

CHAPTER 73
ROTTERDAM MARRIOTT HOTEL
ROTTERDAM, THE NETHERLANDS

I had no answer to what Toys had just said. We both knew he was dead right.

Instead, I got up, took clothes from the dresser, went and turned on the water mix in the shower, then stood for a moment in the bathroom doorway.

"Order room service," I said. "Get some for Ghost, too. I don't know when's the last time I fed him. I'm going to take a shower."

"That's it? I come all this way and you decide to take a shower?"

"That's all I can do for now," I said honestly. "Order something to drink, too, and I don't mean coffee. We'll eat, and then we'll see if there's anything more to talk about."

He studied me for a long, cold time. I expected some caustic remark, but instead, he merely nodded. I went into the bathroom and closed the door.

I stripped off the clothes, wadded them up, and shoved all of it into the trash can. I'd collect it later and dispose of it somewhere else. Then I stepped into the shower and stood for a long, long time with the hot water smashing me between the shoulder blades.

"Junie . . . ," I murmured. "Junie, my love . . . I'm so damned sorry."

Saying the words to myself because I was too ashamed and too much of a coward to call her. Too weak to even send an email for fear that it would somehow infect her with the darkness that seemed to own my body and soul.

JONATHAN MABERRY

"I'm so sorry."

I wondered, not for the first time, if I would ever see her again.

I did not have to wonder if I would ever deserve to see her. I already knew the answer to that.

The shower curtain was opaque and rippled from the breeze created by the water. I saw it darken a moment and was about to growl at Toys to tell him I didn't need him to wash my back, but when I peered around the edge, the bathroom was empty.

That was strange. I was positive there had been someone standing on the other side of the plastic. I let it settle into place again and waited.

Nothing happened.

After almost a full minute, I began to sneer at myself for being spooked by the shadows in my own head. So, I poured some shampoo into my palm and began working up a thick lather. I scrubbed my scalp until it hurt, rinsed, repeated.

The shower wasn't huge, and my shoulder kept pushing against the curtain.

And then something pushed back.

I recoiled, then whipped the curtain back, my eyes still filled with soap, but my hands ready to fight.

There, in the blear of vision, in a microsecond before the water rinsed the suds from my eyes, I saw a figure. Only a hazy outline, but there for sure. A tall man, big as I, but older. He was turned away from me, but I could see his face in the mirror.

My knees buckled at once, and I sank to the bottom of the stall as water splashed on me and bounced out, pooling on the floor.

The figure was gone as soon as I blinked my eyes.

I'd seen it, though.

The set of the shoulders, the dark hair, those familiar eyes.

Eyes I'd known my whole life but set into a face of charred flesh and exposed bone. A smile missing all the teeth that had been blown out when the bomb went off.

It had been my brother, Sean.

And even though he was gone—the illusion or hallucinogen or whatever it was ended—there was a scent lingering in the air. The sharp, rancid, cooked-meat stink of burned human flesh.

CHAPTER 74
ROTTERDAM THE HAGUE AIRPORT
SOUTH HOLLAND, THE NETHERLANDS

Stafford's phone rang as soon as he cleared customs.

Because only one person had the number of that burner, he answered right away.

"Talk to me, son," said Kuga.

"I'm in Rotterdam."

"The fuck are you doing there?"

"My job," said Stafford.

"You know where he is?"

"I know that he came here," said Stafford.

"Where is he?" asked Kuga. "I mean exactly."

"Not sure exactly. His MO is to check into a large hotel. A dog-friendly one, which limits things. And usefully located. I'll find him."

There was a pause.

"Son," said Kuga, "I'm a patient guy, but . . ."

"I know," said Stafford and ended the call.

CHAPTER 75
ROTTERDAM MARRIOTT HOTEL
ROTTERDAM, THE NETHERLANDS

When I came out of the bathroom—god only knows how much later—Toys was busy with a fillet of Dover sole in a parmesan and herb crust. A bottle of Puligny-Montrachet rested in an ice bucket.

"Ah," he said, "you didn't drown." He sounded sad about that.

Ghost was on the floor beneath the window eating some kind of sausage links with the odd delicacy he always displays when eating. He glanced up at me, but I got no tail wag.

I sat on the edge of the bed in slacks and an undershirt and lifted the silver lid on the tray intended for me. There was a steaming bowl of pea soup and a large plate of beef served on a salad with smoked eel and marinated mushrooms. Instead of ordering wine for me, he'd ordered six bottles of a strong Trappist blond beer. I opened one of those with the supplied church key and drank the whole bottle without taking a breath. And burped as the gases swirled in my chest.

"You're not half-posh, are you?" said Toys sotto voce.

"Go fuck yourself," I said.

"A cogent rejoinder." He sipped his wine with the delicacy of a pampered cat.

The beef was delicious and so rare I thought I'd have to chase it around the room.

The three of us ate in silence for fifteen minutes. I ate every scrap on my plate, and when I saw that Toys had leftovers he wasn't going to finish, I took them.

"Oh yes, please, help yourself," he said.

By then, I was three beers in, and I lined the others up on the night table.

"Why are you here?" I asked.

"As I said, because it would hurt Junie if you died."

"So this is all about her?"

"It is."

"Bullshit," I said. "I've been in the field for years. Never saw you line up to enlist."

Toys sipped his wine, then shrugged. "Does it really matter?"

I sipped some beer. "No."

"No," he agreed.

Ghost finished his sausages and gave a contented sigh. But his eyes were constantly drifting between me and the bathroom and back again.

Toys cleared his throat. "So, do we talk about the elephant in the room?"

"No," I said, "we don't. The last thing I ever plan on doing is to have a heart-to-heart with you."

"Heaven forfend," he said. "But I was referring to *what* you're doing, not why or how." He finished his glass and set it down. "Look, Ledger, I truly don't give a tinker's damn about you. I mean that from the heart."

"Thanks. The feeling is deeply mutual."

"However," he continued, "you're out here shaking the pillars of heaven. You think you're damaging the Kuga operation? Come on. You could kill fifty of their scientists and they'll hire a hundred more. This is a war you can't really win."

"Maybe it's not about winning," I said. "Ever consider that?"

"Yes, I have," he said. "And you almost certainly think it's about revenge. About payback, but here's the simple truth—you can't destroy Kuga's empire. His network is too big, and by all indications, it's largely self-sufficient. I truly believe that even if you literally cut the man's head off, the organization would keep running for years, maybe decades. Any power vacuum you create will be filled, and the machinery of international black marketeering will continue. Because it isn't based on any ideology that could go in or out of popularity with a regime or party change; the nature of what he does remains stable. He's not philosophical and, god knows, not religious. Neither he nor Santoro are any species of zealot. They are businessmen, no different in substance from Big Tobacco, Big Pharma, Big Oil, or the gun lobby. They will always remain as global constants, and nothing you, Church, or anyone can do will stop that."

"We'll see."

"Sure, let's see. And in the meantime, you're pissing them off without crippling their operations or even slowing them down."

"You don't know that."

"I do, actually," said Toys. "I have plenty of contacts among the people who play this game for a living. I won't call them friends, but they are former business acquaintances of the Seven Kings and Sebastian Gault. People who are never named in news stories and who continue to do business even when the countries they live in are at war with someone else. Business does not stop. Ever."

I drank my beer and tried not to believe what he was saying.

"This isn't just about doing damage," I said.

"Then what is it? No, let me guess . . . you're trying to be such an irritant that Kuga will send Santoro out to swat you, and that will give you a chance to kill him. What's that make it? Third time between you two?"

I said nothing.

"Even if you kill that evil little Spanish prick, so what? It's not going to bring your family back."

"Fuck you."

"It won't." Toys leaned forward, forearms on his thighs. "But it might make you lose the family you still have."

That hurt. That one went all the way to the bone.

When I didn't say anything, Toys leaned back, took the bottle from the cooler, and poured himself another glass.

"We don't like each other," he said, "but we have more things in common than you believe."

"Apart from the fact that we both love Junie?"

"Apart from the fact that, despite better judgment, she loves us?" He smiled and shook his head. "No. Not that."

"Then what?"

"Darkness," he said.

INTERLUDE 13
THE PAVILION
BLUE DIAMOND ELITE TRAINING CENTER
STEVENS COUNTY, WASHINGTON
TWO MONTHS AGO

Eve sat on the sixth level of a set of bleachers, watching as the twelve Fixers known as the Righteous went through a knife drill. They wore the latest generation of spider-silk and graphene body armor, which allowed them to duel with sharpened knives. The armor was only vulnerable to cuts and stabs where it was necessarily thinner at the inside of the elbows and knees, undersides of the upper arms and armpits, and the neck. There was no real way to protect areas of flexibility from any kind of weapon. But they had also been trained to move and change angles to reduce the likelihood of injuries to those spots.

Santoro watched with a keen eye, lips pursed, fingers steepled together over his heart. He had not said a word in nearly forty minutes, and Eve was beginning to get nervous. Her fingers were knotted together on her lap and squirmed like a cluster of snakes.

Then a bell rang and the partners stopped, exchanged forearm bumps, and sheathed their weapons. Spiro—known now as Cain—barked an order, and the twelve lined up and stood at parade rest. Sweat ran down their faces, but they were not breathing hard. Not as badly as they had when this phase of training began. Eve was a brutal taskmaster, but she also made sure they were properly fed, got all their shots, and received massage and physical therapy. The Righteous had been in great shape to begin with, but now they were incredibly lean, tough, healthy, and powerful.

Santoro sat back and was silent for a few moments.

Then he placed his hand atop hers.

"You have done excellent work here, my daughter," he said. And kissed her on the cheek. "No father has ever been prouder of a daughter than I am of you."

Eve buried her head against his chest and began to sob.

CHAPTER 76
THE SLAAK ROTTERDAM
ROTTERDAM, THE NETHERLANDS

Michael Augustus Stafford checked into his hotel, carried his own bags up, and locked himself into his room. He immediately opened his laptop and contacted Dingo, the head of Kuga's computer team.

"Tell me you have something for me," he said as soon as Dingo answered.

"Maybe," said Dingo, who began the answer to every question that way.

Stafford had to control his temper, but even so, his words came out tight. "Please be specific."

"There are four possibilities," said Dingo. "There were six, but I eliminated one because I hacked the hotel's lobby cameras and the dog was the wrong size. And the other got cut because the hotel wasn't big enough. You said only big hotels, right?"

"Yes."

"Of the remaining four, I could only get into one lobby cam, and the dog's about the right sight but the coloring's off. Don't know a thing about the other dogs."

"Give me the four names."

Dingo provided the names. Stafford considered them and said, "Eliminate the Hotel New York."

"Sure, but why?"

"Says he's from America. Ledger would never be that obvious."

"Maybe he's being *just* that clever," suggested Dingo.

"No. Cut him from the list. I'll check the other three."

"Okay."

"Can you run deep background on those three men?"

"Maybe."

Stafford hung up on him.

CHAPTER 77
ROTTERDAM MARRIOTT HOTEL
ROTTERDAM, THE NETHERLANDS

I sat very still.

"Touched a nerve, have I?" asked Toys.

"You're about to touch the pavement when I throw you out the damned window."

"I'll pencil in two minutes next week to be afraid," he said. "Look, mate, I'm not here for a male bonding exercise, and this isn't bloody group therapy. I think Church let me come looking for you because I know more about personal darkness than you do."

"You think so?"

"I effing well know so. Seriously, you want to match sins with me? I was a fucking criminal, a terrorist, and a murderer." He paused. "*Am* a murderer. That didn't change with my job description. And, sure, you went all *American Psycho* on those lab techs in Croatia, but as far as I'm concerned, boo-fucking-hoo. You did some damage in South Africa and in Italy. Cry me a river. You killed a bunch of right bastards. Sure, without mercy and maybe with a grin and a hard-on. Who knows and who cares? If we're measuring guilt, then my dick is way bigger than yours."

"This conversation is surreal," I said.

"I'm just getting warmed up."

"No," I said, "you're not. You're done. We're not having this conversation. Not now or ever. We are not friends, Toys. If you want to be the bigger Big Bad, fine. Enjoy. Sins are relative, and mine are . . . are . . ."

I actually could not finish my sentence because I could feel—literally *feel*—the Darkness rising inside me. It was like bile and vomit and sickness taking form inside me. If I were a more religious person, I'd think I was possessed. And maybe I was. Whatever it was, there was nothing natural about it.

And I think Toys caught a glimpse of it. Maybe it was a look in my eyes, maybe it was something else. Junie said he was empathic. It's possible she was right.

We drank.

Ghost got up and went over to stare into the bathroom. I heard a low growl, but then he came back, hopped onto the bed, and fell asleep beside me.

"Well, then," Toys said, "let's shift the conversation, shall we?"

"Gladly."

"Have you found anything that's of actual use?"

I had to think about that for a couple of minutes. Partly because I wasn't sure I wanted to trust him. Partly—or maybe mostly—because I was just coming back to myself, and could I trust *that*? Was this a lull between my own psychological storms, or the falsely calm eye in the hurricane that was the Darkness? My gut told me that I was in no way on solid ground. The Darkness had taken hold on me for *weeks*. Why should I have any faith that it was simply letting me go? It's not like there was a breaking point where it lost its hold or I broke free.

Frankly, I don't know why I came out of it as far as I had.

"How do I know you're not gaming me here, Toys?" I asked. "How do I know that you're here with the blessing of Mr. Church?"

He studied the golden depths of his wine. "You could call him."

I shook my head.

Toys sighed, set his glass down, took out his wallet, and removed a black metal American Express Centurion Card, looked at it for a moment, and then flipped it at me. I got a hand up in time to catch it.

The card was in the name of George Harold Sisler. It almost made me smile. Gorgeous George Sisler was one of the all-time greatest baseball players. Started out in 1915 with the Saint Louis Browns—the team that became the Baltimore Orioles—and retired in 1930 from the Boston Braves. During his career, he established a .340 life-time batting average over those sixteen years in the majors, stole 375 bases, and had 200-plus hits in six seasons. My grandpa had Sisler's 1921 baseball card, which he handed down to my dad, and my dad to me. It was in my office at Phoenix House, along with framed cards of Rafael Palmeiro, Davey Johnson, Cal Ripken, Mike Mussina, Roberto Alomar, and others.

"Put your thumb on the centurion," suggested Toys.

AmEx cards have a picture of a Roman soldier on them. Very lantern-jawed and stalwart. I placed my thumb carefully over the image and watched as the card changed color from black to black and orange. The Orioles team colors. When I turned the card over, I saw that the standard credit card text was gone, replaced by a single word written in what was Church's distinctive flowing hand.

FAMILY

I grunted and put the card on the table.

It was a design cooked up by Doc Holliday and not yet in use by any RTI field team. The message could only be read by the person whose thumbprint was encoded, and even then, only if the thumb was warm and had a pulse. None of that cutting off someone's thumb and using it or making a latex cast of a stolen print.

"Okay," I said.

"Okay," he said.

We looked at each other.

"And this is the part where you start telling me utterly fascinating things," said Toys dryly.

"Okay, sparky," I said. "Buckle up."

CHAPTER 78
THE PLAYROOM
UNDISCLOSED LOCATION
NEAR VANCOUVER, BRITISH COLUMBIA, CANADA

Kuga walked through the rooms of his mansion, and the look on his face drove his servants into hiding and made his Fixers snap to attention and avoid eye contact.

He went into his study and slammed the door. Then stood glaring at it for fifteen seconds before he opened it and closed it again, softly this time.

The place was very quiet. No women at the pool. No Santoro—he was down in Texas. No one of enough seniority to open up to. He went over to the wet bar and mixed a tall whiskey and soda, not caring that it was a moral crime to use forty-year-old scotch in any kind of mixed drink. Kuga drank half of it, added more whiskey, and slouched into a leather chair.

His phone rang, startling him, and when he saw who was calling, it gave him two seconds of apprehension, then it made him smile. He punched the button.

"Sunday," he said.

"Mr. Kuga," said the salesman. "How are you doing? Or should I guess? None of my agents have reported finding Joe Ledger's head on a pike, so I can imagine how frustrated you must be."

Spooky son of a bitch, thought Kuga, though he didn't dare say it out loud.

"No," he said.

"And your man Stafford?"

"Just got off the phone with him. He says he's getting close."

"What's that old expression? Close only matters in horseshoes and hand grenades."

"Yeah, yeah. What's happening with plan B? You had me get that stuff from Oslo—Ledger's hair and blood samples from the evidence lockup. I drop a shit ton of money on that because you promised me you could spin some kind of voodoo bullshit, but all I see is him charging around smashing up my labs, killing my people—very goddamned *important* people, I might add. You know what I'm not seeing? I'm not seeing any reports about Ledger going psycho and shooting up a school or tossing grenades into a crowded restaurant. You know what *else* I'm not seeing? Ledger either in handcuffs or on the news because he blew his damned brains out. I'm not seeing that shit at all."

"Give it time," said Mr. Sunday.

"Yeah, well, fuck you with 'give it time.' He's endangering the goddamned American Operation."

"Which, I am reliably informed, is going well. There is not a flicker of talk about it on the net. And clearly no one in the States knows or the whole event would have been canceled. Take a moment and pay attention to the fact that you are doing this very, very well."

"And you're changing the subject to hide the fact that you either fucked up or lied about being able to do this."

There was a soft chuckle at the other end of the call.

"What the hell is so freaking funny?"

"You are, my young friend. You really don't appreciate the way in which this world is wired, do you?"

"What's that supposed to mean?"

"Oh, nothing," said Sunday airily. "Just more of my—what did you call it? Voodoo bullshit, I believe. Adorable."

"Stop being so cryptic, and stop being a smart-ass," growled Kuga. "I'm trying to run a business here, and you are jerking me off. How do I know what you're doing isn't making things *worse*?"

"You don't."

"I want Ledger out of the equation, and I want to know for certain the American thing is not on Church's radar."

"Did I say you weren't?" Sunday snorted. "You'll always be on his radar. He probably has toilet paper with your face on it. And if he ever catches you again, he won't send you back to prison. No, my boy, he'll personally cut your throat—Santoro's, too—and piss on your graves."

"Well, gosh . . . thanks for the cheer-up call. Really made my day."

"Hush now," said Sunday soothingly. "No, what I said was that it is apparent that he is unaware of the G-55 matter. And there is almost no time left even if they *do* find out."

Kuga chewed on that for a moment. "From your lips to . . . well, to whoever's ears," he said grudgingly.

Sunday got a big laugh out of that. Kuga sipped his drink.

"Don't give yourself an ulcer," said Sunday after a moment. "I told you that I was playing my own game on Ledger, and I am."

"How? You don't even know where he is."

"I don't need to know," said Mr. Sunday.

And the line went dead.

On impulse, Kuga decided to call him back, but just sat there staring at his phone. There was no record at all of any recent calls from Mr. Sunday.

"Jesus Christ," he said, and when he lifted his drink to his lips, his hand shook so badly that some of it spilled on his shirt.

CHAPTER 79
BILDERBERG PARKHOTEL
ROTTERDAM, THE NETHERLANDS

Stafford went to a quiet corner of the lobby and called Dingo.

"Checked the guy here," he said. "It's a no go on the first one. Have you gotten anywhere with the background checks on the other two?"

"Maybe."

"For god's sake, Dingo . . ."

"Yeah, yeah, okay. Both of the other guys look good. Hilton and Marriott. Both have emotional support dogs rather than seeing eye."

"And . . . ?"

"The guy at the Marriott has a good Facebook page, and it looks legit. Definitely not Ledger in all the pics."

"That can be faked."

"Sure, but there's a lot of them, going back like eleven years. The time it would take to build all that phony history . . . man, that's weeks of Photoshop alone."

"What about the other guy, the one at the Hilton?"

"Of the two, he has my vote. Has LinkedIn with a picture that could be any of a thousand guys. Not Ledger's face, of course, but a photo with details that match a likely disguise. And his Instagram is all funny memes and business stuff. He sells restaurant software to American chains doing business overseas. His Instagram avatar is a cartoon. Same goes for his Twitter. Lots of retweets from *Forbes* and Bloomberg, some *Wall Street Journal* stuff. And lots of pictures of restaurants all over the world."

"So, you're saying he's trying to be anonymous?"

"That or he really is socially awkward and that's why he has an emotional support dog."

"Okay, I like that. Why's the other guy have one?"

"PTSD. Not from the war, though. The roof of his church collapsed, and he was one of the few survivors."

Stafford looked out the window at a light drizzle falling onto the Rotterdam streets. People hurried to get out of the rain. He watched a very pretty woman with incredible cheekbones and Jamaican braids walking through the shower with a joyful expression on her face.

"Okay," he said, "I'll hit the Hilton first. Stay on it, though. If the other guy makes any kind of move, let me know."

"Sure."

Stafford hung up, nodded to himself, feeling good about the guest at the Hilton. He went out into the rain. He walked directly past a middle-aged woman wearing a dowdy cardigan who walk-jogged through the drops to get into the lobby. He had no idea who Peggy Ann Gondek was and did not even glance in her direction.

She, on the other hand, gave him a double take because at first glance she thought she was seeing Joe Ledger. But that second look convinced her it wasn't Joe, not even in disguise. She turned away, forgetting about the man completely.

CHAPTER 80
ROTTERDAM MARRIOTT HOTEL
ROTTERDAM, THE NETHERLANDS

Truth to tell . . . when I started talking to Toys, I wasn't really sure what I was going to say.

Let's face it, I've been on the world's least fun autopilot for a while. I had information rattling around in my head, but I didn't really have it collated in any useful way. That was the problem. Usually this far into a case, I'd have turned information over piecemeal to the TOC, to Church and Bug, to Doc and whomever else was on deck. Then they'd fire up the analytical monster that was Rogue Team International. They'd bring in MindReader and maybe tap our allies—Barrier, Kingdom, SEAL Team 666, Interpol, Mossad, Chess Team, Sigma Force. Nikki would be looking for patterns, and Yoda would be categorizing data into digestible bites. Maybe we'd call in Dr. John Cmar and his Bug Hunters if there was a bioweapon in play or Dr. Ronald Coleman if this was genetic. All the intellectual muscle would flex and they'd toss me a set of mission parameters that would put me and my team in play.

I'm mixing metaphors, I think. But you get the idea.

But I wasn't playing that kind of ball game. I was way the hell out on my own. Until I started laying it out for Toys, I wasn't even sure that I was chasing anything except blood.

Except . . .

Even though I was literally killing my way up the food chain toward Santoro and Kuga, there was the fact that I kept collecting flash drives and cell phones, laptops and printed files. On some level, the me that was Colonel Joe Ledger was still trying to do his job, to work the case. It made me kind of look inward and give a nod to the very weary Cop part of me. Still treating all this like a case. Collecting clues, processing evidence.

That should have been encouraging. It should have been a comfort.

It made me sad, though, and at that moment, I really couldn't say why.

Toys listened very closely as I went through it from the beginning.

I told him about the lab technicians in the basement of Mitrović's mansion on Trstenik Island in Croatia.

"Some of them talked," I said, and my voice sounded like a specter's—distant, thin, and dead. "Before I killed them, some of them begged to talk. None of them knew where Santoro and Kuga were. None of them had ever met them. So I told them to give me something. A name, a lead, a location. I . . . I told them that telling me was their only chance. That if they didn't, I *would* kill them; and telling me might save them. They told me everything they knew."

I looked down the neck of my beer bottle and found no absolution there.

"I killed them anyway."

I glanced at Toys. His eyes were steady, focused. If there was judgment there, I couldn't see it.

"They told me about a man in Italy. A man named Puccini. Like the composer. He was a middleman in the Kuga supply chain. Nobody of any real importance. There's someone like him in every major city in every country. Someone to pass messages along, arrange for new papers and identities. Someone to provide a bed and a meal, or a key to a hotel suite and a girl. A minor cog with no direct blood on his hands. But he was *inside* the organization. Mitrović was a contractor. Like most of the other people doing research and development. Not in the family."

Toys nodded but said nothing.

"I found Puccini. He . . ." I looked away. "He didn't want to tell me anything."

"But he did?" prompted Toys.

"He did."

"Where is he now?"

"Unless the police have found him, what's left of him is rotting in his basement. Tied to a chair."

"Was he dead when you left him?"

"Very." I sighed. "Did he need to die? Was he a risk for ratting me out? Fuck. I don't know."

"And I don't care. Alive he was a risk."

I shook my head. "You'd have made the worst priest. 'Bless me, Father, for I have sinned.' 'That's okay, kid, it had to be done.'"

He almost smiled at that. "What did Puccini tell you?"

"He told me that Santoro made frequent visits to a lab in Johannesburg."

"That would be Dr. Gerald Engelbrecht of Van der Vyver Biomedical Associates?"

"You know about that?"

"It made the news," he said. "Depending on whose press you watch, it was either a terrorist attack or a theft gone horribly wrong." He finished his wine, picked up the phone, and called room service. More wine for him—a claret this time—more beer for me. And some sliced lamb for Ghost.

While we waited for that to arrive, I went over what I could remember of my trip to South Africa. When I got to the part where I set fire to the place while Engelbrecht was still alive, I saw Toys wince for the first time. And that reminded me that he and Sebastian

Gault had nearly burned to death on my first DMS gig, the Patient Zero case. Not that I had anything to do with it—they blew up the lab where Gault's crazy-as-fuck girlfriend Amirah was turning Seif al Din into an unstoppable doomsday weapon. They say the body has no memory for pain. I've always disagreed, and when it comes to burns, those memories are quite persistent.

Or . . . maybe that wince was because of my callousness. Hard to say, and I didn't ask.

However, he said, "How much of this is you on a revenge kick and how much is the Darkness?"

The waiter knocked at that point, so I went and answered the door, tipped him, and brought the booze over to where we sat. After I was sipping another cold beer, I finally answered.

"I really don't know," I admitted. "The memories are in my head, but it's almost like I'm recalling details I saw in a movie. They don't feel entirely mine, if that makes any sense."

"Yes," he said, "it does."

We drank.

"What was next?" he asked. "Back to Italy?"

"No. Kraków."

He raised an eyebrow. "Poland? Really? I . . . don't think RTI knows about that."

"Kuga probably does," I said.

"What took you there? A sudden jones for cabbage rolls and pierogies?"

"I hit one of their money men," I said. "A banker named Wójcik. More of a bagman, really. He either arranges wire transfers or hand-delivers cash payments."

"To whom?"

"Mostly people on the ground. Buyers working with terrorist groups, PMCs, and militias. A lot of his clients are in the States, and some in southern Canada. White supremacists, but not exclusively. Wójcik made over two dozen trips to the States over the last six years, making payments to radical fringe groups of all colors and all ideologies."

"To what end? I mean, if they're selling arms and providing cash to extreme white groups as well as, say, radical Black groups . . ."

"The hardest thing to remember about Kuga is they're *not* political. They sell product, and they never stand in the way of the gunplay. From what I was able to get out of Wójcik, they're not only selling the weapons but also stoking the fires via social media posts, mass mailings, published pamphlets, and all that. Funding transportation for rallies and counterprotests. Providing payment to help hire social media influencers to give them a bigger visible presence, and a greater potential threat, than they might otherwise have. Some of these groups were no more than half a dozen assholes sitting around in someone's double-wide, drinking Budweiser and talking about how unfair the system was to them because it was trying to make things equal for Black- and brown-skin interlopers."

"Interlopers," said Toys, enjoying the word.

"He said the plan was to keep both sides on the edge of violence so that they're each potential customers. Taking sides cuts your customer base in half."

Toys sighed and nodded. "Somewhere in the great beyond, Hugo Vox is getting an enormous hard-on."

"No doubt."

"This thing with the radical groups in the States," said Toys, "do you think Kuga's trying to start another civil war? Wasn't that a talking point before the last election?"

"I don't know," I said. "From what Wójcik said, any major outbreak of violence would only sell more guns. Kuga has the NRA leadership on the payroll, too. And, for the record, neither Kuga nor any of his people give a rat's hairy dick about the Second Amendment except that maintaining the current interpretation of it is good for business. It's not politics; they're neither left nor right. They just want to sell product."

Toys drank some wine, nodding as he swallowed. "As criminal enterprises go, it's rather clever. Brilliant, actually. Let the ideologues handle the rhetoric and never let them know they're really point men for a sales force. Bloody marvelous."

I shrugged, then also nodded. "It's smart business, if you're a greedy, murderous sociopath."

"Oh, I spit on parlor psychoanalysis."

"Do you disagree, though?"

He sighed again. "Not at all."

I told him about following the money based on the info Wójcik gave me and how that led me to a series of small hits. Each time inching toward someone who might put me on Santoro's scent. However, each time I felt like I was getting closer, all I did was find another bad guy working for the company.

"What happened to these individuals?" asked Toys. "Or is that a pointless question?"

I said nothing.

"Ah," he said. "So, let's see, did all that mayhem finally bring you back to Italy?"

"Yes." And I went over the hit on Fong. "His intel brought me here to Rotterdam, and I got some good intel about someone who actually *does* know where Kuga and Santoro might be."

"Well, that's bloody brilliant," said Toys, brightening. "If you're going out again, I'd be happy to accompany you."

I shook my head. "The guy I'm looking for isn't here."

"Where, then?"

"Germany."

"Where in Germany?"

"Someplace I can't actually go," I said. "Somewhere I can't get to him."

The truth was that I had a name—including a key member of the Kuga organization with the unlikely name of Diego Casanova. However, Casanova was currently incarcerated in a black site prison in Berlin. I briefly considered asking Toys to ask Church about seeing if the man could be extradited and sent to Phoenix House for questioning. De Vries and Fong both said that he was in Kuga's inner circle.

But I didn't say any of that to Toys.

I wanted to, but the Darkness didn't let me. And, yeah, that's real damned hard to explain.

"There's another guy whose name came up from a few of the people I . . . um . . . interviewed. Calls himself Mr. Sunday, though I doubt it's his real name. He's apparently a new hire—last several months or so—and serves as the head of sales. Does sessions with potential buyers via a platform like Zoom or Crowdcast, but on the dark web. Access only via a special encrypted video conferencing platform. I can't find him, so that's something you can tell Church. He can put Bug on it."

"Why don't you tell him yourself? People are actually concerned about you."

"People, but not you."

"Let's be real," he said, and I took no offense. Not sure I'd cry real tears if he got run over by a bus six or seven times. "I'll pass it along, though. And I have something to share with you."

"What?"

"I talked to a few of my old cronies in the black market circles," he said. "Apparently, your escapades have really pissed off our friends. Kuga and Santoro have sicced a specialist on you. A very dangerous chap named Stafford."

I stiffened. "Michael Augustus Stafford?"

"You know him?"

"No, but that name came up. I assumed he was one of the Fixers."

"Oh, he's a lot more than that, mate. Stafford is easily the most dangerous button man in the business. Very discreet, very smart, and very dangerous. Ex–special operations. Expert in all the right stuff—weapons, unarmed combat, disguises, the lot." He snorted. "He's rather like the bad-guy version of you. Your evil twin. He even looks a bit like you, come to think on it. Blond-haired, blue-eyed all-American boy with rage issues and a penchant for scorched earth. Not sure where I'd place my bets if you two chaps were in an even match."

"Let him take his best shot."

"His best shot, Ledger, is likely to be the one you never see coming. He has an unbroken record for closing cases. And now you're his newest target."

I shook my head. "If he's going to try to get between me and Santoro, he'd better be really damned good."

"He is."

"Then he'd better want it more than I do, Toys. And I want it a whole damned lot."

We discussed the American Operation. We agreed that it was probably a misdirection.

Toys took a sip of wine, made a face, and set the glass aside.

"There's one way to find out if there's anything to it."

"Oh? And what's that?"

"Go to America and arrange to let yourself be spotted doing it. Poke around in the militia thing and break some legs, cut some throats. If they send a handful of Fixers after you, then it's no big deal. They just want you dead. If they send Stafford, you'll know two things— that something's really happening in the States . . ."

"What's the other thing?"

"Which one of you really is the better killer."

I smiled at him. "That's actually a pretty good plan. Maybe I will."

"I can help," he said. "You need a bloody minder."

"No doubt," I said. Then I reached under the pillow, took out my Snellig dart gun, and shot him with a nice big dose of Sandman.

He slid out of the chair and into a heap on the floor.

Ghost looked at him and then me.

I said nothing. Finished my beer and began to pack.

CHAPTER 81
ROTTERDAM THE HAGUE AIRPORT
SOUTH HOLLAND, THE NETHERLANDS

Mrs. Gondek was sipping mint tea out of a travel mug when Joe Ledger walked past. He did not look like Ledger, of course. He wore a very old-fashioned suit—fog gray with a faint powder-blue charcoal stripe—and had a very convincing black toupee over his blond hair. His eyes, today, were dark brown, and his mustache was in the clipped Eastern European style. His gait was tentative, selling the fiction of a man who has never quite found his courage in life. Perhaps a businessman who was somewhere on the more useful end of the autism spectrum, but not social, not visibly confident. His dog— white with brown and black patches—walked beside him, and Joe habitually touched the animal as if needing reassurance of the presence of his emotional support. All these items were writ small, so that they had a genuine and lived-in look.

She mentally awarded him a B-plus or perhaps an A-minus.

Her own disguise was one of the thousand variations of her usual kit. A floral dress of the kind popular in rural Italy, a thin white sweater, cheap but not garish necklace, with earrings that nearly but not quite matched. Sensible shoes for walking, and glasses that were merely functional but not stylish. If the circumstances called for it, there were enough separates and other items in her bag that would allow her to become anything from a fashionable tourist to a successful businesswoman to a Sacramentine nun, and she could make the transformation in any toilet stall in under a minute. Mrs. Gondek had been playing this game for a very long time, and she liked being good at it.

As Joe Ledger passed, he never once glanced in her direction. No reason he should. They'd only ever met once, years ago, and before he even had Ghost. The dog did not twitch. Her scent would not be stored in the animal's vast canine vocabulary of scents.

When they were at least eighty feet down the terminal hall, she began to follow. She was able to walk quickly without ever looking like she was hurrying.

She watched Ledger head toward the gate for a flight to Rome. That was what Scott Wilson said he'd do. There was a good-size crowd in the waiting area, and she saw Ledger take out an e-reader, sit down in the section reserved for coach, and begin to read.

Mrs. Gondek nodded to herself and edged away to call this in to the RTI.

She walked past a tall blond man wearing a Società Sportiva Lazio jersey, one of the football clubs in Rome. He was reading yesterday's issue of *La Gazzetta dello Sport* and listening to something through Apple earbuds. He did not glance at her, nor she at him.

And so she never noticed that the man stood at an angle where he could watch the nervous businessman with the big dog.

Michael Augustus Stafford had no idea who Peggy Gondek was or that one of Mr. Church's top surveillance operatives had walked within three feet of him. His focus was entirely on Joe Ledger.

He was impressed with Ledger's disguise and the small personal tics he'd adopted. He filed them away for his own future use. And the dye job on Ghost was subtle and convincing. Stafford had never used a dog as part of a disguise, and he thought it might be fun. He liked dogs and had a mastiff at home that was roughly the size of a stegosaurus. Might be too imposing and noticeable. Maybe something smaller and disposable. Something the cabin attendants would ooh and aah over, giving him a chance to get an email address or phone number.

The challenge was that Stafford did not have a ticket for this flight. He'd followed Ledger here from the hotel, where one of his agents had spotted him. All the intelligence Stafford had gathered indicated that Ledger was following a trail of information that would almost certainly take him to Rome, and from there to one of three possible targets: Tuscany, Sardinia, or Bologna. Kuga had his money on the latter, though Santoro thought Ledger might go back to Tuscany because there was a warehouse near Florence filled to the rafters with components for exosuits that were about to be flown to Canada. Sardinia was the least likely target, mostly because so few people knew about it and it was in a heavily fortified compound.

Stafford's ticket was for a later flight, and he had to change it.

He turned away and made a call to one of the three people stationed here in the airport. When the call was answered, Stafford told the man to get him a ticket for first class if possible. First on, first off. Each of his agents had the right fake credentials to purchase the ticket, but no photo ID was needed to actually board, so Stafford could remain where he was. Then he called Dingo and requested passenger manifests for every plane leaving in the next two hours, especially the ones getting ready to board for Italy.

Once that was done, he turned back.

And Joe Ledger was gone.

INTERLUDE 14
THE PAVILION
BLUE DIAMOND ELITE TRAINING CENTER
STEVENS COUNTY, WASHINGTON
ONE MONTH AGO

Eve stood in the corner, her back squeezed into the cleft of two walls, fists knotted and held to her mouth.

The room was awash in blood.

Two of the Fixers—not her precious Righteous, but highly trained agents nonetheless—lay on the bed. And off it. And across the room. How could all those pieces ever have come from just the two of them?

She was naked, her thighs and breasts streaked with red. None of it hers.

The intensity was gone now, vanishing even faster that it had come on.

How long ago was it all different? She wasn't sure.

At first, it was nice. Beautiful. Two of them—ripped, chiseled, hard, huge. Fucking her. Fucking each other. Doing whatever she told them to do even though neither was gay or even bi. They were hers, and she was Santoro's, and no one said no.

She'd picked them *because* they were so straight. That was a game. Make the straight ones do what she wanted. Kissing, sucking, stroking, fucking. Coming inside each other. That had been an old game. One she used to play with Adam. Find the straight ones, male and female, and try to reshape them. Open them up, liberate their thinking. Expand their minds.

Some—more than a few—liked it.

These men did not, but what choice did they have? If they rebelled, if they walked out on her, Daddy would punish them. No one wanted that. Tougher men than these had broken down crying at the thought. One Fixer had hanged himself because he thought that Daddy was going to punish him in some special way.

Her sessions with them had grown beyond sex games, though. It was during her second or third week at the Pavilion that she'd started with the handcuffs and the riding crop. A week later, it was a bullwhip. Oversize sex toys, including studded dildos never designed for safe anal play.

And on and on.

Things that satisfied her needs one day were pedestrian and pointless the following night. HK let her play, because she, too, was afraid of Santoro.

As for Daddy? He never said a word. Not to her. Not to anyone with authority to stop her.

And now this.

Eve could barely remember taking the filleting knives and the cleaver from the kitchen or the wood rasp from the shop. All she knew was that she had them.

Used them.

All of that, though, seemed to be part of a dream.

All of that happened within fits of a red cloud of lust and hate. A red darkness.

The two Fixers did not look even remotely human anymore. Eve did not want to look in a mirror because she knew that the red darkness was still there, waiting behind her eyes.

Even she, of all people, was afraid of it.

CHAPTER 82
ROTTERDAM THE HAGUE AIRPORT
SOUTH HOLLAND, THE NETHERLANDS

I settled into my seat and made sure Ghost was comfortable.

The jet was a middle-aged Airbus A350–900. Comfortable enough for the flight from Rotterdam to Berlin. I buckled up for safety, opened a bottle of water I'd purchased in the terminal, took a sip, then removed a collapsible rubber dish and poured some for Ghost. He drank noisily while eyeing the pocket into which I had tucked a bag of beef jerky.

"*Du musst warten*," I told him.

Ghost, who did not like waiting even one little bit, gave me a long, withering look of complete disdain. He and I both knew that we weren't even going to be off the tarmac before I caved and gave him some treats.

I wondered how Toys was. Yeah, not a joke. I'd been a real dick doing that to him. But, on the other hand, I hadn't asked him to be my wingman, my father confessor, or my plucky sidekick. Besides, he hadn't liked me to begin with, so I doubted it was going to derail a budding bromance.

Even so.

I'd shot him. And I knew the effects Sandman had. The nightmares. Toys had a lot of skeletons in his closet, and most likely he was going to meet every single one of them.

As I had when I'd been darted by the earlier generation known as Horsey. The original developer, Dr. William Hu, always claimed that shooting me had been an accident, a pistol malfunction.

Bullshit, of course.

Hu was gone now. A victim of one of Harcourt Bolton's master plans. One of many, many victims of the man behind the Kuga mask.

I settled back and waited for the jet to begin rolling.

Before we even got up to ground speed, Ghost was chewing on a piece of jerky.

CHAPTER 83
ROTTERDAM THE HAGUE AIRPORT
SOUTH HOLLAND, THE NETHERLANDS

Stafford stood and listened to the massive silence on the other end of the cell call.

He did not dare break it or ask if the man on the other end of the line was still there.

Finally, Kuga spoke. His voice was much calmer than Stafford had expected.

"You earned a lot of brownie points with the Java thing," said Kuga. "You banked a lot of goodwill currency, but I have to tell you, son, you're burning through it pretty fast. You let Ledger slip away? Jesus H. Christ, esquire."

Stafford said nothing. Apologies were useless and even dangerous with Kuga. Ditto for Santoro, who was probably listening in.

"Where is he going?"

"Best guess? Berlin."

"Why?" asked Kuga.

"Again . . . just a guess . . . but Casanova."

Another silence. "Shit. How soon?"

"Not sure," said Stafford. "If he's going after the processing plant, there are only two ways to get in. Either he needs to get Church to work some kind of magic to get permissions, or he's got to try to break in."

"Alone? That's impossible."

"Maybe we should stop trying to decide what's impossible for this son of a bitch. Much as it actually hurts to say it, boss, he's impressing the hell out of me."

"Hooray," Kuga said icily. "So, sure, we don't underestimate Ledger. Lesson learned. What are you going to do about it?"

"First, I need to catch him, and if I wait for the next commercial flight with an available seat, I'll be here for seven hours. Even with Ledger needing to find the right equipment for a break-in, he'll be ahead of me."

"No," said Kuga, "that's not soon enough. He'll slip your punch. Again." There was a pause. "Let me make a call. Stay at the airport and be ready."

The line went dead.

CHAPTER 84

THE PLAYROOM
UNDISCLOSED LOCATION
NEAR VANCOUVER, BRITISH COLUMBIA, CANADA

Rafael Santoro looked up from his desk as Eve limped into the room. She was dressed in regular clothes—no camo, no low-slung gun belt.

"Eve," he said, smiling, "thank you for coming so quickly."

"Anything for you, Daddy," said the woman as she made her way across the expensive Turkish rug.

Santoro watched her eyes, looking for the flicker of pain with each step. He wondered how much of that pain was physical and how much was emotional. Maybe a twenty-eighty split, he judged. The part of him who was exactly who he was, enjoyed that 80 percent. The part that was the mentor and only surviving friend of the woman felt true empathy for the remaining percentage. It was an interesting mix, and one nearly unique in his personal experience.

"Have a seat, my dear," he said, waving her to one of the two richly upholstered leather guest chairs opposite the desk. "Coffee? No? Tell me how you are feeling today."

"You know how I'm feeling," she said bluntly.

"Hurt, angry, and anxious to put Joe Ledger's head on a pike?" he suggested.

"Yeah, sure, but not in that order."

"And the knee?"

She shrugged. A total knee replacement had been performed a month ago, but there had been some complications, and the doctors were trying to decide if they needed to go back in. The poor function of the new knee required that she go back to wearing the knee brace.

They sat with that for a moment while hidden speakers played the opera *Atlàntida,* a *cantata escénica* based on a Catalan poem by Jacint Verdaguer. It was moody and superb. Two full minutes of it played before Eve spoke again.

"Knee or no knee, I'm telling you right now, Daddy, that if I don't get out there and *do* something, I'm going to go totally apeshit."

Santoro nodded. "I understand, my sweet, but we cannot act rashly."

"Is that some kind of dig because of what happened at the Pavilion?"

He smiled and shook his head. "My angel, what does it matter to me if you vented some of your pressure by indulging your appetites?"

"HK fucking freaked."

"Hers is a more orderly mind."

"More sane, you mean," said Eve, cutting him a suspicious glance.

"No. Are any of us truly sane? We could not be who we are if we were that mundane. No, my daughter, you are allowed to play." She started to speak, but he stopped her with a raised finger. "As long as you do not include the Righteous and the Elites in your fun and games, yes?"

She said nothing.

"Please show me the respect of an answer, Eve," he said, and there was that subtle edge. He never clubbed her, but he did make small cuts.

"Yes, Daddy."

"There's my angel," he said, smiling warmly. Then he changed the subject. "HK has kept me up to date with the training, and our development team has assured me that the equipment we have is more than adequate to our needs."

"Even with Joe fucking Ledger cutting throats all over the place? Seems to me that he's on to us."

"And what if he is?" asked Santoro, raising his eyebrows.

"Isn't the shit he's done going to derail us?"

"Oh no, Eve, it's far too late for his shenanigans to stop what's coming. At best, he'll find us just in time for your Righteous to tear him apart. Tell me, do you know what it means to draw and quarter someone?"

"Sure." She brightened. "Oh, sweet! I can have four of my guys do that."

"Yes," he said, "you can and you should. So . . . if he is on his way, then let him come."

"He'll bring that whole goon squad with him."

"I dearly hope he does," said Santoro. "Even with whatever information Ledger has managed to steal or coerce from our various laboratories . . . he will never be able to stop what's about to happen." He leaned forward. "America will burn, my daughter."

Eve got to her feet, leaned across the desk, took Santoro by the face with both hands, and pulled him to her for a kiss. Not a sexual one—he was her father, after all—but it was full of a certain kind of passion. And Rafael Santoro, who loved his daughter more than anything left alive on earth, allowed it.

Then he pushed her gently back.

"Now listen to me," he said softly. "I have a special mission for you."

She grinned. "Berlin?"

"Yes," he said, "Berlin."

CHAPTER 85
ROTTERDAM MARRIOTT HOTEL
ROTTERDAM, THE NETHERLANDS

Toys woke up with a groan. Sickness washed through him, and he crawled across the floor and into the bathroom, then threw up the excellent food and wine.

It took monumental effort to turn on the shower, strip off his clothes, and collapse into the bottom of the stall. The water pounded on him. He hadn't gotten the water mix right, and the blast was icy.

"You . . . bastard . . . ," he gasped.

The Sandman had conjured inescapable nightmares for Toys, and his worst dreams were always about the innocent people he'd killed before Church had lured him away from that life. Toys had long ago memorized each name, knew details of their lives. They haunted him at the best of times, but in the drug-induced nightmares, they tore him apart endlessly.

Later.

Much later . . .

He took a proper shower, though his legs were still shaky. Then he ordered more food and when it arrived sat staring at it as if it were a plate of steaming offal.

It wasn't until he staggered back from his fourth bathroom trip that he saw the briefcase. It was on a chair across the suite. It was a very expensive case, a Webster X Charles Simon Graphite Mackenzie Aluminum one. The same kind Sebastian Gault used. Very durable, hard to open. Stylish, which Toys took to mean that Ledger had stolen it. The barbarian had no personal style.

The case was unlocked.

He opened it to find file folders crammed with data stolen from the people Ledger had killed. And several external hard drives.

On top of those, though, was a handwritten note.

DON'T COME LOOKING FOR ME AGAIN.
NEXT TIME, I'LL USE A DIFFERENT GUN.

Toys took the case over to the bed and rifled through the contents.

"Jesus Christ," he murmured and scrambled to find his cell phone. However, before he could even dial a call, there was a knock on the door. He frowned, fetched his pistol, and peered out through the peephole. And grunted in surprise. Two people stood in the hall. A short, dumpy young man who looked like Matt Damon—if the actor broke training, lost IQ points, and forgot how to dress; and a tall, fit, elegant, and very beautiful woman with dark hair and darker eyes.

Toys ran fingers through his hair, tucked the gun into his waistband, and opened the door.

The woman gave him a slow up-and-down appraisal.

"Toys," said Violin, "you look awful."

"Yeah, man," said Harry Bolt, "you really look like shit."

Toys stepped back to let them in. "Well, you can both kiss my arse. But . . . come on in anyway. Did Church send you?"

"No," said Violin as she breezed past. "My mother did."

"Looking for Ledger, I assume," he said, closing the door behind them. "Well, you just missed that rotten son of a bitch. He's probably out of the effing country by now."

"Yes," said Violin, "and he's on his way to Germany. Get dressed and packed. I have a plane waiting for us at the airport."

"What?"

"Arklight has had people looking for Joe ever since he went gonzo," said Harry. He was a former CIA agent, and according to everyone who ever worked with him, a truly awful one. He'd only gotten fast-tracked through the academy and into the field because of who his father was. If Harry was the worst, then his father, Harcourt Bolton Sr., was arguably the best the agency ever had. The irony was that the senior Bolton, the most decorated agent in the company's history, had also been the worst traitor. While Harry, however inept at tradecraft, had proved himself to have unbreakable integrity. Violin had taken him under her wing and was teaching him—a task that proved to everyone who knew them both that she had the patience of a living saint.

Toys nodded. "Have a seat. There's still some wine left. And beer, though it's lukewarm by now."

"Works for me," said Harry, taking a bottle. He offered it to Violin, who shook her head. So he twisted off the top and took a long drink.

"What happened here?" asked Violin.

Toys glared at her. "Ledger is a shit-eating arsehole."

Harry snorted beer through his nose.

"Tell me about it while you pack," said Violin, settling back in a chair.

CHAPTER 86
IN FLIGHT OVER GERMAN AIRSPACE

It wasn't a very long flight from Rotterdam to Berlin, but it still gave me time to think.

I felt like a bit of a shit for what I'd done to Toys. The more I thought about it, the more I regretted it. And, of course, once he told Junie what I'd done, that would likely be the last damned straw.

Was I trying to drive her away?

The Darkness whispered one answer to me; the other voices—the Modern Man, the Killer, and the Cop—whispered another. But each answer was another shade of *yes*.

Ghost had his head in my lap and was benefiting from my jangling nerves by getting even more pets and treats than usual. Dog therapy. It's a thing.

The feel of his soft fur and the awareness of his unconditional love were an anchor. Possibly the only clean tether I had left. The only other thing holding me to the desire to remain alive was the fact that Santoro was still sucking air. But . . . what was going to happen if I caught and killed him? Where—and who—would I be then?

At one point, I got up and went into the toilet, locked the door, and stood for a long time looking into my eyes. I'd come out of the total control of the Darkness. I thought. I hoped. But I still had so many questions.

What *was* the Darkness? I mean, exactly. Had my cracked mind completely fractured? Could it ever be put back together again?

At times, during brief moments of terrified lucidity, I wondered if this was more of Kuga's mind games. During the Kill Switch case, he used the God Machine to actually invade my mind. Top's and Bunny's, too. He'd forced them to commit murders. Was that happening all over again? I almost hoped it was. Though even my wishful thinking couldn't help me construct a scaffold of probability for that, because I was doing damage *to* Kuga.

If not that, then what? I even flirted with the possibility that this was demonic possession. I didn't actually *believe* in demons, but there was a bright and silvery thread of hope in that. A chance for this all not to be my fault.

If it was neither of those things, then what was I left with?

Me.

Damaged. Broken beyond repair.

And, no, I didn't think that just because I felt it was my hands currently on the steering wheel that it was over. Nor did I try to lie to myself that what I did, however extreme, was for the good of all. That it was the *right* thing to do. I'd tried that rationalization on back in Italy, but it fit no better then than it did now.

So, where did that leave me?

Who was I now?

What was I now?

And . . . was there any real way to ever go home again?

BECAUSE I
COULD NOT STOP
FOR DEATH
PART 5

The murdered do haunt their murderers, I
    believe.
I know that ghosts have wandered on earth.
Be with me always—take any form—drive me
    mad!
Only do not leave me in this abyss, where I
    cannot find you!

—EMILY BRONTË

One need not be a chamber to be haunted.

—EMILY DICKINSON

CHAPTER 87
DAS VERARBEITUNGSZENTRUM
WANNSEE, BOROUGH OF STEGLITZ-ZEHLENDORF
BERLIN, GERMANY

The place did not exist.

Not officially. That's what I was told. That's what I read in RTI reports.

Not in any computer record or database. It was never mentioned by name in any email or data file sharing. The few people in Germany, England, and the United States who knew about it also knew better than to make any references in any traceable way. Spies were everywhere—in cyberspace and the real world. Someone was always watching or listening.

When the place had to be referred to, even obliquely, it was given the bland nickname of Das Verarbeitungszentrum—the Processing Center. There were thousands of places in Germany that processed something—sales, deliveries, Amazon fulfillment, insurance claims. It was the kind of name that never rang a bell or raised a red flag.

Only eight key people within those three governments knew that the Processing Center was a prison. Which made it the ultimate black site. Prisoners who went there might as well have slipped through a hole in the dimension. They were simply gone.

The staff knew, of course, but they were sequestered in six-month shifts without Wi-Fi or internet. No email, no cell phones, no contact at all with the outside world. Only unmarried soldiers were assigned to the facility, and they were deeply screened beforehand and carefully debriefed afterward. Those employees each signed a nondisclosure document that erased all their rights should they break their oath. A single fracture in the chain of confidentiality would result in arrest, the ruin of their families and their futures, and very possibly incarceration in one of the cells within that forbidding place. Yeah, we live in fun times.

From the outside, it looked like the fiction its designers were selling. A slab-sided block building with few windows, loading bays for trucks, and a security fence that looked absurdly nonthreatening. What passersby could not see were the motion sensors, camouflaged high-def cameras, satellite surveillance, and frequent flyovers by drones designed to look exactly like common hooded crows. And, although the fence was not electrified, there were panels on all the surrounding interior grounds and walkways that were. The default setting was approximately that of a moderate Taser, but during a crisis, they could be dialed up to give a lethal jolt of two hundred milliamps. That'll curl the hairs on your nuts effectively. Those pads were weight sensitive so as not to fry birds, cats, or raccoons.

The windows were false. Each was a rear-screen projection of long loops of footage of real office buildings taken elsewhere. Behind those screens were steel panels. The doors opened with simple key cards, but once inside, there were massive security doors requiring several types of scans—retina, thumbprint, exhaled breath, and spoken day codes. Breaching the walls would require a hell of a lot of explosives, and those walls—and every door—were wired to alarms that rang audibly or quietly but in the right places to send a lot of grouchy German soldiers with guns.

The plan had been direct and effective: to make Das Verarbeitungszentrum fade into the background of a sleepy tourist suburb of a major city and to be essentially impregnable.

"No one can find it," the designers assured the three governments that shared the invisible prison. "No one can beat it."

CHAPTER 88
PHOENIX HOUSE
OMFORI ISLAND, GREECE

"Boss," Bug shouted, leaning his head out of his office and yelling loudly enough to make everyone jump, "I got him!"

Church, who had been in deep conversation with Scott Wilson, wheeled around.

"Where?"

"Germany."

"*Germany?*" exclaimed Wilson. "That isn't on our list of possible targets for him. Are you sure?"

"Pretty darn sure." Bug waved Church and Wilson into his office. Outside, at least thirty staff members had already clustered, craning their necks, jostling one another for a view.

"Someone hit our safe house on Krampenberger Straße in Berlin," he said. "Darted the poor guy stationed there. Guy woke up a few minutes ago and says last thing he remembered was watching a rerun of a cop show. Something called . . . *Alarm for Cobra something-something.*"

"*Alarm für Cobra 11—Die Autobahnpolizei,*" translated Wilson. "Highway police show that's been on forever."

"Yeah. So that rerun started at 2:00 p.m. local time."

Church looked at his watch. "That's nine hours and change." He glanced at Bug. "What did he take?"

"A full field kit, including a MindReader substation and tactical computer. Bunch of drones, weapons, clothes, you name it. And the officer there thinks maybe an old TradeWinds kite."

"For what possible purpose?" asked Wilson.

Church ignored that and instead said, "The substation has a tracker . . ."

"Oh, already on it. Looks like Joe's in the suburbs. Here, let me pull it up." Bug loaded the tracking software, which immediately brought up a map. He pulled in on the screen, which brought up an overlay with town and street names.

"Wannsee," read Wilson, "in the borough of Steglitz-Zehlendorf. Why's he . . . ?"

Then he stiffened so quickly it looked like he was snapping to attention. He turned to Church. "No . . . surely not . . ."

"I think he is," said Church, and there was the faintest hint of an admiring smile on his lips.

"Is . . . what?" asked Bug.

"He's going to try and break into Das Verarbeitungszentrum," said Wilson. "Which, of course, is impossible."

CHAPTER 89
DAS VERARBEITUNGSZENTRUM
WANNSEE, BOROUGH OF STEGLITZ-ZEHLENDORF
BERLIN, GERMANY

So, I broke into the processing plant.

Took about three minutes.

Even brought Ghost, and he loves this kind of thing. Going where we're not supposed to go. Pissing on someone else's floor.

I could have gotten actual permission to enter the facility, but there were three good reasons why I didn't.

First, it would take too much time. The world runs on red tape, and I hate bureaucracy with the fiery intensity of a thousand suns. I'm stealing that quote, though I neither know nor care who from.

The second reason is that going through channels would likely result in me being accompanied by agents of Barrier—the UK's most covert black-operations outfit—some CIA spooks, and a team of busybodies from Germany's own off-the-record group of black-ops shooters, Der Leuchtturm. I wasn't really in the mood for a party. Ghost was all the company I needed, and he was never all that chatty. And, let's face it, with Toys reporting back about me shooting him, and Church evaluating all the intel on my—actions? Crimes? Hard to pick the right word—he'd likely make the calls to ensure that I'd be met by a platoon armed with Sandman darts and a big butterfly net. No, thanks.

And third, a very bad man told me—reluctantly, I might add—that a very highly placed member of the Kuga organization was incarcerated there. Not entirely sure if it was the Darkness or me who asked those questions. My mind is still clogged with mud. For now, I suppose, it's enough to remember the answers I . . . we . . . got.

The prisoner was a Catalonian named Casanova. Actual name. Born Diego Casanova, but later dropped the given name. Maybe he thought that would get him laid more often, but from the surveillance photos I acquired, he was no charmer. Looked like Steve Buscemi, if someone had hit Steve in the face repeatedly with a one-by-three. And he was a brute. Six foot three, three-twenty, with the shoulders and arms of a mountain gorilla. A guy like that wasn't getting laid unless he was paying for it, and even then, he could send even a hardened prostitute straight to therapy.

Casanova worked for Kuga. He worked *with* Rafael Santoro. Which meant that his ass was worth only what value I was willing to put on it. A chatty Casanova who could nudge me a step closer to getting my fingers around Santoro's throat was likely to live long enough to see how good his retirement plan was. A reticent Casanova was going to have a very, very bad night.

What really sucked for Casanova was that he was the one person who might *finally* put me on the path to finding Santoro and Kuga. And by *find*, I mean tear to pieces so I could piss on their corpses. I didn't need the Darkness to want to do that. Or to give me some kind of spiritual or existential permission.

And the fact that Casanova was in one of the counterterrorist community's secretest and most impregnable black site prisons did not worry me all that much. Actually, it amused me in a weird kind of way. Lately, a lot of very strange things amused me. I should probably get that looked at. Rudy Sanchez would likely have a lot to say on the subject. But at the moment, I wasn't much in the mood for analysis, a sermon, or a lecture. I wasn't taking his calls or anyone else's. This was a solo gig. Except for the big white fur monster, of course.

I didn't have my own team with me, either. Havoc Team was composed of the best of the best when it came to tier-one SpecOps shooters, and when things were going south, they could get real mean and damned ugly. But . . . they wouldn't approve of what I was doing. Well, not the *way* I was doing it. Not even a little.

So that left Ghost and me.

To bypass the fence, I used a TradeWinds MotorKite. It was an older one, and the motor was on its last gasp, but I didn't need it to do much. Best it could manage was twenty feet of lift and seventy yards of distance.

We sailed over the fence as the lurid red sunset was fading to a muddy and indistinct purple black. The kite soared over the fence silent as a shadow and approached the building from one corner.

I had a jammer clipped to my belt that would futz with the motion sensors and cameras for the duration of our flight. And the Google Scout glasses I wore helped me avoid the heat signatures from the high-voltage paving stones. I'd stopped by an RTI safe house and took as many goodies as I could. The agent on duty was sleeping off a Sandman dart, and I seriously doubted I'd be getting a Christmas card from him.

Ghost hung from my chest in a Mylar sling, his legs and tail dangling, tongue lolling as if this was fun. The dog's a bit weird. He also likes skydiving, which I really do not.

There were two pairs of security guards on routine patrol, but I'd waited until they were heading around to the far side. It took them approximately six minutes for a circuit of the building, working in different directions. I touched down just as they were each turning opposite corners, walking the kite to the wall as I hit the button to collapse the wings and released Ghost's sling. He immediately turned and watched my back, hunkering low, eyes moving over the landscape. The whole kite rig collapsed down to the size of a folded beach umbrella, and I quickly stowed it behind a line of manicured hedges.

I was dressed all in black, with a balaclava that hid my face, with thin but very tough limb pads and body armor. It was a blend of Kevlar and spider silk around layers of D30, a gooey substance that in its raw state flows like syrup, but when struck locks together, absorbs, and disperses energy as heat before returning to its semifluid state. The body armor can stop most bullets, even .223, 5.56, and 7.62×39 rifle slugs; and the spider silk–polymer blends can turn a knife, which Kevlar alone can't. I also wore the latest generation of shock-reducing ballistic helmet. Sensors sewn into the fabric of my clothes sent real-time data to one screen of my glasses.

Raiding the RTI safe house was a bad risk, but the gear was necessary. And it felt oddly comforting to be back in an official combat rig. Though, yes, that also conjured guilt for what I'd done to my friends over the last month.

Inside my head, the Darkness laughed as if saying that I would never live long enough for those kinds of regrets to matter. Ghost whimpered as if he could sense or even hear those thoughts.

The door I wanted was a bland, metal variety set into the wall eighteen feet from where we'd touched down. As I reached it, I removed two small devices. The first was the size of a postage stamp and painted a neutral gray, with a clear plastic strip on the back. I peeled that off to expose photosensitive chemicals and then pressed it to the side of the metal door for three seconds. When I finished counting Mississippis, I pulled the strip off and saw that it was now the same color as the door. I turned it over and removed the tape from the other side, exposing a strong adhesive, and then pressed it to the door at about knee level, below where the eye would not naturally fall. Unless you knew exactly where to look, the thing was invisible, blending in completely with the paint. The little chameleon bug had incredible pickup and could relay info up to a quarter mile.

Next I took a gizmo about the size of a nickel, removed the adhesive backing, then placed it on the underside of the key card box that was mounted to the right of the door. I then took one of our blank magnetic key cards and went through the process of having MindReader load it with the proper codes.

Of course, I knew that using that Q1 tactical computer meant that what I was doing would be sent to Bug. He would tell Church I was in Berlin, and *where* in Berlin I was. Ah well—couldn't be helped. Made me wonder how quickly the big man would send someone to intercept me. I doubted it would be Toys. Who did that leave? Perhaps Violin? Or my old buddy Oskar Freund? Whoever it was, it was inevitable someone would come, and I needed to finish and get the hell out before they arrived.

I pulled the door open, and Ghost followed me inside. Then I eased the door shut, and the lock clicked comfortingly as if nothing at all had just happened.

Total elapsed time from lifting off with the MotorKite to hearing that click was three minutes. Impregnable, my ass.

CHAPTER 90
BERLIN BRANDENBURG AIRPORT
BERLIN, GERMANY

Michael Augustus Stafford ran down the steps of the private jet Kuga had loaned him for his mission. After the fiasco in Rotterdam, Stafford had appealed to him for better logistical support. The jet—a 2006 Gulfstream G150, which was the closest one available—was comfortable and fast, and Kuga's logistics team stepped up and convincingly fudged diplomatic clearances. It amused Stafford that he was flying as a representative of the World Health Organization on the hunt for a new COVID mutation. Everyone tripped over themselves smoothing the way for him.

There was a car waiting for him, with a driver who knew the area exceptionally well.

"Where to, sir?" was the only thing the driver said.

Stafford told him, and the car—a roomy and luxurious BMW X5—set off.

That driver also provided a box of goodies for him, and while they tore along the darkened streets, Stafford outfitted himself with knives, guns, explosives, and electronics.

"I'm coming for you," muttered Stafford. The driver, on the other side of a closed glass partition, heard nothing. "I'm going to skin you alive, you prick."

CHAPTER 91
BERLIN BRANDENBURG AIRPORT
BERLIN, GERMANY

The sleek black Dassault Falcon 8X luxury jet touched down fourteen minutes after Stafford's wheels hit the tarmac.

The clearances had all been arranged by Annie Han, the computer hacker who officially worked for the South Korean government but who owed her truest allegiance to Arklight.

The jet had a capacity for sixteen passengers, but there were only three aboard. Two men and a woman. They were met at customs by Oskar Freund, who had the papers and the authority to smooth their way through customs.

A woman in driver's livery stood waiting at the curb.

"He was spotted when he came out," she told them. "We have a bird in the air."

The bird was a medium-range radar-deflecting surveillance drone originally designed for the Russian military. Plans and prototypes were stolen by an Arklight hit team. The designer, his staff, and eight soldiers were killed in that raid, and one of Annie's tapeworms was introduced to the computers and internet to hunt down and completely erase all traces of that line of research. It was later learned that Putin's security officers placed the blame on a traitor within their own ranks. He denied it, of course, all the way up to the moment when a bullet punched through his brain. That he was innocent of that particular bit of internal espionage was outweighed by actual crimes for which lives had been lost. Annie and Lilith had no sympathies. Not a shred.

"Where is he now?" asked Violin.

"Heading out of town, it appears," said the driver.

"Catch him," said Toys as he, Violin, and Harry Bolt climbed into the car.

"Ma'am?" the driver asked of Violin, and she nodded.

"Catch him as fast as possible."

The car peeled away from the curb, but before it could go half a kilometer, Violin's cell rang. The caller ID was a steeple.

"Hello," she said warmly.

"Are you on the ground yet?" asked Church.

"Yes, we're following Stafford."

"Change of plans," said Church. "We know where Outlaw is going, and there's every chance he's going to need backup."

CHAPTER 92
DAS VERARBEITUNGSZENTRUM
WANNSEE, BOROUGH OF STEGLITZ-ZEHLENDORF
BERLIN, GERMANY

I tapped my Scout glasses to switch from outside sensors to a floor plan of the processing plant. It was a big oblong building that was laid out for prisoner isolation rather than the standard prison cellblock structure. Lots of small hallways leading to dead ends, and offices, crew quarters, the mess hall, ops center, and other key areas used as buffers between the cells. The idea was to prevent prisoners from ever making contact with one another. Even the walls were baffled to suppress screams and yells. All of which was fine for me, since I neither wanted to be seen nor heard.

I removed two different kinds of tiny drones made to look like bees. They had unfortunate nicknames hung on them by Doc Holliday— Busy-Bees and Killer Bees.

The Busy-Bees were designed to extend MindReader's scanning range in order to hack internal surveillance, and they had good cameras and mics. I activated two dozen of them and tossed the whole bunch into the air. Their wings began buzzing, and off they went, flying fast down the corridors, staying high near the ceiling.

While I waited for their feeds to reach my Q1 screen, I tapped some keys to let the supercomputer's intrusion software hack into the central security systems. That took about eleven seconds, and then I owned the place. I set all the hallway cameras to record video loops that were keyed to sensors in my clothing. As soon as I approached the operational range of the cameras, the prerecorded loop would kick in, which meant I'd never appear on the monitors in the security office. *Stealthy* is my middle name.

The same sensors were on Ghost's harness in case I had to send him wandering off without me.

I knelt and gave Ghost a few short commands. One of which was *Pax*, Latin for "Peace." It meant that for the duration of the mission, and unless told otherwise, he was not to kill anyone. The staff here were not our enemies. If any of them got hurt during this invasion, then it was on me. I was okay with breaking and entering, but I wasn't looking to spill innocent blood. Ghost was a very smart and very well-trained combat dog, and he would follow my orders.

While I waited, I deployed the other kind of drones, the Killer Bees. These were a bit larger and fitted with tiny dart shooters filled with Sandman. I'd have gone with Murder Hornets as the name for them, but I don't hold the patent.

The feed from the Busy-Bee drones came in and told me that there were nine security personnel actively walking the halls, three on duty in the monitoring office, five more in a lounge watching a DVD of the latest Marvel movie, and ten sleeping in a pair of bunkhouses. It was a large staff. The bees also confirmed that there were thirty-nine inmates in the various cells scattered throughout the building. None of the prisoners were named in the computer records. That was fine.

My informant said that Casanova was in cell number 13. I thought that was funny. Unlucky 13.

I clicked through the various feeds to put eyes onto the facility staff and get a sense of them. Then I froze when I saw a group of people standing in one of the remotest hallways. There was an older man— tall, blond, square-jawed, wearing an excellent suit. Beside him was a slightly shorter man with darker hair who held the hand of a very pretty woman. Two kids stood in front of them, and the woman had a small but noticeable baby bump. A big puppy with a goofy grin sat between the kids. They looked directly up at the swarm of drones. As if they could somehow look through the bees to see me.

I knelt there, staring at the faces. Even though the screen was tiny, I could somehow see them all with incredible clarity and detail. To the small scars on the arms of the woman, to the stitches on the baseball the little boy was throwing up into the air and catching in a worn leather glove.

Every.

Single.

Detail.

It froze me.

No, that's not right. When you freeze, it's like all the heat dies in the universe, all the way down to the atoms in your molecules. This wasn't that. This was hotter. I could feel actual heat, as if I crouched next to something burning.

Like a house.

Like bodies.

Like hope.

I squeezed my eyes shut and sagged against the wall.

"Please," I begged. "Please, please, please . . ."

I did not open my eyes until the heat dwindled, dwindled, and faded completely. Even then, I couldn't move. My heart was racing, and shivers ran down my arms and spine. I was in a deep hole, and there was no rope to use so I could climb out. There was only a little light, but it was fading.

No, that wasn't right, either. It was not that the light was growing weaker but that the dark shadows all around me were getting stronger. Overwhelming the light, dominating it, consuming it. There was so little of that light left that I knew it couldn't last. The Darkness was winning.

"Please," I said again, but in that moment, I couldn't tell if I was begging for mercy, for the light to flare, or for the darkness to come and take me, body and soul.

Then . . .

Then I felt pressure against my elbow and only then dared open my eyes to see Ghost nuzzling me, his doggy eyes filled with concern.

My mouth was dry, and my eyes were wet. I had no exposed skin for Ghost to lick, so he kept pushing at me with his nose. I reached for him with arms that weighed ten thousand pounds. I pulled my dog to me and wrapped my arms around him and clung to him.

The screen on my computer showed an empty stretch of hall. No one there. Of course there was no one there. Tears burned behind my eyes. Ghost pushed his whole body against me, whining so softly only I could hear him. Trying to tell me that he understood. That he was there for me. That I wasn't alone.

"It's okay, boy," I said. "It's all okay. I'm okay."

Ghost never cared that I told those kinds of lies.

I did not want to let him go, but I had to. The clock in my head was ticking, and we were deep in the badlands here. Ghost backed away a pace but stayed close as I struggled to get my shit together. It was getting harder and harder to do that.

This was not the first time I'd seen ghosts. I just hoped moments like this didn't get worse, because I was already close to the edge. I'd been fooling myself that because the Darkness was not in total control, it meant I was coming out of it. That I was edging back toward being sane.

Goddamn.

CHAPTER 93

DAS VERARBEITUNGSZENTRUM
WANNSEE, BOROUGH OF STEGLITZ-ZEHLENDORF
BERLIN, GERMANY

I came back to myself, but there was effort in that process. General or abstract thinking won't get that done, so I forced myself to think about specific mission details. It helped, but I found myself not wanting to look at the screen on my tactical computer. I ground my teeth and looked anyway.

I checked the signal from the Busy-Bees again, but all they showed were more empty halls except where there were bored guards on patrol. Lots of locked doors. Only that.

Only that.

"Unclench," I growled under my breath, "and get your screwed-up head out of your ass, Ledger."

At any given time, I have three distinct personalities vying for control. The Modern Man is the idealistic optimist who is probably the person I would have become had it not been for a traumatic incident when I was a teenager. My girlfriend, Helen, and I had been jumped by a group of older teens. They beat me nearly to death and gang-raped Helen. Although we both technically survived that attack, we were never the same. I became psychologically fractured, retreating from who I truly was into a series of jagged-glass pieces of other personalities. Therapists helped me clean house, but three remained, of which the Modern Man was the purest. Then there was his polar opposite, the Killer. Ruthless and violent . . . but always directing his rage at the people who did the kinds of things that had been done to Helen and me. In defense of the innocents, he will do things I never tell my friends or Junie Flynn. It was the Killer, as much as any part of me, who'd kicked in Helen's door when she'd not answered her phone in days. It was he who'd gathered her cold body into his arms and howled like some demented thing. And it was he who'd steered me first toward the army, then the cops, and then my wet work as a shooter, first for the Department of Military Sciences and more recently for Rogue Team International. He knew there was a war to wage and was constantly ready to take it to the bad guys under a black flag. Well . . . let's call it a different kind of black flag. The Killer never hurts the innocent. Ever.

Most of the time, though, I was the Cop. Reasonable, informed, precise, thorough, and pragmatic. A solver of problems, a logician, and strategist. The Cop was the sense of order in my otherwise chaotic head.

I was trying to get into the Cop headspace now. Like my other aspects, he'd been shoved to the back by the Darkness, so much so that he seemed to stop being anything but a memory. Now I really needed him. Desperately. To solve this, to make sense of this crazy hunt I was on, to pick up the pieces of my fragmented memory and puzzle them into some shape that had order and purpose. As random and obscure as the Darkness was, there was a method in there. A plan. And I was sure that at the end of the chain of logic—no, I won't call it *dark logic* because that sounds too much like I'm playing Dungeons & Dragons with myself.

Only this logic was skewed, slanted. It was like trying to understand a word puzzle in a different language. It had a different kind of emotional logic from the one I understood. I was fighting for understanding and fighting for control, and it was anyone's guess as to whether I was gaining ground or being fed crumbs by this new, dangerous, warped, and ugly aspect of myself.

Funny, but when I was first aware of it, I'd told Rudy, and he was the one who gave it the name. He called it *the darkness,* but for him, it was lowercase, not a proper noun. I knew differently. It was every bit as real a person within me as the Modern Man, the Cop, and the Killer. It wanted to live, just as they did. It wanted control because, just like the others, it had work to do. Unlike them, it did not want to share its secrets, its methods, or its toys.

Earlier this year, after I got out of the hospital, I'd speculated about what a person does when they turn out all the lights. At first, I'd relied on the old military answer to that: you learn to *use* the darkness. But that was wrong. It was too commonplace an answer for a person as damaged as me. It wasn't that I learned to use the darkness imposed on me during that act of transgressive horror.

No.

In that moment, I *became* the Darkness, only I didn't know it yet.

I think by accepting that it was a real thing, I gave it license and access, neither of which I seemed able to *take* back. I didn't delude myself into thinking I was clearheaded now, because I'd won any heroic internal struggle.

"Head in the fucking game," I told myself, and I realized I was so jangled I'd nearly said it too loudly. Even Ghost gave me a sharp, questioning look. "Sorry," I told him, pitching my voice much lower.

Ghost gave an eloquent grunt of reproof.

The Busy-Bees helped me map out the safest route, and so we set off. Ghost went first, and I relied on his nose and his instincts every bit as much as my electronic doodads. We moved silently along the dimly lit halls, pausing now and then to allow foot patrols to make a turn down a corridor before we entered that passage. Everything was so quiet. We were near the staff lounge, and I couldn't hear the explosions and dramatic music of superheroes and villains beating the snot out of one another. Nice. Made me want to send a box of chocolates to whomever designed the acoustics. Maybe give him a foot massage.

One confusing thing was that the cells were so scattered that it was tough to follow the numbering system. Nor were there arrows on the walls or those colored lines you see in some factories to guide you to key points. Likely that was to make it even more difficult to find any specific person. That would have been frustrating if I didn't have a tactical version of the world's most sophisticated computer on my arm.

It took me under five minutes to locate cell 13. It was snugged way back into a corner, with the adjoining rooms proving to be dry storage for office supplies on one side and the electrical room on the other. And that was lucky, too, because the machines in the electrical room generated a constant audible hum, further masking incidental sound. Luck seemed to be on my side.

Ghost and I peered around a corner, saw the foot patrol making a left at the far T junction, and then we hurried to the cell. Some jokester on the staff had used a Sharpie to draw a big red heart on a sheet of printer paper and had taped that to the door. For the great lover, Casanova. Cute.

I knelt outside his room and spent a couple of minutes sending new protocols to my swarms. The Busy-Bees fanned out and landed high on walls near the corners, positioned to watch for foot patrols coming my way. By resting on the walls, they conserved their batteries. As for the Killer Bees, I sent two to each intersection. If things got freaky, the Busy-Bees could paint approaching guards with tiny lasers, and the Killer Bees would zero in on each specific guard and send them into slumber land. I didn't want to have to do that, but the way my luck's been running, I figured I'd have to. Once I was outside again, any bees I could not retrieve would be sent a detonation code that would activate minuscule thermite charges. There'd be nothing left for a forensic analysis and no way to trace it back to me or RTI. No way for Bug to track me, either.

I attached another of my doohickeys to the lock on the cell door, sicced Q1 on the security links, and then used the key card–cloning tool to bypass the lock. When all this was over, whoever designed this place as impregnable was going to need crisis counseling.

Then I looked at Ghost to see if he was ready. He was—his brown eyes were very cold and his muscles tensed for action. I opened the door, and we stepped inside.

CHAPTER 94
DAS VERARBEITUNGSZENTRUM
CELL 13

Casanova was reading a book. For some bizarre reason I will never know, it was a copy of *A Wrinkle in Time*. Seemed an improbable choice.

He looked up at me, frowning at my weapons and gear. His frown turned to apprehension when he saw Ghost. Casanova picked up a torn piece of toilet paper, placed it to mark his page, set the book down, then looked at us with all the blank anticipation of a schoolboy ready for his lesson.

I closed the door, sealing us in the soundproofed cell. When I needed to leave, all I had to do was approach the door and the Q1 interface would convince the locking mechanism that I'd swiped the key card again. The wonders of modern science.

　　　　　　　　　　　JONATHAN MABERRY

His eyes narrowed, then he glanced up at the video camera that was protected behind a tough wire screen. The little light was on, but he had no way of knowing the feed was on a continuous loop.

"Morning, lover boy," I said brightly. I said it in Spanish. His native tongue was Catalan, but everyone in Catalonia also speaks Spanish. Besides, Catalan wasn't one of my languages.

"What is this shit?" he asked, but without emphasis. The way a surly prisoner would, but not one who wanted to risk his privileges.

"This shit," I explained, "is a private conversation. It will go like this: I'll ask questions, and you will give honest and very complete answers."

"Is that what you think will happen?" He seemed amused.

"It is. You may not think so, but . . . yeah . . . that's how it's going to play out," I said. "And in case you have doubts, there are penalties for wrong answers. But let me say right now that you really don't want to find out what they are."

I put some real edge into it, but whether I approximated the voice of the Darkness, I will never know. The memories of those other interrogations give me some of the words but none of the true flavor. Was that good or bad? No way to know.

Casanova eyed me, taking inventory of the off-market body armor, the computer strapped to my arm, and my various weapons—a pair of Randall Mark 14 Attack knives strapped upside down to my armored vest, a Sig Sauer 9 mm in a shoulder rig, and a gun of a type he'd likely never seen before in my hand. That was a Snellig 22A-Max gas dart gun, which is proprietary tech, made exclusively for Rogue Team International. No one else has it. All Casanova knew was that the barrel of a nasty-looking pistol was pointing at his favorite crotch.

He had a lot of reaction choices, but Casanova opted for nonchalance. He sat back, his shoulders resting against the cold concrete. "You come in here with your dog and . . . what do you call that? Some kind of ninja costume? All black and scary?" He spat on the floor an inch from my shoe. Not a lot of sputum, but enough to make a statement. "I will tell you what I told the last ten interrogators."

"Oh," I said, "and what was that?"

"I told them to go fuck their mothers up their asses," he said calmly. "And to not bother with lubricant. Really. You should do the same. It's how your mother likes me to fuck her."

He grinned. Casanova had large horse teeth, and one of the front ones was gray, evidence of a dead nerve.

"Here's the thing, buttercup," I said. "That's usually a good line if you want to start a fight. And you're a pretty big lump of shit, so maybe you've made somebody piss his pants once upon a time. Maybe you've pushed buttons that made other people lose their cool and swing on you, which is a nice way of canceling an interrogation. Blah blah blah. Sad truth is you don't have the gravitas or the cool to sell that line to someone who's actually in the game."

He got slowly to his feet and did his level best to loom. "Fuck you and your mother."

Ghost stepped forward and gave a menacing growl, but I clicked my tongue, and he immediately sat down. Ears up, tail flat, eyes merciless.

"I'm not afraid of you or that fucking dog," he said.

"Statements like that speak poorly of your ability to read the room," I said.

There must have been some quality in my voice because I saw a flicker on his face. He looked me up and down, head cocked to one side as if trying to remember where he might have heard my voice before.

"Who are you?" he asked.

I took off my helmet, removed my goggles, and pulled off the black balaclava I wore beneath, and then let him take a good long look at my face. I didn't have to say my name, and I could see the exact moment when he recognized me. His eyes slowly widened, and his lips parted to say a single word.

"No," he breathed.

I said, "Yes."

CHAPTER 95
DAS VERARBEITUNGSZENTRUM
SECURITY OFFICE

Korporal Heinz Kepler looked up from the duty sheet he'd been filling out and stared at one of the twenty-eight video screens on the wall over his desk. Most screens showed nighttime stillness. A few showed guards patrolling the halls. However, there was movement in one of the exterior screens—the one covering the front gate. A big white Mercedes Vario was idling on the turnaround. It was similar to the supply trucks used to deliver supplies to the processing plant, but no deliveries were expected, and certainly not at this hour.

Kepler tapped his shift partner on the shoulder. "Hey, Grunner, look at this."

Grunner, who had been reading a copy of *Der Spiegel,* looked up over his reading glasses. He grunted. "Lost," he said. "Maybe looking for directions."

The driver's door opened, and a slim woman slid down to the ground. She had a blond ponytail sticking out of the back of a blue billed cap and wore a blue windbreaker, tight jeans, and a black leg brace around her left knee. She walked up to the fence and stared directly into the camera. The blonde blew a kiss to whomever was watching, then turned and walked toward the back of the truck.

"What the hell?" murmured Kepler.

They leaned forward to study the video.

Grunner touched the screen. "Hey, what's that? Who's that with her?"

CHAPTER 96
DAS VERARBEITUNGSZENTRUM
CELL 13

Casanova knew he was in trouble.

All the pieces clicked. I'd come in wearing nonregulation clothes and equipment and had not brought the usual kind of backup. No other guards with shock rods or Tasers. This was clearly off the books.

That . . . and he recognized me. He knew he was in a very small room with Joe Ledger and a nasty dog.

He was bigger and heavier than I was, but he shrank away, backing up until he thumped into the wall, eyes clicking left and right as if magical doorways would suddenly appear. The door behind me was closed. The fact that the cell was soundproof was something he'd already know about.

That left him in the exact center of shit creek. Not a paddle in sight.

So he tried for it.

He suddenly pushed off the wall and swung a punch at me that had every ounce of his massive body weight behind. If it had connected, he'd have broken my jaw at the very least, and possibly my neck. His fist was the size and hardness of a bocce ball. Then all he'd have to do was fight Ghost, who would not attack unless I ordered him to, or if he perceived I was losing a fight. And by then, Casanova might have been able to take a gun from my body as I fell.

If he'd connected.

I saw the muscle flex of his waist as he began that push-off, his power turning to put torque into his attack. I saw it and walked right into the center of that turn and smashed my right forearm across his upper chest while chopping at his punching arm with my left elbow. His mass and momentum collided with my surge and precision. The physics were all wrong for him—he had momentum but no balance. He crashed back against the wall, grunting out a deep *huhhh* of breath. I pistol-whipped him with the Snellig and then swept the inside of one ankle with the arch of my shoe; and as he dropped, I pounded down on both shoulders with the bottoms of one fist and the butt of the dart gun. Really damned hard. His ass hit the floor, and there was a muffled wet crack that I knew was his tailbone breaking.

His scream was incredibly shrill for such a big man.

I stepped between his thighs and placed the sole of my boot on his scrotum. Not hard. Not yet.

In a very quiet voice, I said, "Shut. The fuck. Up."

He did.

Ghost was on his feet now, baring his teeth, ready to take a piece.

JONATHAN MABERRY

I moved my foot, and Casanova fell over onto his side, pulling his knees up to protect his balls and to take some pressure off the damage to his coccyx. He groaned and sobbed and started to say something else about my mother but stopped himself. Probably weighed the risk-reward thing and didn't like his odds.

I didn't like those odds, either. And, no, not because he dissed my mom. She died years ago, though if she'd been alive, she'd have fed him his own dick. Mom had always been a sweet lady, but only up to a point. Let's just say that someone calling me a mama's boy was something I'd take as a compliment.

I sat on the edge of the bed.

"Listen to me, asshole," I said quietly. "You're between a rock and a hard place. Rafael Santoro will kill you if you talk to me. So will Kuga. We both know that."

He'd been squeezing his eyes shut, but he forced them open to look up at me. He was sweaty, his skin was gray, and there were tears in his eyes.

"Rafael Santoro murdered my family. All of them. Even an unborn baby. No . . . no, don't close your eyes. Don't you dare look away. I want you to see my face. I want you to look into my eyes and listen to my voice and then decide if you are more afraid of those men—who are hundreds, perhaps thousands of miles away—or *me*. The guy who is right here with you this very minute."

I gave him a few moments on that.

"By now, you'll have heard about what I did in Italy. In Johannesburg, Kraków. I've been having some fun out there. Have you heard? Yeah, I can see it in your eyes," I said. "I guess you have someone feeding you information. Good."

It took him a moment to find his voice. "You're just going to kill me. Why should I tell you anything?"

I shrugged. "You *only* heard about Italy, Johannesburg, and Kraków, but you didn't hear about the other places I've been? Want to know why?"

He said nothing, but he was as attentive as a schoolboy.

"You didn't hear about the other places because I didn't leave blood on those walls," I said. "How do you think I *found* those other places? Those other labs and warehouses, the other safe houses? I've had conversations like this quite a few times, sport. I've had meaningful chats with some people just like you. Or maybe they were smarter. Maybe they valued their own lives enough to answer my questions without trying the sucker punch crap. Don't get me wrong, though, sometimes I had to ask in very specific ways. You think you're in pain now? Imagine how you'll feel if you fuck with me or stonewall me. I'm leaving here with information, that's one of life's few certainties. The question is whether I get all cranked and cut your balls off and feed them to my dog first . . . or whether I leave happy and you get medical treatment for a slip and fall. Your face isn't marked, so no one here will ever know we had this chat."

His eyes were huge, but I could see him working it out. He glanced at the door, then at Ghost, and back up at me.

There were beads of greasy sweat on Casanova's upper lip and forehead. Some of it was pain, and some was fear. Equal portions, I'd guess.

"How do I know you won't kill me?" he asked.

"You don't," I said. "You have to roll the dice. Except that one thing you *do* know is that if you *don't* talk, you *will* die, and you'll die badly. Soundproofed walls, a hungry dog, and a motherfucker who doesn't give one little, tiny roach turd about you. That's one of two outcomes. Take a moment and think about which option sounds more fun to you."

I stopped talking and let him work on it.

The clock in my head was telling me to speed it up. The guard I darted at the safe house was probably awake, pissed off, and making calls. Which meant Bug knew, and Church knew. Maybe someone was already on their way. I wondered . . . would Church send Toys after me again? Or would it be Top and Bunny this time? Either way, someone would come.

I could feel the Darkness in my head wanting to reassert itself and do very awful things. Even if Casanova gave me what I wanted. It was so damned hard to keep the lights on in my soul.

"Tick tock," I prompted.

His eyes were jumpy, as if he were a cornered rat, and the sweat was running down his cheeks. I made a small and unobtrusive finger

JONATHAN MABERRY

gesture, and Ghost immediately came over and sat close enough so that his hot breath blew against Casanova's face. Dog drool spattered the man's orange prison onesie.

"*Okay,*" he blurted. "Okay, okay, okay."

"Okay . . . *what*?" I asked quietly.

"Okay, I'll tell you what you want to know, goddamn your eyes."

"What is it you think I want to know?" I asked.

"Look," he said, "I don't actually know where Kuga is. I've heard rumors. Somewhere in Canada, somewhere in Texas, who knows? I don't know. No one does, but I *can* tell you where you can find Rafael Santoro."

My heart was throwing haymaker punches against the walls of my chest. I pushed Ghost out of the way and leaned close so that it was my own furnace breath, my own hot spit he felt on his face.

"Where. Is. He?"

It came out as three words, three beats. He flinched as if each one were a physical blow. Casanova looked absolutely terrified. Of me. Of the dark things he saw in my eyes.

He said, "If you want to find Santoro, you need to go to talk to Die Katze."

The Cat. A code name for a guy our friends at Barrier had been tracking. No one knew his real name, but he'd been a key lieutenant in the old Ohan international black market operation, though before that had worked in the sex-trafficking business. A real evil son of a bitch. Heartless and mercenary in the extreme. After Ohan got his throat cut, the Cat had become a free agent. I hadn't heard that he was tied in with Kuga, though it made sense.

"That's only useful information if you can tell me where to find Die Katze," I said.

"At the Hotel Timișoara," blurted Casanova. Now that he was talking, he seemed to want to please me. Smart move, since his life depended on it. There is no actual honor among thieves. There's only fear, and he was more afraid of me at that moment than of anyone else. "You need to promise me that you'll kill Santoro. If he ever suspects I told you . . ."

"Oh, bet your whole allowance on that," I promised.

The big man studied me for a moment, then nodded. "Okay, go to the Hotel Timișoara. Die Katze will be there in four days. He's overseeing a sale on behalf of Mr. Sunday."

"Who's that?"

Casanova licked his lips. "He's the head of sales for Kuga. I never met him and only ever saw him on ShowRoom."

He explained what ShowRoom was, and I wondered if Bug already knew about this. If not, I was going to have to break the silence and tell him. The further I moved away from dominance by the Darkness, the more I realized that I needed the RTI infrastructure.

"What is Die Katze selling?"

"I don't know exactly. Some kind of drug. Not for street use. It supposedly has military applications. You'll have to ask him. But whatever they're selling, it's important enough for Santoro to have sent the Cat."

"Three quick questions and then I'll leave you to get a Band-Aid on your ass."

His eyes were wary and jumpy.

"First, I keep hearing about the American Operation. Tell me what you know."

Casanova went a shade paler. "You . . . you can't know about that."

"Clearly, I can." I made a small hand signal, and Ghost, right on cue, gave a nice hungry growl.

Fat beads of sweat were running down Casanova's cheeks. "I don't know the details. All I know is that it's going to bring America to its knees. It's going to make 9/11 look like a fucking birthday party."

"When and where?"

"I don't know. Truly. All I ever heard about is that the staging area is in Texas. Near a place called LaBorde."

I grunted. I knew a couple of guys who lived there, out in East Texas.

"What about G-55?"

He shook his head. "I've heard that code, but I don't know what it means. Not my department."

Crap.

"Okay, let's go back to the meeting with Die Katze. Tell me

JONATHAN MABERRY

everything I need to know. If you trick me, you'd better hope I don't live through it because I'll let *everyone* know who put me onto that buy."

From the stark terror in his eyes, I knew he believed me. He gave me some details and then said, "But, listen to me, Ledger, you'll need to use a code phrase."

"What phrase?"

Casanova said, "It's—"

And then half the fucking building blew up.

CHAPTER 97
DAS VERARBEITUNGSZENTRUM
CELL 13

The explosion was so massive it picked up all three of us—Casanova, Ghost, and me—and hurled us across the cell.

We hit the wall with crushing force as the deep boom of the blast deafened us. We collapsed down onto the hard floor and lay in a gasping pile, none of us able to move a muscle. Dust plumed from cracks in the walls and ceiling.

I heard, as if from miles away, the sharp, high-pitched yelps of Ghost in pain. Everything was muffled, and the air was filled with swirling clouds of smoking dust. I rolled sideways, and there was another sharp cry from Ghost, then I felt him twisting under me, fighting to get free. I fought my way to palms and knees and turned to see the big white dog standing there, a yard away, quivering with pain and confusion.

"Ghost," I croaked, "report." This was a command that had taken me a long time, and the help of a top dog psychologist and trainer, to make him understand. If he was hurt—really hurt—he'd bark twice. A single bark would tell me he was ready to play. Or fight.

He took a moment and then gave a single bark. Not a lot of authority in it, but he emphasized it with a half-hearted wag of his bushy tail.

"That makes one of us," I groaned.

My body felt like I'd been dropped six stories into a rock quarry.

The D30 composite materials inside my body armor had absorbed a lot of the foot-pounds of impact, but I still hurt. A lot. And I'd taken off my helmet to interrogate Casanova.

I turned to see how Casanova was doing, and he stared at me, and through me, and through the wall. He did it from a funny angle, his right ear pressed against one shoulder, and there was a sickening bulge in the side of his neck. The side of his skull had a weird, flattened appearance, and it was clear he'd hit the wall hard enough to crush his skull and break his neck. Ghost and me landing on top of him had ensured that whatever he'd been about to tell me was something Casanova was going to take to the grave.

I wanted to hang my head and beat my fists on the floor and yell. This was my last best lead to Santoro. I closed my eyes. I wanted to give up. I wanted to cry.

I wanted to die.

"Get up, Cowboy."

The words jolted me. *Cowboy* was my old combat call sign from when I ran with the Department of Military Sciences. But the voice I heard, speaking to me there in that cell, did not belong to one of my former SpecOps colleagues. No. Nor was the use of the nickname related to my job. This was the voice of the person who'd hung that name on me a long, long time ago. A voice that could *not* be here. Not now, not ever.

"Go away," I said.

"Screw that," said the voice. "Get your sorry butt up, or I'm telling Mom."

No, no, no, my mind growled.

Aloud, I said, "You can't be here, Sean. You can't."

There was the scuff of a foot and then the creak of mattress coils as someone sat down on the bed. It took so much of everything I had left to open my eyes. To turn. To see my brother sitting there.

He looked the way he had when we were kids. He was wiry and had the look of combined exasperation and humor he wore whenever I did something dangerous or stupid. Or both. Like when I tried to base jump from a tree using a parachute made from black plastic trash bags. Or when I tried for a somersault into the pool at school. He had skeptical eyes and a scuffle of sandy hair, and a scar on his jaw from when he'd run halfway through a privet hedge while we were playing Frisbee in the front yard.

Sean.

My only brother.

Blown to red rags on Christmas Eve. Bones in a box and laid to rest between our father and Sean's wife and kids.

"No," I said. "You're not here."

He shrugged. "You say that, dingus, but you're actually talking to me."

"No, I'm not," I said.

"Whatever, dude. You're just being weird."

"And you're a ghost."

Sean cocked his head to one side. "I don't know . . . am I?"

"Or am I crazy?" I asked.

He spread his hands in an *if the shoe fits* gesture. Then he tilted his face up as sunlight fell on him. There was no sunlight anywhere, there couldn't be. Just on him. I watched his shoulders rise and fall as he took a long breath and sighed it out. Without looking at me, he said, "He's coming for you."

"Who?" I asked. "Santoro? Let that motherfucker come. I *want* him to."

Sean turned to look at me, and in the fragment of a second it took his head to turn, he changed. Now he was the Sean I'd only glimpsed on that awful day. Older. Thirty, with the eyes of a cop whose heart had not yet been thoroughly broken by the job. Wearing an ugly Christmas sweater, with a smudge of green cookie icing on his cheek from where a child might have kissed him.

"No," said Sean. "*He* is coming."

His eyes, which were always as blue as mine, suddenly changed. It was as if ink were leaking into the iris and sclera, tainting them, staining them with ugly shades of green and brown. As if reptile skin had been run through a blender and turned to paint. Even the Darkness inside me recoiled.

"*He's coming for you, Joe,*" said Sean in a voice that was low, raspy, rumbly, and entirely obscene. "*If you keep hunting Santoro and Kuga, you'll find him. And he really wants you to find him, Cowboy. Oh yes, he does. He wants that so much.*"

As he spoke, his breath plumed out. Not cold breath, but hot. It was like being next to the open mouth of a great furnace. I could *feel* the heat on my cheeks and lips and eyes. I recoiled in horror and fumbled for my gun. I think I screamed, but I'm really not sure. God knows I needed to.

But then I blinked and the bed was empty and I was alone with the corpse of Casanova and my combat dog. The heat, so intense a moment ago, faded now, and I could smell the stink of piss and blood from Casanova, his bowels having emptied as his muscles slackened in death.

I turned to Ghost and saw that he'd backed all the way into the corner, tail tucked between his legs, the white hair on his back standing as stiff as needles. He was panting hard. Not from effort or pain but fear. Drool flecked his muzzle.

"It's okay, boy," I said, but those words and the tone of my voice lacked all conviction. It was not okay. Not even a little bit. Either I was losing what was left of my mind or the world was broken. Maybe both.

He is coming.

I thought I knew who *he* was, but I didn't dare say the name. I refused to let myself think that name.

"It's okay," I said and reached a hand toward Ghost. He still trembled, but not as violently, and he summoned the courage to reach out and lick my gloved fingers. "He's not here, boy. We're okay. We're safe."

It was only then I realized that the room had been utterly quiet while Sean was there. Now real sound flooded back. I could hear alarms and yelling, and saw that the door had been knocked ajar. Not much, but enough to break the soundproofing seal. Thin fingers from something burning were clawing at the edges of the door, mingling with the paler dust from the jagged cracks in the ceiling and walls.

Another sound punched into my awareness, coming from outside but close.

Gunfire.

JONATHAN MABERRY

CHAPTER 98
THE TOC
PHOENIX HOUSE
OMFORI ISLAND, GREECE

Doc Holliday arranged for her presentation to be held at the TOC instead of her lab because it had bigger screens. Church and Wilson together, with Bug, Nikki, Yoda, and a dozen other department heads clustered around. Isaac Breslau and Ronald Coleman sat at the front near Doc, who stood and addressed the group.

"Okay," she began, "we've been going over this for weeks, and as puzzles go, it's got that ol' Gordian knot beat six ways from Sunday. The challenge here is that we have a lot of pieces to that puzzle, but we are only just now getting a sense of what exactly this is."

No one commented. Church nodded for her to continue.

"I'm going to give this to you point by point. Most of you know some of it because you've been working on your piece of it. I know most of it because . . . well, hell, guys, I'm the one giving the presentation, now, aren't I?"

She picked up a small clicker and put up the first image.

"This is a 3D model of one of the exosuits based on the schematics we found. This is the K-110 fighting machine, which is the most recent one of its class described in the recovered data. Looks like a robot version of Quasimodo, all hunched over, but see there? The back is articulated, and there are servos so the driver of this nifty gizmo can stand straight."

As they watched, the computer inserted a person into the suit, and it stood up.

"Now it looks more like the love child of Iron Man and one of those Transformer thingies," said Doc. "Or, as Bug insists, something—god help me—called BattleTech."

"Gundam!" yelled Nikki.

"Mazinger Z," countered Yoda, "or Super Dimension Fortress Macross."

Scott Wilson turned and gave them a withering look until they fell silent.

"And now we have this," said Doc, and she fed a short video clip—poor resolution and from a distance—of a single fighting machine going through its paces. "This is footage we got from the button cam worn by Top Sims. As you can see, this isn't something they're just *thinking* about building. Top reports that they had several of these, and drivers—as you can see—are actively training."

She ran the footage three times.

"According to the specs," continued Doc, "these suits are coated with an off-market hardened shell built with layers of heat-resistant and shock-absorbing blends of natural and synthetic fibers. Similar in concept to Kevlar, Nomex, and Technora, but at least two or possibly three orders of magnitude more durable. This is a whole new class of aramids, blending polymers, graphene, spider silk, and other composite materials. Frankly, fellas, I've never seen anything like this, and I suspect no one else has. It's new, and it's almost certainly proprietary tech that is, or will soon be, the cornerstone of Kuga's line of equipment for the PMC trade."

"What are its limitations?" asked Church.

"There were test results in with the material Ledger gave to Toys. Unless this is science fiction, it'll stop armor-piercing bullets up to and including hardened steel, tungsten, and even tungsten carbide in a copper or cupronickel jacket."

Wilson said, "Good lord."

"Not sure the good Lord himself could penetrate this stuff," said Doc. "There's a whole set of test results insisting that this thing can take an RPG in the chest and keep going."

The room was silent.

"And," said Doc brightly, "it gets worse."

"How much worse?" asked Church.

"Well, the unit itself has a max load capacity of fourteen hundred pounds, not including the driver. The carapace has fittings to attach a modified M134 minigun and two five-thousand-round belts. Other nifty options include a launcher for 40 × 46 mm grenades, with an auto feeder capable of twenty shots. That launcher can carry a variety of party favors, too, including high-explosive M441 and XM1060 thermobarics."

Wilson's face was pale, and Doc wasn't sure he'd blinked once since she started.

"There's some reference to a flame unit," continued Doc, "but because of tank size, my guess is that it would be attached to a second unit."

Bug cleared his throat. "So . . . if I'm hearing this right, we're talking about a bulletproof, flameproof personal tank?"

"Yes, and a right spritely one, too. There's a mode for normal pace, but if they want to push the batteries, it can run, climb stairs, and turn on a dime. So it's a tank that can chase you up a flight of stairs, outrun you, and send you to Jesus faster than you can spit."

Doc, who was always at her most cheerful when things were at their worst, positively beamed.

"Now," she said brightly, "want to hear the really bad part?"

CHAPTER 99
DAS VERARBEITUNGSZENTRUM
CELL 13

Ghost found his voice and gave a sharp bark of warning, turning, his tail whipping up, muzzle wrinkling. There were voices outside, closer than the gunfire, coming toward this cell. Two men speaking. Not in German or English. Or in Catalan, for that matter. They spoke Romanian.

I heaved myself to my feet and drew my Snellig dart gun, waving Ghost to a position where he'd be out of sight once I opened the door. My ears were still muzzy from the blast, but I was pretty sure these guys were no more than a dozen paces up the hall.

I eased the door open half an inch wider and peered out. The hallway was thick with smoke, and the Klaxons were much louder. I saw two figures moving toward me through the smoke. They were big and misshapen, like a couple of mountain gorillas, and it took my dazed brain a moment to realize that the figures were wearing body armor of a kind that was bulkier than the sleek stuff I wore.

Their words were distorted, but I caught some of it.

"*Este chiar aici,*" said one of them in Romanian, gesturing toward cell 13. *It's right here.*

He was the shorter of the two. Subtracting the helmet and the thick soles of combat boots, he was probably five foot ten. The other guy was four or five inches taller. Both were broad-shouldered and fit. What was strange, though, is that they moved casually like they were taking a stroll through the park on a spring afternoon. Not the physical dynamic one typically sees in a prison break—which is what I assumed this was.

The bigger guy said, "*Spaniolul a spus că primim cu toții un bonus frumos pentru asta.*"

That made my pulse quicken. *The Spaniard said we're all getting a nice bonus for this.*

The Spaniard!

Rafael Santoro.

Son of a bitch.

"*Sigur,*" said the other, "*dacă vrăjitoarea nu ia totul.*"

Sure, if the witch doesn't take it all.

The witch? I had no idea who that was and no time to think about it.

They had guns in their hands, but they held them sloppily, barrels pointing nearly down at the floor like they didn't give much of a fuck about anything. I shifted the Snellig to my left and drew the Sig Sauer with my right, whipped the door open, and leaned halfway into the hall, pointing one barrel at each man.

"*Sper că voi doi sunteți angajatori,*" I said.

I hope you two are undertakers.

They stopped and stared at me. I couldn't see their eyes through the lenses of their goggles, but I could *feel* their surprise and knew they were trying to make sense of what was happening. I watched the same process with them I'd seen with Casanova—recognition and awareness.

"Ledger," said the shorter of the two, almost spitting my name. "*Este diavolul.*"

It is the devil.

The taller one said, "*Futu-ți Cristoșii și Dumnezeii mă-tii.*"

That doesn't translate well into English, but it's not a nice thing to say to anyone pointing a gun at you.

"Unsling your weapons and drop them to the ground," I told them, still speaking in Romanian. "Do it right now, or I will kill you."

Then they laughed.

And charged at me like a pair of demented bulls. Like men who thought they were invincible, invulnerable. Insane.

I fired both guns.

And it did no damned good at all.

CHAPTER 100
THE TOC
PHOENIX HOUSE
OMFORI ISLAND, GREECE

Doc Holliday clicked a new image onto the screen. It showed a man dressed in more normal body armor—helmet, chest shell, limb pads, and a stomach-groin shield. This was an actual photograph of a man—presumably a Fixer—in a field-testable prototype. He had a sidearm on one hip, a large fighting knife on the other, and carried a standard Special Operations Forces Combat Assault Rifle.

"Well," said Wilson weakly, "at least that's a bit less frightening."

"No," said Doc cheerfully, "it's really not."

CHAPTER 101
DAS VERARBEITUNGSZENTRUM

The taller of the two stepped between my guns and his partner while simultaneously rushing at me. It happened in the blink of an eye.

The Sandman dart exploded uselessly on his shoulder, but the 9 mm round hit him center mass. Even with Kevlar, the brute force of the lead slug should have staggered him. All he did was grunt. It wasn't even a cough or cry of controlled pain. A grunt. Like a bullet fired from five feet away was—at most—an irritant.

Oh . . . shit.

I stepped forward and raised the pistol to fire into his face. See how he'd like that, but then he swatted me aside.

That's the best word I can think of. It wasn't a punch. It wasn't an attempt to deflect my aim before I could correct for a face shot. His hand moved so fast it was a blur, and his open palm hit the ballistic padding over my deltoid. I barely saw it coming, and the blow picked me up as surely as the explosion had and smashed me into the doorframe. I am over six feet and weigh north of two hundred, and that openhanded smack knocked me through the air as if I were a scarecrow stuffed with straw. I hit hard and dropped down to my knees, head ringing and the world doing some kind of drunken jig around me. My hands were empty, and I couldn't even see where my guns went.

If I'd been alone, they'd have had me. No doubt about it.

But then a white missile blew past me and crunched into the tall man's stomach, doubling him more from surprise than anything. The tall guy staggered and went down, and Ghost went for his throat.

The smaller man was caught in a moment of indecision—help his friend or finish me off. That split second gave me a doorway back into the fight. I pushed off the frame and tried a swat of my own to knock aside the rifle barrel he was trying to raise, but hitting his arm was like striking a seasoned oak tree. I hit hard, but all I accomplished was to move the barrel two inches to one side as he pulled the trigger. The bullets caught me on the side as I tried to turn to avoid them. My armor is really good, but the angle of impact was bad, and the impact spun me.

I took that force and let it turn me all the way around, and as I completed the pirouette, I chopped him across the point of the jaw with the bottom of my fist. Armor or no, that is a lot of torque and leverage, and the blow whipped his head to one side. It should have given him whiplash at the very least. It didn't. He cursed and pivoted back, tried for another shot, but I was moving now, my balance on the balls of my feet. Not sure what kind of body armor he had or how it could possibly have sloughed off the damage from my hit to his chin, and I didn't care. I had a tiny window of opportunity, and the Killer in me was fully in the game now.

The Killer. Not the Darkness. Small mercies.

I grabbed the handles of the two Randall Attack knives and snap-released them with downward jerks. The matched knives had

JONATHAN MABERRY

seven-and-a-half-inch Bowie-style blades and brass double guards. Fourteen ounces each. I usually prefer the much smaller and lighter Wilson Rapid Release folding knife, but I was far from home and working with the equipment I could scrounge. These blades are excellent, and they don't give a damn about body armor. I proved that by slashing down at his forearm with one and across his face with the other. Did it the same way a samurai cuts with a sword—chopping down while drawing the blade fast and smooth, letting the length of cut give me depth of injury. Both knives bit deeply, and a reddish-gray gel of some kind oozed from the slashes.

The killer did not shrug it off. No, sir. This time, he screamed in pain, staggered back, and in doing so lost his grip on the rifle, which dropped to hang on its sling. Blood poured from both wounds.

They were bad wounds. Very deep. The kind that awaken thousands of outraged nerve bundles and flood the brain with white-hot agony. *But he didn't stop.*

Through the lenses of his goggles, I saw the pain register . . . and then I saw his eyes change. The white of his eyes suddenly seemed to darken, turning to a vicious bloodred. Then he rushed me, pawing at the knives like an enraged bear. Not sophisticated movements, but so fast and strong that I lost one blade and had to do some fancy footwork to avoid him taking the other.

His whole body seemed to move at a different rate of speed. Faster, with much quicker reflexes.

I counterattacked with slashes that tore his combat gloves to ribbons. The manufacturers advertise those kind of gloves as being knife-proof. I beg to differ. Depends on the knife and the man using it. Did not stop him, though. If anything, he leveled up. Again.

Christ.

I moved in a rapid half circle, avoiding a series of incredibly quick and powerful swings, keeping an empty hallway behind me instead of a wall. Ghost was still fighting the second guy on the floor. The Kevlar was slowing the dog down, but that kind of armor is necessarily thinner around the throat, allowing for mobility. Thin protection means exactly jack squat against a big dog with titanium teeth. There was a lot of blood.

But no screams.

The man was still fighting Ghost, despite obvious serious and savage damage. And in a flash, I saw his eyes. The sclera had also turned a vivid, furious red.

What the actual fuck? Everything since I'd walked into Casanova's cell felt like it belonged in *The Twilight Zone*.

He is coming.

The man I was fighting kept trying to grab my knife wrist instead of actually fighting me. It was freaky. He ripped off his goggles and tore off his balaclava as if it were all choking him. My knife had ripped him open from side to side, giving him a red smile like the Joker. Blood poured from it, splashing his clothes and the wall as he came at me with renewed vigor, red eyes blazing.

But as he attacked, he made a little series of yippy noises like a child so lost in a fit of rage he was unable to form words. It chilled me. I've never seen anyone lose their shit like this before. He was clearly a trained soldier—whether regular military or private contractor—and yet there was absolute madness in his actions. It made no sense at all, even with the severity of the injuries. It was so weirdly out of place that if this were a movie, it might have been comical. But there was nothing funny in real life. He slapped and pawed and bled as I tried to chop him down.

Even with all that, he was so goddamned fast.

His hands blurred. I kept shifting and turning to evade his grabs. His blood spattered me, the walls, the floors. Drops of it seeded the air, punching small holes in the thickening smoke. I feinted left and shifted right, snapping out with a kick to his groin. My shoes have steel tips, and I kick really damned hard. The blow connected, and I could see the shock of it register on his face. He uttered a high-pitched whistle of pain and staggered, and so I kicked him again. And again. Driving the Kevlar groin cup hard into the pubic bone. Even with the alarms ringing, I could hear bones break.

And yet he kept coming.

His ferocity, his animal drive absolutely terrified me. He was hunched over now, white flecks of spit on his bloody lips; his feet losing their sense of control. He was not reacting to the pain in any normal way. It seemed to both increase his pain and fury while driving him into some whacked-out headspace.

I jagged to the other side and stamped down in the inside of his left knee with the flat of my heel, exploding the joint. He cried out, but in the voice of a hurt child. It was the strangest, eeriest thing I've ever heard from someone in a fight. It was as if the man I fought had retreated and his inner child—wild and terrified—had emerged and that was who I'd just hurt.

As he fell, I followed him and stabbed downward, my blade slicing through the thin sheath of protection around his throat. He gagged, spurting dark blood from the wound and from his mouth.

I whirled away from him and saw that Ghost was *still* fighting the other guy. I've never known my dog to have anywhere near that much trouble with anyone, body armor or not. The man was bloody and screaming, but he was still trying to win. I moved in and shouldered Ghost aside and drove the blade down like a spike, smashing through the right lens of his goggles and deep into the man's brain.

Then I half toppled away onto hands and knees. Ghost stood there, trembling with bloodlust and fear, his eyes wild. The sounds of gunfire were somewhere close by. Down a hall, around a corner.

I saw that Ghost was looking past me, but not in the direction of those shots. He began to snarl, and I turned to see something I would have thought impossible. With a broken knee and dozens of cuts, with a crushed pelvis and a slashed throat, the first of the men I'd fought was struggling to sit up. He pawed at a holstered pistol, still trying to fight.

Still trying to be alive.

I gaped at him, speechless, horrified.

I scrambled over and slapped his hand away from the pistol, drew it myself, put the barrel under his chin, and blew the top of his head off. He flopped back.

But he still did not stop twitching.

It was insane.

I recoiled as an atavistic dread surged up inside me. I felt as if I were fighting something inhuman. Something that could not *be* killed.

Then I saw thin tendrils of smoke curling up from under his body armor. Ghost barked sharply, and I turned to see that he was staring at the other man. Smoke was rising from him, too.

"Oh, shit!" I cried. And then I was moving. I scooped up my weapons, yelled for Ghost, and we ran. We ran really goddamned fast.

We got halfway down the hall when the two dead men exploded.

CHAPTER 102
THE TOC
PHOENIX HOUSE
OMFORI ISLAND, GREECE

Doc said, "Don't focus on the weapon he's carrying and look at the armor. It's similar to our best—and by that, I mean *my* best—but as much as it twists my panties into a real tight bunch, it is better. A lot better. It's made from the same kind of composite aramid materials as is used in the K-110 fighting machine. Not as dense, so it can't take an RPG in the breadbasket and might not stop a sniper firing armor-piercing rounds, but don't bet your lunch money on it."

She clicked and changed the image to a page of very technical specifications. Church leaned forward and studied the arcane notations very carefully.

"From a distance," said Doc, "what we're seeing is basically next-gen combat body armor. That's scary, but what makes this more frightening than the K-110 fighting machine is what's built into the armor."

She used a laser pointer to indicate a series of formulae on one side of the screen.

"Each of the suits is fitted with pockets for chemicals," she said, "very similar in theme to the thermite A91 we have in our own gear for post-action disposal when that gear cannot be recovered. But these slippery sons of bitches have gone and upped the ante. One of their mad scientists has found a way to get the big bad bang of azidoazide azide, which has fourteen nitrogen atoms, with most of them bonded to one another in successive, unstable nitrogen-nitrogen bonds, which makes them very prone to going bang! That stuff was developed by my old drinking buddy Thomas Klapötke about a dozen years ago. Normally, any attempt to handle the chemical at all causes those bonds to break and turns them into multiple molecules of rapidly expanding nitrogen gas, which creates a hell of a lot of heat and boom. But these cats have found a way to stabilize it, and I wish to hell the entire formula was there because I'd like to steal it, patent it, and sell it. Just contracts with construction companies alone would net me enough money to buy, oh . . . Mars, and turn it into a luxury resort." She paused. "I know I keep saying this, but it beats the living hell out of me why Kuga doesn't go straight and, like I said, patent it and become richer than God."

"Because he steals the research?" suggested Dr. Coleman, who was a big, burly, and bearded man in contrast to Isaac's small and slender appearance.

"Yeah, yeah, yeah," Doc said, "I know. Just grousing. Anyway . . . this stuff is packed into airtight stabilizing pouches throughout the suit. About seven pounds of it."

"Why do they need that much?" asked Nikki. "Is the body armor that hard to melt down?"

"No, no, no, no," said Doc, "it isn't for after-action disposal. With that modified azidoazide azide, you'd only need three ounces to turn the suit and occupant into smoking fairy dust. Nope. This, ladies and gentlemen, is crime and punishment here. You see, they had a tricky little system of wires synced with telemetry from modified RFID chips. As long as the person wearing the suit maintains a pulse rate above a certain number, all's fine and dandy. But if that person were to die? Well, then, there's a triggering mechanism that sends little electric shocks to each and every darn one of those chemical pouches. The resulting explosion from nine *pounds* of that stuff? Well, if one went off in, say, a high school auditorium, then no one would be graduating that year. You see, they didn't just stabilize that chemical, they upped its kick."

She clicked back to the photo of the Fixer in the body armor.

"Our boy Kuga has developed the most powerful suicide vest in the history of global terrorism. If a Fixer walks into any environment, he can either fire with impunity or kill as many people as he wants. Not because of the armor's toughness—and remember it's really tough—but because anyone firing in self-defense who gets lucky and pops the guy will trigger a blast that will kill every single living thing inside of fifty yards."

She paused, letting that sink in.

"Now imagine a team of them going into North Korea's Rungrado First of May Stadium, which has a capacity of 140,000. Or Michigan Stadium in Ann Arbor. That's 114,000 people dead in a flash."

Church said, "Dear god."

"Where are they planning on using these . . . these . . . *things*?" asked Nikki.

"That, sweet cheeks," said Doc, "is what we *don't* know. And I pray to whichever deity is taking our calls that this is what our boy Joe Ledger is trying to find out."

CHAPTER 103
DAS VERARBEITUNGSZENTRUM

The young blond woman with the brace on her left knee stood in the gaping hole of what had been the main entrance to the processing plant. Now it was a cavern of rubble, torn bodies, and shattered glass. A chemical stink of high explosives hung in the air, pushed around by sluggish clouds of brick dust. Twisted sheets of metal stood up like broken ribs from some gigantic corpse.

Eve grinned at it. Explosions always made her happy, and she'd been told that a big one was needed to breach these walls because they were concrete reinforced with steel. That intel had been correct, and she'd made sure that the first try was enough to do the trick. The blast had been so big that it destroyed the entrance to the building. It tore a line of hedges from the ground and threw them burning into the decorative trees. Those trees now burned like a row of tiki torches.

Nothing of the original doorway remained, and although the blast hadn't damaged the inner air lock, it had completely obliterated the walls into which it was set, so the air lock lay atop the rubble.

"Awesome," she gushed. "That was so *rad*."

A pair of heavily armored killers stood nearby. Cain and Abel.

"The team's located the cell, Miss Eve," Abel told her, his fingers still touching his coms unit.

"About time," said Eve. She looked at her watch, which was set to mission time. It was three minutes since the breach. Standard response time for police at this time of night was five minutes, twenty seconds. Way off in the distance, she could hear a siren.

"The team's encountering some resistance inside," added Abel. "We've lost signals on two . . . no, wait, four. Losing feeds on Ephraim and Asher."

As if to punctuate his comment, there was a heavy one-two *ba-whooom* from inside, and a cloud of hot gas and burning debris belched out at them.

"Two down, for sure," said Eve dryly. "Fucking idiots." She gave Abel a scathing look. "Are we still in control of the scene? Will we get the package?"

"Yes, ma'am," said Abel. "We anticipated some losses, but we still have the numbers and the advantage."

Cain said, "And we're on schedule, Miss Eve."

"You'd better be right," Eve said with a venomous sweetness, "because Daddy will be really unhappy if we come back empty-handed. Really fucking unhappy."

Those words drained the color from the faces of the two big men. Cain turned aside, touched his coms unit, and began growling orders. Abel might as well have turned to stone for all the expression he showed.

Eve turned away to hide her smile. She loved making these boys jump. All she had to say was "Boo," and they pissed their pants. Genuine toughness, she'd been taught, was not a quality of height, gender, or muscle mass. It was all about potential. To reward and to punish.

Eve checked her watch again. "Make sure Enoch's in position."

All her Righteous had biblical combat call signs. She no longer recalled, or even cared, what their real names were. When she got back to the Pavilion, all she had to do was accept two new replacements into her cadre. They would become the new Ephraim and Asher. Real names offered the danger of actual emotional attachment, and Eve was done with that. Forever.

The Righteous served her and entertained her. They kept her from screaming into her pillow every night. They were also without emotional challenge. Eve felt nothing for any of them. Not even when they made her come screaming. It was sensation, not emotion.

Maybe once her network located Joe Ledger and brought him in chains to her, she'd feel something. Maybe after she skinned Joe Ledger, she'd allow herself to become alive again.

God, the things she wanted to do to Ledger before he died.

She wanted to force-feed him Viagra and then fuck him as he coughed out his last breath. She wanted to stab him with every single one of the 206 knives she'd collected.

Would that make the pain go away? Would it chase the shadows out of her mind?

She didn't know, but she swore to herself she would find out. Who knew, maybe she'd even be able to fall in love again. Though, as far as Eve believed, there would never be anyone she loved like she'd loved Adam.

Poor Adam. He had saved her life. He'd *been* her life.

And then Ledger had stolen him from her in Norway last December.

"Enoch's locked and loaded," Abel assured her, cutting into her thoughts.

She blinked, coming back to the moment. "Huh? What? Oh, good . . . good. And the choppers?"

"Inbound, ma'am. ETA four minutes."

Eve measured out a tiny slice of a smile. "Good," she said again.

CHAPTER 104
DAS VERARBEITUNGSZENTRUM

The blast was big.

A one-two punch that sent a tsunami of superheated gas racing after us.

Ghost was faster and made it to the T junction at the end of the hall a half step before I did. The heat caught me, though. It picked me up and hurled me through the air. But I twisted and curled and hit the floor rolling. The main fireball passed over me; it spread out along the ceiling on both sides of the T, dispersing and fading and then burning out completely, leaving all the walls scorched black. Ceiling tiles melted and rained down, and I had to roll around on the floor to put out fires on my goddamn fire-resistant body armor.

I'd never seen a blast like that before. If we hadn't run as fast and as far as we did, we'd have been reduced to ash.

Ghost whimpered, terrified. He began to get up, but I snapped at him to stay down.

Despite the pain in every molecule of my body, I got up into a low crouch and scuttled like a half-cooked crab to peer around the corner. The hall in front of cell 13 was gone—burned and shattered, with sections of the roof leaning drunkenly down. The paint on the walls closer to the blast was burning sluggishly, though most of the flames had been extinguished by the blast.

There was no sign of the two men. They had literally been blown to bits, and those bits still burned.

I straightened and stood for a moment, trying to understand everything that had happened in the last two minutes. Forcing myself to make credible statements of practical analysis. Despite the wreckage inside my head, old and new, I needed to be in the moment. To *understand* this.

A team of some kind had attacked the processing plant. Who they were or what their agenda might be was unclear. Certainly not regular military. No, these cats had to be PMCs on the payroll of someone who wanted to free one or more prisoners. They'd mentioned the Spaniard. Did that mean these guys were Fixers? If so, it meant that they were *enhanced* Fixers wearing ultrasophisticated body armor that exploded when the men wearing them died.

Yeah, find a comfortable chair for that to sit in.

I glanced at Ghost, who was spattered with blood and soot.

"Well," I said, "it's finally happened. The world's now officially crazier than I am."

For no damned reason at all, he wagged his tail. He's a weird damned dog.

The gunfire was getting louder, but not closer. A hell of a battle was raging, and it was getting intenser. I tapped my tactical computer to bring up the feeds from the Busy-Bees and saw that parts of the prison had become full-tilt war zones. There were bodies all over the place. Most of the cell doors had been torn open—literally ripped from their hinges—and the corpses of prisoners lay twisted and dead. I saw one man with a distinctly Somalian face and a torn orange jumpsuit trying to crawl away, but he left such a thick blood trail that I knew he wouldn't make it far. His left foot was missing.

There were other bodies, too. Uniformed guards, sprawled and dead, their limbs shattered, flesh ripped apart with a level of savagery that was appalling.

Then the bees found the main source of the gunfire. It was the staff quarters. A handful of guards—possibly the only ones left—were crouched behind a stack of overturned tables and chairs. Some were dressed, but most were in underwear or pajamas. A dozen of their comrades lay dead around them. They were firing at four more of the armored Fixers. I saw no Fixer corpses anywhere and wondered if that accounted for some of the explosions. Did they all wear suicide vests? Was it some variation of the "no man left behind" concept? Incineration rather than recovery? Were the explosives tied to some kind of telemetry, likely a heartbeat? If so, how'd they ever convince any of the Fixers to strap on those vests?

I wanted—needed—to interrogate one of these spooky sons of bitches, but that presented its own set of problems. They were stronger and faster than I was, and there were a bunch of them. If I had Havoc Team with me, that math would be in my favor. Top, Bunny, Belle, and Andrea were a match for any squad of killers. At least I thought so.

Backup plan was to exfil right damn now, locate their vehicle, and either plant a tracker or tail them.

But . . . there were a bunch of innocent folks fighting for their lives a few corridors away from where I stood. If I left now to save my own skin, I'd be leaving them to die.

Inside my head, the Darkness whispered bad things.

Let them die, it told me. *Saving them isn't the mission. Find Santoro. What else matters?*

It was as real as any voice I've ever heard. It was my own voice painted black.

Let them die.

I would like to say that I was in no way tempted to do exactly that.

JONATHAN MABERRY

To slip away in the smoke and confusion and stick to my goal. Saving these people fell under the heading of "mission creep," adding to the scope of work I already had. It would put me in danger. It would put Ghost in danger. We might not even succeed in saving anyone and die in the process, leaving Santoro free to destroy more lives. More families.

I watched the gun battle on the computer screen.

And for a few brittle moments, I saw my family there. Standing to one side of the barricade. Clustered together. Not watching the battle. They were all looking at me. I saw my father's lips move as if he were talking.

To me.

But I couldn't hear what he was saying.

"Dad . . . ?" I breathed. "Dad, for god's sake, tell me what I should do."

He stopped talking and just looked at me. And then, one by one, they turned their backs and walked away into the smoke.

It came close to breaking me.

"*Dad!*" I yelled. Actually yelled it out loud.

He thinks you're abandoning him, whispered the Darkness. *They all do.*

Tears, hot as acid, burned in my eyes.

I looked down at Ghost. His gaze was dark and scalpel sharp. He bared his gleaming metal teeth.

I holstered my dart gun, then released the magazine of the Sig Sauer, replacing it with a full one.

Together, we ran into hell.

CHAPTER 105
DAS VERARBEITUNGSZENTRUM

We used the smoke and confusion to move through the building, following the gunfire. We came upon one of the processing plant's guards sprawled near another T junction. He was torn apart. Literally. Both arms and his jaw had been savagely ripped from his body. It was a hideous thing to see, and I only prayed he'd at least died quickly.

Around the corner, I found his partner. He sat against the wall with a gaping, ragged red hole where his throat should have been. It looked as if someone had taken a fistful of his windpipe and torn it out, discarding the mess by throwing it against a wall.

There's killing in combat, and even a measure of savagery that sometimes happens in the heat of the fight, but this . . . ? This was a kind of malicious mayhem that spoke to a pernicious delight. These Fixers were having *fun*. Playing with whatever faux superpowers were granted them by their armor.

Even so . . . it scared the absolute hell out of me.

But it also made me angry.

Really damned angry.

Ghost growled low in his chest, not looking at the corpses but glaring along the hall where bloody footprints showed the path the Fixers had taken.

"Yeah," I told him quietly, "let's go get some."

We kept moving, but as we drew close to the sounds of battle, I slowed our pace so I could check the feed from the Busy-Bees. It looked like the guards were currently holding their own, and I could see why. Two of them had pump shotguns, and the big chunks blown out of the doorframe and walls told me these were loaded with slugs—what hunters used to call *pumpkin balls*. Heavy lead balls that my uncle Jack liked for hunting wild boar. Other bullet holes in the metal frame, the ones that clearly punched all the way through, had to be armor piercing. That kind of ordnance had stopped the Fixers for the moment. Clearly, none of those PMCs had been killed, because there was no sign of explosions, though I wondered if some of the other blasts I'd heard were from more successful counterattacks.

I angled some of the bee swarm to focus on the Fixers. One of them had his goggles off, and I let a bee hover to get a good look at him. The camera was small and didn't have great definition, but it was clear enough to tell me a lot. His eyes were wide, staring, the whites stained with red and incredibly dilated pupils. Bloody tears streaked those parts of his cheeks I could see; the blood mingling with the sweat boiling from his skin. He looked like the kind of junkie who had taken too much of too many different kinds of stimulants and was way, way out on the edge. Proof that these Fixers were not only enhanced but strung out by it.

I looked at my pistol for a moment and then holstered it.

"Plan B," I told Ghost and then spent a few seconds activating the other half of my swarm. The Killer Bees. Wish I had the time to swap Sandman out of their dischargers and replace it with something a lot more toxic. But I hadn't planned on doing any harm at all to the staff here. No way I could have anticipated that the place would be hit by a full team of PMCs. Was it a coincidence? Or had the guy I got the Casanova intel from broken his promise to me and confessed to Santoro?

That would make logical sense, but it didn't feel right. Something about this whole thing was freaky, which meant there was a lot I didn't know.

Which meant that the Sandman might be useful to me, after all . . .

I hastily typed new orders into the swarm software. First, I told the Busy-Bees to engage their laser-targeting systems and paint each Fixer. Then I sent the Killer Bees to follow and sting. I crouched next to Ghost and watched.

The Fixers didn't notice the bees coming, not with all the noise and smoke. But then the swarm struck. There was very little exposed skin on them, but they each wore a balaclava, which is thin, flexible cloth. I sent the Killer Bees smashing into their cheeks and throats and lips. Maybe only one in four hit true and hit well enough to penetrate the material, but it only takes one sting for Sandman to drop them.

And the Fixers began to fall.

"Booyah," I murmured. Ghost answered with a soft *whuff*!

I gave it four seconds and then I broke into a run, drawing my knives as I rounded the last corner. Half the Fixers were down, and I was both astonished and horrified to see that they were not out. Somehow, they were managing to fight the effects of the damned drug, and that was supposed to be impossible. I'd never once seen Sandman fail. Sandman was the latest version of a compound originally designed to knock down grizzly bears so rangers could transport them away from campers and homes. It should have had every single one of those pricks unconscious before they hit the floor.

Should have.

I used Q1 to cycle through the radio channels until I found the one for the security team. I yelled to the guards behind the barricade, telling them not to shoot, that I was a friendly. I yelled in German and in English. I had to repeat it several times before the gunfire slowed and then stopped.

I had the Snellig in one hand and a knife in the other as I moved into the group of Fixers, all of whom were darted now. Two still stood, but they were swaying drunkenly, their weapons hanging from loose hands and slack fingers. Ghost raced past me and jumped at one of them, catching a wrist and dragging the man down. His teeth crunched audibly through bone.

"Ghost—*own!*" I yelled, wanting that man injured but not dead. "Own" was not a command to be nice, though, and I heard the wolf that lives inside my dog snarl with savage glee. And, let's face it, over the last month, he'd been getting a lot of practice.

I went for the other one, bashing aside his gun barrel and then kicking him in the knee. It took two good kicks to destroy the joint, and then I ripped his goggles off and smashed the bridge of his nose with the pommel of the heavy knife. Cartilage and the lip of nasal bone exploded, flooding his eustachian tubes with blood, likely blinding him with the shooting stars of photopsia. I hit him again, this time on the temple, and then again once he was down.

Then I whirled as two guards with shotguns began creeping out from their place of concealment.

"Listen to me," I roared in German, "these men are wearing suicide vests that will detonate if they die. We need to disable and restrain them. I shot them with tranquilizers."

One of the guards hurried out, looked at the men groaning and crawling around on the floor, and then he raised the barrel and pointed it at me.

"Drop your weapon," he ordered.

"Did you hear what I said? I'm a friendly."

"Drop your weapon, or I will kill you," he growled.

JONATHAN MABERRY

"Fuck me blind and move the furniture," I snarled. "I don't have time for this."

I snapped off a Sandman dart that took him in the chest. He went right down, the shotgun falling to the ground before he could pull the trigger. Then I wheeled and pointed the Snellig at his partner, whose gun was still aimed at the Fixers. "Sorry," I said and shot him, too.

There was no win here. Not for me anyway. I barked a command at Ghost. He disengaged with a great show of reluctance, but now the other guards were surging out from behind the stack of tables. This was going south too fast.

"Out," I snapped, and together we fled. Even while we ran, I kept yelling at them to not kill the Fixers because of the bomb triggers synced with heartbeats. But their response was to open fire on me.

We dove for the first turning in the hall as a fusillade pocked chips of stone from the walls.

I sincerely hoped the guards would try to cuff and arrest those dazed Fixers rather than do something suicidal like pop caps in them as a way of getting revenge. I hoped that professionalism would trump the need to avenge their fellow guards.

CHAPTER 106
DAS VERARBEITUNGSZENTRUM

"Miss Eve," said Abel, "we have movement."

The two Fixers raised their rifles and took up shooting positions facing the destroyed entrance. Smoke swirled inside, but now shadows moved within the clouds. Eve slipped a Glock 19 from a hip holster and stood between the two men, making no attempt to find cover. She did not see Cain and Abel share a quick glance. Abel began to say something, but Cain shook his head.

There was a squawk of static, and then a voice spoke on the coms unit. "Jedidiah to command. Coming out the front with the package."

"Come ahead," responded Abel.

The shadows resolved into figures—two of the team, bulky in their body armor, helmets, and equipment. They held handguns and used their free hands to support a very thin man who wore only a chest protector and helmet with a blacked-out visor. The thin man wore prison coveralls and slip-on boat shoes. His wrists were zip-cuffed, and he stumbled—though from injury, shock, or weakness was uncertain.

The Fixers hustled him out of the building and ran to the shelter formed by the parked truck. There they turned him around and leaned him back against the vehicle. Eve hurried over and watched as Abel quickly checked the prisoner for injuries. Then Cain removed the blackout helmet to reveal a white man with a scraggly beard and terrified eyes.

"We verified ID with fingerprint and retina scan," said Jedidiah. "This is he."

Eve smiled like a happy kid on Christmas morning. She bent forward and kissed the man on the mouth, which shocked the prisoner but not the Fixers. They were used to her random impulses by now.

"Dr. Dejan Brozović," she said, mangling the Croatian pronunciation. It came out as *Broozoveek*. The man blinked in fear and uncertainty.

"Who . . . who are you?" stammered Brozović. "What is this?"

"This is a rescue, sugar."

"I don't understand . . ."

Even leaned close. "We're the white knights come to save you from the deep, dark dungeons."

"Who *are* you?" demanded Brozović.

"Let's just say Kuga sends his regards."

Brozović's eyes widened. He echoed the name, then smiled with tremendous relief. "Thank god."

"Thank *me*," corrected Eve.

"I thought they were going to let me rot in there."

"Oh no, sweet cheeks, we need you," Eve said. "We've had some issues with the R-33."

"You've been *using* it?" he gasped. "It's still unstable."

She beamed. "Well, no shit, Sherlock. Why do you think we're galloping to the rescue? It's not your boyish charm."

Brozović looked at the building and then at Cain and Abel. "You're Fixers," he said, peering at their faces. "You're not using R-33. Your eyes . . ."

Abel ignored him and touched his coms unit.

There was another explosion inside the processing plant.

"Jubal is offline," Abel said.

"Dipshit," said Eve, then turned back to Brozović. "We're getting you out of here, honeybuns. Kuga and Daddy have very big plans for you."

"'Daddy'?" echoed Brozović.

Cain gave the scientist a small shove. "She means Rafael Santoro. Now shift your ass."

Eve just laughed.

CHAPTER 107
DAS VERARBEITUNGSZENTRUM

Ghost and I hurried through the smoke back to the door through which we'd first entered. A good portion of that part of the prison was in ruins now, so we simply exited through a hole in the wall. We ran low and fast for the fence, and I only paused when I saw a group of three people standing outside the main entrance. Two Fixers—big ones, real brutes—and a slender blond woman.

I skidded to a stop and turned, clawing my binoculars from a pouch on my belt. My fingers were trembling so badly I dropped it. But then I had it pressed to my eyes as I adjusted the focus.

It was she.

Eve. God damn.

Even without the leg brace over the knee I'd put a bullet through, I'd have recognized her anywhere. Eve. Rafael Santoro's little pet. She called him *Daddy*. She loved him, had killed for him, had become his star pupil in the game of brutal extortion. She and her ex-lover, Adam, had managed to forcibly corrupt Navy SEALs and turned them into mass murderers. While trying to shoot me, Eve had accidentally killed Adam. I'd made a critical mistake by not putting my bullet into Eve's brainpan instead of her knee. Every life she destroyed from now on was on me as much as her.

And here she was, with a squad of spooky-ass enhanced Fixers.

Had she known I was going to be here? Or was this one of those coincidences that make me believe the whole universe is run by demented gods?

As I watched, three more figures came out—a pair of Fixers half dragging, half carrying a prisoner in an orange jumpsuit. I swapped a new magazine into my Snellig and then tapped keys to bring the swarms of bees out so I could stage another assault. I could hear police sirens in the distance, but not too close. Maybe I could take out the Fixers and drag Eve off to a quiet spot for a little game of Truth or Consequences. But before I could even begin to formulate a plan, the air was chopped by the *whup-whup-whup* of helicopters coming in low and fast. I turned to peer into the night sky, hoping they were also police or maybe a military sent in response to alarms from the processing plant.

They weren't.

A pair of unmarked black choppers came roaring out of the night. One was a muscular NH90 medium troop transport, and the other was a deadly UH Tiger that bristled with rocket pods, chain guns, and missiles.

I may be crazy, but I'm not *that* crazy. This wasn't a fight I could win.

Ghost made low growling sounds of frustration. He knew it, too.

So instead, I set some Busy-Bees to get pictures of Eve and the prisoner.

We waited until the bees completed their task. I collected them, and then Ghost and I vanished into the night.

CHAPTER 108

THE TOC
PHOENIX HOUSE
OMFORI ISLAND, GREECE

Doc Holliday was not done with her presentation.

"What we don't yet know is where and how they plan to use this tech," she said. "As of right now, they could walk right into any venue, any stadium, any public office, or—hell—even any military base and destroy it."

"Do we think the Fixers *know* they're wearing what amounts to suicide vests?"

She thought about it and then shook her head. "I'd have to say no. I mean . . . why on earth would they strap it on knowing that they were that completely disposable? Remember, the Kuga organization isn't a religious or political movement. They're basically the Mafia on steroids. Criminals are not known for heroic sacrifice. They don't want to die for a cause, they want to get rich, get fat, screw down and marry up, and retire old. PMCs are no different. They take risks because it's a job that pays them for that; but in the end, they want to be able to spend that money."

"Maybe we can find some way to tell them," said Bug. "If they stage a hit, then I can try and hack into their coms systems."

"That's good," said Wilson.

"Unless the suits can be remote detonated," said Coleman.

"Thank you, Debbie Downer," said Doc.

"Ron is correct," said Church. "It's doubtful Kuga would make the critical error of sending his troops out without a fail-safe. He really only needs them to get into position. Whatever collateral damage they inflict with guns and grenades amounts to theater. The real goal would be to destroy a very specific target, either for maximum body count or to make a point."

"Like what?" asked Isaac. "Walking into the United Nations?"

"They're diplomats," said Wilson. "Parliament or the Capitol Building are more effective targets. Or the White House."

"Agreed," said Church. "But we need to consider nonpolitical targets. Or targets of a military nature."

"Yes," said Wilson slowly. "If, say, they sold that tech to the Kurds and had a couple of them go after Assad's palace."

"Or to Palestinians," said Isaac. "Or to Israelis, for that matter."

"His preeminent buyer would likely be underdogs in any political or military conflict," said Church. "If ISIL wanted to make a comeback, for example. Or the Taliban. There are endless possibilities, and any one successful strike becomes a catalog page to sell this technology to the next fifty buyers. Being apolitical, Kuga can sell to both parties in any conflict."

"Then we are in real trouble," said Coleman.

"Yes, we damn well are," said Doc, and Church nodded.

"I really, really, *really* hate to ask this," said Nikki, "but is there more? And please say no."

Doc Holliday gave her a smile as bright as the noonday sun.

"Why, sweetie, of *course* there's more."

CHAPTER 109
THE TOC
PHOENIX HOUSE
OMFORI ISLAND, GREECE

"Now we get to the areas where we don't know much for certain," said Doc Holliday. She clicked to change the image. This one showed a collage of several documents with handwritten notes or Post-its, each with a different acronym. Doc used her laser pointer to tick them off one at a time.

"The most commonly repeated code is AO," she said. "There's also a few references to the AO or TAO, which is probably the same thing. Based on the Croatia documents, we had very little to go on, but in the notes Joe gave to Toys, there are references to 'the American Operation.'"

"Which is . . . ?" asked Wilson.

"Beats the living tarnation out of me, duckie."

"We can conjecture that it involves a deployment of the other technology," said Church.

"Sure, but how can we pinpoint the target?" asked Isaac.

"Without a time frame, we cannot," Church said glumly. "We're early in the summer, and with COVID restrictions lifting, baseball season will continue in earnest, with sentimental fans now flocking to the stadiums. The same goes for concerts, and there are outdoor events like Coachella, Burning Man, and many others. If we go into fall, there's football season, schools reopening, election rallies . . ."

He left the rest hang.

"Moving on," said Doc. "There are a few references to G-55. Isaac thinks it's another product line that we don't have specs on yet. Ronny-bear thinks it's a code for a generation of a bioweapon. But we're just guessing."

They all batted theories around, but again, the lack of context foiled them.

"Then we have R-33," said Doc. "That *is a* chemical, and there were extensive notes in the Croatia papers. There were even some samples of earlier versions of it—notably, R-16 and R-31. But I'll let Wooly Bear tell you his theory."

Ronald Coleman got to his feet. He was relatively new to Rogue Team International and not used to giving presentations to Church and his chief of operations. But he took a breath and plunged in.

"I have a theory about R-33," he began. "There are several references to R-33, Relentless, and the 33 Protocols in the notes we recovered in Croatia, and I believe they're all the same thing."

"Excuse me," said Wilson, "but 'Relentless'?"

"Yes. It appears to be a category of designer drug therapies in the eugeroic category. What some people call *nootropic*. Wakefulness drugs. Modafinil is the best-known drug in this category of drugs. It was developed to work for people with narcolepsy. It's now used in all kinds of contexts where people need to stay alert for long periods of time. The air force uses it as a 'go pill' for certain situations. They did a really interesting test where they kept pilots awake for thirty-seven hours and made them fly in a simulator under the influence of it. That has real benefits for the military on long missions, and I know that it's been tested in some countries to help firefighters on long shifts, emergency room staff, and so on. There are clear benefits, but as with all drugs, there are both known side effects and potential misuses. Not accidental . . . I mean deliberate uses for less-than-admirable purposes."

He paused to make sure everyone was following. They were.

"There's a mention in the old DMS files of a case you worked on, Mr. Church, and which was later completed by Joe Ledger. At different times, you were hunting for black marketeers moving a performance-enhancing synthetic steroid. The first generation of a formula that combines the select lean mass–building steroids with a synthetic eugeroic compound that significantly increases and regulates the hypothalamic histamine levels. In normal pharmacology, these drugs are wakefulness-promoting agents often prescribed to prevent shift-work sleepiness. That version was designed to build stamina and wakefulness to a point where the treated person won't tire and won't lose mental sharpness."

"How does that work?" asked Wilson.

"While these drugs do upregulate hypothalamic histamine, they more directly work as a dopamine reuptake inhibitor, which means that they keep dopamine in the brain from being reabsorbed into the signaling neurons. This has the effect of building up more dopamine in the synaptic space, which is the business end of a neuron. Now . . . this works really well for what it is intended to do. A situation where you have to be okay for a long period of time, but not one where you have to be super awesome for a short period of time. Follow me?"

"What does this have to do with Kuga?" asked Nikki.

"Getting there, getting there . . ." Coleman took a drink from a bottle of water. "One problem with most of these drugs is that they take two to three hours to kick in. And it's sort of a gradual and subtle effect. Per the air force study, there is still a 15–30 percent decrease in performance. However, we were able to obtain sufficient material from Croatia to subject it to GC MS and found four distinct compounds—L-Dopa, tetracycline, N-methylamphetamine hydrochloride, and oxycodone. The last two are in the sub-milligram to low-milligram range per injection. Really not enough to get someone high and certainly not enough to cause superstrength and hyper-aggressive behavior, but they are the only parts of the concoction that make any sense right now."

Bug raised his eyebrows. "So . . . these cats are loading up on meth and oxys?"

Coleman said, "In a way. N-methylamphetamine hydrochloride, or meth, has a long history of being used in combat situations. During World War II, the Nazis gave it out like candy to their soldiers. It was distributed under the name Pervitin. By the end of the war, they had created a pill code-named D-IX. It contained five milligrams of cocaine, three milligrams of Pervitin, and five milligrams of oxycodone. R-33 seems to be a continuation of that work."

Church asked, "What about the other components?"

"L-Dopa is a dopamine precursor that is used in the treatment of Parkinson's disease," said Coleman. "And the tetracycline is a common antibiotic. But let me get to the really key part here. Among the recovered materials was this."

Coleman held up a small white packet about half the size of a business card and less than half an inch thick. "According to their clinical records, something like this is intended to be surgically implanted just beneath the skin of each Fixer. And this is an expanded polytetrafluoroethylene pouch that contains hundreds of millions of cells."

"What type of cells?" asked Church.

"Well, you see, boss, that's the really interesting part. RNA-Seq showed that they were most likely chromaffin cells. Those are the cells in the adrenal cortex that are responsible for the release of catecholamines."

"Cate . . . ?" began Wilson, fumbling with it. Coleman stepped right in.

"Catecholamines are the molecules responsible for the body's fight-or-flight response, which was interesting by itself. But when we dug down and did whole genome sequencing, we found a number of genetically inserted tet-on promoters. Specifically, they were attached to inserted versions of DOPA decarboxylase, dopamine β-hydroxylase, and phenylethanolamine N-methyltransferase."

"I have no idea what that means."

Coleman, who was in gear and very excited, tried to scale it down, but he was a lab rat and very rarely had to explain these things to ordinary mortals. "Tet-on promoters are a little bit of DNA that can be used to control when a gene is expressed. Think of it as a light switch for a gene. But this switch is flipped by adding tetracycline. It has been used in biotechnology for a long time, but this isn't just some off-the-shelf version. This is highly specialized to turn on very fast and make *huge* amounts of the genes. And the genes they control are the genes in the synthetic pathway to turn L-Dopa into norepinephrine and adrenaline."

"But . . . but . . . ," fumbled Nikki, "why put the cells in the pouches? Why not just inject them somewhere into the PMC?"

"Because the pouch protects the cells from the immune system of the person it is implanted into, so there is no rejection," explained Coleman. "The pouch lets small molecules and liquid back and forth, but it doesn't allow cells in or out. There is a clinical trial underway right now where similar technology is being used to encapsulate insulin-secreting cells to treat type 1 diabetes. However, in this case, they are using the pouches as small bioreactors to make huge amounts of norepinephrine and adrenaline but only in the presence of tetracycline. L-Dopa is a synthetic precursor for those hormones, so that makes sense, too."

"Okay," Nikki said. "I think I actually understood that part."

"Still clinging on by my fingernails," Wilson said under his breath.

"So the capsules under the skin are filled with cells that have been engineered so that the presence of this antibiotic causes them to create huge amounts of norepinephrine and adrenaline. The combination of those two hormones is what is believed to cause hysterical strength. That's the kind of thing where a mom lifts a car off her baby or whatever."

"Isn't there a great physical cost to that kind of sudden exertion?" asked Church.

"Oh yes," said Coleman. "Very much. Especially with this Relentless series of drugs. If they use this for any significant length of time, it'll probably kill them. The heart is not designed to take such a huge and sustained adrenaline dump."

The room fell silent as the implications of that sank in.

"Bloody hell," said Wilson after a while. "This will turn those Fixers who are already in bleeding-edge body armor into supermen, and then it will kill them, triggering the explosives."

Everyone in the room looked sick and scared. Even Church.

"Footage taken from Top's and Bunny's button cams have shown that quite a few of the Fixers at the Pavilion have surgical scars," said Coleman. "So we can assume these packets have already been implanted. Since Top and Bunny are relatively new recruits, they haven't yet received these implants. The others, though . . ."

"Maybe we can try to tell the Fixers this," ventured Nikki. "Maybe we can tell them that their employers have turned them into suicide bombers."

"That would be great," said Coleman. "But . . ."

"Dear lord, save me from scientists who say 'But,'" pleaded Wilson.

"Sorry," said Coleman, and there was just a hint of the same ghoulish excitement on Doc Holliday's face. "There's a kicker. And it's a kicker that really does make this worse."

"Then just hit us with it," said Church.

"Even though we don't have samples of R-33, which is apparently their latest generation . . . we do know what they intended to add to it to make the super Fixers even *more* dangerous."

"Christ," breathed Wilson, and he literally grabbed the arms of his chair as if bracing for a blow.

"These packets will contain trace amounts of Rage."

CHAPTER 110
DAS VERARBEITUNGSZENTRUM

The black car idled at the edge of the parking lot, and the three passengers watched the processing plant burn.

They saw two helicopters land and several small figures in black, and one in orange, climb aboard. The chopper lifted into the air just as a line of police cars came screaming into the lot from two entrances.

"Holy moly," breathed Harry Bolt. "Did Joe do all that?"

"What do you think?" asked Toys snidely. "That bloke could start a riot in an empty room."

Violin studied the figures still visible as the helicopters climbed into the air.

"Those were soldiers of some kind," she said. "In body armor. Not a style I recognize."

"How can you see that without binoculars?" asked Toys, but Violin only smiled.

Harry said, "She has superpowers. You wouldn't believe some of the things Violin can—"

"Hush now," she murmured. And he hushed.

The police cars screeched to a halt in front of the building, and the officers piled out, some pointing their weapons at the choppers, but there was no chance of a hit. The machines were climbing and turning.

"Any sign of our boy?" asked Toys.

Violin looked around. For a moment, it seemed as if she were about to say something, but then shook her head.

Suddenly, a new series of explosions rippled through the building. And then an absolutely massive detonation lifted the entire roof off and hurled flaming chunks of concrete across the parking lot. The police scattered, but most of them were caught by the blast or knocked down by flaming debris.

"Christ!" gasped Toys.

"We need to help them," said Violin.

"We need to find Joe," said Harry.

"No," said Toys, "she's right. We need to help."

And the car drove into the parking lot.

CHAPTER 111
SCANDIC BERLIN POTSDAMER PLATZ
GABRIELE-TERGIT-PROMENADE 19
BERLIN, GERMANY

First thing I did was find a public trash can on a deserted city street, pull over, and dump the remaining bee drones and my MindReader gear into the metal can. Then I stripped off my own body armor. Last, I activated four blaster-plasters that I hadn't needed to use. I raced back to my car and was halfway down the block when it all blew up. It was a big and very hot fireball that I knew would completely incinerate everything. All anyone would find was slag. Nothing was traceable to begin with, but now it was not even remotely recognizable as what it might have been. While I drove, I muttered apologies to Doc and Bug.

Then I took a long and complex route back to my hotel in Berlin. I stopped my car on a different side road halfway there and spent some time changing out of my combat rig and into a nondescript suit with a drab tie and fake eyeglasses. Cleaning the blood off Ghost took a while, and he whined and glared as if I were doing something truly awful to him.

"Stop being a big baby," I scolded, and he replied with a loud and eloquent fart.

My hands shook as I worked. Partly it was the adrenaline still trying to get my nerves and muscles to fight or flee. Takes a lot longer for that to wash out of the bloodstream than it does to inject it in. Comes with a bit of nausea, too.

Mostly, though, I was scared. And . . . relieved?

I'd done the whole mission without the Darkness taking me over. And that was something I had to actually think about to make sure I was correct. But there were no memory gaps. I could map out every minute of my time inside the processing plant. So . . . *yay*?

On the other hand, I'd seen ghosts. *Spoken* to ghosts. To my brother, Sean.

If it had been Sean.

When his eyes changed . . . that was how Top, Bunny, and Rudy had all described someone else's eyes changing color. It was a name of a person I was sure had died in California at Church's hands. At least, that's what I thought. I hesitated even thinking the name.

But it came anyway, and my lips and tongue and breath stained the air with it.

"Nicodemus," I whispered.

Ghost whined and curled his tail between his legs, as he had back in Casanova's cell.

"He's coming for you, Joe. If you keep hunting Santoro and Kuga, you'll find him. And he really wants you to find him, Cowboy. Oh yes, he does. He wants that so much."

God almighty.

I debated driving to a church—any church—instead of back to my hotel. And if I thought that would have helped, I'd have done it.

Instead, I drove us into town, parked the car myself rather than let a nosy valet have it, and went up to my room. I ordered enough food for six people, and while I waited for room service, I showered and spent a few minutes just standing under the spray. Maybe I lost some time. I don't really know. What I do know is that I have no clear memory of drying off or getting dressed again.

That should have scared me more than it did.

And the fact that it didn't scare me should have *really* freaked me out. It was as if I could stand a few feet away and objectively observe the process of my own psychological fragmentation.

The knock on the door shook me out of those kinds of thoughts. Like any good total paranoid nutjob, I peered through the peephole while pressing a gun barrel to the door panel. But it was a bored-looking twentysomething in a hotel uniform. I slid the pistol into my waistband and pulled the shirt out to cover it, signed the check, added a couple of extra euros to the already exorbitant precalculated tip, carried the tray inside, and closed and locked the door. I set two of the trays on the floor for Ghost. Medium-rare steak on one, chicken fingers on the other, both with lots of fries. Ghost ate them one at a time and with great delicacy.

While I ate, I typed up an after-action report. When I'd hit town, I'd purchased a low-end laptop because I thought I'd have a lot to record. A computer's memory was far more reliable than my own swiss cheese brain. Once I was ready to check out of the room, I'd email the data to Bug and then abandon the laptop here. Even though I was not technically operating under any kind of orders from Mr. Church, there were things he needed to know.

The report had almost all of it—the Fixers, their newfangled tech, the strange psychological weirdness, the suicide vests, the resistance to Sandman, and the presence of Eve.

I omitted everything about Casanova, though, and I didn't bother providing any explanation as to why I'd broken into the processing plant in the first place. That was need to know, and they didn't.

As I typed, I could see them in the laptop screen's reflective surface.

The silent figures clustered behind me as if ready to take a family portrait.

"No," I told them.

Ghost looked at me and then at the wall behind me. He came and put his head on my thigh. "It's okay," I lied. "Everything's going to be okay."

When I looked at the reflection again, there was nothing behind me but empty wall. I could smell something, though. A burned-meat stink. I tried to close it out, grinding my teeth together so hard my jaws hurt.

I finished the report and emailed it off, got up, walked into the bathroom, and threw my guts up in the toilet. Then I crawled back into the shower, wrapped my arms around my head, and totally lost my shit.

CHAPTER 112
PHOENIX HOUSE
OMFORI ISLAND, GREECE

Bug came out of his office at a dead run.

He found Church in the canteen, sitting down with a cup of coffee, a plate of vanilla wafers, and a stack of reports. Bug skidded to a breathless halt.

"What is it?" asked Church.

"It's Germany," he said. "Damn, boss, this is nuts."

"Sit," said Church. "Take a breath and tell me."

"First, Joe trashed his MindReader substation. He's gone dark again."

"That was expected."

"And we now know for sure why he was in Berlin. Toys called me from the parking lot of some black site prison with an unpronounceable name."

Church stiffened. "Das Verarbeitungszentrum?"

"Yeah. That one."

He explained that Toys, Violin, and Harry Bolt had tracked

Ledger to the prison in hopes of making contact and either offering support or—ideally—bringing him in.

"The prison is gone, man," said Bug. "I hacked into the news and police feeds, and it's basically a burning crater. Total loss of life—all the guards and all the prisoners."

"And Colonel Ledger?"

"That's the thing," said Bug. "They saw him get out. Him and Ghost. But they also saw a team of Fixers there, and they were wearing that body armor."

"Which may explain the explosion," mused Church.

"Eve was with them," said Bug. "Violin thought she was running the crew."

"Now isn't that interesting?"

"Toys said that Joe mentioned a place in Germany he couldn't get into and a prisoner named Casanova. I did the background, and he was on Kuga's team."

"Yes," said Church. "Intelligence from one of our agents—Mia Kleeve, call sign Magpie—helped put him there."

"Okay, well, Eve and her Fixers brought someone out, but Violin says it wasn't Casanova."

"How sure is she?"

"You know Violin," said Bug. "She's sure. She gave me a good description, though, and I ran it through Q1. Looks like the guy they liberated was a lot more dangerous than Casanova."

Church leaned back and exhaled slowly through his nostrils. "And you're going to tell me it was Dr. Dejan Brozović."

"Um . . . yeah . . ."

Church picked up a cookie, looked at it, set it down, and pushed the plate away.

"Molecular biologist and organic chemist."

"They broke him out to work on R-33, didn't they?"

"Yes," said Church. "I'm afraid that's exactly what they did."

JONATHAN MABERRY

CHAPTER 113
SCANDIC BERLIN POTSDAMER PLATZ
BERLIN, GERMANY

Peggy Ann Gondek sat in the cushioned armchair beside her hotel bed and punched in a series of coded numbers on a satellite phone.

She nibbled a carrot stick as she waited for the call to go through. There was a towel spread on the duvet. She unzipped a small clamshell case and began lining up the items she needed. Mil-Comm TW25B lubricant, a thin aluminum rod, a bottle of cleaning solvent, and a brush for a .22 barrel. The call had to be routed through several security steps, so she began disassembling the Ruger SR22 that was her personal favorite. The model, not the specific weapon; she always disposed of her guns and knives before crossing borders and then picked up new equipment.

She dropped the magazine, checked the breech, and made sure there was no round in the chamber. Then she rotated the slide lock lever to the vertical to unlock the slide from the frame.

There was a click on the line.

"Hello, Mrs. Gondek," said a cultured voice. "Have you found our friend?"

"I have," she said.

"Good," said Church. "We're going to need to make contact with him. Where is he now?"

"He just got back to the hotel." She gave the name of the hotel but did not know the room. "Don't suppose you heard anything about an attack on a processing plant in Wannsee?"

"That was our friend?"

"It was." Peggy Ann pushed the spring forward toward the barrel very carefully and pulled it outward to remove the spring. "He got to the hotel less than an hour after things went boom. And he looked quite . . . frazzled. So did the poor pooch."

There was the slightest pause on the other end of the call. "Is he safe?"

"At the moment? Sure. Overall? No, I wouldn't say so."

Another pause. "Is he in control?"

Peggy Ann picked up the brush rod and sat tapping it thoughtfully against the gun barrel.

"Define 'control,'" she said.

CHAPTER 114
HOTEL NEUER FRITZ
FRIEDRICHSTRASSE 10
BERLIN, GERMANY

Eve sat against the headboard of the big king bed, trying to muster the courage to make a call. Daddy had given her two assignments—eliminate Casanova and exfiltrate Dr. Dejan Brozović. One task had been satisfactorily accomplished and the other almost certainly so. The whole building was a burning tomb. But almost certain was not the same as absolutely certain. Would it be enough for Santoro?

She hoped so. Daddy giving her this mission was a big thing. The final test before he could tell Kuga that she was a completely reliable field operative.

Cain and Abel were outside, watching the elevator and the door. She didn't want them around when she told Daddy about what happened at the processing plant. She didn't want them to see her cry.

Her cell phone lay on the pillow next to her. Where Adam's head should be. Every time she looked at it, she saw his face overlaid as if he were there but made of hollow glass. Twice she'd tried to touch him, and both times, she'd jerked her hand back from the nothingness.

"I love you," she murmured.

The ghost of Adam smiled at her.

"Love you, too, babe," he said.

Tears rolled down her cheeks, mingled with snot from her leaking nose, hanging from her cheeks, and fell onto her chest.

"I hate you for leaving me, you selfish prick," she snarled and pounded her fist down on the mattress. It passed through him, and he dissipated like smoke. The jolt made the cell phone slide off the pillow. Eve took a steadying breath, pawed the tears from nose and mouth and cheeks, and returned the phone to the pillow.

"I'll always love you, Eve," Adam said softly. He touched her face, and Eve shivered. Goose bumps rippled along her thighs and up the outsides of her arms.

"Big dummy," she told Adam. "Going off and leaving me."

When she spoke to him like this, her voice was ten years younger. The voice of the girl Adam rescued from the home where they'd both been incarcerated. That bothered her.

Eve had swallowed a Xanax, but it hadn't hit her bloodstream yet. The lag time tempted her to take another, but she didn't. Not yet. Last thing she needed was slurred speech or, worse, to puke her guts up while giving her report.

Eve closed her eyes for a moment and looked inward and downward. In her mind, there was a big movie screen playing, and she was seated in the middle of the front row. As she watched, Joe Ledger drew his pistol, aimed it with great care at Adam, who stood with his hands raised in surrender. A cruel smile of sexual delight wormed its way onto Ledger's mouth as he slipped his finger into the trigger guard. Adam's mouth was open, his lips forming words, pleas . . . begging Ledger for mercy. But the big killer's smile became an orgasmic cry of wet delight as he pulled the trigger and shot Adam in the mouth, blowing the top row of teeth in, ripping through tissue and bone and nerve and exiting in an explosion of blood and brains. Adam stared for a moment in disbelief and then the light—that beautiful pure and perfect light—went out of his eyes, and he collapsed back and down.

Eve closed her eyes, squeezing them shut with such intensity that it forced tears out, shedding them between her lashes.

"You got some wires connected wrong, sweetie," murmured Adam. "I mean, you know that's not how it happened, right?"

"Fuck you, fuck you, fuck you," she said helplessly. "It *is* how it happened."

"Okay, babe," said Adam, "whatever you say. Whatever you want it to be. It's all okay."

She felt his hand touch her leg, tracing the outlines of the brace she wore over the knee Ledger had destroyed with another bullet.

"You know I'll always be right here," said Adam. "Right by your side."

It took her a long time to open her eyes. The cell phone was still on the pillow. Adam was barely an outline. But he was—as he said— still there. By her side.

"You'd better make that call," suggested Adam. "Don't want to keep Daddy waiting."

"He'll be mad," she said in a tiny voice.

"So, let him be mad. You got the right guy out of there, didn't you?"

"I suppose . . ."

"Then you accomplished your mission."

"We lost most of the team. Almost all of the Righteous are gone."

Adam laughed. "You think Daddy cares about that stuff?"

Eve sniffed. Shrugged.

"You *still* came out with the right prisoner. And that other guy? Casanova? He's dead for sure. No way he walked out of that place. Daddy's going to be really happy with you, babe."

"But . . . but . . . Ledger was there . . . ," Eve protested. "I saw him on the body cams. He got away."

"That wasn't your mission, Evie sweetheart," insisted Adam.

She nodded but didn't feel entirely convinced.

"Look, babe," said Adam, shifting a little on the bed—enough that the phone slipped off the pillow—"just call him. Pull the bandage off. Let him yell if he wants to, but just know you did what he sent you there to do. You're his daughter. He loves you."

After a long string of moments, Eve reached through Adam's chest and picked up the phone. She did not see his eyes change from their perfect deep summer sky blue to a swirl of ugly green and brown.

She punched in the number and held her breath until the call was answered.

"Hello," said Rafael Santoro.

CHAPTER 115
THE PLAYROOM
UNDISCLOSED LOCATION
NEAR VANCOUVER, BRITISH COLUMBIA, CANADA

Rafael Santoro closed the lid of the flip phone very slowly, quietly, and placed the instrument neatly on his desk blotter, just to the left and below center. He considered it, then adjusted the angle so that it perfectly aligned with the other items on his desk.

He was a small man. Middle-aged, thin, wiry, and fit. There were scars on his swarthy skin. Old, faded ones that were hidden by his tan, and newer ones that looked like flattened pink worms. His hair was intensely black but swirling with silver lines, his lips full and sensual. People who didn't know him well told him he had a gentle smile.

He looked at the phone as if he could see Eve. His fractured little adopted daughter. A prodigy whose abilities outweighed her eccentricities. At least for now.

Then he swiveled his leather chair around to face the tall man who stood by the wet bar, a tall glass of superb Japanese single malt in his hand.

"And . . . ?" asked the other man. Kuga looked like a younger Kevin Costner. Broad-shouldered, all-American good looks, piercing blue eyes, and a very expensive smile.

"Dr. Brozović is on his way to the safe house," said Santoro. "He will be on a plane first thing in the morning."

"He okay? Last thing we need is him with his brains scrambled."

"Eve says that he was rescued without injury. He is confused but is cooperating with her."

Kuga sipped his whiskey. "Good. What about the team?"

Santoro hesitated, searching for the right words to frame his response. "There were casualties."

"How many?"

"Four Fixers exfilled with Eve."

"Only four? Ouch. You can't tell me that a bunch of prison guards took down most of a top-tier strike team. Every goddamned one of them was juiced and jacked. They should have been able to walk into a military base and kick ass. Shit, we're counting on higher levels of opposition for G-55. How in the hell can—"

"*He* was there," interrupted Santoro.

Kuga froze. "Who? *Who* was there?"

Santoro fought to keep his voice calm as he spoke the hated name. "Joe Ledger."

The room went dead still. Kuga gaped at him. And then he whirled and hurled the whiskey glass at the big mirror over the couch, which exploded in a shower of jagged splinters that slashed the leather. He swept his arm along the top of the wet bar and sent $5,000 worth of quality whiskey and brandy crashing to the floor. The bottles smashed apart and filled the air with the abusive stink of a distillery factory floor. The door banged open, and two Fixers entered, their sidearms drawn.

"Get the hell out!" roared Kuga, and they fled.

He stormed through the room, kicking over the coffee table and knocking everything onto the floor. "How the fucking hell is Joe fucking Ledger at that fucking prison? How, Rafael? *How?* Does that mean he knows? Christ on a stick . . . *does Ledger know?*"

Santoro walked into the middle of the storm and stood right in front of Kuga. For a fragile moment, the taller man loomed over him, fist bunched, arm cocked, ready to strike. Santoro's arms were at his side, and fast as he was, there was no way he could have blocked or evaded that blow.

And it stopped Kuga cold.

The tall American stood panting, face flushed to a hypertensive scarlet.

"Does he know, Rafael?" asked Kuga again, and this time, his voice was soft. Desperate. Even afraid. "Does Ledger know? Why else would he be there? Does Church know?"

"I don't know, my friend," said Santoro, placing his hands on Kuga's broad shoulders. And it was a mark of how important this moment was that he *meant* that word. Friend. He meant it, and Kuga felt it.

"Do . . . do we need to stop the plan?"

Santoro gave Kuga's shoulders a squeeze, then dropped his hands. "Eve said that Dr. Brozović was liberated from his cell without incident. The violence at the processing plant was centralized in two places—the bunkhouse where the staff was sleeping and the corridor outside Casanova's cell."

Kuga turned and walked over to the window, his lips pursed, eyes narrowed and calmer.

"Casanova doesn't know about the American Operation. As far as I know, all he was ever told was that there was one planned."

"Yes," said Santoro. "He knows that, and he knows about R-33. It was Brozović who possessed the knowledge that could damage us. Eve insists that Ledger got nowhere near the wing where he was kept."

Kuga nodded but said nothing.

"As for Mr. Church," said Santoro, wincing a little at the name, "I believe Ledger is still acting alone. There's been no team action, even when such a choice would have been tactically necessary to prevent Ledger from taking undue risks. No, he's out there on his own."

"He's doing a hell of a lot of damage alone," said Kuga caustically.

"He is. And sometimes a single man may accomplish what a full team cannot." Santoro paused and then came at it from a different angle. "My surmise is that there are other hits we don't know about. Maybe several. I think our Colonel Ledger is not merely slamming around collecting scalps. I think he is more in control than we give him credit for. Bear in mind, he was a police detective before he worked for the demon Church, and he's learned a lot about international politics and espionage tradecraft. Including interrogation strategies."

Kuga grunted and sat forward. "Well, that's an ugly damned can of worms. You think he's been getting names from his showier hits, killing some and using coercion on others?"

"It's possible, even likely."

"And those blabbermouths wouldn't fess up because they know how *we'd* react. Anyone who talked to him would take that information to their graves rather than risk a visit from a Fixer . . . or from you."

"Sadly, yes."

Kuga suddenly laughed. It was short and bitter, but genuine. "Goddamn, Ledger is pulling a Rafael Santoro on *us*."

The little Spaniard's face showed no amusement. "We need to

review what each of the people at those locations knew. Most are like Casanova—they know there is an American Operation and that it is tied to materials coded as G-55. But our circle of factual knowledge about the actual operation—the dates, location, intent, and timing—is very tight. I cannot offhand think of a single person, not even Alexander Fong, Gerald Engelbrecht, or Mislav Mitrović, who knows enough to matter."

Kuga rubbed his eyes and blew out his cheeks. "So . . . who does that leave?"

"The leaders of the four Fixer teams and HK, of course, but they've all been confined to the Pavilion," said Santoro. "Gerald Crumby in London, the Cat in Romania, and maybe three others who are here in this house."

Kuga walked across the room and back, avoiding the debris and broken glass. He stopped and stared out the window, hands thrust deep into his pockets.

"Then we need to make sure each of those targets is covered."

"Oh yes," said Santoro. "I will make those calls now."

CHAPTER 116
SCANDIC BERLIN POTSDAMER PLATZ
BERLIN, GERMANY

Peggy Ann Gondek stood in the middle of the hotel room and looked around. She'd closed the door after bypassing the key card lock and stood now with a Snellig dart gun in her right hand. The Ruger SR22 was tucked into a discreet clip on her belt, hidden by a baggy cardigan. She also had a double-edged stiletto strapped to her left forearm under her sleeve.

The closets and bureau drawers were empty, room curtains and blackout drapes drawn, bed messed. A small laptop lay on the desk.

She walked into the bathroom and surveyed the damage. The shower curtain was torn from almost all the rings, the plastic slashed. What was left of the mirror lay in glittering pieces on the tiled floor, each piece smeared with red. There were two words written in what she was absolutely certain was blood, scrawled on the wall.

Umbra.

Tenebris.

"Darkness," she murmured.

Mrs. Gondek set her dart gun on the closed toilet seat lid and knelt. Something about the broken, red-smeared mirror troubled her, so she squatted down and took the pieces and began reassembling them. As she did so, what had originally appeared to be just smears formed two more words. They were written in a similar, but slightly different hand.

The words broke her heart.

The words terrified her.

Save me.

A SHADOW IN THE EAST
PART 6

The ignorant mind, with its infinite afflictions, passions, and evils, is rooted in the three poisons. Greed, anger, and delusion.

—BODHIDHARMA

Instead of a man of peace and love, I have become a man of violence and revenge.

—HIAWATHA

CHAPTER 117
BERLIN AIRPORTCLUB LOUNGE
BERLIN BRANDENBURG AIRPORT

Peggy Ann Gondek sat primly in a padded chair in a corner of the lounge where she could easily see the other customers coming and going. She had a tall glass of iced coffee on the table beside her and the colorful coils of a scarf trailing from her busy knitting needles. Like many travelers, she wore a Bluetooth headset. People smiled at her, and she beamed back at them. Not a smile of invitation, merely pleasant.

Whenever someone came close enough to hear her quiet voice, she changed the subject to talk about stitches. Garter, purl, stockinette stitches as well as moss stitches, ribbing, and the basket weave stitches. She knew how to pitch her voice so that any subject could sound dreadfully dull, even knitting, which was her passion. People generally did not want to sit within earshot and listen to her drone on and on about it.

"Alone again," she said as another person decided somewhere else was tranquiller and less lethally dull. "Is he available yet?"

"Hold on," said a woman with a distinctly Brooklyn accent, and a moment later, a man's voice spoke on the line.

"Were you able to determine where our friend is heading?" asked Mr. Church.

"Oh yes," said Peggy Ann. "Timișoara, in Romania. His flight leaves in a little over an hour."

"Can you be on the same flight?"

"Not a chance, dear heart," she said. "He got the last seat. Who would have thought so many people wanted to go to Timișoara?"

"That's unfortunate."

"I'm on standby for another flight," said Peggy Ann.

Mr. Church paused for a moment, then said, "Will you be able to locate him in Timișoara?"

"Oh, honey, of course."

"Let Bug know if you need any additional resources." And the call ended.

"Well," said Peggy Ann to herself as she continued working on the scarf, "and a pleasant good afternoon to you, too." She shook her head. "Not even a proper goodbye. Hmph."

She worked for another ten minutes, finishing the row, and then packed up her things and headed down to find her gate.

CHAPTER 118
HOTEL TIMIȘOARA
TIMIȘOARA, ROMANIA

I had another blackout.

Another day lost to the Darkness.

I have dim memories only of going to the airport. I had to search my pockets for the boarding pass I used. It told me I was in Romania.

Why Romania?

My hand hurt, and I realized it was bandaged. Somehow I'd cut the side of my fist. Had that happened at the processing plant?

No, I didn't think so.

I looked around. This was a nice hotel room, but which hotel? There was a directory of numbers attached to the phone, and it gave the name of the hotel and my own room number.

Seeing that information began a process that had now become familiar. Details floated back, often without context, and I struggled to make sense of them. I had four different room key cards. They were laid out on the desk, and it took some effort to fish inside my broken head for what they represented. Not sure if that process took five minutes or an hour. All I know is that understanding came, slowly and reluctantly. These were keys for other rooms I'd booked.

Then I jolted.

"Ghost . . . ?" I called.

But there was nothing. No sound. I ran into the bathroom, looking in the closets, under the bed, but Ghost was not in that room.

Panic tried to punch its way out of my chest.

I found my shoes and put them on. Found a gun. A Snellig. How in the fuck did I get that through customs? Nothing made sense, and the thought that I—in my fugue state—had either abandoned Ghost or . . .

I couldn't go there.

I grabbed the room keys, tucked the gun into my waistband, and ran into the hall.

"Ghost," I sobbed. "No . . ."

CHAPTER 119
THE PAVILION
BLUE DIAMOND ELITE TRAINING CENTER
STEVENS COUNTY, WASHINGTON

Mia Kleeve huddled in a treetop with Belle.

It was midday, and the Fixers were creating thunder with live fire drills. A third of them were in body armor and a dozen in the K-110 fighting machines. During the night, they'd received intel from Scott Wilson about what the science team had been able to piece together. It was truly terrifying.

The two women, though hidden and unsuspected by the enemy, were shaken to their cores. As was Andrea, who was at his post on the far side of the camp. His bird drones sent images to them and to the TOC.

"God, I wish we could just call in a strike," muttered Mia. "Drop a fuel-air bomb and just erase this whole place."

"I am in harmony with that, Magpie," said Belle.

"Plan B would be to just go in and cut some throats."

"Again, this is a good plan."

They smiled at each other, though both of them knew neither plan was ever going to be approved. Knowing part of what the enemy was doing was not enough. Sure, a powerful and direct military action could take out this camp, even with the Fixers and their fighting suits and body armor. But what if this wasn't the only camp? What if this was only one of many such camps? What if taking this place out would cause the other camps to go into hiding? What then?

The answer to each question was the same.

And it was a terrifying answer.

CHAPTER 120
HOTEL TIMIȘOARA
TIMIȘOARA, ROMANIA

I found him in the last hotel room.

Of course not the second or third. The fourth.

I opened the door and there he was. On the bed. Unmoving.

My heart sank.

"No!" I cried and ran to him, flung myself onto the mattress and pulled him to me. He came. Limp, boneless, eyes half-open, tongue lolling.

I pressed my head to his chest, praying that for once the universe wasn't that completely cruel. Kill me. Don't hurt Ghost. He's a dog. Dogs are pure love. They are mean if we make them mean, and they're not if we love and care for them.

I listened to the vast nothing inside his chest.

And then . . .

The slow, steady *thump . . . thump . . . thump.*

It was only later—much later—after holding him for a long time, that I found the fragments of the Sandman dart pasted to the fur on his shoulder.

Where I, in my deepest darkness, had shot him.

CHAPTER 121
ARKLIGHT SAFE HOUSE
BERLIN, GERMANY

Toys stood looking out the window, hands in his pockets, shoulders slumped, head bowed.

"You've been there for hours," said Violin. "Come and sit. Have some breakfast."

He shook his head.

Harry, who was at the stove pushing globs of eggs, onions, and diced potato around a pan, leaned close to her and in a confidential tone said, "What's his beef? He doesn't even like Joe."

"Hush, Harry," she said and walked out of the kitchen and went to stand by Toys.

After a few minutes, he said, "If you're going to give me a lecture, don't."

"Why would I lecture you?"

He turned his head and looked at her.

Violin had her long dark hair up in a loose bun and wore a baggy sweatshirt that made her slim body look thinner than it was. She wore no makeup, and that aged her, revealing tiny lines at the corners of her eyes and mouth. Toys had no idea how old she actually was. There were rumors that she was well into her fifties, though she looked—at most, even in the unforgiving sunlight pouring in through the window—about thirty. Her mother, Lilith, had the same timeless quality and could reasonably be guessed at forty, fifty, or sixty; though Junie said she'd heard that Lilith was quite a bit older. Good genes? Or something else? He wasn't sure.

For his part, he felt his years. He was not yet thirty-five and felt ninety. His twenties had been spent doing harm to the world, and his thirties were, so far, some kind of holding action. FreeTech had given him purpose, but it also bored him to tears.

He said, "You would have laughed if you'd been there when I appealed to Church about getting back into the field. God, I was so righteous about it."

"You must have been convincing."

"Oh, sure," he said bitterly, "I convinced him that somehow I, of all people, would be able to find Ledger and bring him back safe and sound."

"Well," she said with a wry smile, "you *did* find him."

"And he bloody well shot me."

"Be happy he used a dart gun."

"Tell me, have *you* ever been shot with Sandman?"

"No."

"It's not exactly fun."

"Joe is capable of doing much worse."

Toys snorted. "Frankly, darling, I think I'd have preferred a beating."

Cars passed as people left their homes to go to work. The sight of that normalcy, that ordinary life, made him sad.

"Look at them," he said, "everyone hurrying to get to their cubicles or their shops. Getting the kiddies off to school. Thinking about picking up dry cleaning at lunch and going to the pub for a cold one after work with their mates. Maybe a PTA meeting or helping the kids with homework."

"They," said Violin, "are who we fight to protect."

He leaned his forehead against the glass, which was cool despite the sunlight. "I never had that. Not even as a kid. Always got knocked around at home. Started getting into trouble when I was eleven, and it only ever got worse. Then I fell in with Sebastian Gault, and that turned out to be a right shit show." He sighed and straightened. "When I was in that life, I loathed those people. Truly hated them. Held them in the highest contempt for being what they were. Ordinary. Nothing was more unappealing to me. Then Ledger blundered into my life. And Church. That unnerving bastard Church. And . . . Junie."

"She thinks the world of you."

"She shouldn't."

"Why would you say that?"

He avoided her eyes. "Because I'm not worthy of anyone's admiration, or fondness, or kindness. Those people out there? Even the most boring, mundane, mindless worker bee is worth fifty of me. A hundred."

"You are valuable to the war."

"The war is the war," he said, echoing one of Church's favorite sayings. "Yes. I'm a good killer, so that makes me valuable as a person."

"We're both killers, Toys," said Violin. "And I have considerably more blood on my hands than you do."

"Are you so sure about that?"

"Yes," she said, "I am."

He turned to study her.

"That sounds like a longer conversation than we have time for now."

"Yes, and perhaps it's one we'll never have. Time will tell." She

JONATHAN MABERRY

paused. "So where are you going with your self-loathing? I mean . . . I don't want to sound callous, but are you going anywhere with this?"

He laughed. "Nowhere of use, that's for sure."

Violin folded her arms and leaned against the wall beside the mirror.

"Tell me something . . ."

"Sure."

"Would it help if I were to slap the self-pity off you? Or would you prefer to go upstairs and flagellate yourself for a while? I can braid a rope and cake it in rock salt."

He stared at her for several long seconds.

"Dear god," he said, "I'm actually whining, aren't I?"

Violin held her fingers up half an inch a part. "Just a little."

Toys looked up at the ceiling, and then he burst out laughing. After a moment, Violin joined him. In the kitchen, Harry—who was a good way into burning the eggs—glanced over his shoulder and wondered what the heck was so funny. They were still laughing when the smoke alarm went off.

Which made them laugh even harder.

CHAPTER 122
HOTEL TIMIȘOARA
TIMIȘOARA, ROMANIA

I sat with Ghost all through the day and into the night. Even when, deep inside his drugged sleep, he peed the bed. It got all over me, but I didn't care. He could bite my face off, and it would be less than I deserved.

And yet, when he finally woke up, he looked up at me with those big, liquid brown eyes and gave a sad, apologetic wag of his tail. He whimpered and pressed his muzzle against me. Asking for my forgiveness for whatever wrong he'd done to deserve what I'd done to him.

I don't know that I have ever felt more ashamed of anything in my entire life.

I held him and rocked him, and then I carried him into the shower, sat down fully dressed in the stall with him, and let the water rain down. He licked water and tears from my face.

"I'm sorry," I told him.

And I said it a thousand times.

CHAPTER 123
ARKLIGHT SAFE HOUSE
BERLIN, GERMANY

Toys was shaving in the upstairs bathroom when his cell phone rang. It was Church. He took a steadying breath before answering.

"Look," Toys said instead of hello, "before you tell me what a failure I am, let me—"

"Save it," said Church. "Tell Violin her jet is fueled and waiting for the three of you."

"What? Why? To go where?"

"Romania," said Church. "Mrs. Gondek thinks she's found Ledger."

"I—"

"No time," said Church. "Go."

CHAPTER 124
RTI SAFE HOUSE
KRAMPENBERGER STRASSE
BERLIN, GERMANY

Otto Jäger was not a happy man.

Partly because he was deeply embarrassed. He had been in various covert ops groups for thirteen years and had worked with Aunt Sallie and Mr. Church for much of that time, following seven years in the Deutsches Heer, where he'd been a *stabsfeldwebel*, and one of distinction. Being appointed the in-country liaison to Rogue Team International had been a big thing, a sign of trust, and a position of which he was rightly proud.

And then Joe Ledger had knocked on the door and shot him with a Sandman dart. Just like that. There wasn't even a good brawl to look back on. No one would have expected him to win such a fight, but at least the anecdote would be better. In the right circles, he could dine out on tales of a knockdown bout of fisticuffs with the legendary Colonel Joe Ledger.

But no. Just a dart. Not even a conversation. Ledger had not gone so far as to show him the courtesy of a cover story or even a simple greeting. The door opened and the lights went out. Jäger woke on the couch with a blanket over him and a nice pillow under his head.

So, Otto Jäger was not particularly cheerful.

What made things worse was now Mr. Church, Scott Wilson, and the others at Phoenix House were being nice to him. Nice. He was getting emails from staff members asking if he was okay.

He spent most of the day wandering around the safe house cursing Joe Ledger and everyone in his family going back seven generations.

Inventorying what Ledger stole was his ostensible job, but that only took ten minutes. Now he had to "rest and feel better, old chap," as Wilson had said three times.

"*Leck mich am arsch*," he snarled, and wished he had a picture of Ledger—and maybe one of Scott Wilson—that he could piss on. Or wipe his ass with.

When he heard a knock on the door while making coffee, he froze.

Was it him again?

There were no other RTI agents in Germany that he knew of, and no one else knew this place was anything more than a house where a bachelor lived a quiet life.

Fool me once, he thought and tapped a concealed button to release a section of the wall behind which were a half dozen handguns. One of them was a Snellig loaded with Sandman. Jäger pulled it free, checked the magazine, and crept to the door, smiling and thinking the blackest thoughts he owned.

"*Wer ist es?*" he asked, leaning close to the door.

He peered through the peephole, and there he was. Tall, broad-shouldered, blond. Wearing a thick leather jacket.

Ledger.

Du Hurensohn! he thought, raising the pistol as he unlocked the door.

He whipped it open just as Ledger turned around.

Except it was not Joe Ledger. This man could have been his brother, but it wasn't Joe. It was a stranger.

And the stranger held a gun.

A pistol with a long black sound suppressor.

Jäger brought his own gun up, and both weapons fired at exactly the same time. The glass dart struck the sleeve of the leather jacket and exploded harmlessly.

The man's bullet took Jäger in the hip, tearing through meat and exploding the bone, spinning him, detonating incredible agony all through his body. The man shoved Jäger inside even before the agent could fall; then he kicked the door shut. The stranger slapped the Snellig from his hand and buried the hot barrel of the suppressor under Jäger's chin.

In very good, very clear German with a definite American accent, the blond man said, *"Wo ist Joe Ledger?"*

Where is Joe Ledger?

CHAPTER 125
HOTEL TIMIȘOARA
TIMIȘOARA, ROMANIA

I washed Ghost and myself.

I brushed him and pampered him. I ordered his favorite stuff from room service. I took him for walks and played with him, and spooned him when we needed to sleep. I'm pretty sure he knew I was feeling guilty and was milking the hell out of it.

That's fine. He deserved it.

We went and visited the other rooms I'd booked during my fugue, and in the second one, I found the notes I'd written after my abortive conversation with Casanova. So much of that had been shoved back into the recesses of my brain because of the fight with the Fixers. It took a while for me to remember that I'd written it down already and emailed it to Bug. Which meant Church and everyone who mattered knew about what happened at the processing plant.

That was good. It was important, and I had a feeling it was even more critical than it seemed. Those Fixers had cutting-edge gear and were wearing suicide vests. Ones that went boom in a way that was out of all proportion to what I knew of explosives.

The possibilities were staggering. However, I trusted Church, Wilson, Bug, and Doc to grasp that potential and put the right wheels in motion.

For now, though, I had to concentrate on this part of my mission. My self-imposed mission.

Was this getting me anywhere close to Santoro?

In a very weird way, I found that I almost didn't care.

I was becoming weary of hate. That was something I didn't think was possible.

My family was seven months in the ground. Nothing I did would change that. Not even their ghosts showing up.

I was probably clinically insane, and this course of action sure as shit wasn't driving me in the direction of a cure. I wasn't sure if I could finish this mission.

No, let me correct that, I wasn't sure if I should.

Not that mission. Not finding and killing Rafael Santoro.

It took me a lot of hours pacing in my hotel rooms, walking Ghost, lying in bed staring at the ceiling to work it through. If this were a movie, I'd have covered a wall with three-by-five cards, Post-it notes, and colored pushpins, and tied everything neatly together with red string. But that was the movies, and this was my life.

The Darkness had receded further this time. I could barely feel it back there in some corner of my mind. Don't know why; didn't care. What mattered was the picture coming together from what I'd learned in Italy, Poland, South Africa, the Netherlands, and Germany. On some level, I was pretty sure I had nearly all of it.

The cybernetics.

High-end body armor.

Fighting machines with human drivers.

Some kind of mind-altering chemical compound that drove the Fixers mad while giving them extra speed and strength.

The suicide vests and whatever high explosive they were packed with.

Something called the American Operation.

Those pieces had all floated around loose because I'd collected them piecemeal here and there. And sometimes while in a fugue state.

But now, a bit more clearheaded, I could see how there was a sense to it. A cohesion.

Somewhere in America, Fixers with chemical enhancement, cybernetics, bulletproof armor, and advanced weapons were going to stage a strike. Knowing Kuga and Santoro, it was going to be big. Something that would draw a lot of attention, but at the end of the day, Kuga wanted to sell more weapons of conflict. Just as the Rage attacks in the two Koreas and at the denuclearization summit in Oslo were never really about unifying North and South Korea or stopping the proliferation of nuclear weapons. Just the reverse. Kuga wanted to keep the world always on the brink of war, because when things are peaceful, no one's buying as many guns.

This, quite simply, made sense.

I was here in Romania to see someone called Die Katze. The Cat. A salesman high in the Kuga organization. Someone who might actually *know* what this American Operation was. Or at least give me enough so I could keep going.

"Keep going," I said out loud.

Did I want to? Need to? Have to?

Or was it time to lay down my sword and shield and let Church take it from here?

I smiled up at the ceiling. Yeah. Sure. Let me go sit on the sidelines and have a foot-long and a cold beer while the world blows up.

Let me sit it out while other people—better people—put themselves in the line of fire in my place, because I was too sad and weary.

"No fucking way," I said.

Ghost looked at me and thumped the bed with his tail. When I looked at him, he bared his titanium teeth at me. Maybe it was a snarl, maybe it was him laughing.

He wasn't buying that bullshit, either.

I looked at my watch.

"Game time, furball," I said.

CHAPTER 126
HOTEL TIMIȘOARA
TIMIȘOARA, ROMANIA

They were being very careful.

I stood with my face pressed against my door, peering through the peephole at the four men who stepped off the elevator. Three were big, with the kinds of faces that would pretty much guarantee they'd never work in customer service. Lumpy, craggy, with crooked noses and humorless, unimaginative eyes. They wore sport coats that they unbuttoned the moment they stepped out of the lift. Even from a third of the way down the hall, I could see the bulges beneath their jackets. Two right-handers and a lefty. All of them should have had THUG tattooed on their foreheads.

The fourth man was approximately the size and shape of a mailbox. No neck, but not because he was overmuscled—he was simply very short and very obese. His face was florid and beaded with sweat. He had a sparse beard and mustache and a sharp nose that he could have used to pcck a hole in tree bark. He was the one I cared about. He had the briefcase filled with money to buy something I wanted very much.

Something he was going to buy from Die Katze.

The four of them walked past my room, the guards clicking their eyes left and right, looking for threats but clearly not expecting any. It was a nice hotel. Elegant and quiet.

As I watched the men in the hall, I could feel Ghost watching me. Patient and just as hungry as I was. He remembered what we'd had to do to get this far. Questions had to be asked. I always ask nicely the first time. Not so much if they stonewall me.

The men stopped at a door only four down from mine. The upside was that I now knew the room number; but the downside was that it was at a bend in the hall where someone inside that room doing exactly what I was doing might see me coming.

That was a problem to be solved in motion.

For now, I waited and watched.

The small man with the woodpecker nose rapped four times on the door. Two distinct sets of two beats. He paused and repeated it.

Someone inside spoke, but I couldn't hear it; however, I did hear the small man reply.

"*Dragoş m-a trimis.*"

Dragoş sent me.

I had no idea who that was and assumed it was just a code word. Like the old speakeasies. Lefty sent me.

Then he repeated the double rap again.

There was a three count, and then the door opened. The small man entered the room accompanied by one of his guards. The other two turned their backs to the door. Normally, you'd think that would skew the math, but it didn't. With two guys watching the door, no one was likely to be peering through the peephole. I could work with that.

I checked my weapon and made sure the magazine was full. There was a Sig Sauer 9 mm snugged into the waistband of my trousers, firm against my left kidney, and two extra mags for it in my right pants pocket. Nothing else in there to interfere with grabbing one; and the pocket opening was sewn with a strip of elastic so it would stretch for an easy pull.

However, the pistol I held in my hand was my Snellig dart gun.

Why the dart gun? Partly because it was whisper quiet. Partly because I wasn't sure if some of the people in that room were noncombatants or nonhostiles. And partly because I wanted the option to exfil someone with a pulse so I could ask a bunch of questions they couldn't answer if they were dead. The Sig was there in case things went sideways and I wanted to send some of these assholes to Jesus on a fast train.

I paused to take a look at myself in the mirror. Nice, quiet business suit. Hair combed. Fake glasses and a fake mustache. I looked ready to sell used cars in Akron. I even tried on a smile. I wanted it to look convincing, affable, nondescript. But it felt wrong on my face and looked phony in the mirror.

I haven't been smiling all that much lately.

I heard a soft *whuff* behind.

"You can keep your opinions to yourself, fleabag."

He *whuff*ed again. Eloquently.

"You want to sit there being snotty or do you want to go play?"

His bushy tail thumped on the duvet.

"Well, then stop lying around eating bonbons and get your furry ass in gear."

He immediately launched himself from the bed and went to stand glaring at the door, giving me "hurry the hell up" looks.

"Let's go be naughty," I said, and opened the door.

CHAPTER 127
THE PLAYROOM
UNDISCLOSED LOCATION
NEAR VANCOUVER, BRITISH COLUMBIA, CANADA

Kuga got through after six failed attempts.

"Hello, my friend," said Mr. Sunday.

"Fuck you with hello," growled Kuga.

"Well, you seem like you're in quite a state. Someone piss on your new shoes?"

"Cut the shit, Sunday. I want to know what the hell you're playing at."

"At the moment? I'm playing with my dick."

Kuga closed his eyes and resisted the urge to hurl the phone across the room.

"You said that you were going to mess with Ledger."

"And I am."

"Oh, really? He's out of his mind, but he's also tearing my organization apart."

Sunday gave a long, exaggerated, and comical sigh. "Haven't we had this conversation before? Is it nine times now or ten?"

"He is out there killing people."

"And you are there, safe and sound, planning to kill a lot more people than he is," said Sunday. "I've been having some lovely chats with our friends in all those well-regulated militias. We're going to have such fun."

"Yeah? And what if Ledger gets to them and makes them talk?"

"He won't."

"How would you know? You haven't stopped him from killing my guys in South Africa and Italy and all those other places."

"I haven't because I did not try."

"*What?*"

"Let me rephrase that," said Sunday.

"Yeah, I think you'd fucking well better."

"I haven't stopped him from killing those people because I don't *care* about them. I really don't. They are nothing to me because they have already done what I—and of course, I mean 'we'—have required of them. Ledger is cleaning things up for us while thinking he is doing you harm."

"You're insane."

Sunday laughed. "If that is the worst thing that you think I am, my friend, then I am very disappointed."

And he hung up.

Kuga stared at the phone. But he did not throw it.

CHAPTER 128
HOTEL TIMIȘOARA
TIMIȘOARA, ROMANIA

We stepped into the hall.

Ghost can look like a middle-aged house pet when he wants to. And I can look shorter and slower than I am. It's a posture thing, and the way you set your shoulders and how you walk. And I composed my facial features to sell it. My lips were loose, rubbery, as if I were lost in thought; and my line of sight was vague, as if I were in my own head and not looking at anything or anyone. I stood in the hallway patting my pockets like an absentminded guy making sure he had his car keys, billfold, and cell phone.

There were security cameras in the hall, but I'd already hacked into the system using gear I'd lifted from the safe house in Germany. I'd recorded six minutes of empty hall and fed it back in on a loop.

Then I clicked my tongue for Ghost, and we began walking along the hall, angled so there was no sense of obvious interception. Just a man and his dog.

Until we were six feet away.

Then I brought the Snellig out very fast and smooth and shot them both in the face. They went down right away. No pause, no groans, no cries of alarm. Sandman does not ask, it tells.

I rushed forward and caught them both, groaning under their combined weight, and dragged them back from the door before laying them on the dark red carpet.

I needed to get in, but modern hotel doors are notoriously hard to kick open. Especially in the better hotels. Last thing I needed was to raise a ruckus kicking the thing four times, or to lame my foot. So, I removed a small device roughly the size of three stacked quarters, peeled off the film on the back to expose the adhesive, pressed it to the locking mechanism, pushed the little silver button, and backed up quickly, raising the gun.

The device—known affectionately as a party popper—blew the lock apart. I kicked the door and rushed into the room, firing through the thin veil of smoke.

"Ghost," I growled. "Hit, hit, hit!"

He hit.

We both did.

There were seven people in the room. Six men, one woman. Ghost hurled himself like a pale missile at the closest man, a big bruiser who had to be six eight. Over the years, Ghost has lost ten teeth in combat. Each one has been replaced with a titanium fang, and there's some additional reinforcement to allow the dog to use those chompers to maximum effect. Ghost bit into the muscular forearm of the big man as the guy was pulling his pistol. Even with all the noise, I could hear bones break. Man and dog went down hard.

I fired at everything that moved. It was a hotel room, a suite, and one of good size, but everyone was clustered around a coffee table. My shots caught them rising, in confusion, reaching for weapons but not actually able to point them. Not in time. Sandman works at the speed of nerve conduction.

Ghost left the big man screaming and went after the third of the guards who'd come with Woodpecker. That man went down with a savaged thigh, and he had a choice—try to shoot or use both hands to clamp down on a torn femoral artery. The man chose wisely.

A man swung a pistol toward me, but I blocked the wrist with a blow from my left hand and shot him in the cheek.

Suddenly, six men were down, and the only person standing was the woman. She gave me a look of mingled terror and lethal hate and dove over the back of the couch, coming up with a neat little handgun I hadn't seen on her. She rose up firing, but I was moving, changing angle and distance, and the range was bad for her but good for me. I chopped down on her wrist hard enough to break things, then kicked her in the stomach. She folded into a knot that was tight as a fist.

Then I shot the two men Ghost had injured. One was going to bleed out and die. Fuck it. The other was going to need a lot of surgery. Too bad.

The whole fight took about four seconds.

I looked down at the woman, shrugged, and shot her with Sandman. Then I left them all there and found a housekeeping closet, tricked open the lock, and grabbed a big canvas laundry cart on wheels. I took it back to the room and loaded my three sleeping beauties into it and then hid them with towels and sheets I pulled from the bed.

"In," I said, and Ghost jumped into the cart, and I covered him with a duvet.

The briefcase Woodpecker had been carrying was on the coffee table next to an identical one. Both were locked, both went in with the laundry, along with everyone's wallets and cell phones. Then I was out the door, wheeling the cart to the elevator. There was nothing in the room where Ghost and I had spent the night. My borrowed gear was downstairs in the first room where I'd awakened from my fugue. And, besides, I didn't want to be anywhere near this room. So we took the service elevator.

I got into that elevator just as the main elevator doors pinged open and two security guards and an assistant manager hurried out to investigate reports of a disturbance. I pushed up my sleeve to allow access to the thin, flexible tactical computer strapped to my forearm and disabled the video loop. They never saw me.

I rode the car down to the fifth floor, fed the empty-hall loop to those cameras, exited, and—after making sure the hall was clear—wheeled the cart to the other room I'd booked. Got inside, reactivated the security cameras, and sent a signal for MindReader to erase all

JONATHAN MABERRY

traces of my hack, closed and locked the door, leaned against it, and exhaled, blowing out my cheeks.

Ghost raised his head and peered at me, grinning to show his bloody metal teeth.

CHAPTER 129
HOTEL TIMIȘOARA
TIMIȘOARA, ROMANIA

Ghost hopped out of the cart, taking a particularly stinky and stained bedsheet with him, and I had to bribe him with doggie treats to relinquish it. Last thing I needed was my dog rolling around in someone's love puddle. Silly damned mutt. I over-bribed him, and he went off happy, wearing the kind of look successful con men use when their scam has worked exactly as planned.

He settled down in the entrance to the bathroom, belly on the cool tiles, head and front paws in the bedroom, nibbling the treats.

I removed my stolen jacket and hauled the dozing bad guys out of the cart, used flex-cuffs on their ankles and wrists, and sat them in a neat row against the wall. This room was a corner suite, and I booked the only adjoining room, which was empty, under another fake name. I turned on the radio, found an opera channel, and dialed the volume high.

There was a small medical kit on the bedside table, and I removed three small syrettes and placed them on the edge of the bed. The woman looked like Cruella De Vil, but without the obvious warmth or humanity. She sat on one side of Woodpecker, with Slenderman on her other side. I sorted through the IDs, ran them through the MindReader unit—making a mental note to send poor Otto Jäger something really nice for Christmas—and was in no way surprised when they all pinged as phony. So I used the touch pad on my tactical computer to take their fingerprints, and also sent clear photos, and I kicked all that stuff over via satellite to the MindReader mainframe in Greece.

Bug would be going nuts, and once more the RTI crew would know where I was and what I was doing. Somehow that mattered less to me then than it had before. I felt, one way or another, my time of hiding and running was coming to an end.

Which, of course, made me think of Junie.

I love you, babe, I thought, wondering if somehow—intuitive as she is—she could hear me. *You deserve so much better than me. But I love you with my whole heart.*

Ghost gave a single short bark. And when I looked at him, I swear to god he nodded. Only once, but I damn well saw it.

Jesus.

While I waited for replies, I set about examining the two cases. They were both the same make, model, and color, with nine-digit keypad locks. Very expensive, and this kind of case had steel mesh beneath the leather exterior. Pick-proof and cut-proof.

For just about everyone except cats like me.

I attached tiny leads to the keypad of the first one, connected the other ends to my tactical computer, and let MindReader sort out the combination. Took longer to connect the wires than get the code. The lock obliged by clicking open. I repeated it with the other case and was amused to see that it was the same combination, suggesting that the bags were intended to be swapped.

I was briefly unnerved to discover that each case contained a small explosive device wired to the locks. They were rigged to blow if those locks, or the hinges, were forced. The bombs weren't big, but they would have very effectively blown me in half had I been less careful.

"God damn," I said.

In the Woodpecker's bag, I found lots of money. Six hundred and fifty thousand dollars in bearer bonds. Two bundles of cash in mixed Romanian leu notes bound by rubber bands. I thumbed through the bills and estimated around five hundred grand in lei, which shakes out to a bit over one hundred Gs in American dollars. There were also ten bundles of euros in two and five hundred denominations. About twenty-two thousand euros, which made it just shy of twenty-seven thousand bucks. I figured the euros were a partial payment for Cruella's team, since they were black marketeers who worked this part of southeastern Europe, while the lei were for paying local help. At the bottom of the bag, I found a burner phone with a single number programmed in. I ran that through MindReader, too, and it accessed a system for wire-transferring much larger amounts. Once a call was made and a certain code typed in, ten million euros would be transferred to a numbered account in the Seychelles. I did not have that code, but I had a whole afternoon ahead of me, so anything at all could happen. I waved a stack of cash at Ghost.

"There's almost enough here to keep you in doggie treats for a week."

He wagged at me.

I pointed at the three prisoners. "They're evil. Bet you want to chomp on them some, dontcha, boy?"

More wags.

My dog is as bugfuck nuts as I am. This is not a news flash.

I opened the other case and found a smaller container inside. White Styrofoam sealed with red biohazard tape. No labels, though, and nothing inside the case or container to indicate what I'd just found.

"Rut roh," I said in my best Scooby-Doo voice.

I left the tape in place, closed the case, and picked up a syrette.

"Eeny meeny miny moe," I said, "catch a psychopath by the toe."

Cruella De Vil lost, and I jabbed her in the arm.

"Wakey-wakey."

Normally, Sandman takes hours to flush out of the bloodstream, but Doc Holliday came up with something she calls JumpStart. It wakes a Sandman victim up pretty fast, but there are some unfortunate side effects. The woman's eyes popped open. She pissed herself, and then vomited onto her lap.

Despite her feeling what was probably a level-ten pounding headache, and the obvious humiliation of having puked and soiled herself, the woman's head snapped toward me. She fired off a tirade in Romanian that would have stripped the flesh from a rhino carcass. The woman had a truly poisonous mouth, and I let her vent for maybe fifteen seconds, impressed with her creative vulgarities. They were very specific. She told me I was the slimy aftermath of a Turkish ass-fuck orgy. She accused me of fornication with my mother on Easter morning. She said that I buggered baby goats.

It was the baby goats one that pissed me off. I like baby goats. Ever see those videos of them in pajamas? Adorable.

I removed the fake glasses and the fake mustache, then squatted down in front of her. I said nothing. Her words trickled down and stopped as she caught sight of my smile. And then my face. Despite the side effects, JumpStart clears the head pretty quickly. It's intended for situations like this. The drugged glaze cleared away, and I saw the exact moment when she recognized me.

Her eyes snapped wide and filled with horror. Her skin blanched to a corpse pallor, and her lips began to tremble. "No . . ."

I smiled. "Yes."

CHAPTER 130
HOTEL TIMIȘOARA
TIMIȘOARA, ROMANIA

"You're him. Oh, sweet Jesus on the cross, you're going to kill me," she said, not framing it as a question. She spoke in Romanian, which was fine. That was one of my languages, and I'd brushed up on it in anticipation of this moment. Not with her, specifically, because I still had no idea who she was, but for a moment like this.

She tried to shrink back through a hole in the dimension. She tried to twist free of her bonds. She tried to kick me. She tried to scream, but all I did to stop that was to lay my hand on the pistol next to me and give a single shake of my head. She fell into a shivering silence, tears cutting lines down her cheeks.

I gave her the old Joe Ledger smile. The one that crinkles the skin around my baby-blue eyes and makes my teeth look like an ad for good dental hygiene.

"I have questions," I said softly. "You're going to answer them."

She forced a smile onto her face and moistened her lips and—god help me—tried to look seductive. Despite what looked like Campbell's Chunky soup smearing her mouth and lap, despite sitting in a cooling pool of her own urine, she was actually trying to work her charms on me.

"Oh, for fuck's sake, sister, skip the bullshit," I said. "I'm not the audience for that crap, and you're not the type to peddle it."

She dropped the act, and for a moment I saw the real her. Cold, calculating, and vicious. Then fear crept back and clouded that.

"What do you want?" she asked.

"I want two things," I said. "The first is the code for the wire transfer. No, don't look surprised. Don't play dumb and don't lie to me, either, because you won't like how that works out."

She stared at me, trying so hard not to cry.

"I'll only ask this once," I said. "The code." Something in my voice reached her, and she suddenly rattled off the code. I punched it into the burner and then, once the deposit was underway, fed the target account number to MindReader. The funds would go to an account I set up called WC—shorthand for War Chest. Whatever I didn't need for my hunt would eventually be donated to FreeTech.

"Good," I said to the woman. "That's very good. You're earning brownie points. You'll need them. Next question is what's in the bag you were going to hand off?"

"I—"

I cut her off by holding up a single finger. "If the next two words out of your mouth are *don't know*, you won't like what happens next."

"Don't hurt me," she said in a much more fragile voice than she probably wanted to use.

"That will depend on how you finish that sentence, won't it?" I asked calmly. Or at least my voice sounded calm. Inside my head, though, a furnace was burning toward overload. It scared me how easily I could joke, and function, and sit here having a chat while the Darkness inside of me was so damned hungry.

She kept trying to look away, and each time, I snapped my fingers, loud as a gunshot, to bring her back to focus. To me.

"Do I need to ask again?" I murmured. "Right now, we're having a conversation, but if you'd rather play Truth or Consequences, say so. I can work with that. Hell, I could have fun with that."

Despite her toughness, there were tears in her eyes, and her breath was shallow and rapid. Panic breathing. It took her a few tries to get her voice.

"It's a chemical agent. R-33. That's what they call it."

I thought the word *aha*. I'd seen references to that all through the files I'd been stealing.

"What does R-33 do? What's it for?"

"I . . . I'm not—"

"Remember the rules," I cautioned.

"No, I really don't know," she insisted. "At least I'm not sure. Please, you have to believe me. I'm telling the truth. All I know is that it's some kind of enhancement thing. An energy booster, but I don't know how it's to be used. All I really know about it is the code name and the cost."

I gestured to the other two. "Do they know?"

She turned to them and considered. She nodded to Woodpecker. "He's a local broker. He'd know who he was taking it to and where. But that's all."

"Okay. And the other guy?" I said, indicating Slenderman.

She licked her lips again. Not to try the seduction thing but to stall. "I don't know him. Not even his name. He uses a code name. Die Katze."

The Cat. How interesting.

I said, "Aha." Aloud this time.

I grilled Cruella for another twenty minutes, but it was clear she really didn't know anything more.

"Thank you for playing," I said and shot her with the dart gun.

Mind you, it was tempting to just freaking strangle her. I wanted to. Or maybe the Darkness wanted to. Hard to really say. But there was no proof she had blood on her hands. I had her prints, a scan of her face, and I took a swab of the inside of her mouth to capture her DNA. All of that would go into the system, and god help her if she came onto my radar again.

I left Woodpecker to sleep. He was too much of a small fry for my needs. Lucky him.

The Cat—Slenderman—was another matter entirely. I jabbed him with a syrette of JumpStart and watched him twitch and cough and piss and puke his way out of Sandman's arms and into the awful realities of the moment.

I watched him pull at the threads of what he last remembered and tie them into the fabric of what was happening. What was about to happen. The woman had blanched, but the Cat turned an even whiter shade of pale as he realized who I was.

"Ledger," he gasped, making it sound like the name of the devil.

He was not far wrong.

　　　　　　　　JONATHAN MABERRY

CHAPTER 131
THE PLAYROOM
UNDISCLOSED LOCATION
NEAR VANCOUVER, BRITISH COLUMBIA, CANADA

Kuga was alone at the pool when Mr. Sunday walked out onto the patio.

Brooding clouds hid the sun, and the trees were filled with ugly birds. Kuga did not get up but instead let Sunday drag a chair over and sit down. The salesman wore crisp blue jeans with a razor crease, hand-tooled cowboy boots with hummingbirds and roses on them, an embroidered Western shirt with the same pattern, and a brown sport coat with leather elbow pads. He even had a white cowboy hat on his head.

"Christ, Sunday," said Kuga, "you look like you're either going to try to sell me a certified used pickup truck or run for office in some little redneck town."

"I believe I would enjoy either of those pursuits."

Sunday sat down in an Adirondack chair. The black birds in the trees screeched at him, but when he looked up at them, they fell silent and stood shuffling their wings.

"Cockroaches with feathers," he said.

"Why are you here?"

"Because I knew you'd be alone," said Sunday. "Your little Spanish extortionist is busy elsewhere."

"You really don't like each other, do you?"

"I don't trust him."

Kuga grunted. "Santoro? Why the hell not?"

"More to the point, my friend," said Sunday, "why do you?"

"He's never given me any reason *not* to trust him."

"No, of course not. The world's subtlest and most effective manipulator of people would never dream of making you—the cash cow whose tit he's been sucking on—distrust him. Heaven forfend."

Kuga picked up a cold cucumber slice from a chairside tray and bit it in half. "You're out of your mind."

Sunday merely smiled.

CHAPTER 132
HOTEL TIMIȘOARA
TIMIȘOARA, ROMANIA

I gave him the same charming smile I'd given Cruella.

"Pisica," I said, using the Romanian word for *cat*, "let's have a nice little chat."

He literally shot to his feet—something that's mighty damned hard to do with ankles and wrists bound and all sorts of complicated drugs playing merry hob in his bloodstream. Ghost also jumped up, and suddenly, the goofy dog with a pile of treats transformed into some prehistoric proto-wolf.

Just.

Like.

That.

It's terrifying to see. Ghost's entire body language changed. Not sure how he does it, but his shoulders bulge up to look bigger, he lowers his head and glares with merciless, hungry eyes. His muzzle wrinkles to show those titanium fangs. The total effect will give any sane person serious pause.

The Cat stood there, shivers rippling up and down his body as if a winter wind were blowing on him with blizzard force.

I said, "Sit."

He sat.

Ghost did, too. Like a gargoyle in the middle of the floor. Watchful. Ready.

"I have a few questions," I began. "Now . . . do I really need to go over the rules? Pretty sure you know how this works."

"Why should I tell you anything?" he asked, sneering as he spoke. "You're going to kill me regardless."

I nodded to the other two. "I didn't kill them."

He ignored Woodpecker and studied Cruella. It was clear from the mess around her that she'd gone through the same fun wake-up process as he had. I saw him watching her chest to see if she was breathing. Then he turned back to me. He had eyes like a Vegas bookmaker, and I could tell he was working out the odds. His whole attitude suddenly shifted from hostage about to be fucked with to a business guy wanting to get to the bottom line. Maybe it was a front, maybe it was his way of regaining some measure of agency over the moment, or maybe he really was as pragmatic as that.

"What will get me out of here alive?" he asked frankly.

"Information is your best shot," I said, equally reasonably. "First, tell me about R-33."

He looked momentarily shocked, then narrowed his eyes. Then he ticked his head toward Cruella. "So, the stupid cunt couldn't keep her mouth shut."

I made a very subtle finger gesture for Ghost, who immediately bared his teeth again. Some people train their dogs to roll over or fist-bump. I use mine for messing with people's heads. Ghost gets biscuits either way.

The Cat flinched back. "*Ce pula!*" he cried.

It means "what the dick?" Local equivalent of "what the fuck?" You don't need to know the local language to guess that. A good chunk of his businesslike calm dropped right off.

"Focus on me," I said coldly. "On what we are talking about. Tell me about R-33. What's the code stand for? What is it, and what does it do?"

He kept glancing at Ghost, who was now sitting like a Sphinx.

"R-33," I prompted.

The Cat cleared his throat. "It's an enhancement drug."

"What kind of enhancement? Are we talking super Viagra here? Something to sell to the old rich sons of bitches you used to peddle little girls to?"

"No. Nothing like that," he said. "This is military grade."

"Meaning what?"

"It's some kind of experimental compound," he said. "It's something new. Something that's supposed to increase physical strength and stamina. That's about all I know. I'm just a salesman."

"And, what, you're here selling it without being able to describe how it works?"

"Maybe I should have said that I'm just a delivery boy."

"Bullshit," I said. "You're on the executive level. Maybe lower tier, but you're no gopher."

The Cat glanced at Ghost and then back at me and switched to

English. Very good English, with a thin veneer of a London accent. "Look, Ledger, I really don't know much, but I'll tell you what I do know, okay?"

"I'm all ears."

"The junk in those vials is something new. Radical. I got a lecture on it, but I didn't understand one word in ten. I was military before I started doing this, then did PMC stuff for Romania and Germany. I'm half and half, so I've done stuff with corporations in both countries. Ask me about a gun or an RPG or something practical and I can give you details all the way down to the metallurgy, but this is chemistry. It's some kind of weird chemistry. Not my area. The regular salesperson for this is missing, maybe dead. His boat sank somewhere off the Bulgarian coast. The boss thinks it was sabotage, but that's a guess. All they ever found was some debris."

I said nothing and kept my face blank.

"R-33 is supposed to be some kind of super juice," he said. "You ever watch those movies about Captain America? About how he got so big and strong? What did they call it? A super-soldier formula? Well, that's what this is supposed to be. Something to give PMCs a real upgrade. Not like they become Superman or anything. Just a boost to strength and stamina, maybe amp up their speed and reflexes so that one man can do the work of four. Cuts down on the number of contractors someone needs to hire for a gig. And they'll work until they drop. That's what the code letter is for. *R* for Relentless."

"Relentless," I mused.

"Right, but it has a double meaning. And I'm afraid if I tell you, you'll hurt me."

I smiled. "If you tell me the truth, then no, I won't."

He thought about it. "Okay, okay . . . The earlier versions of Relentless were just that. But this new generation, number thirty-three . . . it has Rage in it."

I stared at him.

"Yes," he said. "Not enough to go completely insane, not like in Oslo and Korea. Just a touch. It makes them want to kill, but they can still tell friend from foe. The designer originally called it Berserker, after those crazy Vikings. But because it's married to the Rage compound, they . . . well, you understand."

"Who developed it?"

"Dr. Dejan Brozović," he said. "He created Relentless for Kuga but got clumsy and was arrested. They needed him to finish the development of R-33. The stuff in that case is a test version, but it's probably not very good. I knew that, but these idiots didn't. We were going to let them test it, and if it *did* work, then we wouldn't need Brozović. We were stuck because he was in a German black site prison until the other night. But I guess you know that."

And another piece of the puzzle fell into place. Eve and her Fixers were there to get Brozović out to perfect Relentless in time for the American Operation. Right. The fact that they staged that hit when they did was suggestive. Maybe this American thing was going to happen sooner than later.

"Where's his lab?"

He snorted. "They don't tell guys like me, Ledger. Everything is compartmentalized. Wherever the lab is, they keep all information about it on a need-to-know basis, and the sales force doesn't need to know. When I need to deliver a product, I get an email or text about where to pick it up. A warehouse or paid storage unit somewhere, or—in this case—a coin locker at the airport."

"Okay," I said, "then tell me about the American Operation."

He jerked at the mention of that.

"Holy shit," he said. "How do you even *know* about that?"

"Let's go with the fact that I do, and I know a lot," I lied. "I want you to tell me what *you* know and if the two stories don't line up, it's going to be a bad night for you, Kitty Cat."

If he was scared before, then he was absolutely terrified now.

"They . . . Look, Ledger, I'm serious . . . They'll do more than kill me if they find out I told you *anything* about that. They know where my family lives. My ex-wife, my kids. You have no idea what they're capable of."

I said, "Christmas Eve."

But he shook his head. "That was ugly, sure, but it was quick. Santoro and his little blond scorpion—"

"Eve."

"You think he's psychotic? She's way past him."

"I don't care," I said. "If you tell me, I'll have my people get to your family and take them somewhere safe. And then I'll make sure Santoro and Eve are cleared off the checkerboard. That's the only option you have. At least with me, your family has a chance."

His eyes were wet, and his lower lip trembled. I let him think about it for a full thirty seconds.

"I don't know much," he said, "and that's the truth. All I know for sure is that it's going to be soon, and it's going to be loud and messy. Multiple hits. I've heard talk about a concert or a sports thing. They've been waiting to see how things open up now that the COVID vaccine is out there."

"What's G-55?"

He frowned. "I have no idea."

Sadly, I believed him.

"Look, Ledger," he said, "I know what you've been doing. Raiding labs and killing people. People I knew, including friends of mine."

"Boo-hoo," I said.

"No, listen . . . I know that I haven't given you much here. Not about the American Op because I don't know much. Please don't hold that against me. Don't let them kill my ex-wife and kids because I'm a piece of shit. Okay, maybe my ex, she's a bitch . . . but my kids, man. They're just kids."

"How many kids are going to die if this American Operation happens?"

He shook his head. "Let me do this," he said. "Let me give you something else."

"I'm listening."

"You need to run. Get the hell out of Europe. Go home, back to the States. I can give you a name or two to check out there. Maybe they'll know more, because if anyone's going to be part of the actual event, it'll be them."

"Give me the names."

He did, and also addresses. Deacon Donnelly in Fort Lauderdale and Jimmy-John Harris in LaBorde, Texas.

"Who are they?"

"Militia."

"What?"

JONATHAN MABERRY

"Those white supremacists you Yanks are always scared of. Like those Proud Boys and Boogaloos. Like that. Those idiots who are all jacked up about the Third Amendment."

"Second Amendment," I corrected.

"Whatever. Kuga's using them. He has his sales guy, Mr. Sunday, recruiting them, and they're sending guns and money to them. I think they're going to use them along with the Fixers for whatever this operation is."

I digested that. It was a new puzzle piece, and I wasn't yet sure how well it fit. The problem with this kind of interrogation was that the guy in the hot seat may be giving a lot of intel that is only part of what he really knows, but there's no way to verify it in the moment.

"And there's one more thing," he said.

"Hit me."

"There's a shooter on your ass," said the Cat. "Michael Augustus Stafford. Very dangerous guy. Top of the game."

"I've heard."

"Maybe you have, but last I heard, he was only about a step behind you. If he catches up, then you're dead."

"I can handle my own."

"No," he said, "you can't. Stafford's the best there is."

I smiled. "Let me try."

The Cat shook his head. "I'm giving you fair warning. I've seen him in action. He's as good or better than Santoro. No, that's not right. With knives, guns, or hands, he's better."

"I'll take my chances," I said. "Last question. Where can I find Santoro?"

"Who the hell knows? Last I heard, he and Kuga were in Canada, but that's probably misdirection. People aren't allowed to know where they are. One thing I can tell you, though, is if you get close to Jimmy-John Harris, he'll know how to get in touch with Mr. Sunday, and Sunday will absolutely know. Play it that way."

I grilled him for a while longer, but his well of information was dry. He sat there, head bowed, sobbing. "Please," he begged. "Please, that's all."

I watched him for a long time. A minute, maybe two.

I lifted my pistol. The Sig Sauer, not the dart gun. I began slowly screwing a sound suppressor onto the threaded muzzle. He looked up sharply.

"*Wait* . . . I told you everything I know."

"Sure," I said, "and thanks for that."

"Then what are you doing with that gun?"

I cocked my head and smiled at him. "What did you do before you did this kind of thing? Before Kuga. Before you went to work for Ohan. Tell me what you did."

He looked startled. "What . . . The girls? What the fuck's that to you?"

"Yes," I said, "the girls. How many of them did you sell?"

"I . . . I don't know. What does it matter?"

"It matters," I said and shot him.

No witty quip. No "see you in hell" bullshit. All I did was point the gun and fire a single shot. The bullet punched through the crown of his head and blew a hole the size of a lemon out of the base of his skull. His body never even twitched. Just fell over.

Ghost gave a single *whuff*, but otherwise did not move a muscle.

I sat on the edge of the bed for a very long time.

CHAPTER 133
NOWHERE

Mr. Sunday sat cross-legged on the floor. He had tarot cards spread around him. There were bones he'd cast. Some were animal bones; others once belonged to children. He remembered their faces. So sweet and beautiful.

Candles burned in bowls and holders. Six times six candles.

He was naked, because he preferred being naked. It was so pure. In the corners of the room, flies buzzed and reptiles wrestled and spat.

He was about to turn over a card. The Magician. The trickster card. His favorite.

But the card was upside down, and that made him frown.

"Someone is speaking my name," he said aloud.

JONATHAN MABERRY

Mr. Sunday turned another card. It was the Destroyed Tower. It was another favorite card. It foretold so many delightful things. None of them good. He set it down next to the Magician.

One of the candles guttered and went out.

Mr. Sunday stared at it with eyes whose colors swirled and changed, changed and swirled.

CHAPTER 134
HOTEL TIMIȘOARA
TIMIȘOARA, ROMANIA

I spent a long time in the shower.

Washing off the day. Reliving what I'd just done. It had been a strategic choice. I could not take him into custody or even turn him over. Kuga had too much influence backed by an apparently bottomless bank account. And he had Rafael Santoro, the world's most effective extortionist. They would do whatever it took to silence Die Katze, and there was zero doubt in my mind that innocent people would be hurt or killed in the process.

On the other hand, if I'd left him unconscious along with the others, then he would be free. He could plead innocence and there was no proof he was involved in any crimes. At worst, he'd lawyer up, make bail, and then go dark.

No, the math was simple.

Except nothing is simple.

I leaned back against the cold shower tiles and let the hot water boil me. Last year, my lover, Junie Flynn, asked if I was becoming blasé about the killing that I sometimes have to do in my job. She was concerned that I was becoming unemotional about it. Detached.

I did a lot of soul-searching over that. But then, on a small island off the coast of North Korea, while leading Havoc Team on a mission to discover what had killed all the inhabitants, I had an epiphany. We found the body of a young woman. No ID, no way to ever know her name. She lay in an artless sprawl, her dress hiked up, body robbed of all life, all emotion and potential. Her senseless murder became the focal point for me. I swore to her that I would find whoever did this and tear their world apart. It was for people like her that I did this. It was because there were predatory monsters in this world who will kill the innocent for the political leverage it offered, for profit, for strategic gain, to make a point, or a dozen other criminally obscene reasons. I did not know then that I was hunting Santoro and Kuga.

We stopped that plot and another that was piggybacked onto it. Hooray for the good guys, right?

Not really. Everyone on that little North Korean island is still dead. As are more than half the population of a South Korean island hit by the second wave of that bioweapon. And scores of people at the D9 denuclearization summit in Norway. Thousands of innocent victims. And why were they killed? It wasn't to prosecute a political or ideological agenda, and it wasn't a religious crusade. No. The whole thing was to make a profit.

Kuga used the attacks on the two Koreas as a practical demonstration of the kind of mayhem his organization peddles. And the ruin of the D9 summit destabilized the global sense of safety, which in turn sent governments and private corporations scrambling to arm up because the shit was hitting the fan. Kuga's black market for weapons ranging from bacteria to high-end combat drones had exploded with new sales.

Bottom line? He won.

But because I'd done a little bit of damage in the process, Kuga sent Rafael Santoro to slaughter my family. Part of me died that day, too. Not my spirit, not my drive or resolve. No, what they killed was some crucial part of the control I normally have. Last year, I would not have done what I'd just done to Die Katze. Last year, I would have found some other way. Last year, I had a different set of restraints.

Maybe last year I was more human.

I don't know. I should probably talk to Junie about it. Or my best friend, Rudy Sanchez. Or someone.

Instead, I kept it all bottled up inside. Pushed in, stamped down. Like shoveling too much coal into a furnace.

The woman and Woodpecker were low level, and they were local criminals, not part of the Kuga empire. Die Katze was. When I'd left America to go hunting for Santoro and Kuga, I'd done it under a black flag. That was the only banner of war for the Darkness. For what I'd become.

I knew I'd just committed murder. An execution.

What would Junie say?

What would Rudy say?

What did I feel about it?

The water pounded my skin as I stood there. I could see the hazy outline of Ghost through the shower curtain. He was not troubled by moral dilemmas. He was part of my pack of killers.

I turned off the water and stepped onto the tiled floor. Not caring about leaving puddles. The mirror was fogged, and I hand-wiped it clear, then stood looking at my reflection. Midthirties, with blond hair darkened by water. Blue eyes filled with ghosts. Scars everywhere. I still had the habit of running my tongue over the bridgework from where Santoro had knocked a few teeth out. My nose was more askew than it used to be. Hard to believe I was the man in the mirror. He looked alien to me now. Like a monster wearing a skin suit and only pretending to be human.

What did I feel about myself?

What did I feel about having just executed a helpless prisoner?

What did I feel about the real possibility that even if I won this fight, I'd lose myself to the Darkness forever?

What did I feel about any of that?

I'm not sure I felt anything at all.

CHAPTER 135

THE PLAYROOM
UNDISCLOSED LOCATION
NEAR VANCOUVER, BRITISH COLUMBIA, CANADA

It was another late call in a string of them.

Knowing that Sunday was probably going to call made Kuga start drinking early so that by the time the phone rang, the bourbon would have sanded off all the edges. Even so, that first ring hit his nervous system like a bucket of cold water.

As always, Kuga took the call in his room—though it seemed that Sunday had some creepy way of knowing when he *was* alone. That had bothered Kuga for months, so he had his people do regular sweeps of his bedroom, walk-in closet, bathroom, sitting room, and even the hallway outside his personal suite. No bugs.

And yet Sunday never called except when Kuga was alone.

He pressed the button. "Hello."

"You sound grumpy."

"It's late. The hell do you want?"

"Oh, it's something I've been meaning to discuss with you—not as an employee but as a friend and advisor."

"'Friend'?"

"Oh yes," said Sunday, "we are friends. We are very close, even if you don't invite me over very often. How many times has it been now? Oh, that's right—once."

"Sorry if your feelings are hurt."

"I'm sorry to see you so stressed all the time."

"Who says I am?"

"It's in your voice," said Sunday. "It's in your attitude. And it's obvious in that you never leave that fortress of yours. Time was when you'd have been bouncing from one place to another, living the high life, getting laid in only the very best places. Now . . . you've become a nervous hermit."

"Well, it's not like half the first world nations don't want my head on a pike."

"And whose fault is that?"

"What's that supposed to mean?"

"It means," said Sunday, "that had a certain someone not bungled Oslo and allowed the authorities to make an educated guess as to who 'Kuga' really is, your life would be a lot more comfortable."

"Hey, that was as much my fault as Rafael's."

"Was it? Tell me—and don't lie because you know I always know—if Santoro had not gone totally against policy and physically been on-site in Oslo, would the world governments have actually connected the Rage attacks directly to you? To you personally? No, I don't think they could have. Before he was videotaped engaging in pointless fisticuffs with Joe Ledger, your involvement was only a rumor. But since you and he were the only two people broken out of that prison two years ago, the connection became obvious."

Kuga said nothing. He wished he'd brought a fresh bottle and some ice with him to bed.

"Moreover," continued Sunday, "if Santoro hadn't forgotten about the golden rule of 'not taking things personally,' he'd have never tried for revenge against Joe Ledger. Killing Ledger's family was Santoro giving a consolation gift to Eve for losing *her* family. Adam. And what's the result? Ledger has slaughtered his way up the food chain looking for him and for you."

"I . . . ," began Kuga, but he had nowhere to go with it.

"Santoro used to be the king of subtlety, the author of the best long-range plans of manipulation and coerced control. Now what is he? An emotional wild card. A liability who is endangering the American Operation, our entire operation, and you personally."

"I thought you were taking care of Ledger. Is that what your mumbo jumbo Lord Voldemort crap was all about? The Darkness bullshit?"

"You talk as if that is as certain as a bullet fired from point-blank range," said Sunday. "I've done real damage to Ledger—and even if he survives, he'll never recover—but the rage Santoro awakened in him has its own power. There is a war for control of his soul, and what Santoro did is in danger of canceling what you wanted me to do."

"Fuck . . ."

"But the real reason I called was to suggest that you take steps."

"If you think I'm going to put a contract out on Rafael, then you're out of your—"

"No, no, no. Nothing like that," laughed Sunday. "I'm suggesting something more immediately practical. I think you need to make sure that someone else has access to the overall network. Command, I mean. I think you need to delegate some of the responsibilities."

"Oh, sure. To whom? To you?"

"That's not what I'm suggesting," said Sunday. "Perhaps to a kind of board. Under your authority, but clearly sharing the responsibility for plans drawn and actions taken."

"Why the hell would I want to do that?"

"Because you have enemies, my friend," said Sunday. "Ledger may be out there crashing and burning because that level of madness isn't self-sustaining . . . but Church undoubtedly sees you as the principal threat. And, let's face it, he's not at all above sending assassins out to take you off the board. He believes that if he cuts off the head of the dragon, the whole empire will collapse into infighting. I doubt he's wrong about that. I mean, if—god forbid—something happened to you, can you see Santoro, as emotionally compromised as he's become, running *your* empire? On the other hand, if there is a clear infrastructure in place, you stop being a critical winner-take-all target."

Kuga sat on the edge of the bed.

"I'm listening," he said.

CHAPTER 136
HOTEL TIMIȘOARA
TIMIȘOARA, ROMANIA

After the shower, I got dressed and then sat at the small desk in the suite and hacked into the hotel security channel and the local police frequency. Things were hysterical for a while, but by four in the morning, things were settling down.

I looked at Cruella and Woodpecker, but they were still sleeping. I wondered what their dreams were like. I considered shooting them, too. Just in case.

Thought about it but didn't do it.

So far, the Darkness was there—moving within me, fighting for dominance—but hadn't totally overwhelmed me. So far, the three other aspects of my broken mind were in control. Barely, but there.

So far, I wasn't in the same room with Rafael Santoro or Kuga. When that happened, I knew the Darkness would own me, own the moment, own the world.

I both feared and prayed for that moment.

I wiped down every surface, packed up my equipment, buckled Ghost's service vest in place, put on dark glasses, and we made our way carefully from the hotel.

CHAPTER 137
HOTEL TIMIȘOARA
TIMIȘOARA, ROMANIA

The street outside was busy, with dozens of official cars and news vehicles parked at crooked angles to the front of the hotel. It was dark—dawn wasn't even a rumor. A crowd of people were gathered to rubberneck. In the lobby by the front door, a worried-looking hotel official flanked by two stern cops was checking everyone's ID, matching it against the guest registry and—in some cases—taking individuals away for pat-downs.

My credentials were unbreakable. The identification they scanned was not associated with the room near where the exchange happened or the room where I'd interrogated the three black marketeers. I'd been very thorough when I'd set this up. My ID was attached to a room with no particular view, and I was an Italian national on a lecture tour of Central Europe. I taught computer keyboarding for the vision impaired.

The cops opened my suitcase and checked through clothes, books, toiletries. They searched my laptop case and found a computer with a braille keyboard and other devices that you'd expect to find. None of these were brand-new but obviously well used, even down to some muffin crumbs stuck between keys. One of them actually waved a hand in front of my eyes. They also checked the service animal serial number on Ghost's vest, ran it through their system, and finally repacked my stuff for me.

The R-33 materials were sealed inside the shell of the laptop, and some of the cash was wrapped in plastic and rolled up inside two cans of dog food, with the smelly glop on top in case they opened the cans. The rest of the cash was on the floor with the three people I'd interrogated. I'd taken a roll of bills and shoved them in each of their mouths. Sure, it was a juvenile and cruel thing to do. So what? It was a kind of mobster gesture that would likely send the cops off in the wrong direction.

The search was done well, but they weren't looking for someone like me. They probably figured that whoever hit that room was long gone. They hadn't even knocked on my door. There would be a street-by-street search and then a national manhunt.

"Thank you," I said in Italian-accented Romanian as I took my papers back. Ghost sat there the whole time, staring into the middle distance. He really can act, and I foresaw some treats and belly rubs in his near future.

"Do you have a driver?" asked the hotel official.

"I was going to take a taxi," I said.

"It's beginning to rain, sir," he said. "I'll have someone fetch you a cab."

He handed me off to a doorman, who, indeed, flagged a lemon-colored taxi, put my bag in the trunk. Very polite, very considerate of the poor blind guy and his docile service dog.

CHAPTER 138
TRADE UNION BUILDING
STRADA MĂRĂȘEȘTI
TIMIȘOARA, ROMANIA

The sniper had the perfect vantage point, and the weather gods were being kind to him.

The building across the intersection from the hotel had a low wall around the roof, with the big metal housing for the air conditioner snugged over to one corner. The correct corner. In the niche between the AC and the wall, there was a comfortable place to wait, and he'd waited for hours. That was fine. The sniper was a very patient man.

His name was Sydänkäpy. Only that. It meant "heart pine cone." A nickname whose significance was lost to time because the group of fellow soldiers who'd hung it on him were all dead. Long dead, each lost to this war or that. Or to this covert job or that.

Only Sydänkäpy remained. He did not consider himself a fighter. His hand-to-hand skills were only ever okay. He did not like hump-ing eighty pounds of equipment through deserts or windy mountain passes. Sydänkäpy always joked that he was the world's laziest man, which was why he'd picked sniping as a profession. You got to sit around a lot. Relax. Wait. Watch.

As he was watching now. It was one of the skills that his mentor—his master—Michael Augustus Stafford had taught him. Watching. Being patient. Letting the target come to him. Letting the target prove through incaution that he wanted the bullet.

He'd arrived before the meeting between the local black market chaps and Kuga's team. His brief was simple—if a man fitting a certain description and accompanied by a large white dog left the hotel at any point, Sydänkäpy was to take him out. That order had been reissued with a stern demand that it be done with extreme prejudice. Apparently, the meet had gone south and the players taken off the board. That meant the package Kuga's agent was to hand over to the Romanian had been taken. The target would likely have it.

The target would be in disguise. That didn't matter to Sydänkäpy. He had the eyes of a predator bird—a hawk or falcon—and was not distracted by false mustaches, wigs, or a phony limp. He'd studied this man, seen footage of him. And would know him in a snowstorm.

Sydänkäpy spent time setting up his equipment. A small laptop fed real-time information to him through earbuds. A folding stool kept him comfortable, so he didn't have to kneel for hours. And, of course, there was the rifle. A Finnish gun that Sydänkäpy had used many times. Not the same gun but one like it. He tended to use one of three or four different weapons for jobs like these. Guns he knew intimately. His pick for tonight was a Sako TRG 42 long-range sniper rifle. Without a doubt one of the finest sniper rifles in the world. It was a much-improved version of the old Sako TRG 41 on which Sydänkäpy had learned his trade.

The TRG 42 had a new and very comfortable stock design. And the weapon was designed to handle more powerful cartridges with a maximum length of 95 mm. It was a manually operated, bolt-action rifle chambered for .338 Lapua Magnum cartridges. That gave him an effective range of fifteen hundred meters. During daylight hours, he used the Picatinny-type scope, but as a coming storm darkened the day and night fell, he switched to a night vision scope, the kind adjusted to accept some artificial light—streetlights and the neon around the hotel entrance—without blinding him. Very expensive and very subtle technology.

The other bit of tech he added was a sound suppressor of a kind that also reduced muzzle flash. Sydänkäpy liked things nice and quiet.

As the hours passed, he watched the arrival of police and crime scene units. He saw ambulances appear and then vanish. He saw crowds gather to watch, dispersing only a little as the first raindrops fell. He listened to police chatter via his coms unit and got updates from his handler. He knew everything that took place inside the hotel.

Almost.

The target had vanished, presumably to a bolt-hole within the place. The computer team working logistics and intelligence did pattern and keyword searches on the guests booked into each room. Only one of them had a dog.

A blind man. And one whose credentials were beautifully constructed, even down to small details on social media platforms. Very sophisticated.

That made Sydänkäpy smile. He appreciated good tradecraft.

It was full dark when the blind man and his white service dog stepped out of the hotel. Sydänkäpy shifted into position. The rain was blowing toward the hotel, which meant that the air conditioner housing blocked it from splatting on him. The angle of the wind kept almost all droplets off his scope. Nice.

The blind man was blocked for a few seconds by a helpful member of the staff and the driver of a cab. A suitcase and laptop case were put into the trunk. No bags that resembled the ones taken from the meeting room, but he didn't expect to see those.

He tested the wind and made very slight adjustments to his sights.

Ready. Patient.

The man then moved away from the hotel staff member and the driver and the shot was clear and easy. Sydänkäpy slipped his finger into the trigger guard, took a breath, and exhaled as he pulled the trigger.

CHAPTER 139
THE PAVILION
BLUE DIAMOND ELITE TRAINING CENTER
STEVENS COUNTY, WASHINGTON

Bunny was out walking.

He and Top took turns strolling around, making sure that they were never directly looking at anything important, but letting their button cams pick up details.

"Turn just a little bit to the left," said Andrea, who was somewhere in the woods processing the intel. "Gorilla balls! What is that?"

Bunny, of course, said nothing.

Forty feet away, a group of Pavilion technicians were using a forklift to place K-110 fighting machines into huge crates. There was a line of nine such crates, and three more on the back of a stake-bed semi. Other techs were busy securing the loaded crates to the truck bed with canvas straps and chains. The crates were marked: MEDICAL EQUIPMENT—C-19.

"*Accidenti!*" cried Andrea. "What clever bastards they are. *Che palle!*"

Bunny lingered for as long as he could—no more than a few seconds—and then moved on to complete his daily morning walk. Later, Top would go jogging through here.

CHAPTER 140
HOTEL TIMIȘOARA
TIMIȘOARA, ROMANIA

But just as I was about to step into the car, I heard a strange sound. A soft whisk of air past my cheek and immediately a light *thunk* of something striking asphalt nearby. There was so much hustle and noise on the street that no one else seemed to have heard it. I ducked my ass immediately into the car and shifted to the center of the rear bench seat, pushing Ghost down on the floor.

"Hurry, please," I said to the driver, "I need to make my flight."

He pulled away, and then we were gone.

My pulse was hammering because I knew both of those sounds.

The first had been a bullet passing within inches of my face. How many inches? Hard to say, though I've been in enough firefights to know that's what it was. Four inches? Less? There is a distinctive way the lead cleaves through the air. And the other sound was that same bullet hitting the blacktop on which I stood. It had been a very solid impact, too.

A rifle bullet.

Which meant there was a sniper positioned in some high, hidden elevated shooting position. He'd tried to shoot me—which meant he knew who I was—but something had caused him to miss with that first shot. He hadn't taken another. Snipers are fast, so maybe his angle was obscured, or maybe I was lucky enough to have been getting into the car already when he fired.

But luck was a funny thing. I don't have that much of it, and I don't trust it worth a hollow damn. So, why had the shooter missed?

I sat tense as fuck, crouched as low as I could—pretending to adjust Ghost's harness—expecting the rear or side window to implode with the next shot as the sniper corrected the angle.

However, there was no next shot. He'd missed his shot and hadn't tried again. Why not? He could have extrapolated where I was once I was in the car. Three spaced shots in a line, twenty or so inches apart and at that angle, would have hit some part of me, no matter how I hid in the back.

"Hurry, please," I snarled, and the car pulled out into the street.

I crouched, breathless, terrified, trying to block Ghost. The dog whimpered softly in fear and frustration. He was always in tune with me. He knew we were in trouble. Very bad trouble.

We sped through the rain-swept darkness.

The cab headed to the airport, and I don't think I started breathing for three full blocks. At the airport, I went into the terminal and straight to the closest men's room. I changed my clothes, then went to a coin locker to retrieve a different set of travel documents and ID and headed to security, and—as an Austrian music historian traveling with his emotional support dog—boarded a jet for Innsbruck Airport. Below us, the land fell away, and we rose above the clouds and vanished into the night.

CHAPTER 141
ROOF OF THE BELVEDERE RESTAURANT
TIMIȘOARA, ROMANIA

The woman knelt there, a figure wrapped in darkness, lost in shadows. Invisible.

She studied the rooftop across the street through a Nightforce Optics 5.5–22×56 NXS Riflescope mounted on her Accuracy International's L115A3—the best .338 rifle on the market. Finding the other sniper had taken time and patience, but she knew he had to be there. Somewhere.

All her intel and all her instincts said he must be there. In the dark. A ghost, like she was.

He was good, though. No rookie errors of allowing the metal or glass of his weapon to reach into the path of any stray light. Finding an expert is one of the most challenging and frustrating parts of the game. Snipers know how not to be found.

But in the end, the sniper needs to take a shot. The woman calculated the best angle for the kill and balanced it against the sniper's need to escape. In daylight, at a distance of eight to twelve hundred meters, the muzzle flash is minimal unless they are looking right at it. Bullets travel faster than sound, so the target never hears it, and the report is difficult to echolocate. However, the woman followed the sniper's line of sight to the street, where a man in an overcoat and black glasses—a blind man—was getting into a cab with his dog. The man was big and had pale hair. The dog was white as snow.

The woman tucked the stock of the rifle against her shoulder and fired.

The timing was very nearly tragic. The sniper was more prepared than she'd thought, and he fired at the same moment.

Or . . . the tiniest fraction of that moment.

Her weapon fired a bullet at the approximate speed of sound—340.3 meters per second—and it struck the sniper in the eye as his finger pulled the trigger. The difference was one ten-thousandth of a second. At that angle, at that distance, with the reduction of the sound suppressor, that was enough. His bullet hit the asphalt twenty inches from the blond man's right shoe.

Her bullet blew the sniper's head apart.

Below, the cab rolled away and vanished into the Timișoara night. There were no yells or whistles, no sirens. The sniper's shot had missed and, in the confusion, gone unnoticed. Had Joe Ledger noticed? She thought so, from his body language and how fast he'd gotten out of the line of fire. How fast the cab had moved off.

Joe Ledger must think he was lucky or that the shooter had misjudged. That was fine. He was not a lucky man—not in most ways—but he had some good fortune. He was lucky in his friends. Lucky to have people who loved him.

"Be safe, Joseph," murmured the woman. Even Ledger did not know her real name. Like most people, he called her by a nickname. A code name. A combat call sign.

Violin.

The cab was gone now. Violin packed up her weapon, and then she, too, faded into the darkness to where Harry and Toys waited for her.

CHAPTER 142

THE PLAYROOM
UNDISCLOSED LOCATION
NEAR VANCOUVER, BRITISH COLUMBIA, CANADA

Sunday called Kuga late in the evening.

"Jesus," growled Kuga, pawing his eyes clear so he could see the caller ID. It was an icon of a coyote. "Why are you calling at this hour? Is something wrong?"

"Nothing's wrong, my friend," said Sunday smoothly. "Just calling to see how you are."

"I'm drunk and tired is how I am," growled Kuga. "And this is hardly the time for a little chitchat."

"I wanted to tell you three things. First, I closed the deal with our militia friends in Florida. That makes fifty groups now. A complete set."

"Yeah?"

"Yes, indeed. The incentives and product samples did the trick. And they said that they are very much on board for our little party."

"Okay, that's awesome. But you could have told me this tomorrow."

"It is tomorrow," said Sunday.

"Technically, but I just got into bed. What's the second thing?"

"HK is shipping the *support* materials out."

"Again, that could have waited until tomorrow."

"This last little bit of gossip can't wait," said Sunday. "Joe Ledger is on a plane to these United States. His flight left not five minutes ago."

Kuga was completely awake now. He sat up and swung his legs off the bed.

"Are you sure?"

"Of course."

"Where's he going?"

"Fort Lauderdale."

"*What?*"

"Yes. Isn't that interesting? Clearly, he knows something, and I wonder how he could have gotten wind of anything related to our little venture. Tell me, Kuga, who all knew about that?"

"Just you, Santoro, and me."

"Yes," said Sunday. "I find that very interesting. You didn't blab, and I know I didn't. I wonder . . . I wonder how Ledger got wind of this?"

Kuga got up and walked to the window. The mansion was huge and the night outside vast, but suddenly, it felt like all the walls were closing in on him.

"Where's Stafford?"

"I sent him after Ledger in your fast little jet," said Sunday. "It's what Rafael should have done."

PATRIOTS
PART 7

But I've a rendezvous with Death
At midnight in some flaming town

—ALAN SEEGER

If you could hear, at every jolt, the blood
Come gargling from the froth-corrupted lungs,
Obscene as cancer, bitter as the cud
Of vile, incurable sores on innocent tongues,—
My friend, you would not tell with such high zest
To children ardent for some desperate glory,
The old Lie: *Dulce et decorum est*
Pro patria mori.

—WILFRED OWEN

CHAPTER 143
TIMIȘOARA TRAIAN VUIA INTERNATIONAL AIRPORT

I found a quiet place in the airport and made a call that I didn't want to make.

No, not Junie. I was still too much of a coward for that. Maybe I'd never find the courage. Maybe I wouldn't live long enough to have to.

God, what Rudy would make of that thought. Me thinking that death was an easier, healthier, better choice than calling the woman I love. What a hero.

So, the call I actually made was to Church. His private line. Last thing I wanted was to have the call broadcast over the speakers at the TOC.

Church answered right away, and his voice was, understandably, cautious.

"Outlaw," he said.

"Boss."

"You've been busy."

"A bit."

"The intel you sent has been quite useful."

"It's scaring the hell out of me," I said.

"There's some of that around here as well. How secure is this line?"

"It's a burner. Never used before," I said, "and I'll trash it after. I'm in a place where no one can hear me, so we can talk."

There was a last-call announcement for a flight.

"You're at the Brandenburg airport," he said.

"Yeah, but that wasn't my flight." I paused. "Look, I don't know how much you've been able to piece together. You have a lot of what I've learned, but not all of it. I think we need to compare notes."

He said, "Cybernetically and chemically enhanced Fixers with superior body armor, some in fighting machines. The Fixers are driven by a compound called R-33, which is a mix of a new generation of eugeroic therapies code-named Relentless. The latest version is mixed with the Rage bioweapon. There is something called the American Operation, possibly code-named G-55, in which those Fixers intend to stage an attack resulting in mass casualties." He paused. "How am I doing so far?"

"You got all that from what I sent?"

"From that and from the materials, samples, and data files recovered from Croatia. Am I missing anything?"

"Do you know about Mr. Sunday?"

"Yes, the sales director for Kuga. Bug is trying to find a way into his presentations on the darknet."

"ShowRoom," I said.

"Yes."

"I have no other intel on him."

"What else do you have?"

I was near a window, looking out at the big planes landing and taking off. I saw a bunch of the same night birds standing in a line on a disused in-flight-catering truck. Maybe sixty of them, and I swear they were watching me.

"Do you know about the militia groups?"

"No, that's not in our materials. What have you learned?"

I told him what the Cat told me. It wasn't much.

"That's new," said Church. "I'll have Bug put people on it."

"I'm going to follow up some leads of my own," I said. "I'm on my way back to the States. But look . . . I don't want backup and I don't want a crowd scene. Let me do this my way."

"Is there anything else you can tell me?"

"The guy who told me about the militia thinks they're going to hit a stadium. Maybe a sports game or concert. He didn't have details but thought it was going to be sometime in the next month. Sorry I can't be more precise."

"You've given us a lot, Outlaw," said Church. "If it hadn't been for your actions, we would be considerably behind the curve."

"Maybe we still are."

"Or maybe now we have a chance to react in time when something happens. At the very least, we'll be able to make contact with some of my friends in the government and elsewhere and give them a heads-up."

"Yeah, but our challenge is always that we're by nature a reactive organization. That's why I'm following these leads. I can't just sit and wait."

"You don't need to justify your actions to me, Outlaw."

"Boss," I said, "I know you meant well sending Toys after me, but don't do that again. I'm . . . I'm not entirely stable. I think you know that. He's probably told you what I did."

"It came up in conversation."

"I've done a lot of . . . *questionable* things."

"Would it comfort you at all to know that I, in my time, have done much worse?"

"Maybe. I don't know. I'm about a long mile from real perspective."

"Give it time, Outlaw. You're doing better than you think."

"I want to ask you something, and I don't want you to think I'm an idiot or that I've gone completely off my rocker."

"Try me," said Church.

"You know about a lot of supernatural stuff, right?"

"I'm familiar with the scholarship and traditions of the larger world."

"What do you know about flocks of black birds? Not just crows but all kinds, flocking together?"

There was a pause. "Tell me," he said, his voice devoid of all emotion, "are they by any chance particularly ragged-looking? As if they're all molting or windblown?"

I looked at the birds. Now there were more than a hundred. "Yes," I said.

"Tell me where you've seen them."

"My flight will be boarding soon."

"Tell me."

So I told him. And as I did so, I realized that there were more incidents than I'd been consciously aware of.

"And these night birds have been following you since Croatia? They first appeared after the incident in the basement?"

"Yes. What did you call them? *Night* birds?"

"Two words: night birds."

"How scared should I be?"

"Very," he said, and now there was a new note in his voice. "Not of them—no, definitely not of them—but of who it is they hate."

"I . . . have no idea what the hell that means."

"Outlaw . . . Joe . . . listen to me, the night birds are omens. They warn people of certain kinds of threats. There is a great deal of literature about this. But what you need to know is that they have often been reported during times when a certain person is awake and alive in the world."

"'Awake and alive'? You just went all Bram Stoker on me. Who are you . . . ?"

And my words trailed off because I realized *exactly* who he was talking about.

"No," I said. "No fucking way. You killed him."

"I never said I killed him," said Church. "I merely stopped him. For a time."

"You're saying *Nicodemus* is involved in all this?"

"Yes," said Church. "I'm sorry to say that he is."

CHAPTER 144
PHOENIX HOUSE
OMFORI ISLAND, GREECE

Church set down the phone, removed his glasses, and pinched the bridge of his nose. Old scars on his skin flared with remembered pain. Deeper wounds that ran all the way to his heart ached with fear and weariness.

"Nicodemus," he said to the soft shadows in his office. "Too soon."

Then he picked up the phone again and began making a series of calls.

The first was to Lilith. To tell her and suggest she warn Violin.

"Ledger is seeing night birds?" she asked.

"He is."

"That means he is very close to the veil," she said. "He is more in death's kingdom than this one."

"Yes."

"You may never bring him back, St. Germaine. Not this time."

"I know."

His next call was to Bug, to make sure his people included the new information from Ledger.

"Militia guys?" asked Bug. "Is he sure?"

"His source was sure."

"Okay," Bug said, sounding as comprehensively tired as Church felt. "I'll spin this up. And Joe wants us to look at something in the next month or two?"

"Yes, but my gut tells me that this will happen sooner than later."

He called Scott Wilson.

"I was just about to ring you," said Wilson by way of a hello. "We just heard from our team at the Pavilion."

"What's happening there?"

"Seems as if our bad guys are loading some of the combat tech for transport. The feed from Bunny's cam was clear, so we have visuals and a license plate number. I've already instructed Andrea to put a drone on that truck."

"What is the drive time to East Texas? Same question for Fort Lauderdale, Florida?"

"Twenty-eight to thirty-two hours to that part of Texas. Forty-five to fifty for Florida. More, if you count stops for food, fuel, and sleep."

"Assume this is straight through. I want routes plotted, and make sure there's a backup to the drones."

"Very well," agreed Wilson.

"Two more things," said Church. "First, Ledger is inbound. Not sure which of those two locations he's heading for. Check flights from Brandenburg leaving anytime from right now to four hours out."

"Easy enough. What's the other thing?"

"There's a new player in this."

"Friend or foe?"

"Definitely foe," said Church. "Nicodemus."

"God save the queen . . ."

Church called Toys.

"I was rather expecting you to call," said Toys. "Violin just had a rather disturbing call from her mum."

"No doubt. Put this call on speaker."

He gave them all of it, including the intel from Bunny.

"We're on our way," said Violin. "At the airport now."

"Hurry," said Church.

CHAPTER 145
FORT LAUDERDALE–HOLLYWOOD
INTERNATIONAL AIRPORT
FORT LAUDERDALE, FLORIDA

I tried to sleep on the plane. *Tried* being the operative word. Much of the flight was a blur, though. Not because the Darkness owned my ass again—I don't think that happened. No, it was more that I was tired beyond words, jacked to the eyeballs with caffeine, heartsick, and scared.

Scared of Nicodemus.

Scared of what I had become, especially if that meant I was a puppet and Nicodemus had his hand up my ass.

Scared of what Kuga was about to do.

Just plain scared.

Now that Church was up to speed with everything, I probably should have felt comforted, but . . .

Ghost was on the seat next to me, and in his sleep, he moaned. It sounded like he was in pain. When I put my hand on the nape of his neck, he shuddered and settled into a deeper place in his dreams. The place where the mind is vulnerable and the fear can't escape even through involuntary sounds or movements.

We flew on.

When we landed in Fort Lauderdale, the wheels hitting the tarmac jolted me out of a doze I wasn't aware I was in. Ghost yipped, and I realized that in my surprise I'd squeezed my hand on his ruff.

"Sorry, boy," I said.

He gave me a withering look.

We deplaned, and I did my trick of going into the bathroom and changing clothes from what was in my carry-on. And switched Ghost from emotional support to "just a dog."

We went to Enterprise, and I used a fake ID to rent a bland white Ford Edge. Once in the car, I drove us out of the airport and to a grocery store. Loaded up on dog food, dog treats, a new rubber ball—also for the dog—and a handful of items for me. I also bought a tourist guide to the area and four burner phones. The clerk raised an eyebrow at those, and I gave him a ninja death stare until he looked away. He no doubt thought I was in the drug trade.

Packages in hand, we walked to the Edge, which I'd parked next to a whitewashed stone wall.

A man stepped out from between my car and a white panel truck parked next to me. He was roughly the size of Godzilla and had a face like an eroded wall and wore a DON'T TREAD ON ME ball cap and a windbreaker with a tattered American flag on the right chest. Out of my peripheral vision, I saw another man, thinner and with flaming red hair like the comedian Carrot Top, come up on my right. A third, wiry and fit, covered with tattoos of snakes coiling around swastikas, came around the front of the truck.

Godzilla had his hand inside a nylon windbreaker.

"Joe Ledger," he said, smiling.

That's the moment when you're supposed to freeze, look shocked beyond words, maybe say something like a stuttering, "Wh-what?"

From Godzilla's shit-eating grin, it was clear he was ready to milk that kind of reaction.

I threw the shopping bag hard at his face and heard the meaty *thunk* as six cans of Alpo caught him on the mouth, but I was pivoting left, reaching for Carrot Top as Ghost went in and left and slammed into Snakeman.

Carrot Top was quick and tried to raise the gun he'd held down behind his thigh so it would be out of sight of witnesses. Fast, sure, but I'm faster. I hit him on the bridge of the nose with the side of my balled-up fist. His nose exploded, and the force knocked his head back, exposing his throat. So I pivoted and whipped him across the Adam's apple with the left forearm.

He went down, gurgling and thrashing, while I spun back to Godzilla, whose face was bloody and already beginning to swell. The impact had spoiled his draw, and the big Glock snagged on the inside of the jacket. I used my left palm to pin his wrist against his chest and caught him across the point of the jaw with my palm. If you do it just right, moving your hand in a sharp, very fast circle, the blow spins the jaw all the way around, much faster than the body can deal with. The result is a sprained neck, dislocated jaw, concussion, and a total disruption of the synovial fluid in the inner ear. He staggered and collapsed back against my SUV. I boxed his ears and kicked his kneecap loose, but before he could fall, I tore his jacket open and took the Glock.

I whirled toward Carrot Top, but he was down, no longer making sounds. No longer breathing.

Ghost had Snakeman on the ground, and titanium fangs had turned the man's throat to ground beef.

All of it in three seconds. Maybe two.

"Ghost," I snapped. "Done. Off."

He disengaged reluctantly.

I grabbed all three of their guns and my sack of groceries, unlocked my car, and ordered Ghost to get in, but as he ran around to the open driver's door, someone opened up with another handgun. I ducked down as the bullets knocked jagged splinters from the wall. Ghost screamed in pain, and I couldn't tell if it was a splinter or a bullet. His shoulder was pouring blood, and when he tried to run toward the open doorway, his legs buckled.

More shots punched into the hood of the car and the windshield, filling the glass with spiderweb cracks.

I pivoted to return fire, but the gunman crouched behind an open car door, and there were terrified pedestrians behind him—some running, others frozen in shock.

So I scooped to pick up Ghost, and it was a measure of his pain that he snapped at me. But I got him in and pushed him over and down into the passenger footwell. I started the car, keeping low,

JONATHAN MABERRY

released the brake, and stamped on the gas. The Edge lurched forward, and I drove it right at the shooter, ducking low as he blew out the windshield. But then the left front fender smashed into the door behind which he was standing. I heard an awful shriek and the tire thumped over something, and immediately, the scream stopped.

I muscled between that car and another and then cut left across the parking lot to the first exit. The passenger-side window burst inward, and I heard more shots, but I couldn't see the shooter. I was too busy driving.

We got the hell out of the parking lot and drove one block and pulled into an underground garage beneath an office building. It took me only seconds to break into another car and ten more seconds to disable the alarm. Easy when you know how. I transferred Ghost, who was whimpering piteously, into the back seat. Then I exited the lot and got the hell out of the area.

Ghost needed a doctor, and we both needed a place to lie low. And I knew exactly where to go.

CHAPTER 146
OAKWOOD PLAZA
HOLLYWOOD, FLORIDA

Stafford disconnected the call and sat behind the wheel of his rental Jeep Gladiator.

Four dead.

Four.

"Jesus Christ," he said aloud. And then repeated it over and over while banging his fist on the steering wheel.

He'd sent a six-man team, all experienced militiamen from the New Founding Fathers, one of the most radicalized of the teams on Mr. Sunday's list. Men who'd been involved in serious operations—the shooting of an anti-fracking senator, the kidnap and execution of a CEO who was moving his plant overseas and taking seven hundred American jobs with it, and counterprotesting at voting sites from Miami to the Rust Belt. Men who should have been able to handle one man and a goddamned dog.

He debated calling Kuga, which he was supposed to do, but the boss had seemed a little twitchy lately. No, better wait until there was *good* news to report.

Stafford took his tablet from the open briefcase on the passenger seat and called up the profile on Joe Ledger. Looking for where he might be going here in Lauderdale. Stafford did not think Ledger knew where he *should* have been going. If that were the case, if Ledger knew where the Fixers were getting their gear ready, that cocksucker would be leading the entire National Guard right there. Since that wasn't happening, then the likelier scenario was that Ledger had gotten the name of the city from the Cat—which was all that idiot knew—and was going to hole up while trying to plan his next move.

Fine.

That meant that Stafford now had the time he needed to figure out where exactly that was. Unlike Ledger's visits to the cities in Europe and Africa, this was home turf, and the whole Ledger family had ties to Fort Lauderdale. This part was just legwork, guesswork, and—if things went as he expected—gun work.

CHAPTER 147
THE PAVILION
BLUE DIAMOND ELITE TRAINING CENTER
STEVENS COUNTY, WASHINGTON

Top and Bunny had been taking a lot of walks and doing a lot of jogging over the last few weeks. Partly to establish these things as habits, but primarily to gather intel.

It was a strange time for both of them and by far the longest they had been undercover in any operation, before or since working for Mr. Church.

It was also deeply frustrating because they could not effectively sweep their rooms for bugs and so had to assume they were under constant surveillance. Even the old trick of running the shower and having a huddled conversation protected by the wall of sound wouldn't work, because bathrooms could be bugged pretty easily these days. And the only way to find those devices would be during a concerted search, which would appear, on video, to be exactly what it was. Once in a while, they would jot a note on a tissue or a few sheets of toilet paper, but writing those notes could not be done anywhere in their rooms. Bunny did his in a porta-potty on the far side of the camp, and Top did his in a bathroom stall attached to the main training gym.

And so they were roommates, forcing themselves into routines and conversation habits that reinforced their credibility as disgruntled ex-military who were training to be upper-tier Fixers.

Every day, they went to classes to study the technology, the strategies and tactics, the politics of likely client nations, and similar classes on corporate structures for multinational businesses who routinely hired private military contractors. They did physical training in the morning, with long runs in full kit, clanking iron in the gym, swimming laps in the pool, climbing trees using hand and foot spokes, and hand-to-hand combat drills. Top had risen to the rank of assistant instructor, working with a Chechen ex-commando. They disliked each other at once, so there was no male bonding going on. However, they made a good team.

Day by day, though, Top faced the reality that he was actually training killers to be even more lethal.

Bunny kept his skill level from showing, though he got high marks on the gun range. Of the two, he was the better shot, though not by much.

And every other day, groups of Fixers were trained in the use of the high-tech battle gear. The guns and armor were easy. The fighting machine took practice. Only for Top, though. Bunny was far too big to be a candidate for a K-110 driver. But Top found he actually liked being inside the shell of that machine. The servos were so responsive that it wasn't like lifting weights, which was how it looked. The level of resistance was less than walking chest deep in a pool, which was why all the drivers spent two hours a day practicing in the water. Top hated the first ten days of that, and then his body seemed to shuck the years. His muscle tone was as fine as when he'd been a spry twentysomething running with the 101st Airborne.

He gave his machine a nickname—*Hot Mama*—and painted that on the cowling.

Over the last few weeks, the camp had begun to empty out. Truck-loads of Fixers had rolled out already, and there was only a skeleton crew left behind—thirty Fixers, five scientists, six techs, and a dozen support staff that included the mess cook and room maids.

On the same day Joe Ledger was racing through the streets of Fort Lauderdale with a bleeding Ghost, Top saw HK pulling a suitcase toward a big Lincoln Navigator. He'd been out jogging and was both surprised and alarmed that HK seemed to be moving out as well.

"Hey, boss lady," called Top, slowing to a walk and falling in beside her, "don't tell me you're leaving, too."

"It's that time," she said, giving him one of her brilliant smiles.

"Well . . . damn," he said, smiling back. "Won't be nothing left here but ugly-ass Fixers to look at. You're taking all the pretty with you."

HK's eyes flickered a bit at that, as if deciding whether his comment was charming or a step too far, but she kept her sunny disposition.

"I'm sure you'll find something to keep you occupied, Mr. Guidry."

He offered to stow her suitcase in the back of the car, and she shrugged and allowed it.

"In all seriousness, HK," said Top, "Buck and I really appreciate you taking us on here. We feel like we found a home with y'all. A family."

Now the smile changed, mingled tones of surprise and warmth. "That's sweet of you to say. We try our best."

"That's obvious, ma'am, but hey . . . we'd like to earn our keep. Everyone else has rolled out, and it's obvious there's something big about to happen. You can feel the excitement. You can taste it, though I don't know what it is. It's all hush-hush. When do Buck and I get a chance to join in the fun, maybe kick a few asses and take some names?"

She looked up at him for a few seconds, and he watched her eyes and calculated the wattage of that smile. It was obvious she was deciding on how much to tell him.

"We have plans for you and everyone else left here at the Pavilion," she said. "Your team isn't part of the other operation we have running. No, Mr. Guidry, your unit will be shipping out overseas.

Can't say where exactly, but I can say that I hope you like heat and humidity. Though your *Hot Mama* is, after all, air-conditioned."

"Oh, okay," he said. "That's cool. But I made some friends in the other squads. Wouldn't mind seeing some of those cats again."

"Oh, sorry. They won't be coming back here," she said, making a little sad face. "That's why their gear's already been forwarded. But . . . who knows, maybe we'll all have a big class reunion. Have to run now. Bye!"

And she punctuated that with a big wink.

Then she got into the back of the Escalade, and Top watched the vehicle drive off.

He didn't linger and instead went back to his daily run.

The path took him through all the small buildings used as suites for the Fixers. There were no guards back there, and Top slowed down, pretending to be out of breath. He walked slowly through the now deserted alleys between the buildings. Every now and then, he leaned on a windowsill, ostensibly for balance as he stretched his quads, but really to catch quick glimpses through the windows. What he saw made him grunt in surprise.

Because he was wearing a T-shirt and shorts for the run, he did not have his button cam. So he walked back to the suite he shared with Bunny and gave his partner a small gesture to indicate they should both go outside. It was a lovely day, and they strolled in the general direction of the pool.

When Top was sure they were out of range of likely surveillance, he told Bunny what he'd seen. Bunny frowned.

"Their stuff's still here?" asked the big young man.

"Yeah. In every window I looked. Seems like they just walked away from it. Clothes, gear, personal stuff."

"And HK said they weren't coming back?"

"So she said."

"Why would she lie about something like that?"

"Maybe 'cause she doesn't want the rest of us 'Fixers' to know that we're all single-use products."

Bunny stared at him.

"Well . . . shit . . ."

CHAPTER 148
ABOARD THE *SOPHIA YIN*
FORT LAUDERDALE, FLORIDA

When I got to Lauderdale, I didn't like the way the cut on Ghost's shoulder was looking. I'd cleaned it off, but he seemed to be in a fair amount of pain. And he was getting grouchy and even snippy about it.

In perhaps the only bit of luck I've had in who knows how long, I actually knew a veterinarian in town—one of my dad's friends, Jean McGee-Thompson, a fifty-three-year-old general practice animal doctor who had a curious sideline of doing what she called "private salvage" work. Jean's not exactly a private investigator—she just does the occasional favor for friends. Hiding me out is one kind of favor. Like her father before her, Jean is smart, shrewd, funny, idealistic, and pretends to be a cynic. But she has a huge heart. I first met her at her husband's funeral twelve years ago. He was apparently killed in a failed mugging, but Jean didn't believe that's how it played out. So she went hunting, looking deeper than the police bothered to. A week or so later, there was a news story about what a sad coincidence it was that her husband's business partner fell off a roof. Terrible luck, the reporters said.

My dad told me that Jean deconstructed the situation and found that her husband's partner had picked clean every bit of money their underwater photography business had and borrowed right up to the hilt against the physical assets. Dad said she got a bit more than half of it back. He never told me how she'd managed it or how the partner managed to be on the roof of their boathouse. Or how he somehow tripped and took that fatal fall.

I knew he had his suspicions, but even if he had proof, I doubt he'd have called one of his cop buddies in Lauderdale. His dad, my grandfather, had been a close friend of Jean's dad, and there were some tall tales about what the elder McGee had been doing his whole life. All Dad ever said was, "Joey, there's the law, and then there's justice."

I got to know Jean better after Junie and I came down for one of her legendary boat parties. Twelve couples, including Rudy and Circe, my brother, Sean, and his wife, and some folks who were strangers when

　　　　　　　　　　　　　　　　JONATHAN MABERRY

we set off and friends when we docked. Jean and Junie had spent a lot of that trip talking, walking together on beaches, drinking wine in a drifting skiff. Junie never said what they talked about, and I have never asked.

Jean kept a low profile except among the tight community of permanent boat people, and she'd extended the invitation for one or both of us to visit anytime. And, at the end of that ten-day excursion, when Junie was already in the car and I'd come back for the last of my scuba gear, Jean took me aside and told me that if I ever needed a place to lie low, to come see her. She'd been shaking my hand when she said it and maintained her firm, dry, powerful grip for an extra second or two. Not as any kind of come-on but the way one soldier might do with another. The message was clear, and I thanked her.

So I used one of the burners to call her. She said she was home and to come right over.

Forty minutes later, I was there.

Jean is tall, with long, wiry red-gold hair, pale eyes, and a look of constant, amused skepticism. She had that rare blend of relaxed vitality and obvious high intelligence. A brainy doctor in a jock body. And she was sunbaked to a golden brown. There were some interesting little scars here and there that could be reasonably accounted for by either her profession as a veterinarian or her avocation as a boat bum. I knew knife scars when I saw them.

She took Ghost down below and said that there was a splinter of something buried under his fur. Apparently, the shot that missed me and grazed him carried a piece of the stone wall with it. It was pressing on some nerves.

"I need to put him out and remove it," she said. "And I'll shoot him up with antibiotics. Won't take long, but he'll need to sleep it off, so while I'm working, you'd better go out and do some shopping. I don't have toiletries for a guy, and you need a shave, shampoo, and shower. And maybe some fresh clothes."

I thanked her, kissed Ghost's head, and went out. I bought more than toiletries and clothes, though. There's a woman in town who is part of the Arklight extended family. I told her what I needed, and she said to give her an hour. My guess is that most of that time was making calls to Lilith and Violin. By the time I arrived at her place—which looked like an LGBTQ bookshop—she had what I needed. I tried to pay her, but she got so offended I apologized.

I took the stuff around the corner to my rental car, and it took me nearly an hour to find the three tracking bugs she'd hidden in the big suitcase. An hour was a long time, which meant Violin was likely at the airport now and would be here by morning.

Then, reasonably sure my new gear was clean, I headed back to the marina to see how Ghost was coming along.

CHAPTER 149
THE TOC
PHOENIX HOUSE
OMFORI ISLAND, GREECE

"Okay, guys," said Nikki Bloom, "we put together two lists of events in the areas Joe said might be strike zones."

She sent the data from her laptop to the big screen at the front of the room.

The tactical operations center was packed to the rafters. The brightest minds from each department were there, along with the regular mission command team. Church, Doc, Wilson, and Bug stood at the foot of a wide aisle between rows of workstations.

"If we start at the two-month mark," continued Nikki, "you can see that there's something like two hundred and fourteen events with estimated populations over two hundred. More if you include the Lauderdale metropolitan area. And for LaBorde, we don't know which part of the county is a possible target."

Long lists of events appeared on the screens. The green list was LaBorde County, and the blue was Lauderdale.

"There are convention centers, high school and college stadiums, baseball and football stadiums, track-and-field meets, summer camps, car shows, gun shows, political rallies, music concerts, art shows . . ."

Doc leaned close to Church. "Oh, lordy."

"Indeed," agreed Church.

Wilson said, "Have you assigned values to these events?"

"Sure," said Nikki. "About a zillion different sets of metrics. Largest anticipated crowd density, indoor versus outdoor, recurring versus onetime, entertainment versus governmental; and we have breakdowns by political parties. Though, since we're between elections in midsummer, there isn't a lot of political heat right now, and the ones that are scheduled have some of the smallest potential crowds."

"What are the political ones?" asked Wilson.

"There's an anti–stem cell research rally at a library in Hollywood, Florida. Based on previous events by the same group, they expect a hundred people. The speaker is a former state senator," she said. "There's the governor's conference on police funding in Nacogdoches—which sounds like it would be hot button, but it's not. Mostly reading of proposals and photo ops. A bipartisan thing that's so dull it's struggling to get press. Figure maybe two hundred. And the other is a little likelier, a Second Amendment event set for the week before the new background check legislation comes up for a vote in the Florida state senate. A lot of opposing groups are blasting about it on their social media, so you can expect everyone from BLM to the Proud Boys to show up for that. It's in two weeks and will be held outside the Greater Fort Lauderdale Broward County Convention Center, where the Florida Gun Show will be held. Much bigger numbers."

"That has my vote," said Wilson, and Doc nodded.

"Don't matter which side of the issue you're on," said Doc, "when Americans start arguing over guns, you're gonna have trouble."

"It has potential as our target," said Church, "and the timing is right."

"If you want to jump to really big crowds, the next couple of megaevents are coming up," Nikki said. "The biggest is Going Viral, that big beg-a-thon concert to raise money for families hit hardest by last year's shutdowns. But no one's throwing stones at that because people right across the electorate were affected. Right, Left, whatever. They expect the concert to raise something like eighty million, between ticket sales, merch, and online donations. And because this is in the South, there's a high proportion of country artists, though there are R&B and hip-hop, too. A bit of everything."

"How many people are expected for that?" asked Wilson.

"At the venue? Eighty-five thousand, not counting tailgate parties and all that. Lots of small ancillary events, too. Autograph booths, celebs visiting local families. That kind of thing."

"When is the concert?" asked Church.

"This weekend," said Nikki. "It's all over the news, trending on social media."

Wilson looked at Church. "Are you thinking that's the target?"

"It fits the profile for a big-ticket hit," said Church.

"Right, but the trucks from the Pavilion would barely have time to make it."

"*Barely* is not *can't*," said Church. "Reach out to the organizers, call in any markers you have. If we can't shut it down, then we need to have our people in the venue and with official status. Get Homeland on this as well. You know who to call."

"On it," said Wilson, and he left the room at a brisk walk.

Church stared at the long list of other events.

"Walk us through all of it," he said.

CHAPTER 150
ABOARD THE *SOPHIA YIN*
FORT LAUDERDALE, FLORIDA

Ghost was fine.

"The big thing, apart from potential infection," said Jean, "was the pressure on a nerve cluster. Once he wakes up, he'll be pretty much pain-free. Just be sure he drinks water and eats as much as he can manage."

"He can manage a lot."

"Good. A juicy steak will help. All that protein."

"He'll love you forever."

"He's *your* dog."

I smiled. "I can't thank you enough, Jean."

"He's your dog," she said again. "That makes him family."

It was an oddly touching thing for her to say.

I nipped out and came back with some truly heroic steaks, which we grilled and ate with steamed vegetables, mashed sweet potato, and wine. I put Ghost's steak—which looked like it was cut from a woolly mammoth—in the fridge because he was snoring.

Jean and I went up to the sundeck where we watched a line of pelicans coast on the thermals, and we sipped dark Mexican beer. There was a sun tarp angled to block casual observation from the pier, and I had a hat with a floppy brim, a Miami Dolphins T-shirt, and sunglasses. Protective coloration.

For reasons that I can never adequately explain, I opened up to her. Sometimes what one needs is a disinterested third party. Like a lawyer or a shrink. Not a friend, per se, but an ally. Someone who understands the way the world is assembled and who put which piece into place. Jean was like that. Few people are on her level of insight.

We sat together for the next hour before she broke into my brooding silence. I caught her studying me for long periods of time, and after trying to ignore it, I said, "What?"

It came out more belligerently than intended.

She smiled. "Have to say, Joe, you look like fifty miles of bad road."

"I thought the expression was 'forty miles.'"

"Have you looked in a mirror?"

"Funny."

"No," she said, "it's not. By any metric, you're a goddamn mess. You've lost too much weight, your skin color can best be described as an unhealthy pallor, your fingers keep twitching, and there's a sense of *wrongness* about you."

"Wrongness? Since when are you metaphysical?"

"Since never. Just telling you what I see."

"I'm fine."

"Ri-i-i-i-ight," she said. "And I'm the queen of all the mermaids."

I drank my beer. The sun inched toward the horizon, lengthening the shadows.

"You haven't called Junie yet, have you?"

I shook my head.

She said, "I nearly did while you were in the head taking a shower."

I looked at her. "Why didn't you?"

"Because you didn't say it was okay," she said.

I sipped my beer. "Thanks."

"But I'll call her after you leave."

"Please don't."

She shook her head. "You don't get to ask that."

"Why the hell not?"

"House rules," she said. "No deliberate cruelty."

"It's not your business, Jean."

She snorted. "It became my business when you came on this boat." She paused to drain her bottle and then fished a pair of fresh ones from the cooler between us. She unscrewed the tops with deft twists of her strong brown hand and offered one to me. I took it. We didn't clink because it wasn't that kind of day. "I don't know you that well, Joe. I knew your dad better. Actually had my eye on him for a while, even though he was older than I was."

"Oh god, don't tell me that."

"Hush now," she said. "Your dad talked about you a lot. I know what happened when you were a kid. I have some idea what it did to you and what it's still doing. To use precise clinical terms, Joe, you're out of your freaking mind."

"I can see why Dad liked you. It's the sexy technical jargon."

She threw a peanut at me. "My point is that Junie knows all of this, too. Probably better than anyone except that ol' teddy bear Rudy Sanchez. She knows about your damage, and she loves you anyway. Loves you with her whole heart, and that is a considerable thing to say, especially when there's no exaggeration in the observation. And before you open your mouth and say something dumb, I have a bit of insight into her, too. We had a lot of long, good talks. She opened up to me. I know about her—how should I phrase this?—*unusual* genetic history. I know that she has been badly hurt a few times because she's in your life. That maniac who shot her, all those glass cuts she got during that hospital attack, and then getting impaled Christmas Eve."

"That's my point," I said. "All I can offer her is pain. I'm nothing but bad luck to her. And, besides, she doesn't know about the Darkness."

Jean got up, walked over to stand in front of me, leaned down to place both hands on the arms of my chair.

"You listen to me, Joseph Edwin Ledger," she said sternly. "Junie Flynn is my friend, and you will not sit on my sundeck and bad-mouth her."

"I didn't," I protested. "I'm talking about myself and—"

"Do I have to hit you? I know you're fast, but I bet you I'll get a damned good one in if you keep talking like that."

I said nothing.

"Do you think that Junie defines her life, her happiness, her love on whether you can keep her safe? Do you think she's such a fragile maiden that she needs you to protect her from the big bad world? God, and here I thought you were one of the enlightened ones. A male who doesn't think his woman revolves around him like a moon."

"I—"

"Do you think she's so shallow that she'd just bail when it all got tough? She was *born* to a tough life. Every bit as tough as yours, but without the support system you had with your folks and with Rudy. She's brave and brilliant and, for some damned reason, is committed to you. Sure, there's no marriage certificate, but she's in it for better or worse, in sickness and in health."

"She doesn't know what I've done," I said. "What I've been through since—"

She was right; she did get in a good one. Two, actually. A sharp slap that knocked my face sideways and a backhand that banged me straight again. Then she leaned forward until her nose was an inch from mine.

"You think *you're* in hell, Joe," she snarled. "Imagine the hell Junie's been through these last weeks. Do you know how many times she's called me? And I've called her? And you have the audacity, the arrogance to think she's so weak that this will break her? Sure, she's a vegan post-hippie new age tree hugger who doesn't like guns and would rather watch a chick flick than binge-watch the latest season of *The Boys* with you, but that doesn't mean she's weak. Don't forget your history, Ledger. Benevolence, compassion, honesty, loyalty, honor—qualities that define her were also tenets of the goddamned samurai."

My face stung, but the burn of my flushing cheeks hurt more.

"You call her soon, or so help me, I'll find you and break something you don't want broken."

She pushed off the arms of my chair and slumped back into hers. We drank.

We drank a lot.

After an hour, she got up, yawned so loudly her jaw creaked, gave me a long, frank, disapproving glare, and trundled off to bed. By then, the sun was down and I stayed there, drinking the last beer very slowly, watching the sky to see what stars were going to catch fire. There was laughter and music from nearby boats, and the soft-heavy slap of water against the hull as the last of the day's fishing boats made their way to their slips.

CHAPTER 151
ABOARD THE *SOPHIA YIN*
FORT LAUDERDALE, FLORIDA

It's the small things that can kill you or keep you alive.

I fell asleep in the deck chair and drifted into some truly awful dreams. Nicodemus hunted me through a burning city. Towers flared like candles and melted like wax. The glass windows of every store were a cracked mirror reflecting hundreds of distorted versions of me. Each aspect was that of a dying man infected by some horrific plague that was quickly turning my skin to a sickly red black. Ragged black birds fled across the sky, but the fingers of flame reached up from the buildings and set them alight. They fell, burning and screaming like children.

Behind me, Nicodemus stalked in relentless pursuit. He was a hundred feet tall, and his eyes were fire. A black serpent's tongue lolled from his laughing mouth, and his teeth were filed to dagger points.

There was nowhere to run, no safety to find. No shelter from the awareness that I was fighting something that could never be defeated. A monster without pity or reason or vulnerabilities.

I was aware that I was dreaming, but no matter how I tried, the dream would not let me go. I couldn't escape it.

And then I heard a creak of a heavy foot on wood. Even way down deep in the dream, I could tell that it was stealthy, because it stopped

JONATHAN MABERRY

so suddenly and there was a hiss of a voice. No words, just the kind of sound one person makes when someone else has been incautious.

And I knew that I was in trouble.

I came awake all at once and launched myself out of the deck chair, diving, rolling, coming up ten feet from where I'd been just as lightning cracked and thunder boomed. Only it was really a muzzle flash and a bullet punching into the chair.

In that split second of fiery light, I saw them.

Two men, guns in hand, standing at the top of the gangway.

I had no gun, but there was a shark rifle under the topside control panel. I dived for that, tore it from the clips, and came up firing.

A hollow click. Of course it was unloaded here in port.

I was already in motion, though, using the darkness, swinging the rifle like a club even as both of them fired. Something burned a line along my right side, but I didn't care. The rifle stock caught the first man on the temple. I'd put all my strength and all my fear into that swing, and his face disintegrated. He sagged sideways and would have fallen if not for the hand ropes.

The other man turned and fired at me, but I was ducking and surging forward in a driving tackle that took us both down the gangway. His next shot went high, and I kept ramming until we were on the dock. The angle of the gangway and the force of my impact made him stumble and fall, and I landed on him, dropping my knee into his crotch with devastating effect. He screamed, but I chunked him in the forehead with the stock of the rifle, and the scream died.

Lights were coming on in the neighboring boats. People began yelling, telling whoever was setting off fireworks to damn well stop.

There were no more shots.

I crouched over the second shooter.

"Sorry!" I yelled into the darkness, trying to make my voice sound like a drunk's.

The unseen neighbor told me to sober up and go the hell home.

My heart was hammering as I fished for his handgun, but it was gone. Dropped in the fight. I rose up into a crouch and scouted around, sticking to the darkest shadows. No one else seemed to be moving.

I ran back up the gangway and saw a shape detach itself from the blackness. There was a glint of moonlight on a pistol barrel.

But it was in Jean's hand.

"Joe . . . ?"

CHAPTER 152
ABOARD THE *SOPHIA YIN*
FORT LAUDERDALE, FLORIDA

It took some effort and a lot of stealth to get the two attackers aboard, below, and trussed up. The one I'd hit in the temple was in bad shape—not dead but clearly a skull fracture. Jean did what she could for him, which demonstrated a level of kindness that I did not share.

"He needs an ER," said Jean. "And a lot of surgery. You really mashed him. They'll be picking bone chips out of his brain, and he may lose an eye."

"He's lucky the shark rifle was unloaded," I said coldly. "And maybe he's lucky you're standing right here."

She studied me, then gave a small shake of her head.

The other man was hurt and maybe had a fractured pelvis, but he'd live. She gave him some painkillers. I searched the two men, found car keys and extra magazines for their guns. Then I went topside, found the pistol the first guy dropped, and went prowling. The keys belonged to a Chevy pickup truck with a camper body parked in the marina lot. I did a quick search and saw food wrappers, more ammunition, duct tape and plastic bags, and a bundle of leaflets for a group that called itself the New Founding Fathers. The rhetoric was all about a skewed set of American values, the righteousness of God's plan for the white race, and a lot of anti-Semitic garbage.

Then I returned to the *Sophia Yin*. Jean made coffee while I went through the stuff in their wallets. Head Wound was Brett Kovacks, thirty, of Saint Louis Street in LaBorde, Texas. Cracked Pelvis was Al Carson, twenty-seven, also of LaBorde. Their voter registrations listed them as Independent. Guess there wasn't an option for *asshole* as party affiliation.

Carson began to snore.

"How much painkiller did you give him?" I asked.

"Enough to put him out and keep him out."

"I wanted to question him."

Her eyes were hard and uncompromising. "I know, Joe, and I have a pretty good idea of *how* you'd phrase those questions."

"I—"

"No," she said, cutting me off. "This is my boat and my home. I'm not exactly a pacifist like Junie, and I'm okay with you doing whatever damage you needed to do to keep from getting killed, but I won't be a party to torture. I won't have that in my house."

And there was no way to move her from that stance.

Sure, I could have hit her with humanism and patriotism and all of that, but . . . I really did understand.

"They're probably not on the policy level anyway," I said, then sighed. "What do you want me to do? It's still dark. I can carry them up the pier a bit, dump them there, and make an anonymous call."

"That seems best."

So, that's what I did. Let the cops and the doctors at the local hospital figure out what happened, who gave them first aid, and what happened to their truck, because . . . yeah, I stole it.

Ghost slept in the camper body, and I drove. It was sixteen hours to LaBorde at posted speeds. I was pretty sure I could do it a lot faster.

CHAPTER 153
THE PAVILION
BLUE DIAMOND ELITE TRAINING CENTER
STEVENS COUNTY, WASHINGTON

Another group of Fixers was in the main turnaround, loading more crates and gear onto a truck. There were more of the fighting machines, and what concerned Top was that they had their ammunition packs already in place. That would only make sense if the machines were about to be deployed into combat.

Then Top saw the humped stack of parachutes. Personal ones— enough for every Fixer—and larger cargo chutes. Armed sentries stood guard, and HK's last administrative assistant was there to oversee the process.

Top and Bunny watched this from the jogging path.

"Population's getting a might thin 'round here," said Bunny. "Guess we're next."

When Top didn't answer, Bunny turned to him.

"What . . . ?"

Top shook his head. "What the hell are we doing, Farm Boy?"

"What do you mean?"

"We got all the intel we could," said Top, "but I'm starting to feel like the circus left town without us."

"This was the job, old man. Watch and report."

"And then what? Sweep up after?"

Bunny shoved his hands into his back pockets. "Hey, if you got something in mind, I'm all ears."

"Yeah," said Top, "I got something in mind."

He tapped the fake mole beside his ear and opened the Havoc Team channel. "Pappy to Jackpot, hear this. I need a Q1 unit and combat pack times two. Drop in on the jogging track closest to our suite. Pappy out."

Bunny grinned. "Well, shit, Top. Why didn't you just say it was party time?"

CHAPTER 154
I-75 FLORIDA TURNPIKE
COLUMBIA COUNTY, FLORIDA

I called Church as soon as I got onto the turnpike. When he answered, I told him where I was going and how I'd gotten that information.

"I'll have Scott smooth any legal issues for Ms. McGee-Thompson," he said. "And Bug can take care of media coverage."

"Thanks."

"What shape are you in?"

"Vaguely human."

"Amusing. It was a serious question."

"I know, and that's about as good an answer as I can give."

"And the Darkness?"

"Sleeping, I hope."

There was a considerable silence. "Outlaw," he said with surprising gentleness, "perhaps it's time to stand down and let someone else handle this from here on out."

"No," I said. "Screwed up or not, I've been making wins during this. I've been getting the intel that's allowed us to see the shape of what Kuga is planning. Call me superstitious, but I need to stay in the game until the final buzzer."

"Is that an objective assessment or hubris?"

"Bit of both, probably," I admitted. "But it's what I'm going to do. My question is whether you're going to lecture or help."

Was there a faintness of a sigh on the other end of the call? Not sure.

He said, "Tell me what you need."

"For starters, a full field kit," I said. "The works. Body armor, a coms unit, an ass-load of weapons, blaster-plasters, Q1 substation and tactical computer, Lightning Bugs, Busy-Bees and Killer Bees, a new Snellig and plenty of Sandman, a Wilson knife—you know the style I like. And anything else you think I could use."

"Done. I can have someone meet you with it."

"No. I want it waiting for me when I reach LaBorde. Have them drop it off at my dad's friend's house. Hap Collins." I gave him the address.

"Very well. What else?"

"Intel on that group the New Founding Fathers. If they have a clubhouse or something, I want to know where. If you can get names and addresses of their leaders and key members, get me that, too. Can you do all that?"

"Of course," he said. "What about backup?"

I hung up on him.

CHAPTER 155
THE PAVILION
BLUE DIAMOND ELITE TRAINING CENTER
STEVENS COUNTY, WASHINGTON

Top and Bunny walked into the administration building as if they had every right to be there. Stealth, they knew, came in a variety of forms, and sometimes brashness was the right method.

There was no one there, however.

The assistant was still overseeing the loading of the team's equipment.

Bunny carried the camouflaged gear bag Andrea had quietly left for them. He unzipped it, and they strapped on gun belts and shoulder rigs—the former for their Sig Sauers, the latter for the dart guns. Another item in the bag was Bunny's favorite playtoy, an Atchisson assault shotgun with a thirty-two-round drum magazine. He slapped in the drum and smiled like a kid on Christmas morning.

"Be careful with that, Farm Boy," said Top.

"You tell your grandma how to suck eggs?"

"No, my granny didn't blow the fuck up when she did."

"Yeah. Okay. There's that," said Bunny. "Guess I'll have to shoot them real careful like."

Top shook his head, muttering, "'Shoot them real careful like.' Jesus, Mary, and Joseph."

They stuffed their pockets with the small Lightning Bugs and fitted extra magazines into the belt slots and in pouches on chest harnesses. They did not have body armor, and neither wanted to wear the versions available for the Fixers. Wearing suicide vests had little appeal for either of them.

Bunny stood watch as Top set up the small MindReader Q1 substation, attaching various cables to the desktop computers. MindReader cracked through the sophisticated Pavilion security in under a minute. Top began opening transportation and logistics folders and suddenly froze.

"Ho-leeeee shit," he breathed.

"What is it?" asked Bunny, turning from the window.

"I know where the last team went and where this one is headed."

He turned the monitor so Bunny could see. The big young man leaned down.

"Going Viral?"

"Yeah."

"Oh shit."

"Yeah."

And immediately, Scott Wilson was on the line. "Pappy, we're seeing the same intel. This is it. This is what we've been waiting for. Excellent work."

"The concert's tonight," said another voice. Bug.

"Doesn't matter," said Top. "Looks like they're going to Spokane and then fly. I saw them packing parachutes, too. That venue is an open-air stadium. You'd better make sure someone gets control of that airspace and maybe shoots that goddamned plane down."

"Count on it."

"But this is only the *last* shipment. Two other teams headed down there days ago. Plenty of time for them to be in place. Not sure what it's going to take to cancel this thing."

"The venue is already in use," said Wilson. "There have been concerts from non-headliner bands since midnight last night."

Bug said, "I'm looking at the venue computers now. Shit, guys, there's twenty-two thousand people in there right now."

"Then *do* something," growled Top, "because I'm looking at medical services reports that tell me that more than half of the Fixers sent out have already had the R-33 packets implanted. You need to stop this."

Wilson's voice sounded lost. "I don't know if we can . . ."

"You damn well find a way," Top snarled and tapped out of the channel.

He looked up at Bunny.

"Yeah," said Bunny, reading the look in his eyes, "let's rock and roll."

CHAPTER 156
ON THE ROAD

I was on I-10 with a lot of miles to go. At the last rest stop, I checked on Ghost. His sleep seemed to have changed from the utter slackness of anesthesia to a more normal doze. Bit of a nose whistle. I stroked his fur for a minute and then got back on the road.

After forty minutes of outlining all the reasons I *shouldn't* do it, I summoned the courage and called Junie.

The phone rang for so long that I thought it would go to voice mail, but then she answered with a cautious, "Hello? Who's calling?"

She wouldn't have recognized the burner's number.

"Junie," I said. "It's me."

And we both began to cry.

CHAPTER 157
ON THE ROAD

It took us a long time to form words.

I kept telling her I was sorry.

She kept telling me she loved me.

Miles blurred.

"Joe," she said at last, her voice thick with emotion but clearer than it had been, "I spoke with Mr. Church. He told me about the Darkness and about . . . Nicodemus."

"Christ."

"That's what this is, Joe," she insisted. "He's doing this to you."

"I . . . I don't know, babe. It's still my head. It's still *me* doing all this."

"No, it isn't," she said sharply. "Goddamn it, listen to me. Was it Top's and Bunny's fault when Kuga took over their minds with the God Machine and made them kill those people that time? Were they monsters?"

"No, but—"

"So, how is this *your* fault?"

I tried to explain. This was a conversation I'd rehearsed a thousand times in my head. But everything that came out of my mouth was either an apology, an explanation for things she already understood, or lines cribbed from old books and movies. I felt like a bad actor reading scripts written for someone else who actually *had* talent. It was that level of depression where I felt like I was a minor and rather disappointing supporting character in someone else's story.

And with all that, Junie was there with me. For me.

In me.

I know that some of my colleagues in covert ops don't understand the connection I have with Junie. Hell, even Top and Bunny were rooting for me to make it work with Violin because she was a fellow soldier and that was a certain kind of family. Junie was an outsider. She walked a peacefuller path and, in her way with FreeTech and her own ideals, likely did more measurable good than a barbarian like me ever could.

But that's the nature of love, isn't it? You don't have to be cut from the same, or even similar, cloth. You don't need to compare scars won in combat to share commonality of essential truths.

Junie had her own scars, and yes, some of them had come through violence. Directly or indirectly, some had been cut into her skin and her soul by Nicodemus and Kuga and Rafael Santoro. It's sometimes too easy for a soldier to forget that civilians are fighting the war in their own way. It's easy for a trained fighter to perceive and respect the natural courage of those not in uniform.

Top was the first to understand this. Then Bunny. I suspect Church knew all along, and that's probably why he called her to share the truth. He knew what I doubted—that Junie was stronger than I am in some key ways.

The miles whipped by and the tires hummed on the road, and my woman—my dearest friend—did what I could not do and which none of my armed and battle-hardened soldier brothers could do. She brought me home.

CHAPTER 158
THE PAVILION
BLUE DIAMOND ELITE TRAINING CENTER
STEVENS COUNTY, WASHINGTON

Top tapped his coms unit and spoke to Havoc Team.

"You all heard?"

"Hooah," they said.

"We can't let these sons of whores leave," he said.

"Hooah." This time, there was a growl in it.

"Then here's what I want each of you to do." And he told them.

"Dinosaur balls!" gasped Andrea.

"Yes," said Belle, her voice low and without a shred of mercy.

"Sounds fun, boys," said Mia.

"Let's not be nice about it, either. Combat call signs from here out," Top said. "And we do this until it's done."

There was no stunned silence as the meaning sank in. Not with them. They gave a last *hooah*.

Top turned to Bunny. "You good?"

The big man from Orange County grinned. "Top, I've been doing exactly jack and shit since we came here. I'm so far past good you can't even see me."

Top held out his hand, and Bunny looked down at it. They shook and held the clasp for a long moment before releasing. It had the feeling of a farewell, but that was okay. They'd been through the Valley of the Shadow so many times. If this was the end, then they were both at peace with it.

"I heard the team plan, but what's *our* plan?"

"Plan? I intend to shoot a lot of motherfuckers. See where that gets us."

"Works for me."

They grinned at each other like kids about to slash the tires on the school bus.

They walked outside, bumped fists, and split up. Bunny plunged into the woods, and Top began walking along the path that would take him to the gymnasium.

CHAPTER 159
LABORDE, TEXAS

I reached LaBorde and got lost twice trying to find the place where my dad's old buddy lived. I'd been there and even had the address, but the GPS in the pickup kept taking me onto dead-end streets.

Then I saw the house.

The porch was shaded by old trees, and two older middle-aged guys—one white and one Black—were sitting on the porch. I parked and walked up to the foot of the stairs.

"Permission to come aboard," I said.

"Come on up," said the white man, and he got up with creaking knees to offer his hand.

Hap Collins was thin, unshaven, and looked like he'd spent the night getting beaten up behind a bar. There were bruises all over his face, and he had two black eyes and a big piece of bloodstained tape across the bridge of his nose.

"Jesus," I said, "what happened to you?"

"Someone took a serious dislike to him," said the Black man. "And you can't fault him for that."

Leonard Pine was the same age, with a bit of a beard going gray and a pale cowboy hat that had seen better decades. Like Hap, though, he was on the wiry side of lean and had the kind of calluses on his knuckles and other parts of his hands you only get from hitting heavy bags. Or heavy people.

"You're the son," he said.

"I'm the son." We shook.

"Met your dad a couple of times. Knew his way around a fishing line. We hauled in some bass. Nothing for the record books, but good to eat." He paused. "Sorry to hear about what happened."

I nodded. "Thanks. He told me some tall tales about you two."

"If he ever said Hap was good-looking, well hung, or kind to old ladies, then he was lying."

"Those three things never came up."

"Set a spell," said Hap, waving to a plastic milk crate on which someone had placed a rather pretty blue pillow. I sat.

The stories my dad had told me were often long, funny, painful, and insightful. Hap was a bleeding-heart liberal who'd gone to jail rather than Vietnam. Leonard, despite being a gay Black man, was a fiercely devoted Republican. All of which shows you that you can't go by assumptions. Deep South—the Black guy votes right and likes men; the white guy votes left and isn't much of a fan of country music.

When my dad first met them, Hap and Leonard were working in the rose field, cutting long stems for shit wages. But over the years, they'd gone through a number of adventures that—if Dad wasn't exaggerating—meant that they were serious badasses. Lately, they'd gone into business with Brett, Hap's wife, and were now officially licensed private investigators. Which, I assumed, was what accounted for Hap's face.

They had glasses of iced tea, and Hap went inside and got me one. He also brought out a plate of cookies. Goddamned vanilla wafers.

"Have one," said Hap, offering me the plate.

I smiled. "Thanks, but no."

"More for me," said Leonard and took the plate from Hap. There was a small tug-of-war about, but Leonard won. He smiled as he bit into the first one.

Seriously, what is it with vanilla wafers? Was Leonard Church's long-lost son? Was it some kind of cult thing? I had no idea.

I sipped the tea. It was excellent, with mint leaves floating in it.

"Got a couple of goody bags someone dropped off for you," said Leonard. "All kinds of *Mission Impossible* shit."

"Not that we looked," lied Hap.

"Hell yes, we looked," countered Leonard. "Don't know what half that shit is."

"Some of it goes bang," I said.

"Yeah, well, I didn't blow my dick off, so we're good."

I drank some tea.

Hap said, "This guy who called me, Mr. Church? He told me to tell you that you should tell us why you're here."

"Did he?"

"Said that we're—and I quote—'family adjacent.'"

I had to laugh. "Okay. That's a bigger thing than you know."

"But what's it mean?" asked Leonard.

I gave them the bones of it. They listened and asked good questions, but we didn't have any light bulb moments.

"So, you came all this way to poke around at the convention center with a bunch of governors people from their own states don't care about?" asked Leonard.

"Pretty much."

"We've heard about those New Founding Fathers," said Hap. "Not the usual militia crowd. Fewer beer bellies, more military tats. And they are almost genuinely well regulated."

"They're dangerous honky assholes," observed Pine.

"They are that, too," agreed Hap.

Leonard kicked my foot. "Hey, your truck's barking."

And it was. I went and opened the back and was assaulted by Ghost, who was sore, confused, hungry, and had to poop. Leonard and Hap came down, and I introduced them. Ghost seemed to understand immediately that they were dog people and that treats might be involved.

Ghost was limping pretty badly, though, so once he was done with his business, I picked him up and carried him into the house. Hap's idea. My dog met his dog, did the sniffing thing, and then Ghost decided that after his long sleep, he needed a nap.

"Not to be mean or anything," said Hap, "but you could use a shower, hoss."

"I don't think I can spare the time."

"Four minutes, for the sake of public safety?"

I relented, realizing that I smelled worse than what Ghost had dropped on the curb. I took the camo pants and black T-shirt from one of the two big black cases. No underwear, so I'd have to go commando, and that irony was not lost on me.

The shower felt great after fourteen and a half hours in a smoker's pickup truck. I even used Hap's deodorant and a little cologne.

"Hey," I said, "can I hit you for one more favor?"

"Not if it involves you eating my vanilla wafers," said Leonard.

"There's so little chance of that."

"Shoot," said Hap.

"Can I leave my dog here until I get back? He's in no shape to go with me."

Hap smiled. It youthened him. "Sure, no problem."

"Yeah, the dog's okay," agreed Leonard.

We shook hands, and I took my bags of nasty goodies and went out to my stolen truck.

CHAPTER 160
THE PAVILION
BLUE DIAMOND ELITE TRAINING CENTER
STEVENS COUNTY, WASHINGTON

Bunny met Mia in the woods. Even though they'd been in proximity for weeks, it was the first time they'd seen each other. At five two, she was more than a foot shorter than he was and half his weight.

"How's it hanging, Donnie Darko?" she asked.

"Might turn out to be a good day, Magpie."

They grinned at each other and moved like cats through the forest. The Fixers were nearly done loading the crated fighting machines onto the truck and were handing up the carefully packed parachutes. None of the Fixers doing the loading wore sidearms, but there were six guards with rifles.

"Where's Pappy?"

"He's coming," said Bunny, "but we don't need to wait for him. Fact is, we need to gather some intel 'cause what we find out is going to help whoever has to face the bigger squads down in Florida."

"What kind of intel?"

Bunny took a Lightning Bug from his pocket. "What we don't know—and what wasn't in the data Doc and her boys are looking at—is whether an EMP shutdown of their body armor will nullify the R-33 packets and the explosives or—"

"Or make them go boom," finished Mia.

"Yeah."

"Well, crap."

"Yeah."

Mia said, "Guess there's one way to find out." She patted his bulging biceps. "Bet you can throw that sucker farther than I can. So you do that, and I'll see if I can get some mischief going on 'round the other side. Worst case, we catch them in a cross fire and shorten the odds. And Mother Mercy's up there somewhere watching our backs. She'll want to play."

"I like this plan," said Bunny.

They split up, with Mia circling wide to come up on the other side. Bunny was always impressed by how she moved and wished she was on Havoc Team instead of Chaos. Maybe after this, something could be worked out.

He gave her a couple of minutes and then worked his way along a ridge, keeping low behind thick shrubs. When he was within fifty feet, he thumbed the switch on the Lightning Bug, rose up, threw with all his strength, and dropped back behind cover.

The device had just enough heft to make for a good throw. It arced over the truck and, just on the far side, detonated. In bright daylight, it was only a flash that was nearly invisible. And its mild *pop* was buried beneath the sound of men working. Bunny flattened out with the ridge crest between him and any resulting explosion.

The forklift jerked to a stop, a crate almost level with the flatbed.

"What the hell?" he heard someone growl.

Men clustered around the forklift, offering the kind of useless suggestions people always thought worth sharing. There was no explosion.

Until there was.

But it wasn't the massive blast Wilson had told them to expect. This was a good, deep solid *crump* of a standard-issue fragmentation grenade.

The blast caught everyone by surprise and punched the crated fighting machine off the forklift. The crate slammed against the side of the truck and then crashed to the ground, burning wood showering men who lay dazed and bleeding.

The other Fixers scattered.

Mia rose up and hosed them with her M5, burning through a full magazine and tearing two men to rags. Then she dropped down, rolled into a gully, and ran like hell as return fire from the sentries tore apart the place where she'd been. One of the sentries suddenly jerked forward, the entire front of his face disintegrating as a sniper round found him.

Bunny laughed. This was Magpie and Mother Mercy doing what they did, the fierce women scoring first blood.

As unarmed Fixers ran around to hide behind the truck, Bunny laid his combat shotgun on the ridgetop and opened fire.

A bird drone soared past him and buzzed one of the sentries, who spun and fired at it, but in doing so came out from the cover of the open truck door. Magpie and Mother Mercy both hit him, and the man seemed to become a cloud of red mist.

"Hoo-fucking-ah," laughed Bunny as he poured fire down the hill.

CHAPTER 161
EAST TEXAS CONVENTION CENTER
LABORDE, TEXAS

It was drizzling when I pulled into the parking lot for the convention center. There was a sea of cars, with perhaps a bias toward pickup trucks of every make, model, color, and condition. Not particularly surprising in the South. A whole roped-off area for black SUVs, too, and lots of cops on foot and motor patrol. No hordes of Fixers in evidence, but I hadn't really expected any. On the way there, I'd gotten a call from Church informing me that Top had discovered the real target—the Going Viral charity fundraiser back in Lauder-damn-dale, where I'd just left.

Ah well. Maybe I didn't need another gun battle, you know? My nerves were totally shot, and I hadn't slept in two days. I was, at least, a freshly washed zombie.

Checking this place out was the tactical equivalent of dotting the last *i*.

Then what?

Home.

To Junie, who was at FreeTech in San Diego.

Home, maybe for good.

The Darkness in my head was quiet. Was it gone? Had Church's revelation that Nicodemus was working mojo on me somehow broken the spell? I looked around for night birds, but if they were there, then the rain hid them. Or maybe they were off scaring the piss out of some other poor schlump. It didn't exactly make me weep with longing that they weren't here.

Oh yeah, and fuck Nicodemus. Maybe Church didn't do the job right. Maybe the old stories are true, and you have to drive a stake through his black heart. No, that doesn't mean I think he's a vampire. It just occurs to me that a sharpened piece of lumber through the ticker tends to do the trick. I'm not above beheading, either. There's a reason those have been fan favorites for a long while. Just saying.

In a weird way, it almost made me smile. I was legitimately considering the possibility that supernatural evil existed and that I was a victim of a real-world magic spell. It is to laugh. The world, it seemed, was even crazier than I was, and that was not a low bar.

I found a spot and parked the truck, killed the engine, and opened one of the cases. From it, I took a nylon shoulder holster and snugged the gas dart pistol into it, then clipped a Sig Sauer to my belt. There was a jacket with lots of pockets padded to hide the magazines I was shoving into slots. As promised, there was a tidy little Wilson Rapid Response folding combat knife there, and I clipped it to the inside of my right pants pocket. It has a three-and-a-half-inch blade that locks into place with the flick of a thumb. It's short, but the weapon weighs so little that it puts no drag on the hand, allowing for top speed and dexterity.

There were several sets of IDs in the bag, all nicely built around identities Bug had set up for me. I picked one that said that I was a special agent of the Secret Service. Anyone running that ID would discover it was rock solid, because that's how Bug rolls. And Church would have made a few calls to ensure that I was allowed total access.

I was about to pop the door when I decided what the hell and stuffed a few of Doc Holliday's electronic goodies into my pocket because—no apologies—I am a pessimistic sumbitch on my best days.

Then I got out and jogged through the rain to the building. There was a big banner strung across the front of the convention center, welcoming the United States governors. It occurred to me that I doubted I could name five of them, let alone all fifty. I am, by nature and inclination, apolitical. I kind of despise the people on both sides of the aisle because they are typically self-serving con men and op-portunists. Sure, I vote, even with absentee ballots sent from Greece, but more than half the time, it was a coin toss. Or me edging toward the lesser of two evils. If it were up to me, I'd replace the system with a roomful of wombats, and I think history would validate my decision.

A hell of a lot of umbrellas created a decorative river flowing into the convention center. Texas was an open-carry state, but even so, I was amazed that anyone was being admitted with a sidearm to a rally with all these political figures.

I bypassed the lane and walked right to the door, where a guard tried to wave me back into the press until he saw the ID wallet I held up. The door guards did their due diligence and checked me out, then gave me a snazzy clip-on badge and waved me through.

"You get hung up in traffic?" asked the guard. "You almost missed the show."

"Wouldn't want to do that," I said and gave him a quick profes-sional smile. The kind that only reaches the mouth and means noth-ing. He reciprocated in kind.

Inside, it was more crowded than I'd expected, though still mod-est as political events went. There was so much lingering exhaustion from the last presidential gutter fight. The floor was damp from wa-ter running from folded umbrellas and lots of yellow rain slickers and cowboy Stetsons. Bit of a Marlboro Man convention, but that was okay. Lots of farms in Texas.

I tapped into the TOC channel for the first time in a month.

"Outlaw," said Wilson, "my dear fellow. Let me say what a great relief and pleasure it is to have you back with us."

"Sure," I said blandly. "Hooray."

I told him where I was and that everything looked nice and calm and wonderfully boring.

"Rather a delight to hear it," he said.

"No joke."

Church came on the line. "Outlaw, be advised that Havoc Team has engaged a group of Fixers at the Pavilion. Will provide details as we get them."

That stopped me. "Do they have backup?"

"We have assets in the air, but this was an impromptu mission," said Church. "Pappy called the play based on activity unfolding on the ground. We rolled Bedlam Team from their staging area in Spokane, but they're still an hour out. The National Guard is sending helos, but they are forty minutes away."

"Shit."

Regret stabbed me, because had I not gone on my weird mission, I would have been with them and could have helped.

And . . . I realized how arrogant that thought was. Top was a brilliant, brave, and extremely experienced soldier and leader of troops. If not for his loyalty to me, he'd have easily earned his own team years ago. Bunny, too. They didn't need me to do their jobs at an exceptional level.

Yeah, Rudy was going to have a real piece of work cut out for him when he finally got me on his couch again. I did not envy him that.

To the folks at the TOC, I said, "I'll hang around here for a couple of hours. Talk to the heads of the various security details, look backstage and whatnot. But I think this was, at best, a feint or maybe a plan B. Lauderdale is where the fun's going to be."

"We are in the process of evacuating that venue now," said Wilson.

"Hey, sugar buns," said the sweet voice of Doc Holliday. "Got some potentially good news for you."

"Jeez," I said, "*please,* for the love of god."

"Bunny said that so far it *seems*—and notice how I'm leaning ever so slightly on that word—that my little Lightning Bugs can scramble the eggs of the Fixer tech without causing it to go boom."

"Well . . . hell . . . that's actually awesome."

"And Mr. Church has talked the president into putting a plane in the air heading for Fort Lauderdale, with an e-bomb in it. Mind you, it'll fry cell phones, cars, and computers and do about five billion dollars' worth of damage to the city infrastructure, and it won't do anyone any good if they're in surgery or wearing a pacemaker . . . but it will keep those K-110 fighting machines from turning a hundred thousand people into hot dust."

"So, when you say *good news,* you're being facetious?"

"Just a little."

"Swell. Maybe go look up what *good* means and . . ."

My voice trailed off as I looked up at a digital sign above the huge dais set up. It was a welcome message for the governors.

The fifty governors of the United States.

And the governors of American Samoa, Guam, Northern Mariana Islands, Puerto Rico, and the U.S. Virgin Islands.

It stopped me dead in my tracks.

There weren't fifty American governors. Not when you added the five territories.

There were fifty-five.

And they were all here.

"Jesus Christ," I said.

"What?" asked Church.

"G-55. It's right here."

CHAPTER 162
THE PAVILION
BLUE DIAMOND ELITE TRAINING CENTER
STEVENS COUNTY, WASHINGTON

Bunny kept firing as he moved laterally along the ridge. He was firing explosive rounds, and the whole area around the truck was pocked with smoking craters. Half a dozen bodies lay in the path of his barrage, and more lay where Mia or Belle had dropped them.

But now the Fixers were rallying. Those who were unarmed had crawled under the semi while two brave—and foolish—techs climbed onto the truck, opened a crate, and were handing guns and ammunition belts down. Mia shot one of them, but the other was at an angle that afforded no clear hit. Until, that is, he moved to his right to hand a belt of grenades down to another Fixer, and as he leaned out, it gave Belle three inches of his forehead to aim at. Even at 180 yards, that was enough.

The Fixers under the truck loaded their weapons and opened up, and the fusillade drove Bunny down behind the ridge. Two of them shimmied to the end of the semi and began trying to pick Mia off, and she, too, had to find better cover.

Belle was providing as much plunging fire as she could, but the Fixers were making maximum use of the semi.

There was a roar, and an armored personnel carrier came rocketing along the road from the front gate, with a Fixer in full armor standing behind a Browning .50-caliber machine gun, and he filled the trees with a deadly swarm of bullets. Belle's sniper fire stopped, and Bunny's heart sank.

He ran down a gully and burst out onto the road around the bend from the battle zone, swapping in a new drum for his shotgun. A Fixer in full armor came out of nowhere and swatted the weapon from his hand, and the brutal impact was so intense that it sent Bunny sprawling.

The Fixer laughed loudly and wickedly, and as Bunny scrambled to his feet, he saw that the man's eyes were turning a weird and dangerous red. R-33 was already at work, sending that deadly mix of chemicals that powered him up and drove him to madness and rage.

"Oh shit!" cried Bunny as the man charged at him, raising an AK-47. Bunny dived for cover, rolled, and came up with his handgun in a two-handed grip, firing center mass. The bullets barely staggered the Fixer, who burned through half a mag trying to kill him. But Bunny was moving, using trees as cover, letting their trunks soak up the rounds as he took running potshots, hoping to get a head shot.

On the far side of the truck, Mia was running low at the bottom of a rain gutter, swapping a new magazine in, and then coming up at an angle that put one of the semi's double rear tires between her and the shooters. She saw a foot sticking out past the tires and blew it off with a three-round burst.

As she ran, there was a sound that made her blood run cold. It was a mechanical noise like a hydraulic loader powering up. A moment later, one of the crates burst apart as a K-110 fighting machine rose up. It spun toward her, and the six barrels of the minigun whined as they spun, sending a barrage of death at Mia.

CHAPTER 163
EAST TEXAS CONVENTION CENTER
LABORDE, TEXAS

I glanced around the room, and suddenly everything looked like a threat.

All those big men in concealing rain slickers and cowboy hats—were they Fixers? Were they with the New Founding Fathers? The swirling crowds held umbrellas that I knew from spy craft could conceal guns and knives. I knew the attendees had come in through metal detectors, but I also knew how subtle Santoro was in his long game. There was every chance he could have applied his cruel techniques of coercion to force them to allow Kuga's killers in through security. Hell, maybe the event staff itself was under Santoro's thumb. I'd learned the hard way that no one is safe from that little murderous bastard.

My thoughts were so tangled that I was not paying sufficient attention to the droning voice over the PA system, but the sudden applause smacked me back to full awareness. I turned to see lines of well-dressed men and women filing out of doors on either side of the dais. Local and state police, along with a mix of Secret Service agents, stood facing the crowd, eyes watching.

The fifty-five governors were coming into the room.

"Grendel," I said, using Wilson's call sign, "we need to shut this down right now."

"I'm on the phone with the chief of security—"

I lost whatever else he was going to say, because suddenly a big man stepped out of the crowd and removed a folded sheet of cardboard that he spread wide as he raised it over his head. In big black letters, it read:

TRAITORS TO THE AMERICAN WAY

And below that were the letters *NFF.*
New Founding Fathers.
But then another man held up a sign:

All around the room, people—men and women—were raising signs. Some were slogans, but most had an acronym, a logo, or the actual name of some group. There were at least a dozen different extremist militia groups, including a few that had figured prominently in last year's BLM riots, but there were also Black Lives Matter signs, Blue Lives Matter, the Second Amendment Coalition, and others, including one claiming to be Antifa. The hall had suddenly become a microcosm of American political hot-button contention. White, Black, and brown people were suddenly waving their placards and shouting while onstage the governors stood in uncertain clusters, glancing at security, jabbering with one another, and a few trying to calm the protesters. In the crowd, I could see everyone with a cell phone taking pics.

There was not one part of this that made sense.

All the protesters had used essentially the same tricks—sneaking signs in—and they were spaced too evenly, too thoroughly throughout the audience. The signs had a cliché nature to them, as if they were movie props intended to sell the theme of the moment.

Which, of course, they had to be.

And another few pieces of the puzzle clicked into place. This wasn't misdirection to draw focus from Going Viral. I think *this* was plan A all along. Make sure the public got all those signs—and more to the point—each of those groups on cell camera videos. Give it just enough time for those pics and vids to land on Twitter and the other social media platforms. Then start a riot in this convention center. The big play? Maybe capture or, likelier, kill as many governors as possible. There were groups planning that late last year but doing it piecemeal. Kuga never did things small. Fifty-five governors, a big split between red and blue states. People seeded into the crowd who were likely legitimate, though politically manipulated members of those groups; and maybe a goodly number of Fixers playing roles. Let the whole country see that Americans were willing to up the ante and go big in the worst possible way. Put it in a pot and stir until you have a new civil war.

Kuga sold arms and was apolitical; he'd sell them to anyone. To everyone. He was creating a brand-new and enduring client base. This plan was brilliant, and it was scary as *hell*.

And I was right in the middle of it.

I saw the exact moment when the choreography of disaster began.

Two men—one white, one Black—were yelling at each other. Very loudly, and with a lot of jabbing of fingers inches from each other's faces. I know there's a lot of racism in America, but this was too picture-perfect. A large white man with swastika neck tattoos and a Black man with a do-rag and a T-shirt with a picture of George Floyd.

"Shut this down!" I yelled to Wilson or Church or whoever the hell was listening. I began making my way through the crowd, pushing past people, shoving some aside, holding up my fake ID, announcing that I was Secret Service.

I might as well have been invisible for all the good I accomplished, because by the time I reached the fringe of the circle of folks—all of whom were now screaming their hate—both the white man and the Black man pulled guns.

I tapped my com unit. "Christ, send backup. Now."

The whole room became a war zone.

Just.

That.

Fast.

CHAPTER 164

THE PAVILION
BLUE DIAMOND ELITE TRAINING CENTER
STEVENS COUNTY, WASHINGTON

Mia ran fast, but the bullets were so much faster. Two of them caught her between the shoulder blades and punched all the air out of her lungs. She fell hard and rolled badly, coming to rest in a gap between two pines. The body armor had saved her life, but the impact had been tremendous. Pain seemed to pulse outward from both sides of her spine, and breathing was a real challenge.

The minigun chopped at the trees, creating a cyclone of flying bark and pine needles. Mia crawled as fast as she could and tumbled over into a small natural depression as the forest above her was chewed apart.

She tried to make sense of this. Clearly, the Lightning Bug hadn't knocked out all the electronics on those goddamned machines. Maybe the mini-EMP bomb had been too far away, or maybe the K-110's computers were shielded. She didn't know and, in that moment, did not care.

Something whipped by overhead and flew straight at the fighting machine. It was one of Andrea's crow drones. The birds were unarmed, but it paused in midair, hovering like a hummingbird right in front of the driver's face mask. The minigun's angle of fire went totally wild for a moment, and then stopped as the driver tried to swat the drone away.

That gave Mia a chance, and—despite the agony in her back and only spoonfuls of air in her lungs—she got to fingers and toes and scampered away through the brush.

Bunny was still engaged in a running fight, pausing for one second only every few yards to turn and fire an explosive shell at the Fixers. Four of them were on the far side of the K-110 that had fired at Mia, and they were using crowbars and hand spikes to clumsy another of the big crates toward the edge of the flatbed. Belle hammered at the crate, but the bulky container effectively blocked the Fixers.

Bunny knelt beside a tree, aimed, and fired, but his shot went high and hit the top of the crate instead of one of the Fixers. The explosion blew off one side of the huge wooden box, and the fighting machine inside toppled out. The four men scattered, but one was half a step too slow, and the K-110 smashed down on his rear leg. He collapsed screaming. The other men snuck under the truck and squirmed up and out again with the fallen machine as cover. Bunny saw a glint of metal and glass as the access hatch opened and a Fixer wriggled inside. He fired at the cowling, but even though he scored a direct hit, the K-110 hummed to life.

The ungainly device got to its feet, and the driver brought the gun arms up. Bunny hit it again and again with high-explosive rounds, but if it did any damage, he couldn't see it. He had more of the Lightning Bugs in his pocket, but he was way too far out of range. He was going to have to get a lot closer to try to fry those things. Just as he set himself to move, the second K-110 opened up with its machine gun, forcing him to turn and run for cover. Going away from the thing.

He glanced back as he ran and saw that the first machine had turned to return fire from the trees—Belle or Andrea, Bunny couldn't tell—and from that angle, the thing was able to cover the attempt by one of the Fixers to climb into the semi's cab.

CHAPTER 165
EAST TEXAS CONVENTION CENTER
LABORDE, TEXAS

It was a brawl.

It was a gunfight.

It was total chaos.

The white man and the Black man who'd been yelling at each other both drew their guns and fired. What surprised me was that they actually fired. That made no sense if they were Fixers. Was I possibly wrong about this being a staged fight? Had all Santoro and Kuga done was manipulate disparate groups into a situation where violence was inevitable?

No. That was too convenient, too pat.

The men fired as they tried to duck for cover. Neither hit the other, but the screaming civilians behind them were not as lucky. I saw a woman with an old MAGA hat fall, dragging her young son down with her. No way to tell if the kid had been shot. On the other side, a Black man with gray hair and a preacher's Roman collar spun away, hands clamped to a bleeding stomach.

Other people fell, though many were diving for cover.

On the dais, police and security personnel were pushing the governors down into crouches and shoving them in stumbling runs toward the exits.

But then the exit doors banged open, and that's when I knew that

I'd been right about it all. Four big men emerged from the exits, a mix of races, all of them armed and moving as precise military units. These were the Fixers, dressed in civilian clothes. No fancy body armor, no cybernetic fighting machines. Hopefully no goddamn explosives. But from their speed and the bellows of fury they howled into the air, I knew they were being driven by R-33. And they were both relentless and filled with rage as they plowed into the security teams.

I saw so many people go down in the first barrage—cops, uniformed security, aides, tech staff, and some of the governors. No way to tell how many were hit or how badly. All around me, people were fighting. Rioting. And again, no clear way of determining who was a militiaman or radical tricked into coming here, who was a Fixer seeded into the audience, and who was just a civilian whose simmering political anger had boiled over. It was a true melee, a free-for-all.

I saw all of this while moving.

I pulled the Snellig and, as I ran through the thrashing crowd, shot anyone who'd been holding a placard, anyone holding a gun, anyone clearly going after a civilian. I wanted to get to the dais and take out the Fixers, but there was a churning sea of people between me and them.

A fat man with a huge beer belly and massive forearms got in my way and threw a head-smasher of a punch at me. I ducked it, rammed my shoulder into that belly, and used him as a combination shield and battering ram as I slammed into the Black man who'd accidentally shot the woman. I rose up, headbutting the fat guy. I stamped hard on his foot, splintering the bones, and leaned past him to shoot the white guy who'd nailed the preacher. Then I shot the Black guy. All three went down, and I quickly knelt by the preacher, but he was dead, his eyes staring up with profound surprise at the heavens. As I turned toward the woman with the kid, I saw someone else kneeling to help. Good.

As I rose, something hit me hard on the back, and I whirled to see a very old white woman with an umbrella. She began hammering at me and calling me some of the filthiest names I'd ever heard.

I let Sandman hush her up, but I caught her as she fell and laid her gently on the floor. Her hand flopped over and lay almost precisely in the outflung palm of the dead minister. I wonder if *that* would trend on Twitter.

Yeah, the world was mad.

I began moving, firing at active shooters, avoiding counterattacks by the dazed and confused.

When I was within ten feet of the dais, a voice rang out, sharp and clear, even with all the ambient furor.

"*Ledger!*"

My name had been yelled with such anger and shock that it jolted me. I turned and looked up, and there, on the stage, was *Rafael Santoro*.

CHAPTER 166
THE PAVILION
BLUE DIAMOND ELITE TRAINING CENTER
STEVENS COUNTY, WASHINGTON

The K-110 on the back of the semi bashed the crow drone away, sending it tumbling and broken into the grass beside the truck.

More of the bird drones swarmed in, but the fighting machine simply ignored them and kept pouring covering fire into the trees. The sheer destructive power of the minigun was denuding the slope of trees and shrubs, destroying any chance for a stealthy advance.

Fixers were now swarming up onto the semi and attacking the remaining packing crates. Two of them began tossing body armor to the others, who ducked down to gear up. But they froze as an explosion sounded deeper inside the Pavilion complex.

"Pappy," yelled Bunny into his coms, "where the hell are you?"

"On my way, Farm Boy," came the reply.

"Hurry the hell up, old man."

Was that a laugh he heard or a curse? Hard to tell with all the noise.

He was out of the effective range of the minigun and well beyond the useful range of his own weapons, so he broke into a run as he began a wide circle. The fact that the camp was deliberately smothered by thick trees was a blessing in disguise, because it allowed him to make maximum use of cover.

Movement ahead made him drop to one knee and freeze beside an old oak. Two Fixers in full armor were running down the slope toward the road. They must have come from another guard post and managed to suit up before joining the action. They were heading directly his way, but he didn't think they'd spotted him yet.

Bunny weighed his options. Let them pass and use their approach to disguise his own? Or ambush them and at least try to cripple both to prevent them from joining the fight?

He was familiar with the Fixer body armor now and knew that there were vulnerable points. No armor made could protect every single area of the body. The need for flexible and nimble movement came with a price. That was half the challenge; the other half was to stop them without killing either, because he didn't think he could outrun the resulting blast.

He swapped the drum of explosive rounds for double-aught buck, and as they ran past, he opened up on full auto from twelve feet. The heavy sprays of buckshot scythed through the flexible knee joints, and both Fixers screamed as they fell. One of them lost his entire lower leg in a grotesque shower of bright blood.

Bunny was up and moving before either had a chance to bleed out.

He got all the way down to the road when that side of the hill seemed to tear itself free of the earth with a monstrous thunder strike of sound. Pieces of torn turf and shattered trees chased Bunny, hammered him, and finally smashed him to the ground.

The blast plucked Mia out of her hiding place behind a massive dogwood. The leaves of the tree burst into flame as pieces of burning debris landed among the branches.

Flash-burned and half-dazed, Mia staggered away, blinking and pawing away blood from her nose. She suddenly realized that she no longer held a gun, but when she looked back, the entire area around the dogwood was ablaze. The breeze was blowing from the north, pushing little dancing demons of flame into the tall summer grass.

"Oh . . . shit," she wheezed as she turned and ran. She slapped the Sig Sauer from her holster and held on to that for dear life, as much for its deadly potential as for a talisman.

She reached the road ahead of the semi and saw that every one of the Fixers was either firing toward the trees where Belle's sniper fire had come, off to the east where she'd seen Bunny hightail it, or toward the explosion up the slope. No one was looking in her direction.

Then there was a roar as the semi's big engine growled itself awake.

Her heart sank, because there were now three fighting machines on the back of the semi with drivers in them. More than half of the Fixers were aboard, too, using the rest of the packing crates as cover as they waited to simply be driven out of the firefight.

She and her friends in Havoc Team had done a lot of damage, but not nearly enough. These Fixers and their deadly weapons were going to escape.

Gunfire erupted from two different points—the sniper rifle and an M5—on the far side of the loading area, which meant that Andrea had stopped playing with his toys and was joining the fight on the ground.

The K-110 on the ground began stalking toward them, letting the incoming fire spend itself uselessly on its reinforced cowling. A few of the Fixers clustered behind it, using it as cover as they and the machine went hunting.

Mia knew she couldn't help Belle and Andrea. They would survive or fall on their own. She had to find some way of stopping that truck.

A plan began to form in her head.

A very, very bad plan.

CHAPTER 167
EAST TEXAS CONVENTION CENTER
LABORDE, TEXAS

The whole universe froze around us both.

He was on the dais, standing over the body of a Secret Service agent, a dripping red knife in his hand. Blood pooled out around the agent, draining from a slashed throat. There was a Fixer beside Santoro, and well behind him, I saw Eve. She was staring, too, her eyes bugged out with a mix of fear and malevolence.

The whole room swam, and shadows crept in at the edges of my vision. The Darkness asserting itself, needing to be fed. I stupidly wondered if the parking lot was now full of night birds.

I raised the dart gun, but the crimson-eyed Fixer flung himself at me. It was so fast I couldn't get out of the way, and the descending weight smashed me back and down. I twisted as I landed, though, and came up on top of the killer and brought the Snellig barrel up. But just as the Fixer back at the processing plant had done, he slapped it away with such force the pistol went spinning out over the crowd.

I wasted no time and dropped my knee into the pit of his stomach, parried his hands to one side, and drove my right thumb into his eye socket. There was an explosion of red, and he shrieked so loudly, it hurt my head. Instead of writhing in agony, he punched me in the side hard enough to lift me off him. I crashed down and immediately rolled away as he hammered down with his fist. I pivoted on my hip and kicked him in the mouth. Enhanced or not, skin, muscles, bones, and tendons are still vulnerable. My kick knocked his jaw askew.

I hopped to my feet and pulled my Wilson knife from its pocket sheath, thumbed it open with a flick of my wrist, and, as the Fixer lumbered up, I swept his foot out from under him, caught his hair as he fell, and cut his throat.

Then I spun just in time to see Santoro shove Eve toward the backstage door.

"No!" I yelled, and it came out weird. Too big, too rough, too alien. It was the voice of the Darkness speaking through me.

Together—I and that destructive thing inside me—I leaped onto the dais and raced after them.

But the door banged open, and another group of Fixers came out of the back.

I immediately turned and ran like hell.

And saw, on the far side of the room, the main doors open, and three people fight their way through the tide of escaping civilians. One was a short, dumpy young guy; another was a thin man of medium height; and the third was a tall woman with a heavy fall of midnight-dark hair. They saw me and immediately began fighting their way in my direction.

Harry Bolt.

Toys.

And Violin.

CHAPTER 168
THE PAVILION
BLUE DIAMOND ELITE TRAINING CENTER
STEVENS COUNTY, WASHINGTON

The K-110 moved like a predatory dinosaur—a velociraptor for the techno age.

The driver shifted from the minigun to a rocket launcher and sent grenade after grenade into the trees. The forest blew apart in sheets of flame and burning gas, and the machine walked into that hell.

Andrea saw this from behind the corner of the compound's sewage pump house. He had Lightning Bugs, but the machine was still out of range.

"Monkey balls," he said over and over again.

There was nowhere for him to go. If he stayed where he was, the Fixers would find him in seconds. If he ran, he'd be exposed, because the next good cover was at least thirty yards away across the firing range. The irony of that was not lost on him.

His only option, then, was to wait and, in the last second before they cut him down, try to use the EMP bomb to stop the fighting machine.

"Hairy monkey balls," he muttered and touched his chest over his heart, seeing the face of his husband and their little girl. Aching that he would never see them again. Then he set his jaw, took the Lightning Bug in his hand, put his thumb on the switch, and waited for the end.

"*Vaffanculo!*" he yelled as he began to rise up.

But then the wall of trees to the left of the approaching K-110 burst apart as *another* fighting machine slammed its way onto the road, firing grenade after grenade into the Fixers. The men in body armor were hurled through the air like straw in a stiff breeze, and the K-110 staggered and crashed onto its side.

Andrea stared in shock, and then he saw the words *Hot Mama* painted in big red letters on the side of the cowling.

Top Sims had joined the fight.

CHAPTER 169

EAST TEXAS CONVENTION CENTER
LABORDE, TEXAS

Violin crushed me with a quick, fierce hug.

"Thank the goddess you're alive, Joseph."

"Working on it," I said. "Thank whoever that you're all here. This is a shit storm."

"How can we help?" asked Toys.

I quickly explained the situation. Toys and Violin nodded; Harry looked confused and a bit scared, but he gave a nod, too. They all had standard handguns as well as Snelligs.

"I need a dart gun," I said, and Violin gave me hers. "Thanks. Look, you three do what you can out here."

"Where are you going?" asked Violin.

"After Santoro."

Toys caught my eye for a moment, perhaps searching to see if I was alone inside my head. And although there was no warmth or kindness there, he gave me a nod. One fighter to another.

"Try not to kill anyone who's not a Fixer," I said.

"What about the militiamen?" asked Toys.

"Feel free to dent them, but the courts can sort them out. The Fixers are the true threat. You can kill every last one of those pricks."

"Count on it," said Toys.

"As for you, Joseph," said Violin, "feel free *to* kill that evil little man."

I stole Toys's line. "Oh, you can definitely count on that."

We split up, and I ran for the dais once more. Some of the Fixers who'd chased me back came at me, but I put them down. When I reached the doors to the back, I had the dart gun in one hand and my knife in the other. The Darkness was welling up inside me, and I wondered if it wasn't time to let it hold sway over everything else that happened.

CHAPTER 170
THE PLAYROOM
UNDISCLOSED LOCATION
NEAR VANCOUVER, BRITISH COLUMBIA, CANADA

Kuga was at his desk with three laptops open, a cell phone tucked between shoulder and ear, and several maps laid out on the top of his desk. Things were happening, but the timetable was screwed up. The driver of one of the transport trucks was jabbering about a hit at the Pavilion. HK reported in that the venue for Going Viral was being emptied and her team of K-110s were not in position for the hit. She said that she thought someone was ghosting through her computer. Halfway through that call, her line went dead.

But according to the breaking news on TV, the G-55 thing was exploding exactly as planned. And that was the big get. No matter how many of the governors they killed, racial and political tensions in the States were going to skyrocket, taking sales with them. The loss of the Pavilion—if it indeed fell—and the failure at the concert venue were nothing compared to that. Not merely because he'd sell a lot of guns in America for the next dozen years but because it was a model for domestic strikes with limited boots on the ground and limited liability. There were at least thirty-seven client countries whose political leaders would be watching the same news.

He looked up in surprise as the door to his study opened and Mr. Sunday walked in.

"What are you doing here?" said Kuga. "We didn't have a meeting scheduled."

"No," said Sunday, closing the door behind him. "This is a bit of a surprise call."

"Yeah, well, go make yourself a drink or something. I'm kind of in the middle of this right now."

Sunday walked over to the desk and, smiling like a crocodile, reached out and plucked the phone from Kuga's hand.

Kuga blinked in frank astonishment. "Hey!"

Sunday dropped the phone to the floor and stepped on it.

"What the hell are you doing?" demanded Kuga.

"Oh, just making sure you're paying attention, Harcourt."

"I told you before, don't ever call me that. Harcourt Bolton is dead."

"No," said Sunday, "not yet."

That froze the moment.

"What . . . the hell is that supposed to mean?"

Sunday used his forefinger to close the lids of the laptops—one, two, three.

If it had been anyone else, Kuga would have gotten up and comprehensively kicked their ass. Maybe to the point of needing someone to dispose of a body. But this was Sunday.

This was *him*.

And so, he sat very still.

"What do you want?" he asked.

"Oh," said Sunday, "everything."

"The hell's that supposed to mean?"

"It means I'm delighted that you followed my advice about delegating so much of the organization to talented department heads. That's wise of you, but really, it's very convenient for me. After all, most of our customers—and really the world at large—see you not as a person but a brand. Kind of like Colonel Sanders. At the end of the day, does it really matter who wears the white suit and string necktie?"

Kuga slipped his foot over to the alert button on the floor and pressed it. He said, "You may be scary as hell, Sunday, but you'd better not be saying what it sounds like you're saying."

"I'm delighted that you're clever enough to understand the inference. Bully for you." Then he cupped a hand around one ear. "Oh, wait, is that the sound of no one coming to answer your call?"

Kuga's eyes shifted to the door, which remained stubbornly shut.

"It's just you and me, Harcourt," said Sunday. He reached into a pocket and drew out a glittering filleting knife. "And look . . . I brought something for us to play with."

CHAPTER 171
THE PAVILION
BLUE DIAMOND ELITE TRAINING CENTER
STEVENS COUNTY, WASHINGTON

The semi began to roll.

On the flatbed, three of the fighting machines were still firing, and now the Fixers were all armed and adding to the barrage. The whole thing was a rolling engine of destruction.

Mia turned and ran farther up the road, cut through a switchback, and headed toward the guard shack at full speed. Her plan needed cover and it needed height, and she wanted to get to the shack, climb atop it, and then use that as a platform to jump onto the roof of the truck. If she could empty a magazine or two down through the roof and kill the driver, then maybe the truck would crash.

And so, she ran like hell.

Bunny saw Mia running from the truck and tried to figure out what she was doing.

But then he realized there was no time for that. Or for anything else. The Fixers were going to get away. And even if they weren't likely to make it down to Fort Lauderdale in time to add to that attack, they would be free to do more damage. He had no doubt Kuga and Santoro could find other dreadful uses for those machines and all the highly trained and enhanced Fixers.

"No damned way," he snarled as he launched himself down the road. He had nearly a full drum of the high explosives left. They may not pack enough punch to stop the fighting machines, but those grenades would do a lot of damage to that truck. He was even grinning as he ran.

He was grinning when a Fixer rose up from the shrubs right in his path. It wasn't an ambush, just bad luck. Bunny slammed into him at full speed, and the two of them fell and began rolling down the slope. Bunny's shotgun flew straight up into the air and vanished inside a holly bush.

Top used *Hot Mama* to stomp on the other K-110. The titanium alloy feet of the fighting machine, backed by the entire weight of the device and every ounce of cybernetically enhanced technology, did what grenades couldn't do. It smashed the cowling in, crushing it, flattening it, and turning the driver within into a red horror.

"Yeah, and fuck you, too!" Top yelled.

Then he turned as bullets pinged off his own cowling. Two of the Fixers were on their feet, eyes blazing red as the Relentless chemicals flooded through their systems. One kept firing with his rifle while the other grabbed a six-foot length of broken tree branch and swung it like a baseball bat at the machine. The blow was massive, and it staggered Top, making *Hot Mama* backpedal for balance.

Top opened up with the minigun, driving the armed Fixer back and down, but the one with the club kept swinging, going mad with it, laughing maniacally. Top tried to swat him away with the mechanical arm, but the Fixer was fast and ducked under. The killer rose up before Top could check his swing and cracked the branch across the cowling again. The wood shattered, but a small crack appeared in the reinforced glass.

The Fixer dodged another swing, dived, and came up with a rock the size of a grapefruit. He dodged in again, smashing the stone with raw power, but also with precision, attacking the K-110's few weak spots. It was the kind of assault only someone who really understood the fighting machine would know to do.

Out of his peripheral vision, Top saw Andrea kneeling behind the pump house, engaging the last two remaining Fixers in a gun battle. One of them edged around to get a better angle, but three fast shots from the trees sent him sprawling backward, blood jetting from his throat. Belle, by intention or—likelier an accident—had found the vulnerable sweet spot.

"Jackpot! Fixer down, Fixer down! Get out of the—"

It was all he got out before the Fixer's body armor exploded.

CHAPTER 172
THE PLAYROOM
UNDISCLOSED LOCATION
NEAR VANCOUVER, BRITISH COLUMBIA, CANADA

There was no Mr. Sunday in the room anymore. That person had served his purpose and was gone. The skin that had made up the face of the salesman lay on the floor, still clutched in the bloody hand of what had been Harcourt Bolton Sr.

There was no Harcourt Bolton anymore, either. Not in any substantial way.

All there was in the room now was Nicodemus.

His filleting knife rested on one thigh of his crossed legs.

The face that no longer belonged to Bolton lay wetly on his other thigh. Nicodemus tugged at it to make sure it lay flat, inspecting it for tears. There were none. No bruises, either. He'd been very careful not to damage the face.

As for the rest of that man's body . . . it was sprawled nearby. Open. Ruined. No longer beautiful.

"Kuga," said Nicodemus, trying the name with a pleasurable sense of ownership. "Kuga. Yes."

His eyes were a swirling mix of awful greens and sickly yellows and reptile browns.

His smile, although streaked with red, was so wide and bright and happy.

CHAPTER 173
EAST TEXAS CONVENTION CENTER
LABORDE, TEXAS

The Fixers who chased me off were now spread through the crowd and causing all sorts of problems. There were a lot of bodies on the floor, and there was an atmosphere of mingled pain, confusion, and terror permeating the room. However this ended, this would be *the* news story for days.

Which, I supposed, was another goddamned victory for Kuga.

More proof that he could sell mayhem to his clients. As with terrorist groups, multinational corporations, and organized crime, there was no way to get a completely clean win. The world has never been that tidy. There was always a cost, and I could see that coin being paid all around me.

Which made me all the more determined to stop Santoro. He enabled so much of this; his fingerprints were all over it. That had to stop.

And he had to pay for what he did to my family.

To so many families.

I reached the door through which he'd gone and saw only one Fixer guarding it, his eyes still normal, but sweat pouring down his face. I wondered if the enhancer aspects of Relentless were just hitting his bloodstream. How long before the Rage kicked in?

I didn't know and didn't care. He turned toward me, and I shot him in the face. The Sandman dart caught him beside the nose, and he staggered. Like the Fixers at the processing plant, it affected him but didn't knock him out. So, as he reeled against the door, I used the knife. Yeah, that did the trick.

I leaped over his body and crashed through the doorway.

The hall was empty except for a dead security guard. Poor bastard.

I slowed from a fast run to a cautious walk as I approached the corner, then ducked low to take a quick look around the edge.

Had I done that while standing, I would have died right there. A meat cleaver chunked into the wall at the level of where my throat had been, and I looked up into the sparkling blue and thoroughly insane eyes of Eve.

She simultaneously tried to tear the cleaver free and kick me in the face. Bad moves, both of them. What she should have done was not be between me and Rafael Santoro. And I had no damned time to waste on junior-grade psychopaths. As I shot to my feet, I gutted her from navel to breastbone, gave the knife a big push and twist at the top, and sent the tip of the blade into her black heart.

Eve looked at me with such profound confusion that it was as if she were trying to understand how this—her life, her ambitions, her goals—could simply end this quickly. Maybe she'd planned a drama for us, a big battle in which she would emerge victorious. Or perhaps she thought her mentor—her *daddy*—would step in to save her.

I tore my knife free and let her fall.

Maybe I should have pity for the damage that drove her to become what she was. That's something for philosophers, and I'm not one of that brotherhood. I doubted I'd even mention her to Rudy. Why give her even that much? There was too much innocent blood on her hands for me to care.

Santoro was twenty feet away, and he was grinning at me.

I grinned, too.

And I think my smile was a great deal darker than his.

CHAPTER 174
THE PAVILION
BLUE DIAMOND ELITE TRAINING CENTER
STEVENS COUNTY, WASHINGTON

Mia saw the blast through a gap in the trees. She heard Top's warning, and then a fireball enveloped his fighting machine. Then she was too busy to keep watching because the semi rounded the curve. It was packed with the remaining Fixers and the K-110s.

She crouched atop the guard shack, which had been abandoned by the soldiers who'd run down to join the fight. Sadly, there were no weapons there, and she still only had her pistol. It felt bizarrely inadequate against what was rolling toward her. And if she couldn't stop the driver, then this whole fight was for nothing. The help that was on the way—Bedlam Team and the National Guard—were still at least thirty minutes out. If the truck got away, it could vanish into the massive surrounding forests.

"Come on, boys," she said under her breath. "Come and dance with the Magpie."

She could see the driver, a burly man in the dark Fixer's body armor, his head turned to one side as he watched the last of the fight through the sideview mirror. On the flatbed, the Fixers were still firing, but randomly now. No one was looking at her.

The semi was going about thirty miles an hour and accelerating when she flung herself from her perch and onto the roof of the cab.

* * *

JONATHAN MABERRY

Bunny and the Fixer got to their feet. Neither had a gun anymore, having lost them in the collision.

In his body armor, the Fixer was broader and blockier than Bunny, but the big young man was taller and at the peak of his physical strength. His six-and-a-half-foot-tall body was packed with corded muscle. Not the top-heavy bodybuilder muscles but the springy and toned muscles of the professional athlete. A long time ago, he'd played volleyball in the Pan American Games, and, had it not been for joining the Marines, he might have gone on to the Olympics. And during the years since both Top and Colonel Ledger had taught him a lot about how fast a big man can be.

He went right at the Fixer and landed a massive overhand blow that drove the killer to one knee. Bunny immediately shifted weight and brought his knee up sharply to smash the Fixer's nose. Then he boxed his ears with cupped hands.

The Fixer screamed but did not fall.

Instead, in the space of a fractured second, his eyes went a burning red, and his face became a mask of pure rage. Actual *Rage,* as the bioweapon, mixed with the Relentless stamina enhancer, turned man into monster.

Bunny threw another punch, an overhand right that would have broken the man's neck . . . had it landed. But the Fixer moved fast. So fast. He blocked the punch and hit Bunny in the center of the chest with such appalling force that Bunny felt something break inside. His heart seemed to lurch, and suddenly there was not enough air left in the whole world.

CHAPTER 175
EAST TEXAS CONVENTION CENTER
LABORDE, TEXAS

"Hey," said Harry, "look, there's Joe."

Toys barely heard Harry's comment. He was busy defending a group of church lady types from a juiced-up Fixer, and that was proving to be much harder than he'd thought.

Harry saw Joe Ledger edging around the far side of the crowd, and that made him frown. Was Joe leaving? And . . . why had he stopped to change his clothes? Some kind of disguise?

He ran across the room, calling Ledger's name. Joe finally heard him when Harry was a dozen paces away. He turned.

And that quickly, the man stopped being Joe Ledger.

He was the same height, build, color, even down to the eyes.

The man smiled. "Hey," he said, "are you a friend of Joe's?"

"Yeah," said Harry. "Are you with the RTI?"

"Not exactly," said Michael Augustus Stafford as he raised his pistol and shot Harry Bolt twice in the chest.

Toys shot the Fixer in the eye with the Snellig. Twice. Once in each red eye. The man reeled back, screaming, clawing at his face even as his knees buckled. He lingered there, blood and mess running down his cheeks. Toys shifted his weight and balance and kicked the Fixer in the Adam's apple.

He turned away from the dying man just in time to see Harry Bolt get shot.

And he immediately recognized who it was who'd fired those shots. The anti-Ledger. Stafford. The world's most sought-after assassin.

Toys glanced around for Violin, but she was in the thick of it.

"Bloody hell," he growled and went running, making maximum use of cover behind the flailing, fighting people.

Stafford did not see him coming, because he was looking for a different face in all that madness. Toys came up directly behind a burly Latino who was trying to load a pistol but kept fumbling the magazine. Toys gave him a sharp push that crashed him into Stafford. The Latino's gun and Stafford's went flying.

Toys brought up his Snellig, but Stafford was cat quick, and he blocked Toys's gun hand and hit him twice—sternum and high in the chest. It had been an attempt to stall with one punch and crush the throat with the other—a technique Toys himself liked. But it was the kind of thing one did with the great unwashed. Not with another professional.

Toys turned his head and dipped, forcing the punch to land on his cheekbone. It hurt, but he knew it would hurt Stafford a good deal more.

The killer snatched back his hand but wasted no time complaining about the pain; instead, he snapped out a very fast toe kick that, had it landed, would have done terrible damage to Toys's crotch.

Toys took that on the hip and whipped out with a snapping backfist that knocked blood from Stafford's nose.

There was the tiniest pause—much less than a second—where the two men saw each other, less for who and more for *what* they were.

And then the battle was joined with savage, murderous intensity.

CHAPTER 176
THE PAVILION
BLUE DIAMOND ELITE TRAINING CENTER
STEVENS COUNTY, WASHINGTON

Bunny staggered back, his chest on fire from that blow over the heart. Fireworks exploded in the air, and he knew he was in real trouble. The Fixer was superhumanly strong, and that blow had done serious damage.

The choices were slim. Backpedal and try to run, or attack like a sick bear and try to drag the man down to the ground and see who knew the best dirty tricks. In both cases, the Fixer had the edge. He was stronger, faster, and he was not yet hurt.

The killer solved the matter by rushing Bunny, howling like a monster.

Top Sims was in hell, and the fires were really damned hot.

He fought to clear his head, to make sense of what was happening, and clarity of mind brought no comfort. He lay inside *Hot Mama,* and the fighting machine was wreathed in flame. Most of it was burning debris from when the Fixer in the body armor had exploded, and even though the shell of his cybernetic battle suit was heat resistant, the driver could still cook.

Top fought to make the K-110's arms and legs move. They did, but not well. The blast had seriously damaged the servos. He threw all his muscle into turning over. It seemed to take an age, but he finally thudded down on his chest. Next he brought the hands up. No . . . just the left was working. The right arm of the machine wouldn't move at all. Lifting the ponderous suit one-handed was agony. His back was burning in a different way. Something was wrong. A sprain, a strain. He prayed to god it wasn't worse. When the blast happened, he'd been thrown and hit rolling. The suit was never intended to protect the driver from something like that.

He heard gunfire and knew the battle was still going on, so he couldn't have been out for more than a few seconds. Where was Andrea? He'd been by the pump house but had no tech to shield him from either blast or blaze.

Top got to his knees, and after ten thousand years, to his feet.

Walking was a special kind of hell, but with each step, the burning debris fell away, and after ten steps, he was out of the fire.

He hit the release, and the dying K-110 spilled him out into the dirt.

Mia Kleeve clung to the roof of the cab, fighting to steady herself, sloughing off the extra momentum from her jump while compensating for the semi's acceleration. She grinned. They didn't teach *this* in the regular army.

The truck was heading out toward the main road. Once it got there, it would accelerate to sixty or seventy, and that would be the end of her. She had to stop it now.

With her hand braced against an exhaust stack—the heat intense even through her gloves—she knelt above the driver's seat, drew her pistol, and aimed the barrel straight down.

She knew the consequences. The Fixer was wearing body armor, and there was every chance it was going to blow up if she scored a kill shot. Could she kill him and have time to get clear?

The roof of the cab was thirteen or fourteen feet in the air, and the truck was now going at least forty miles an hour. The jump would probably break every bone in her body.

"Yeah," she said, "well, you can kiss my ass."

And she fired. The Sig Sauer P226 had a twenty-round extended magazine, and she fired every last bullet she had. The slide locked back, and the truck instantly began to slew sideways. Mia had to let go of the empty gun to hold on. There was a patch of grass coming up fast on the right, and she scrambled to the passenger side, tensed to spring, and . . .

Her first bullet had punched down through the top of the driver's head, stopping thought, control, breath, and life. His body armor reacted to the sudden drop in pulse, and it blew up.

The explosion punched backward, blowing out the rear of the cab and killing four of the Fixers in the back. Their suits blew as well. Mia never made it off the roof of the cab. She was caught inside a thermobaric fireball that lifted the entire semi, the crated and uncrated fighting machines, all the Fixers, and three-quarters of an acre of road and forest, and threw it all burning into the air.

At virtually the same moment, in one of those cosmic coincidences that seem to be part of the life—and death—of tier-one special operations, there was another explosion nearly three thousand miles away. Two blasts, really, seconds apart as a pair of AIM-120 AMRAAM missiles hit the Fixer troop transport planes. One missile struck just as the first K-110 was trundling toward the cargo hatch, ready to drop into the concert stadium.

Eighty-eight Fixers and sixteen fighting machines, along with the planes and flight crews, filled the sky with fireballs that could be seen for fifty miles in every direction.

Belle walked out of the woods, her rifle raised but no one left to shoot.

Top Sims sat on the ground, his back to the pump house wall, with an unconscious Andrea leaning against him. Except for skin color, they could have been father and son. Belle checked on them and was relieved to find out that, though hurt, they were still alive.

It took longer to find Bunny.

He was on a slope, wrapped in a tangle with a Fixer. Both men were unconscious. Both were battered into bloody hulks. Belle could not wake Bunny up; his pulse was thin and his breathing too quick and shallow.

The Fixer's breathing was labored and kept stopping. That alarmed her, and she ran down to the buildings and found a tarp. It took every ounce of her strength to get Bunny onto the tarp and then pull him down the slope and into a drainage ditch. When the Fixer's heart stopped and his suit detonated, Belle covered Bunny with her own body.

It was nearly fifteen minutes before the first choppers arrived.

CHAPTER 177
EAST TEXAS CONVENTION CENTER
LABORDE, TEXAS

Santoro's smile was genuine, but it wasn't happy. It was a rictus grin, and in it were stress and anger, grief and shock, and a hatred so palpable it was like a fist. I'd killed his pet, his adopted daughter, his—well, whatever else she was.

I'd also blundered right into the heart of his operation. He had no idea that there was maybe 5 percent skill and the rest either blind, dumb luck or the perversity of the gods of war. Or some combination thereof.

What mattered was that I was here to end his plan and end him.

We'd fought twice before. The first time was aboard a cruise liner for the Sea of Hope event. Another charity fundraiser like Going Viral. We'd fought, and he whipped me *and* Ghost. If Mr. Church hadn't come along at the right moment, that would have been the end of us. Church kicked Santoro's ass and then threw him into a black site prison.

The second time was late last year at the D9 conference in Oslo. We'd beaten each other half to death, and maybe I'd gotten the upper hand at the end of it. Not sure, because right as things were going my way, I took a blast of Rage in the face. Next thing I remember is waking up cuffed to a bed because, apparently, I'd tried to kill Church and Belle. However, Belle shot me with Sandman.

This was round three, and the math had changed a lot since last year.

Santoro had murdered my entire family. He killed everyone I was related to by blood or marriage. The bomb that killed them all nearly killed Junie. And in that moment, something died in me, and something was born.

Church thinks that Nicodemus infected me with the Darkness. Maybe he did, but if so, it was an infection laid down on top of something already boiling out of the lowest places in my soul. Maybe the reason that the Darkness did not turn me suicidal or make me take innocent lives was that it was not wholly a product of Nicodemus's magic—if magic was even the right word. Whatever that trickster son of a bitch did to me was added to what Santoro had already conjured in the dark soil of my damaged psyche. The poet Baudelaire wrote about flowers of hate. Yes, they have grown wild in me, yielding strange fruits.

I didn't rush at Santoro, or he at me.

It was as if the madness outside this room no longer belonged to either of us. This hallway was the whole world. I raised the Snellig, barrel pointed to the ceiling. He had a Beretta in his waistband, and he took it out with two fingers. We nodded and each set our weapons down on the floor and kicked them away. Then I took the Wilson knife and drove the point an inch deep into the wall. Santoro nodded again and removed a stiletto from a concealed sheath and did the same.

Now we were unarmed.

I have plenty of soldier friends who would think this was stupid. Two grown professionals in the middle of a war fighting a duel. But those people weren't here. They weren't Santoro or me. They weren't in our heads or hearts. They didn't share our histories. They couldn't and wouldn't understand. Nor would their understanding matter. They, like the rest of the world, did not exist for us as we walked slowly toward one another.

There were no taunts, no gibes, no trash talk. His eyes were filled with strange lights. I could once more see shadows creeping into the corners of my awareness. In my heart, the Darkness was struggling to break free. *It* wanted this as much as I did. The Darkness did not share its reasons with me, and I did not allow it to see into my mind.

There were fewer than six feet between me and Rafael Santoro.

I think we both moved at exactly the same moment.

CHAPTER 178
EAST TEXAS CONVENTION CENTER
LABORDE, TEXAS

Toys had never fought anyone as brutal and quick as Stafford.

Of course, he'd never fought Joe Ledger, and he imagined this was what it would be like. No flashy moves, no concessions to style. Just combat.

Stafford's technique was basic, but his speed and power were incredible.

From the beginning of the fight, Toys realized that he was very likely going to die.

Stafford feinted high and ducked low, throwing a short, vicious hook to Toys's groin, but the young man twisted aside and once more forced the punch to hit bone. Same hand. First the cheekbone and then the hip. This time, Toys saw pain flicker across Stafford's face.

The man shifted left and kicked at Toys, catching him on the thigh with the flat of the heel and knocking him eight feet back. It was a ploy, Toys realized even as it was happening, so Stafford could catch a breath because a few seconds ago Toys had tucked a nice one into the assassin's gut with a straight right.

Toys got his balance but did not charge right in. He needed a moment, too. They'd traded a flurry of crushing punches in the first two seconds, and both of them had knuckle cuts across their faces. Toys spat blood onto the floor between them.

"Who the hell are you anyway?" asked Stafford.

"The Ghost of Christmas Yet to Come," said Toys.

"Okay, sure," said Stafford. "Whatever."

And midway through that last word, he moved, darting forward almost like a fencer with a step-drag motion that closed the gap while giving him a springy and balanced stance for a left-jab, right-hook combination.

Which was exactly what Toys expected him—*wanted* him—to do. He'd shifted to look like his weight was resting on his heels and let his arms sag as if too weary to keep his guard up. Stafford, the faster boxer, blitzed in.

JONATHAN MABERRY

Toys crouched a little and leaned away from the jab but into the line of the hook. The punch was so fast that Toys hadn't yet braced his balled fists against his head so that his whole body would absorb and slough off the foot-pounds of impact. Stafford's punch knocked Toys's own fist into his left eye socket.

But Stafford's already damaged right hand hit the bent elbow. The hand, for all the powerful things it can do, is remarkably fragile and made up of many small bones. The elbow, when bent double, is a club, a big knot of bone. Stafford's fist hit that unyielding bone at thirty miles an hour. His knuckles exploded, driving sections of bone deep into the muscle and cartilage of the hand. Splinters of bone shot out through the skin, and all those bundles of nerve endings shrieked.

Stafford reeled back in agony, and Toys, dazed and bleeding, took his moment. He skipped forward with an instep snap to Stafford's groin, and, as the man folded, Toys grabbed his hair with both hands and dropped into a low squat. The motion, the sudden deadweight drop of his body, slammed Stafford face-forward onto the concrete floor.

Toys fell sideways, his elbow on fire, and his head ringing so loudly it was like church bells on Christmas morning. But he knew he could not stop, so he got to his knees and crawled to his enemy, swung a foot over so he straddled the man at midback, looped an arm under Stafford's head, and cinched it tightly around the neck. But he was not trying to choke the man. Instead, he clamped his other hand around the wrist of the looped arm and simply sat down. He did it as a limp drop and then jerked backward with all his strength. The motion jerked Stafford's head up and back. Too far back and too quickly. There was a double *crack-crack* as the man's neck broke and then the spine between the shoulder blades.

Toys let go and collapsed onto the floor beside the man he'd just killed.

Violin shot a Fixer four times before the Sandman took him down, but he collapsed before he reached her, his hands brushing her boot as he landed facedown on the floor.

Behind him, a tall, slender Black woman and a shorter, heavier white woman were fighting like cats, snarling and biting and rolling around on the floor. Violin shot them, too.

It occurred to her that it would simply be easier to shoot everyone instead of trying to pick who was a Fixer, who was a duped militiaman or radical, and who was a civilian caught up by the hysteria of violence. She had six magazines for her gun, each of which carried thirty darts. That was more than enough to put a third of the room down.

So, she began firing.

Violin's weapon of choice was a sniper rifle, and she had been the one to train Belle in the art. But Lilith had required that she be proficient with every kind of gun, long or short. Just as she was highly skilled with any edged weapon. Years of experience had given her timing and savvy and refined her battlefield judgment.

And so she put her back to a wall and targeted the people with guns first, taking them down before they were aware of her. Then, as bodies began to pile up around her, she shot whoever was closest and the person directly behind them.

Civilians scattered, and she let them go. The patsy militants tried to outshoot her, but she was the better, faster, more accurate, and less emotional shot.

Fixers took several rounds each, but she had darts to spare.

It was only after she'd built a landscape of drugged bodies that she saw two distinct things that broke her concentration.

To her left, Toys sprawled next to a clearly dead Michael Augustus Stafford. Oddly, Toys reached up and patted Stafford's cheek before that hand flopped back down.

To her right, a young man crawled toward her with a terrible slowness, leaving a snail's trail of shining red behind him. Blood bubbled from his lips, and there were tears in his eyes.

"*Harry!*" she cried and broke into a run.

CHAPTER 179
EAST TEXAS CONVENTION CENTER
LABORDE, TEXAS

Santoro dropped and pivoted to swing a vicious Muay Thai shin kick to the outside of my left knee, but I was already in motion with a cutting palm to his chin. Because I was pivoting, his shin hit my knee straight and bent, which did no damage but hurt us both. A lot. My cutting palm missed his chin because he was pivoting and banged off his forehead. The two blows buffeted us backward.

Pain meant nothing to Santoro, and it meant even less to me, so we closed again. Only slightly warier. We were evenly matched for speed. He was smaller and could move his whole mass more quickly; I had a longer reach.

He tried a stamp, missed my instep but mashed my big toe. But I crouched and twisted and drove a two-knuckle punch into the center of his quads. He hissed and chopped me across the side of the mouth with the edge of his hand. My lip split, and droplets of blood followed his hand like the tail of a comet.

I feinted with a low roundhouse kick but then tilted forward to try to put my thumb in his eye. He parried my shot and caught me under the arm with a short, chopping uppercut. It numbed my arm as he knew it would, and he tried to close on that side, but I pivoted in place and swung a spinning elbow at his nose. Santoro leaned into me to nullify the force of the blow, but I'm a big guy and I hit hard, so the sheer torsion I'd generated sent him stumbling sideways.

I tried to correct my balance and follow, but I was still at the end of a pivot, and by the time I'd shifted my stance, he was out of range and beginning to circle.

We played that cat game of walking in opposing circles for a few seconds, reading each other, waiting for the moment, stalking each other on the balls of our feet, knees bent, able to move in any direction. That's how the pros do it. It's what they try to teach students on the first day in the dojo. Don't be flat-footed, keep your weight balanced, don't root yourself to the ground.

I sprang at him, using my left hand to chop down on his guard while I looped my right up and over and down with a smashing palm-heel. He was fast. My lord, was he fast. I had him cold, and he still managed to twist and contort his body to empty the space where he'd just been. A matador would weep for such an evasion; a danseur would kill for that grace.

His evasion turned into a counterattack as—with his back briefly toward me—he kicked up backward in a deer kick that caught me high on the inner thigh with his heel.

I was not wearing underwear, and my balls were right there, directly in the path of the kick.

It hurt. Real fucking bad.

Here's the thing about pain, though. Unless the pain is coupled with debilitating damage, it's just sensation. It can be dealt with. It can be endured and even disregarded. Every boxer knows this, every soldier injured in combat while still a hundred yards from cover knows it. Marathon runners know it, and so do teenagers playing soccer on a Sunday morning. Getting hit in the balls hurts. In a civilized moment, you tend to curl up into a fetal position and pray for death. In action, though, when it's not only your life but the lives of everyone who needs you, counts on you, depends on you . . . it becomes something else. It becomes fuel.

The pain galvanized me, and I hurled myself at Santoro, trying to drive him against the wall. But he was already turning, having seen or sensed my jump. He slapped his arm around my waist, turned away, bent over, and used his hip as a fulcrum and my mass and momentum to throw me onto the floor.

But I grew up in jujitsu schools. Throws and counter-throws, or counters to counters . . . that's my thing. If I'd fed him that technique, it could not have been more ideal. As I landed, I turned like an axle and made him the wheel. The new torque whipped him around me, and then he was on the floor and I was on top.

Last year in Oslo, he'd had a dominant moment like that and, instead of ending it right there, decided to beat me to death. He'd knocked out teeth, fractured an eye socket, and busted bones in my face. He could have used that time to kill me, and it gave me a chance to turn the tables on him. And . . . damn if I hadn't done the same thing. I'd wanted to punish him for the deaths of the helpless

JONATHAN MABERRY

and innocent people on the islands where the Rage pathogen was released.

I should have killed him. Like Santoro a moment before. I *could* have killed him. Both of us had made the mistake of succumbing for the need to use our blows as punishment and as a lesson. Know this, understand this, be aware of why you are being beaten. That's its own kind of arrogance. The price I paid for that was him slipping away and then coming after my family. Their deaths were on me.

On me.

I completed my roll, and for a moment I was on top, straddling him, my hands free.

And the Darkness tried to own me.

It rose up like a tsunami of utter blackness. *It* wanted Santoro punished. It wanted to dominate, to own, to humiliate, to educate. I could feel it spreading through me like a jar of ink poured into a gallon of water. The tendrils uncurled along the paths of least resistance, filled every nerve ending, every muscle fiber. I could feel it behind my eyes, and I wondered if they had turned as black as the Fixers' eyes turned red. I believed that if I opened my mouth, I would vomit out a cloud of stygian horror.

It wanted to steal this moment from me.

And in doing so, give Santoro a chance. In the past, he'd proven that all he ever needed was a chance.

The Darkness was so powerful that I was becoming lost in it, just as I was aware that all of this was happening inside the bubble of a millisecond.

I was the Darkness now, and an awareness stabbed through me, whispering awful truths.

If I gave this moment to the Darkness, then it would have all my moments henceforth. If I became the Darkness, then everything that I was—that Joe Ledger was—would be gone.

Nicodemus would win. Kuga would win.

Rafael Santoro would win because he would have eradicated, however indirectly, the entire Ledger family for all time.

If I yielded to the Darkness, then that would be where I lived forever, and there would be no other home to go to.

There would be no Junie.

There would be no joy, no love.

No light.

The millisecond stretched and snapped.

Santoro and I were just coming out of the roll, I was only then straddling him, looking down at him. In the next moment, he would react.

And so I struck him under the chin with my left palm, tilting his head back, exposing his throat, and I slammed a full fist punch down. I put every ounce of my rage, my hurt, my loss into that punch. Crushing his throat, breaking his neck, *ending* him. I gave everything I had to that punch.

I killed him, goddamn it. Not the Darkness, goddamn it.

I did.

Joe Ledger.

EPILOGUE

-1-

Even the longest night ends.

After darkness, there is light.

-2-

They medevacked Harry Bolt to the best hospital in the region.

Violin went with him, holding his slack hands in both of hers. He was rushed into surgery, and the doctors worked on him all night.

I got there hours later. The aftermath at the venue was titanic, and I was the center of a hell of a lot of suspicion and scrutiny, despite my credentials. It wasn't until phones started ringing in the right hands and voices representing frightening levels of officialdom told them to leave me the hell alone that they did.

Bug made sure my name and face were erased from every news story. That must have pushed MindReader to its limits, but it wasn't the first time I'd been edited out of a slice of history. Which was perfectly fine by me.

While I sat with Violin and Toys in the waiting room, I got two calls. The first was from Scott Wilson. He told me about the fight at the Pavilion. Bunny, Top, and Andrea were all in a Spokane hospital. They were alive, but each was badly banged up. Andrea had burns and lacerations from flying debris. He was in the best shape. Top had some damage to his lower back, but Church was flying in the top spine doctor in the world. No joke. Church has a lot of friends.

As for Bunny . . . he had a broken sternum, four broken ribs, a cracked collarbone, and three broken fingers. His fiancée, Lydia, who was once a shooter back in the DMS days, was flown in one of Church's jets, and a nurse was along for company because Lydia was entering her third trimester.

But we lost Mia Kleeve. She'd gone down hard and taken out the last major lingering threat from the Relentless program. The word *hero* is bandied about too much. Football hero. Guitar hero. There are actual heroes, though. There's no way to calculate how many lives her actions saved. I liked her and had planned to see about her getting a transfer to Havoc Team. Now . . . she would be a star on a wall at Phoenix House. Tales would be told, drinks raised. The public at large would never hear her name, never know how much intelligence and courage it took for her to stop that truck.

Those of us who understand the nature of that sacrifice, though? No, we wouldn't ever forget.

I shared all this with Toys and Violin.

Toys merely grunted. He had stitches and bruises and looked like he'd been the star attraction at a muggers' convention.

Then Church called me to say that Junie was flying in. That news came closer to breaking me than anything else. I had to go into the men's room and just stand there for a while. I used a trash can to block the door.

When I came out, Toys was alone.

"They called her in," he said.

"Harry . . . ?"

Toys took a moment. "They used the phrase *cautiously optimistic.*"

"Shit."

"Yes."

We sat. Time lost all meaning.

Finally, without looking at him, I said, "About Rotterdam . . ."

"Mind if I just sum it up?"

"Uh . . . yeah, sure."

"Fuck you."

I nodded. "Fair enough."

We sat.

"Are you regretting the whole 'going into the field' thing?"

He took so long that I didn't think he was going to answer.

"Actually," he said, "I haven't enjoyed myself this much in years."

"Okay," I said.

"Okay," he said. "But seriously . . . and I mean this with my whole heart, Ledger . . . Fuck you."

We nodded to one another and lapsed into a long silence.

That was me and Toys.

JONATHAN MABERRY

-3-

The authorities arrested eleven Fixers at the convention center.

With Rafael Santoro dead, they seemed a whole lot less hesitant about making deals for reduced sentences in exchange for telling every damned thing they knew. And they knew a lot. Since that day in LaBorde, there have been close to three hundred subsequent arrests, and with Interpol, Mossad, MI6, Barrier, and a slew of other agencies involved, that tally was likely to rise.

As for Kuga?

Only one Fixer knew about his mansion in Canada, but by the time the CRMP descended on it in a swarm of helicopters, there was nothing left to find. Some blood in what was clearly Kuga's office, and it was a DNA match with Harcourt Bolton. But no bodies, no computers, no anything.

One odd little detail that I got from one of the Mounties was that the whole area—from driveway to the backyard to the eaves of the house—was covered with thousands of black birds.

-4-

On a sultry night in early September, I lay on a towel at the high tide line in a small cove of a secluded beach in Kauai. The sun was just starting to edge toward the horizon, the light through the clouds smearing the sky with every color in the paint box. Less than a hundred feet from the beach, two juvenile dolphins leaped and splashed and played; and a big old green sea turtle crawled out of the crystal water and stopped to doze near me. I looked into his ancient, wise eyes and saw peace and understanding there that went miles and miles deep.

There was a splash, and I saw Junie come out of the water pulling off her mask and snorkel. Water sluiced down her long legs, and her blond hair hung in salty rattails down the front of one shoulder. She wore a bikini that made no attempt to hide the scars time and hard use had cut into her skin. She was then, and forever, the most beautiful and complex woman I have ever known. And I've known a few.

She saw me watching her, and a smile blossomed on her face.

There are few smiles like that. Full of understanding and grace, full of love insight. As deep as that turtle's, but with a different kind of awareness. A keen intelligence and childlike joy at simply being alive.

Junie came and sank down next to me. She stretched out, and we kissed for a long, long time.

Then she made a pillow out of my left bicep, snuggled close, and we watched the magnificence of the sky. Even though this was the beginning of the long, slow Hawaiian evening, the sky was filled with light.

And there was not a trace of darkness to be seen anywhere.

THE RELENTLESS PLAYLIST

"**1X1**" by All Them Witches

"**45**" by Shinedown

"**A Place for My Head**" by Linkin Park

"**A Place Where You Belong**" by Bullet for My Valentine

"**Accidentally Like a Martyr**" by Warren Zevon

"**Afraid of Heights**" by Tom Fletcher

"**Again**" by Flyleaf

"**All I Want Is You**" by U2

"**Alone**" by Judas Priest

"**Alone, Omen 3**" by King Krule

"**Angel**" by Sarah McLachlan

"**Angel from Montgomery**" by Bonnie Raitt

"**Angel of Death**" by Thin Lizzy

"**Angry Chair**" by Alice in Chains

"**Animal I Have Become**" by Three Days Grace

"**Anymore**" by Savatage

"**Bad Day**" by Fuel

"**Bad Man**" by Esterly ft. Austin Jenckes

"**Bankrupt on Selling**" by Modest Mouse

"**Barton Hollow**" by the Civil Wars

"**Battle Royale**" by Apashe ft. Panther

"Beginning to End" by Paul Haslinger ft. Nona Hendryx and
    Sussan Deyhim

"Believer" by Imagine Dragons

"Better Than Me" by Hinder

"Black River Killer" by Blitzen Trapper

"Blood in the Cut" by K.Flay

"Blood on My Name" by the Brothers Bright

"Blow Up the Outside World" by Soundgarden

"Brick by Boring Brick" by Paramore

"Bring Me to Life" by Evanescence

"Bruised Orange" by John Prine

"Buffalo Run" by Orville Peck

"Built for Pain" by Esterly ft. Austin Jenckes

"Bullet the Blue Sky" by U2

"Bulletproof" by Godsmack

"Call Me When You're Sober" by Evanescence

"Caught in the Sun" by Course of Nature

"Chain of Sorrow" by John Prine

"Changes" by Charles Bradley

"Circus for a Psycho" by Skillet

"Click Click Boom" by Saliva

"Closer" by Kings of Leon

"Confusion" by Metallica

**"Counting Bodies Like Sheep to the Rhythm of the War
    Drums"** by A Perfect Circle

"Cowboys from Hell" by Pantera

"**Crush 'Em**" by Megadeth

"**Crying**" by Roy Orbison

"**Day One**" by Matthew West

"**Death**" by White Lies

"**Decoration Day**" by Drive-By Truckers

"**Delete Forever**" by Grimes

"**Demons**" by Imagine Dragons

"**Dig Up Her Bones**" by Misfits

"**Dirty Deeds Done Dirt Cheap**" by AC/DC

"**Don't Fear the Reaper**" by Blue Öyster Cult

***Elevator to the Gallows* soundtrack** by Miles Davis

"**Emergency**" by Paramore

"**En vivo Salón Pata Negra (14 de enero '20)**" by Deby Medrez
  Pier

"**Epiphany**" by Staind

"**Every Heart Is a Beating Piece of Shit**" by Miava

"**Excitable Boy**" by Warren Zevon

"**Fade to Black**" by Metallica

"**Forever Autumn**" by the Moody Blues

"**Full of Hell**" by Entombed

"**Give the Bastards Hell**" by the Killigans

"**Glycerine**" by Bush

"**Go to the Light**" by Murder by Death

"**God Is a Bullet**" by Concrete Blonde

"**Going Under**" by Evanescence

"**Golden Brown**" by the Stranglers

"Gone Away" by the Offspring

"Gone Forever" by Paul Williams

"Gone Sovereign" by Stone Sour

"Grace Is Gone" by Dave Matthews Band

"Happy?" by Mudvayne

"Hard Times" by Paramore

"Have You Ever Seen the Rain" by Creedence Clearwater Revival

"Helena" by My Chemical Romance

"Hell or High Water" by Billy Raffoul

"Hells Bells" by AC/DC

"Hemorrhage" by Fuel

"Here Comes Revenge" by Metallica

"Here I Am" by Yelawolf

"Here in the Black" by Gary Numan

"Here Is Gone" by the Goo Goo Dolls

"Highway to Hell" by AC/DC

"Holy Ground" by Napalm Beach

"Hurt" by Johnny Cash

"I Alone" by Live

"I Am the Wolf" by Mark Lanegan

"I Can't Make You Love Me" by Bonnie Raitt

"I Don't Care Anymore" by Phil Collins

"I Hate Everything About You" by Three Days Grace

"I Stand Alone" by Godsmack

"I Will Break You" by Godsplague

"I Will Not Bow" by Breaking Benjamin

"I Will Survive" by Gloria Gaynor

"I Won't Back Down" by Johnny Cash

"I'd Rather Go Blind" by Etta James

"If You Fear Dying" by One Day as a Lion

"In the End" by Black Veil Brides

"Independence Day" by Martina McBride

"Inside the Fire" by Disturbed

"Irresponsible Hate Anthem" by Marilyn Manson

"It's Been Awhile" by Staind

"Joan Crawford" by Blue Öyster Cult

"Jumper" by Third Eye Blind

"Killing an Arab" by the Cure

"Killing in the Name" by Rage Against the Machine

"Last Kiss" by Wayne Cochran (cover by Pearl Jam)

"Last Resort" by Papa Roach

"Lawyers, Guns, and Money" by Warren Zevon

"Let the Bodies Hit the Floor" by Drowning Pool

"Lightning Crashes" by Live

"Lights Out" by Breaking Benjamin

"Like a Stone" by Audioslave

"Lost" by Death Angel

"Love the Way You Lie" by Eminem ft. Rihanna

"Lovin' Arms" by Etta James

"Mad World" by Gary Jules

"**Memories**" by Maroon 5

"**Merry Go Round**" by the Struts

"**Monster**" by Jacob Banks

Murder Ballads **album** by Nick Cave and the Bad Seeds

"**My Heart**" by Varna

"**My Immortal**" by Evanescence

"**Natural**" by Imagine Dragons

"**No Time to Die**" by Billie Eilish

"**Nobody Knows**" by the Tony Rich Project

"**Not Ready to Die**" by Avenged Sevenfold

"**Oh Darlin' What Have I Done**" by the White Buffalo

"**Once in a Lifetime**" by Wolfsheim

"**Only Road**" by Sur

"**Perdida**" by Deby Medrez Pier

"**Pilgrim**" by Fink

"**Pink Houses**" by John Mellencamp

"**Please Don't Leave Me**" by P!nk

"**Poor Poor Pitiful Me**" by Warren Zevon

"**Prayer**" by Disturbed

"**Push It**" by Garbage

"**Pushing Me Away**" by Linkin Park

"**Radiation**" by Gavin DeGraw

"**Radioactive**" by Imagine Dragons

"**Raining Blood**" by Slayer

"**Reaper**" by Wild the Coyote and Badd Wolf

"Reckless" by Lacuna Coil

"Red Right Hand" by Nick Cave and the Bad Seeds

"Redemption Song" by Bob Marley and the Wailers (cover by Joe Strummer & the Mescaleros)

"Refuse/Resist" by Sepultura (cover by Hatebreed)

Repentless **album** by Slayer

Requiem by W. A. Mozart

"Resentment" by A Day to Remember

"Revenge" by Archers of Loaf

"Rise Up" by Andra Day

"Roland the Headless Thompson Gunner" by Warren Zevon

"Roots" by In This Moment

"Running Up That Hill" by Meg Myers

"Sad but True" by Metallica

"Sail" by AWOLNATION

"See You Again" by Wiz Khalifa ft. Charlie Puth

"Señor Sol" by Deby Medrez Pier

"Shallow" by Lady Gaga and Bradley Cooper

"Shatter Me" by Lindsey Stirling ft. Lzzy Hale

"Sinner Man" by Nina Simone

"Snuff" by Slipknot

"Sober" by P!nk

"Soldier's Eyes" by Jack Savoretti

"Soldiers" by Otherwise

"Song of a Sinner" by Top Drawer

"Splendid Isolation" by Warren Zevon

"St. Anger" by Metallica

"Still There'll Be More" by Procol Harum

"Surrender" by Billy Talent

"Take Me to Church" by Hozier

"Tell It to My Grave" by J. B. Beverley

"The Big Payback" by James Brown

"The Blacklist" by Exodus

"The Bleeding" by Five Finger Death Punch

"The Father, My Son, and the Holy Ghost" by Craig Morgan (Live at the Opry)

"The Grace" by Neverending White Lights ft. Dallas Green

"The Grand Massacre" by Ennio Morricone

"The Keeper" by Chris Cornell

"The Kill (Bury Me)" by Thirty Seconds to Mars

"The Killing of Georgie" by Rod Stewart

"The Last" by Agust D

"The Naked Ride Home" by Jackson Browne (cover by James Taylor)

"The Red" by Chevelle

"The Sound of Silence" by Simon & Garfunkel (cover by Disturbed)

"The Thunder Rolls" by Garth Brooks

"The Trick Is to Keep Breathing" by Garbage

"The Ultra-Violence" by Death Angel

"The Vengeful One" by Disturbed

"The Way I Am" by Eminem

"**The Writ**" by Black Sabbath

"**These Boots Are Made for Walkin'**" by Nancy Sinatra

"**Things Have Changed**" by Bob Dylan

"**Think Twice**" by Eve 6

"**This Is War**" by Thirty Seconds to Mars

"**This Means War**" by Avenged Sevenfold

"**Time to Kill**" by Overkill

"**Tom Sawyer**" by Rush

"**Train of Consequences**" by Megadeth

"**Turquoise Jewelry**" by Camper Van Beethoven

"**Twilight and Shadows**" from *Lord of the Rings: Return of the King* soundtrack

"**Ultra Violet (Light My Way)**" by U2 (for Junie Flynn)

"**Unchained Melody**" by the Righteous Brothers

"**Unholy War**" by Jacob Banks

"**Until the Day I Die**" by Story of the Year

"**Uprising**" by Muse

"**Useless**" by Depeche Mode

"**Vengeance**" by New Model Army

"**Violence**" by A Day to Remember

"**Vow**" by Garbage

"**Walk Me Home**" by P!nk

"**War of the Worlds**" by Jeff Wayne

"**When Did You Stop Loving Me, When Did I Stop Loving You**" by Marvin Gaye

"**When the Party's Over**" by Billie Eilish

"Whiskey Lullaby" by Brad Paisley ft. Alison Krauss

"Who Did That to You" by John Legend

"Who Knew" by P!nk

"With You" by Linkin Park

"Without You" by Harry Nilsson

"Wonderwall" by Oasis

***World Painted Blood* album** by Slayer

"Wrong Side of Heaven" by Five Finger Death Punch

"You Ain't Coming Back" by Zeal & Ardor

"You Ain't Seen Nothing Yet" by Bachman Turner Overdrive

"You Better Run" by Motörhead

"You Give Love a Bad Name" by Bon Jovi

"You Oughta Know" by Alanis Morissette

"Your Time Is Gonna Come" by Led Zeppelin

"Zero" by OTEP

ACKNOWLEDGMENTS

The Joe Ledger novels could not be undertaken without the help of a lot of talented and generous people. In no particular order, then . . .

Many thanks to John Cmar, director of the Division of Infectious Diseases at Sinai Hospital of Baltimore, and Dr. Ronald Coleman, CEO of Regentech Incorporated.

Thanks to my friends in the International Thriller Writers, International Association of Media Tie-In Writers, the Mystery Writers of America, and the Horror Writers Association. Thanks to my literary agent, Sara Crowe of Pippin Properties; my stalwart editor at St. Martin's Griffin, Michael Homler; Robert Allen and the crew at Macmillan Audio; and my film agent, Dana Spector of Creative Artists Agency. Thanks to Big FUN Shirt Company in Eureka, California (where Joe Ledger and I both shop!).

Thanks to contest winners Michael Stafford, Mia Kleeve, Peggy Ann Gondek, and Jill Hamilton-Krawczyk.

Special thanks to my friend and colleague Joe R. Lansdale, for his gracious permission to allow Hap Collins and Leonard Pine to have some fun with Joe Ledger.

And special thanks to my brilliant audiobook reader, Ray Porter.

ABOUT THE AUTHOR

Sara Jo West

JONATHAN MABERRY is a *New York Times* bestselling and five-time Bram Stoker Award–winning author of *Deep Silence, Kill Switch, Predator One, Code Zero, Fall of Night, Patient Zero,* the Pine Deep Trilogy, *Ink, Glimpse, Mars One, The Wolfman, Zombie CSU,* and *They Bite,* among others. His V Wars series has been adapted by Netflix, and his work for Marvel Comics includes *The Punisher, Wolverine, DoomWar, Marvel Zombies Return,* and *Black Panther.* He is a board member of the Horror Writers Association, the president of the International Association of Media Tie-In Writers, and the editor of *Weird Tales* magazine.